S.S.F. Public Library
Grand Ave.
306 Walnut Ave.
South San Francisco, CA 94080

D0175132

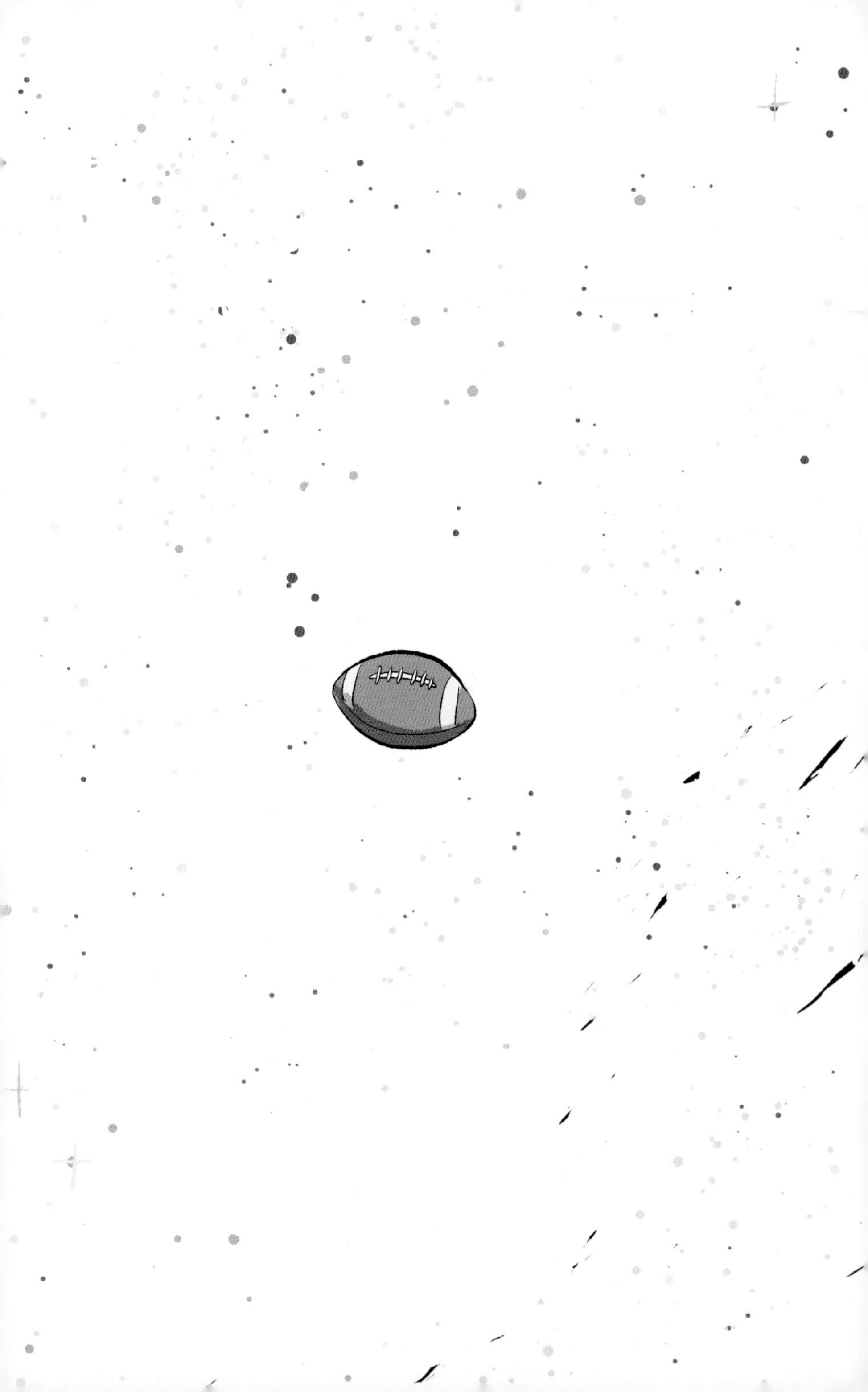

Stephen McCranie's

SPACE BOY

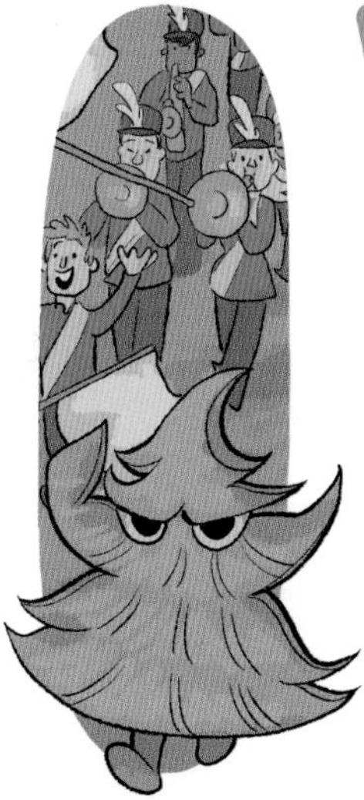

VOLUME 7

Written and illustrated by
STEPHEN McCRANIE

DARK HORSE BOOKS

President and Publisher **Mike Richardson**

Editor **Shantel LaRocque**

Assistant Editor **Brett Israel**

Designer **Anita Magaña**

Digital Art Technician **Allyson Haller**

STEPHEN McCRANIE'S SPACE BOY VOLUME 7

Space Boy™ © 2020 Stephen McCranie. All rights reserved. Dark Horse Books® and the Dark Horse logo are registered trademarks of Dark Horse Comics LLC. All rights reserved. No portion of this publication may be reproduced or transmitted, in any form or by any means, without the express written permission of Dark Horse Comics LLC. Names, characters, places, and incidents featured in this publication either are the product of the author's imagination or are used fictitiously. Any resemblance to actual persons (living or dead), events, institutions, or locales, without satiric intent, is coincidental.

This book collects *Space Boy* episodes 95–110, previously published online at WebToons.com.

Published by Dark Horse Books
A division of Dark Horse Comics LLC
10956 SE Main Street | Milwaukie, OR 97222
StephenMcCranie.com | DarkHorse.com

To find a comics shop in your area, visit comicshoplocator.com

First edition: June 2020
ISBN 978-1-50671-401-1
10 9 8 7 6 5 4 3 2 1
Printed in China

Names: McCranie, Stephen, 1987- writer, illustrator.
Title: Space Boy / written and illustrated by Stephen McCranie.
Other titles: At head of title: Stephen McCranie's
Description: First edition. | Milwaukie, OR : Dark Horse Books, 2018- | v. 1: "This book collects Space Boy episodes 1-16 previously published online at WebToons.com."--Title page verso. | v. 2: "This book collects Space Boy episodes 17-32, previously published online at WebToons.com."--Title page verso. | v. 3: "This book collects Space Boy episodes 33-48, previously published online at WebToons.com."--Title page verso. | v. 4: "This book collects Space Boy episodes 49-60, previously published online at WebToons.com."--Title page verso. | v. 4: "This book collects Space Boy episodes 61-75, previously published online at WebToons.com."--Title page verso. | v. 6: "This book collects Space Boy episodes 76-92, previously published online at WebToons.com." --Title page verso. | Summary: Amy lives on a colony in deep space, but when her father loses his job the family moves back to Earth, where she has to adapt to heavier gravity, a new school, and a strange boy with no flavor.
Identifiers: LCCN 2017053602| ISBN 9781506706481 (v. 1 ; pbk.) | ISBN 9781506706801 (v. 2 ; pbk.) | ISBN 9781506708423 (v. 3 ; pbk.) | ISBN 9781506708430 (v. 4 ; pbk.) | ISBN 9781506713991 (v. 5 ; pbk.) | ISBN 9781506714004 (v. 6 ; pbk.) | ISBN 9781506714011 (v. 7 ; pbk.)
Subjects: LCSH: Graphic novels. | CYAC: Graphic novels. | Science fiction. | Moving, Household--Fiction. | Self-perception--Fiction. | Friendship--Fiction.
Classification: LCC PZ7.7.M42 Sp 2018 | DDC 741.5/973--dc23
LC record available at https://lccn.loc.gov/2017053602

Neil Hankerson Executive Vice President • **Tom Weddle** Chief Financial Officer • **Randy Stradley** Vice President of Publishing • **Nick McWhorter** Chief Business Development Officer • **Dale LaFountain** Chief Information Officer • **Matt Parkinson** Vice President of Marketing • **Vanessa Todd-Holmes** Vice President of Production and Scheduling • **Mark Bernardi** Vice President of Book Trade and Digital Sales • **Ken Lizzi** General Counsel • **Dave Marshall** Editor in Chief • **Davey Estrada** Editorial Director • **Chris Warner** Senior Books Editor • **Cary Grazzini** Director of Specialty Projects • **Lia Ribacchi** Art Director • **Matt Dryer** Director of Digital Art and Prepress • **Michael Gombo** Senior Director of Licensed Publications • **Kari Yadro** Director of Custom Programs • **Kari Torson** Director of International Licensing • **Sean Brice** Director of Trade Sales

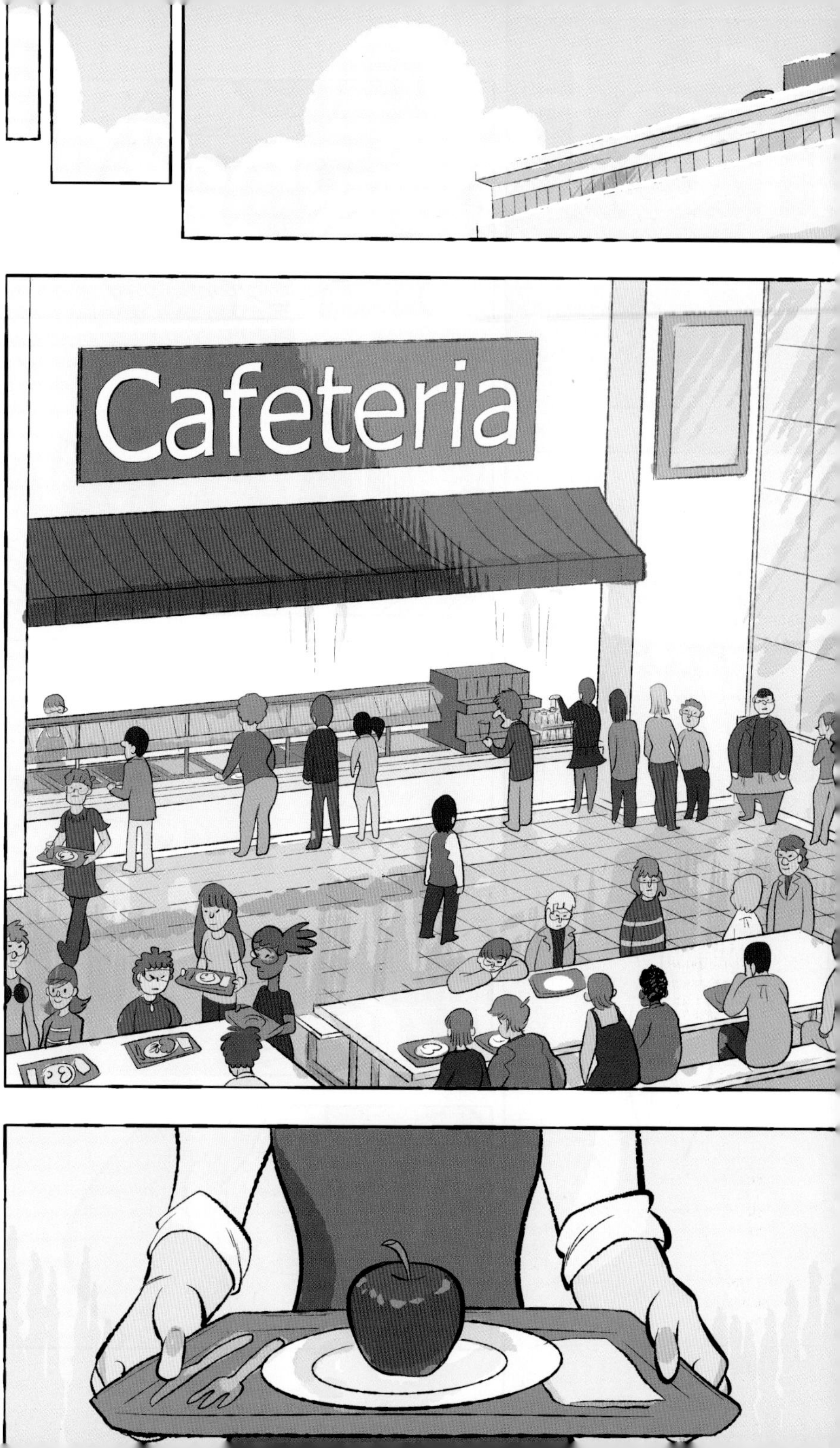
Cafeteria

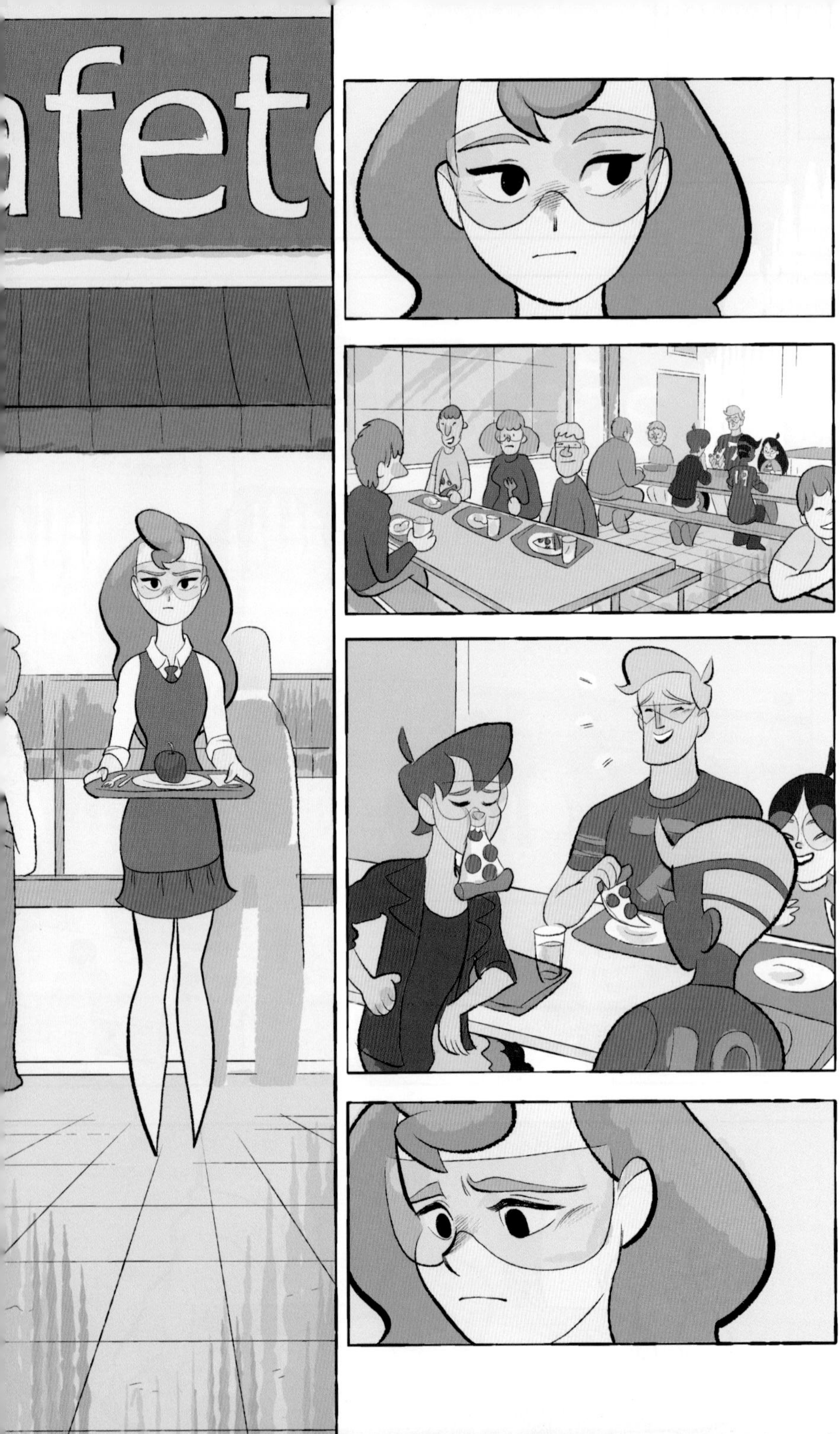
afet

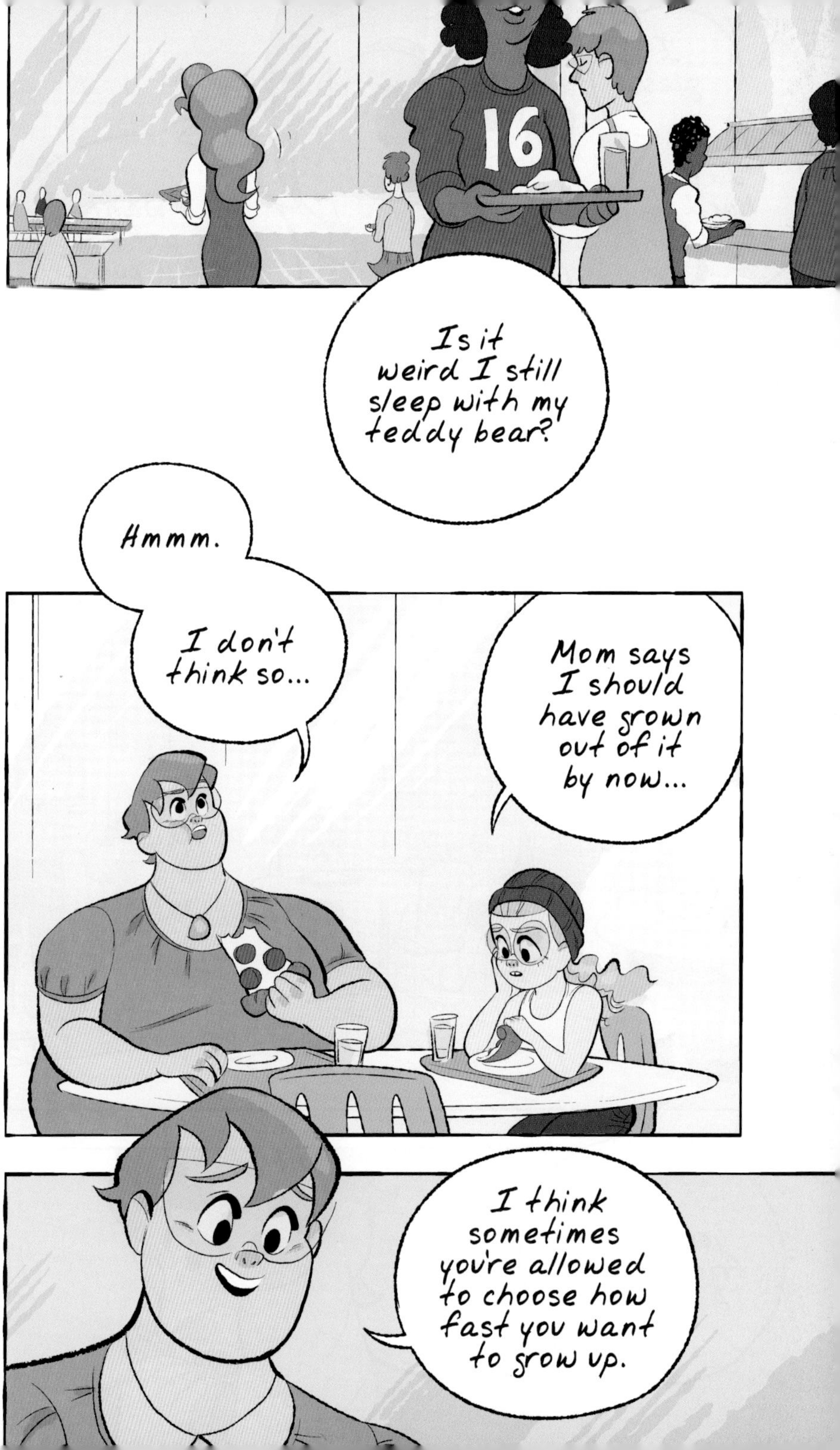
16
Is it weird I still sleep with my teddy bear?
Hmmm.
I don't think so...
Mom says I should have grown out of it by now...
I think sometimes you're allowed to choose how fast you want to grow up.

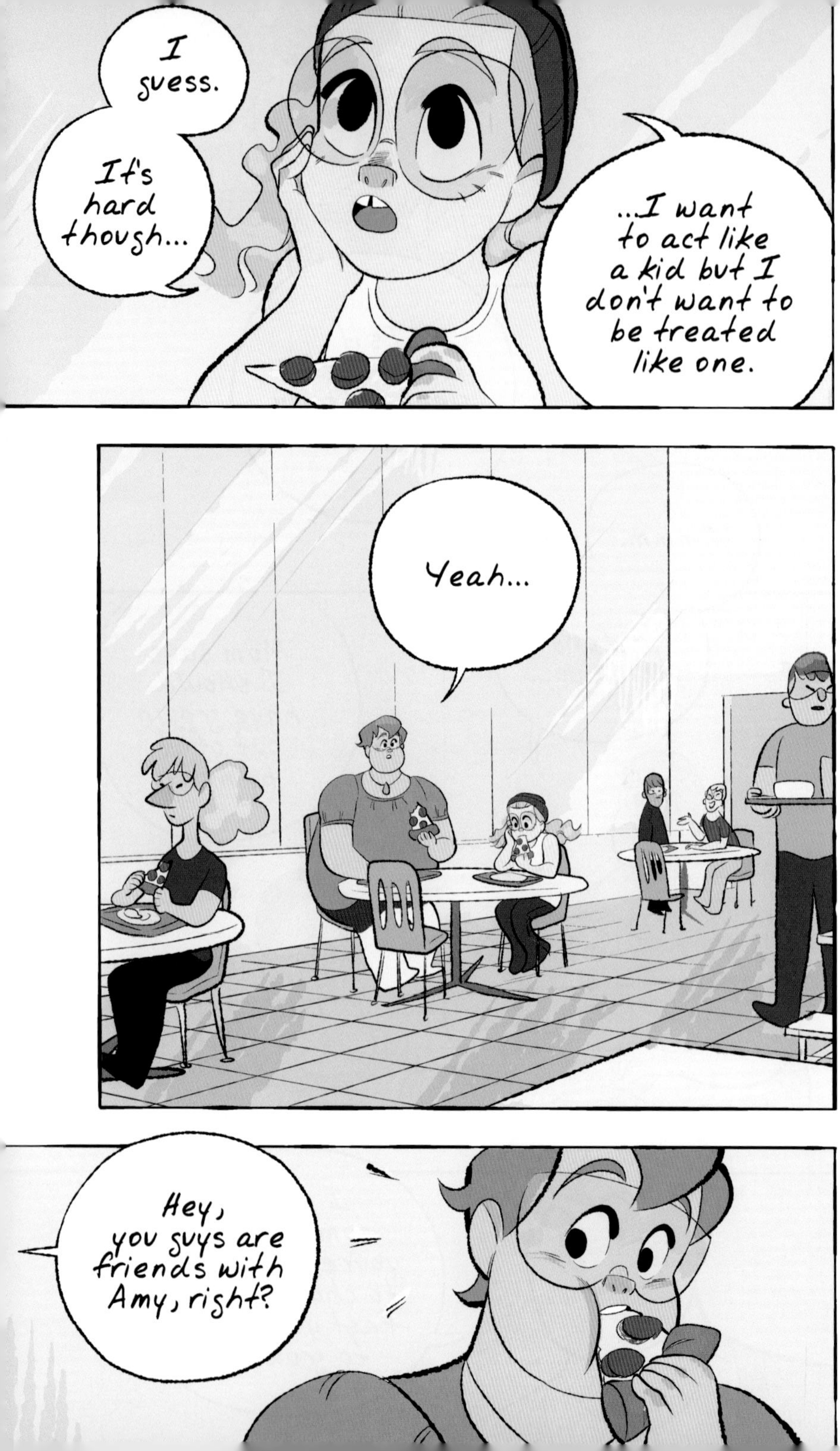
I guess.
It's hard though...
...I want to act like a kid but I don't want to be treated like one.
Yeah...
Hey, you guys are friends with Amy, right?

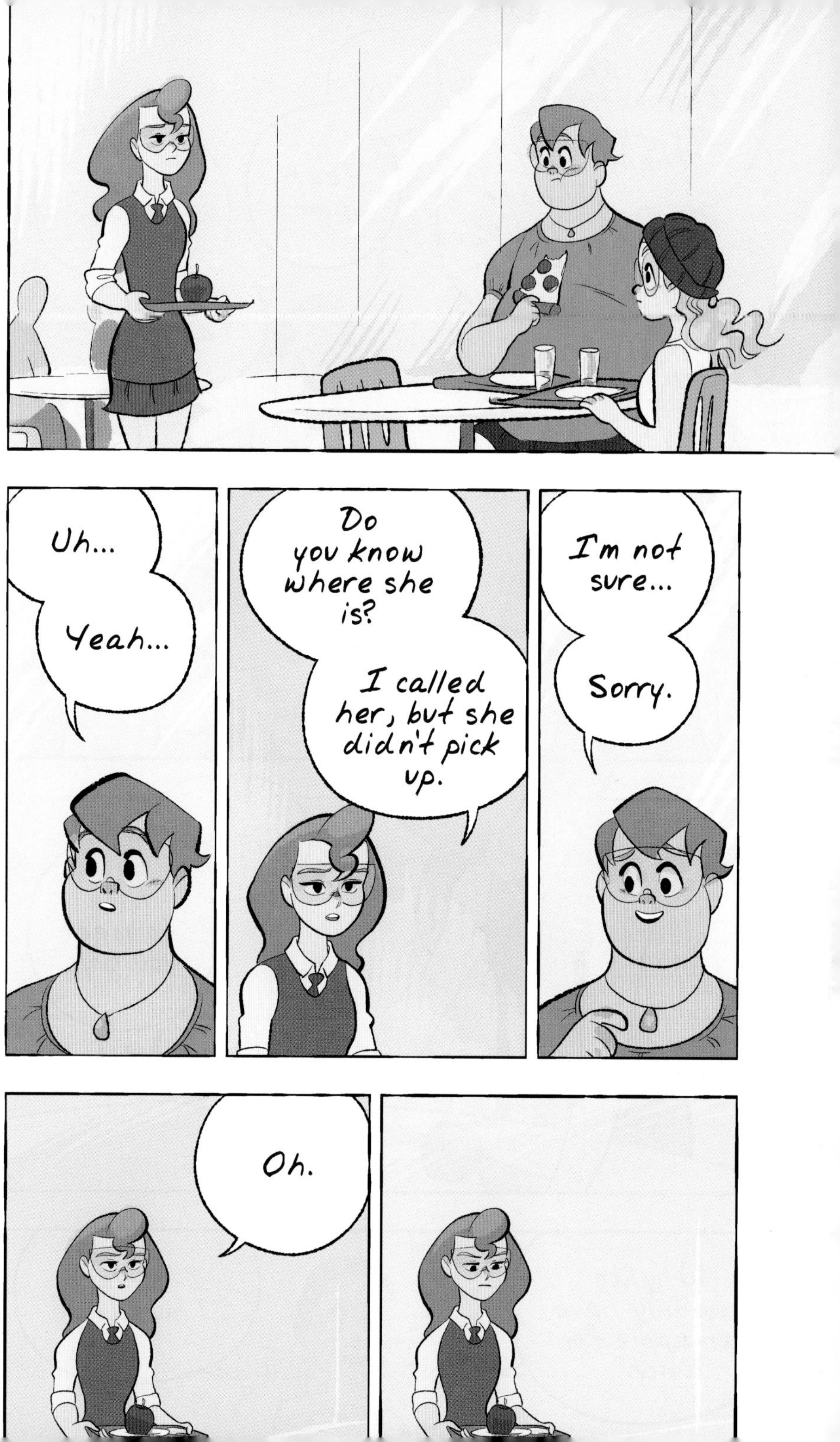
Uh...
Yeah...
Do you know where she is?
I called her, but she didn't pick up.
I'm not sure...
Sorry.
Oh.

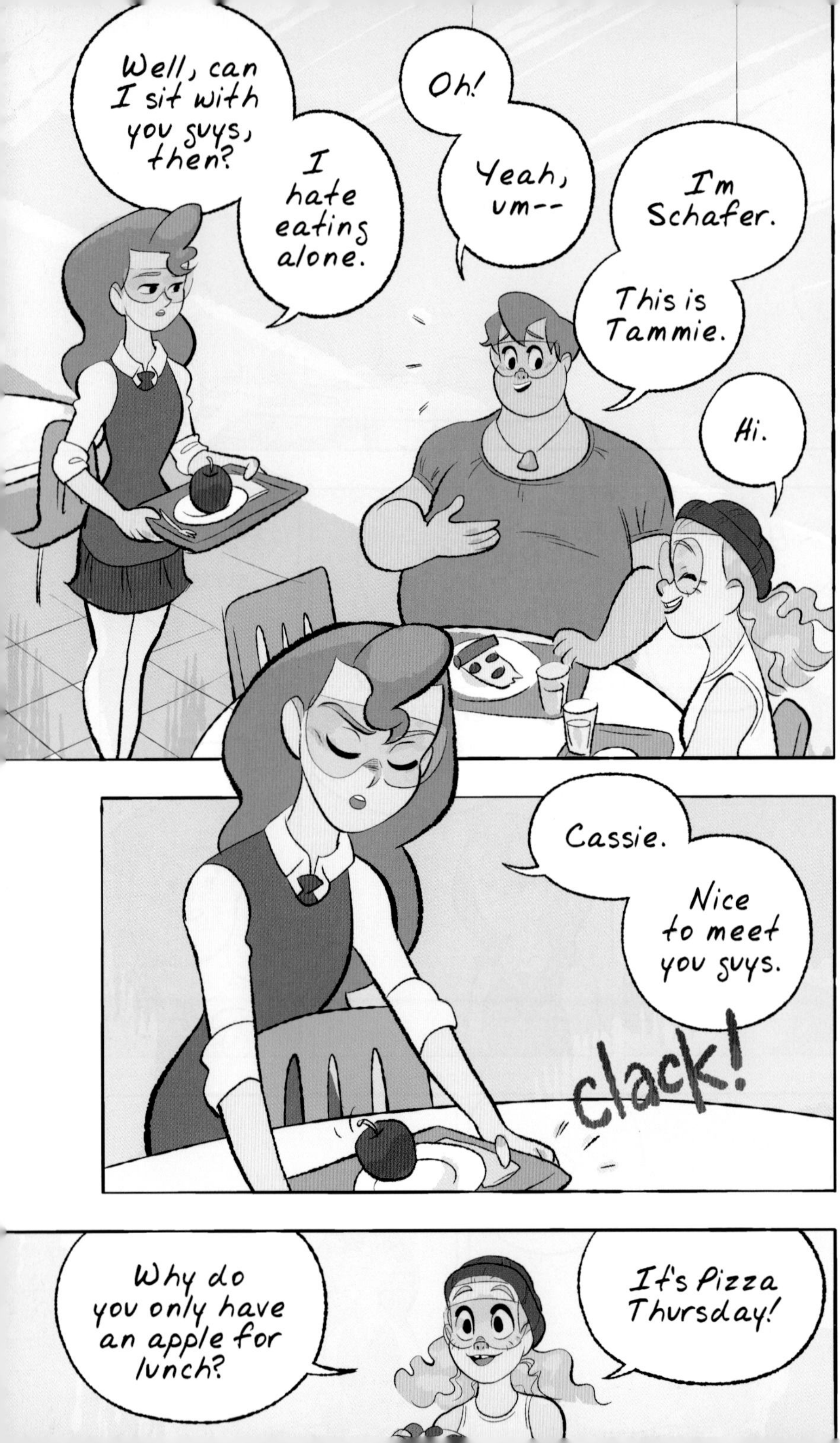
Well, can I sit with you guys, then?
I hate eating alone.
Oh!
Yeah, um--
I'm Schafer.
This is Tammie.
Hi.
Cassie.
Nice to meet you guys.
clack!
Why do you only have an apple for lunch?
It's Pizza Thursday!

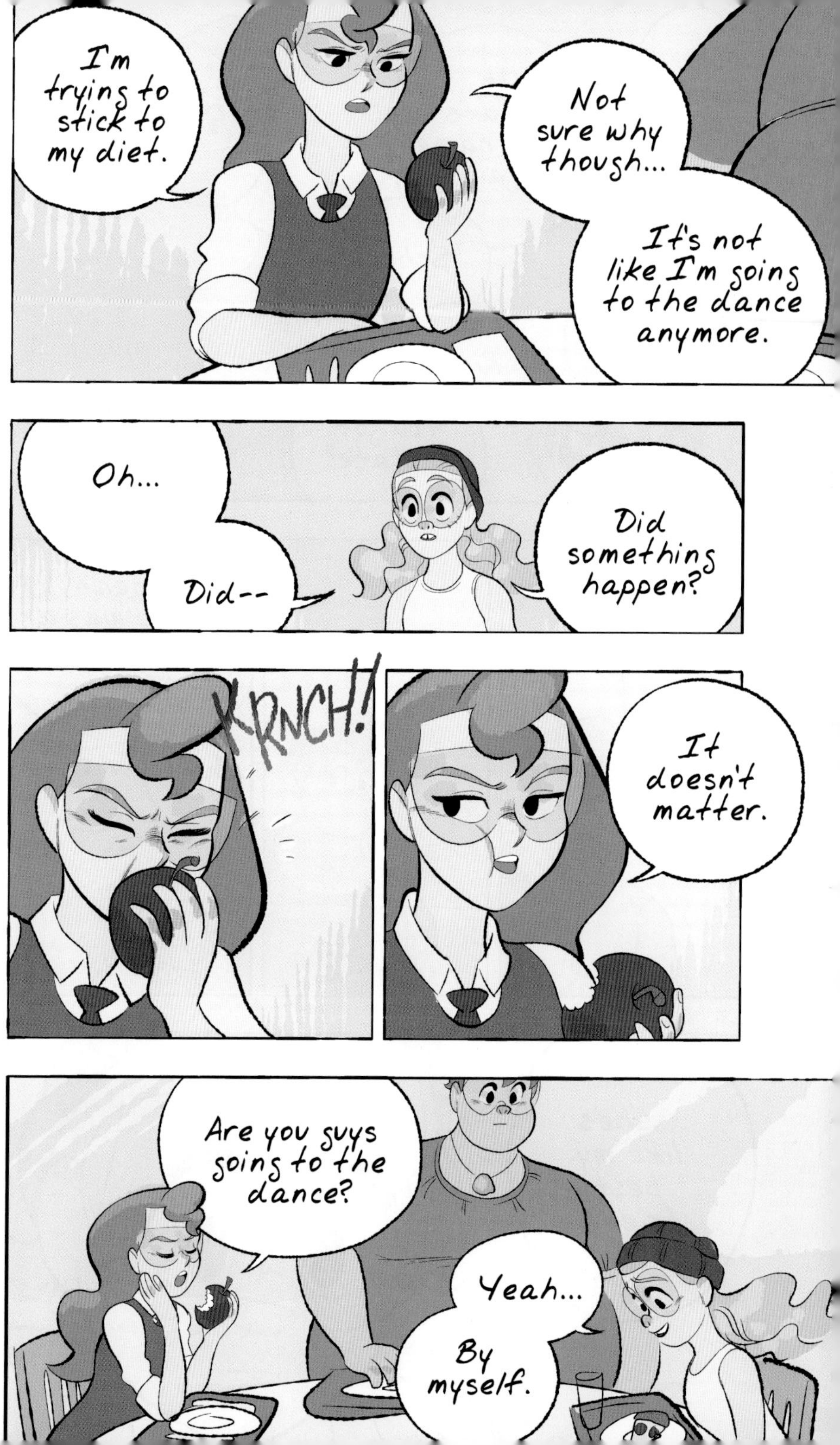
I'm trying to stick to my diet.
Not sure why though...
It's not like I'm going to the dance anymore.
Oh...
Did--
Did something happen?
KRNCH!
It doesn't matter.
Are you guys going to the dance?
Yeah...
By myself.

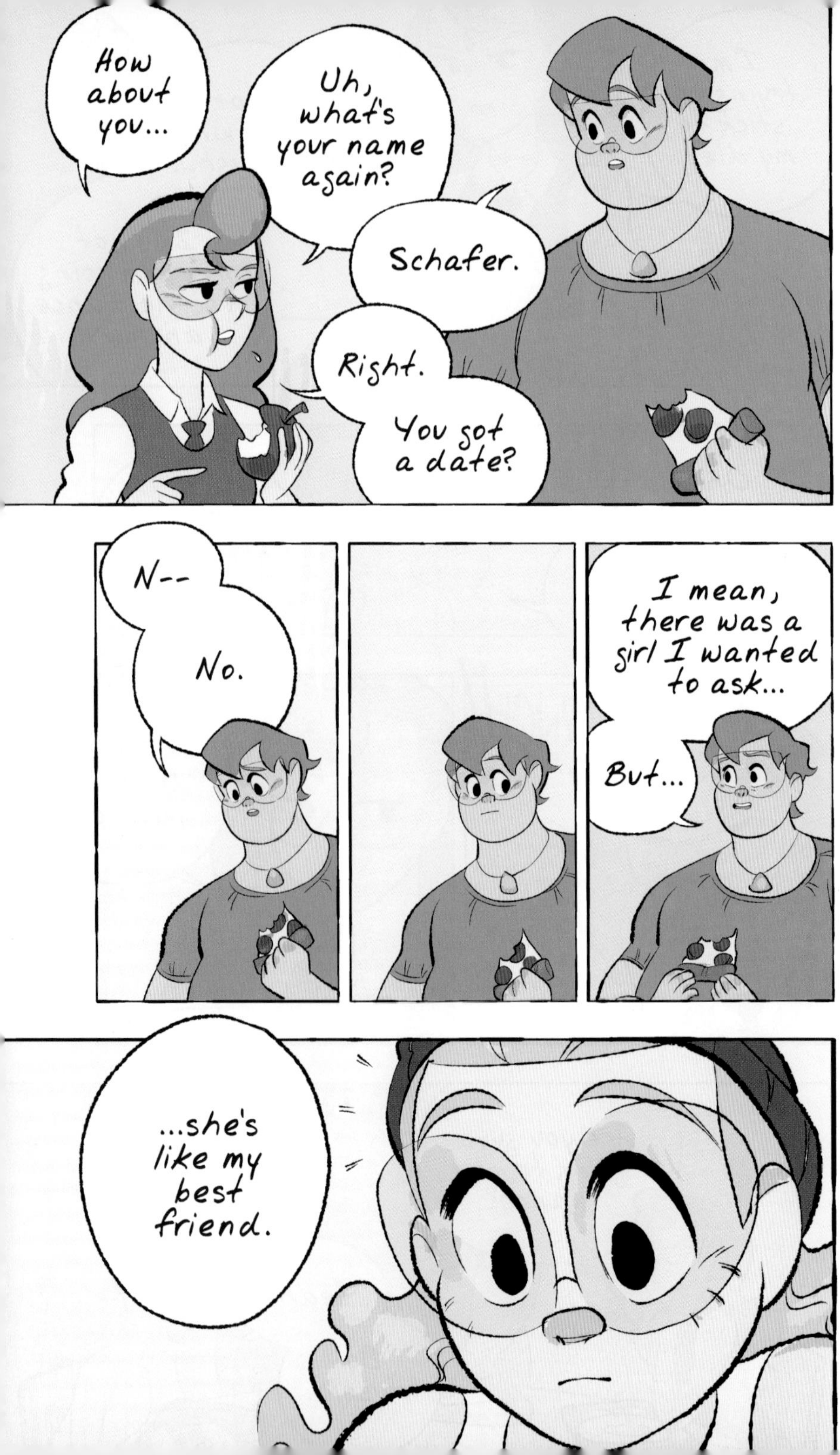
How about you...
Uh, what's your name again?
Schafer.
Right.
You got a date?
N--
No.
I mean, there was a girl I wanted to ask...
But...
...she's like my best friend.

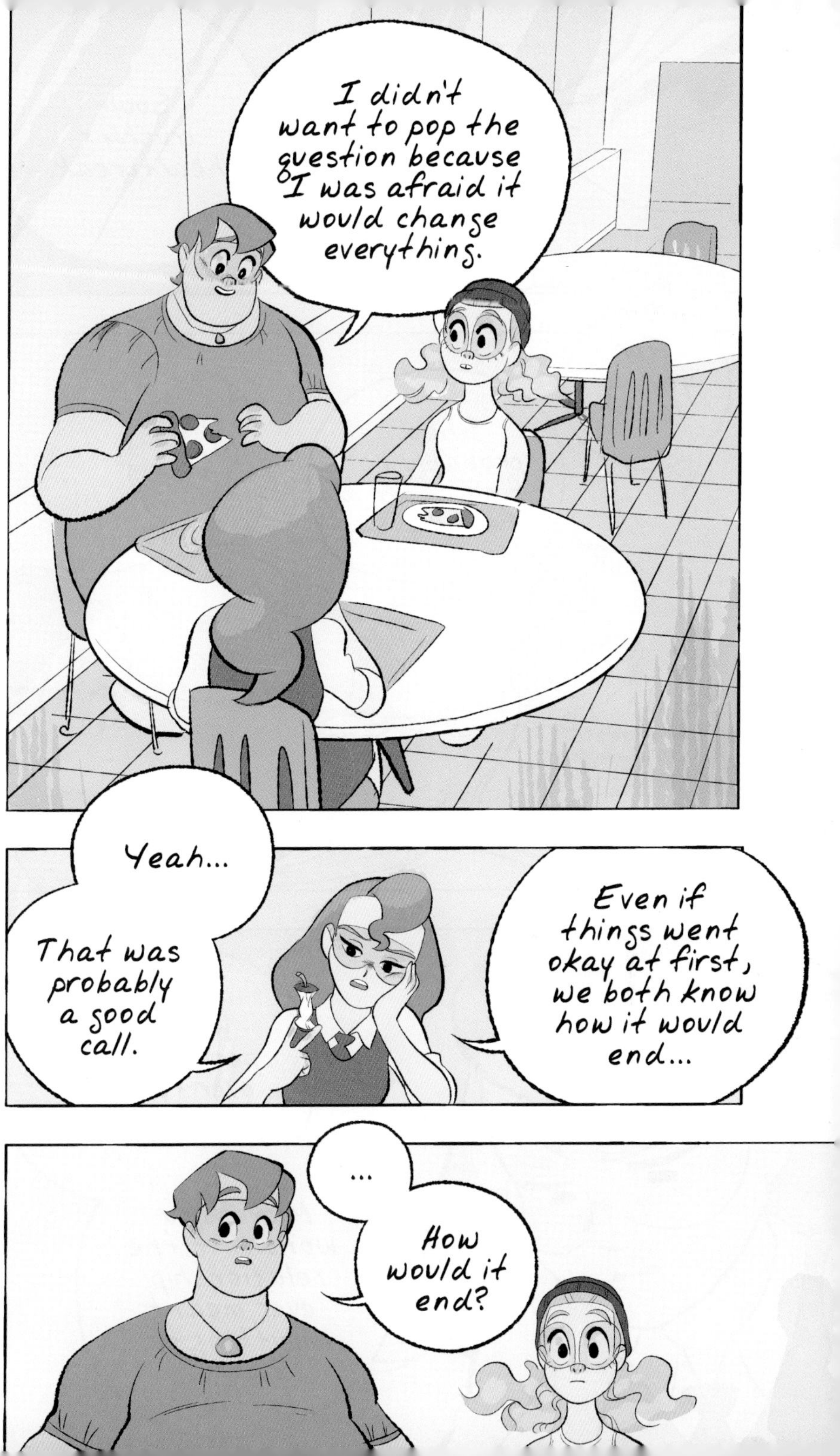
I didn't want to pop the question because I was afraid it would change everything.
Yeah...
That was probably a good call.
Even if things went okay at first, we both know how it would end...
...
How would it end?

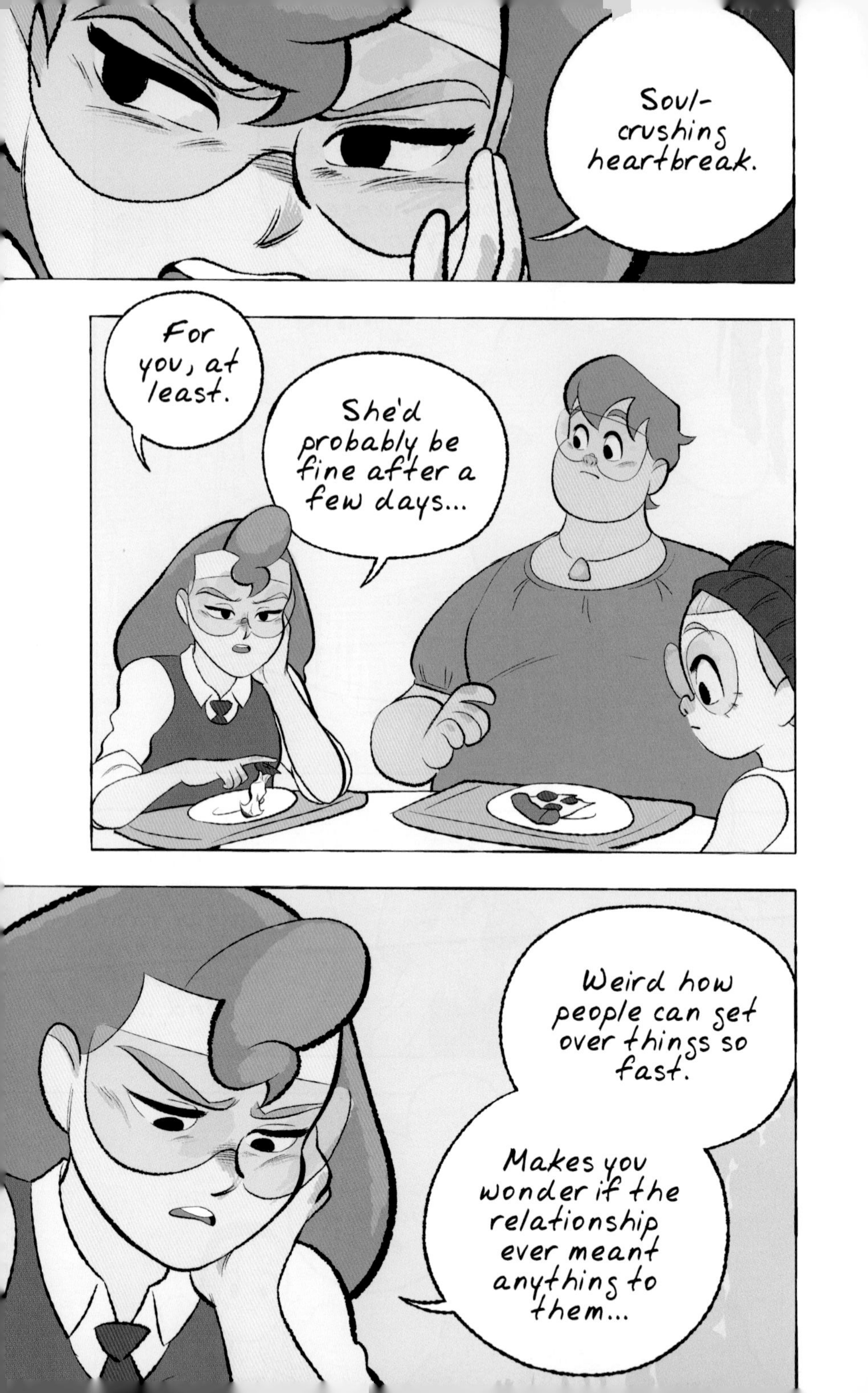
Soul-crushing heartbreak.
For you, at least.
She'd probably be fine after a few days...
Weird how people can get over things so fast.
Makes you wonder if the relationship ever meant anything to them...

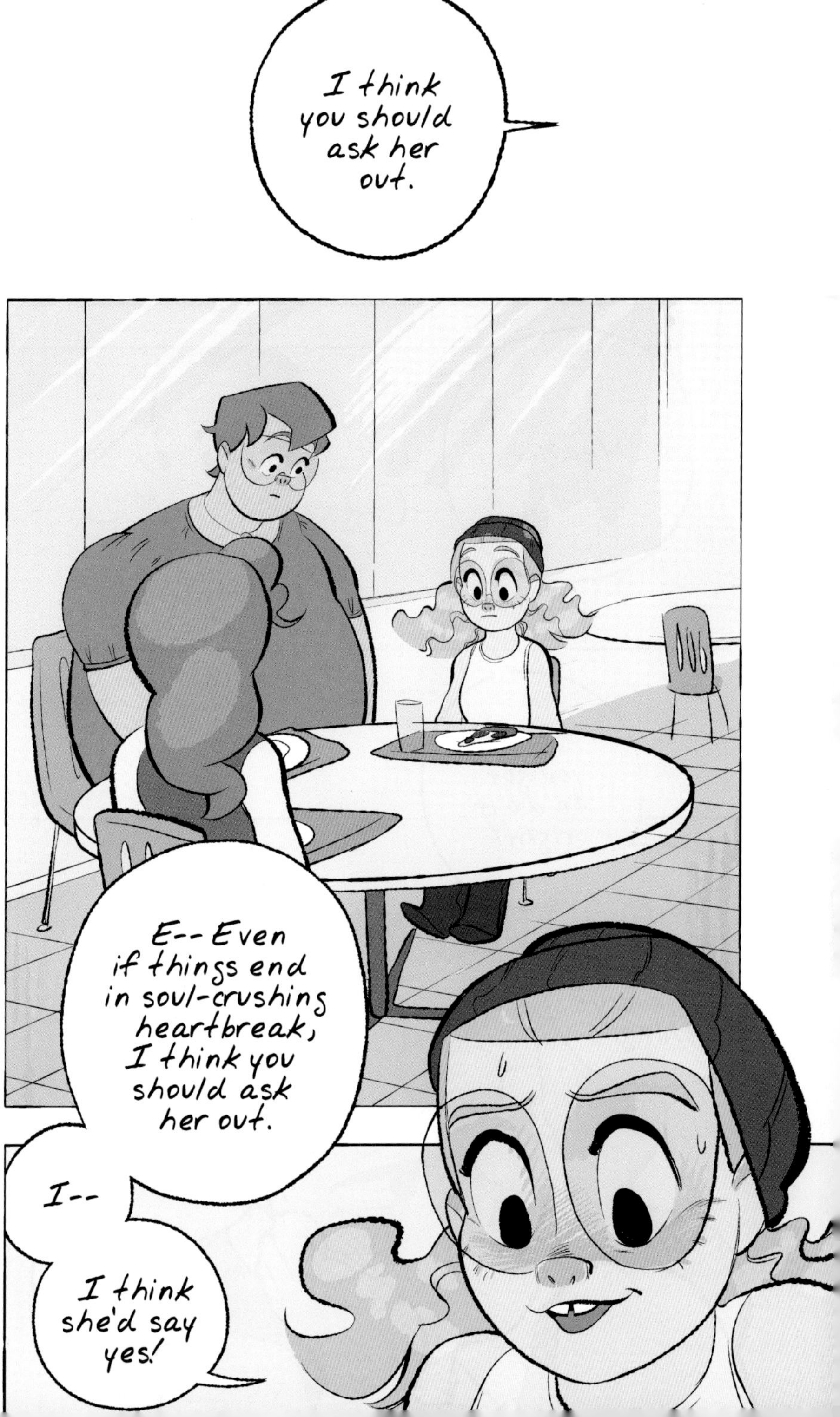
I think you should ask her out.
E--Even if things end in soul-crushing heartbreak, I think you should ask her out.
I--
I think she'd say yes!

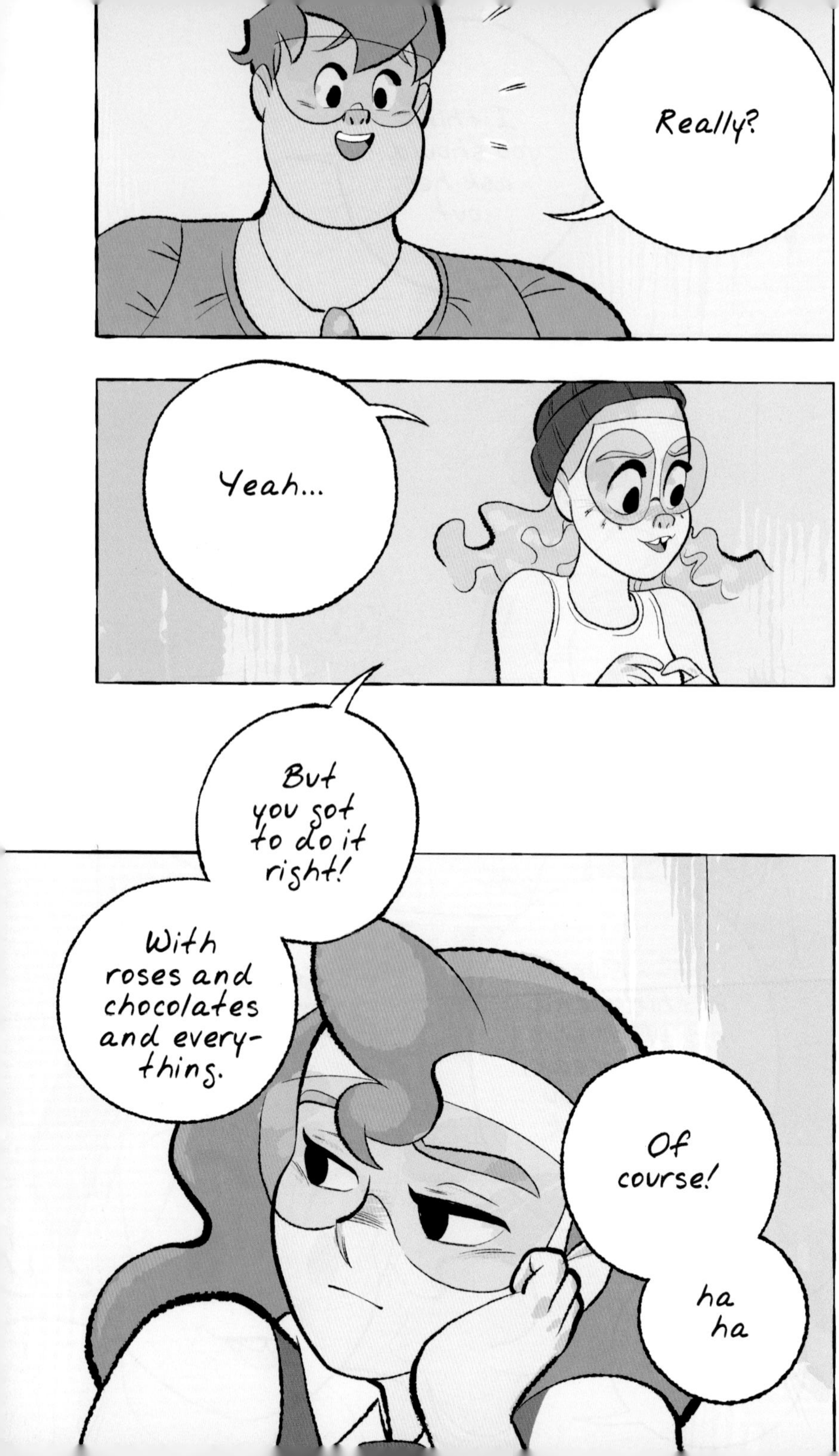
Really?
Yeah...
But you got to do it right!
With roses and chocolates and every-thing.
Of course!
ha ha

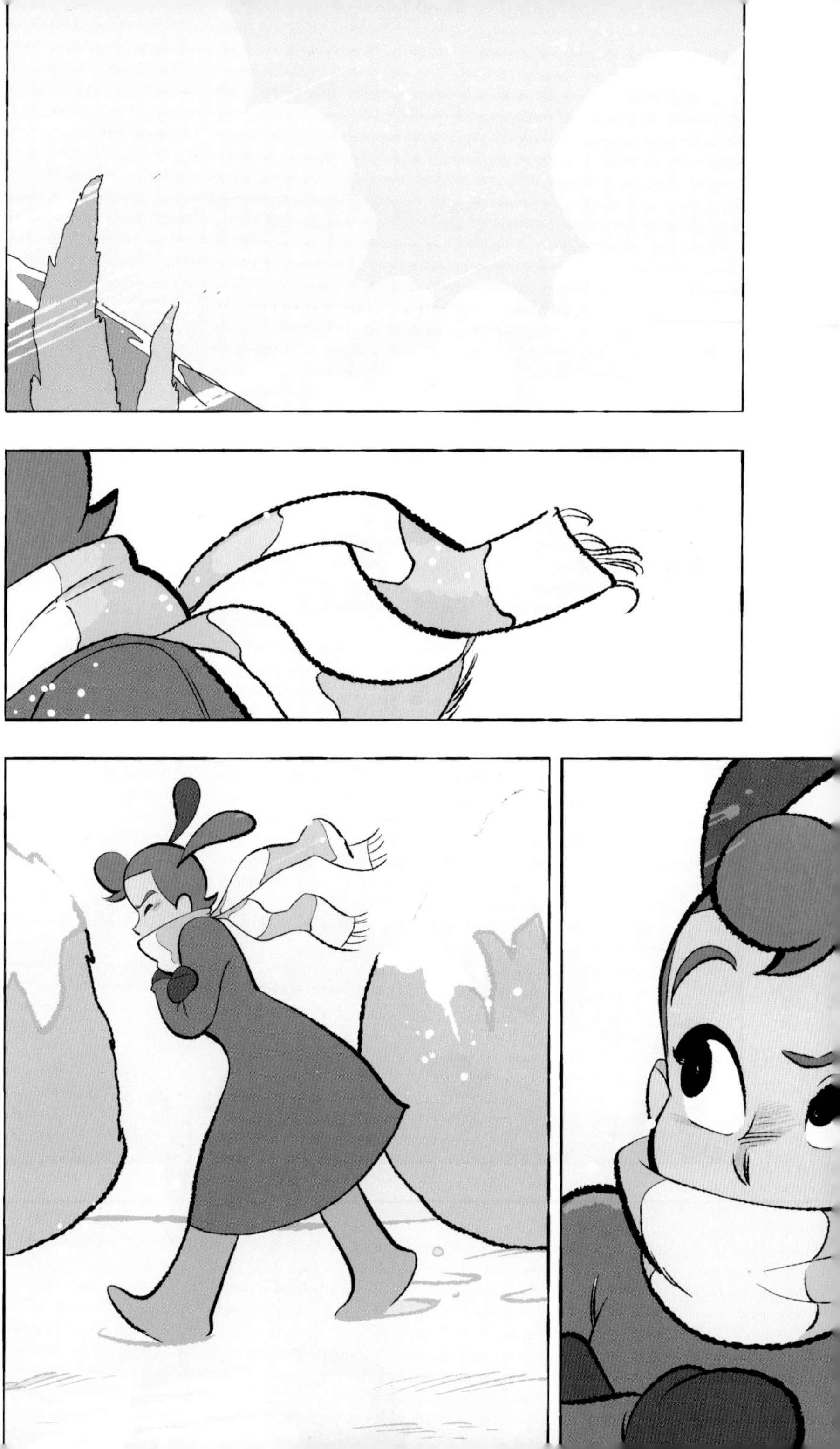

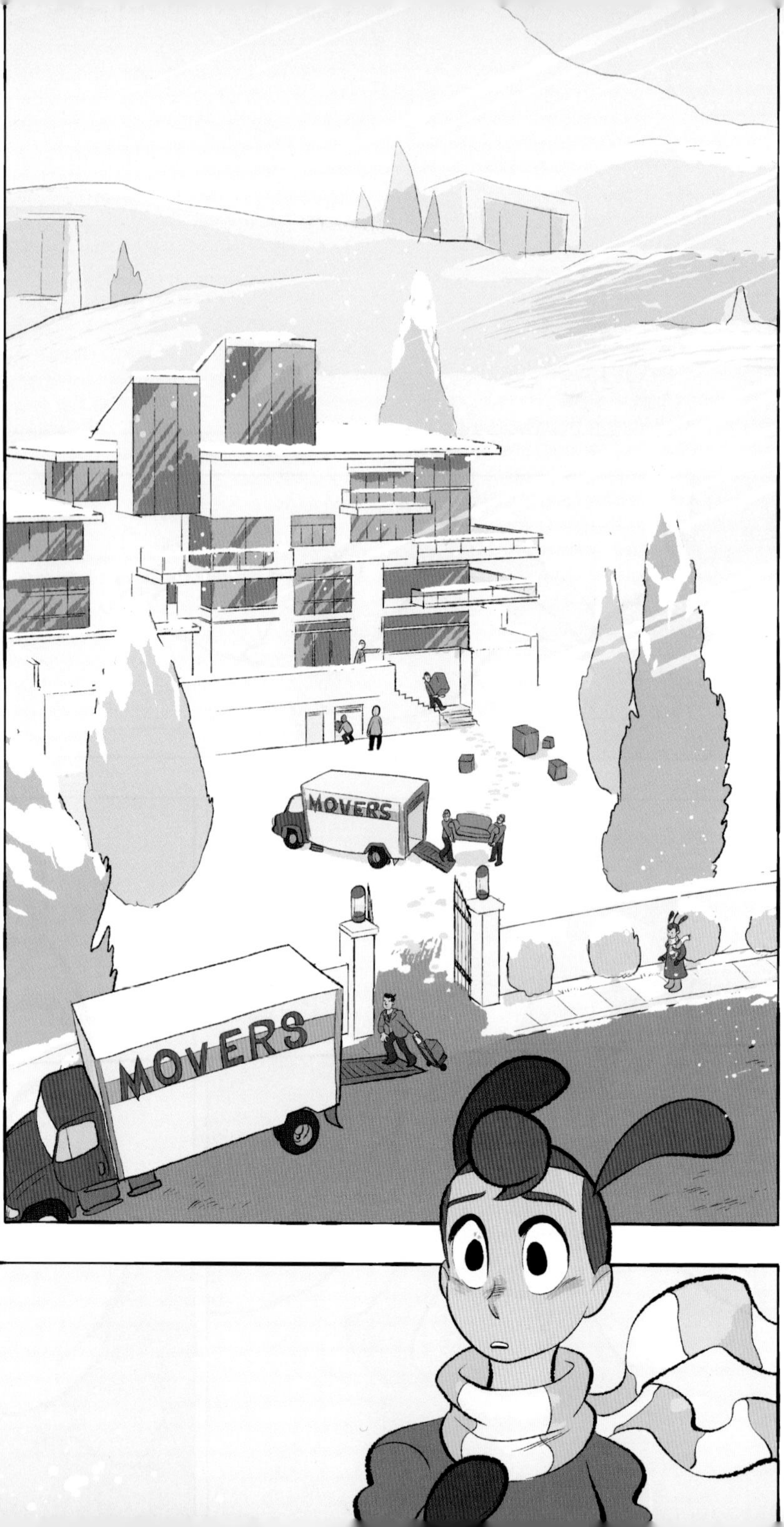
MOVERS
MOVERS

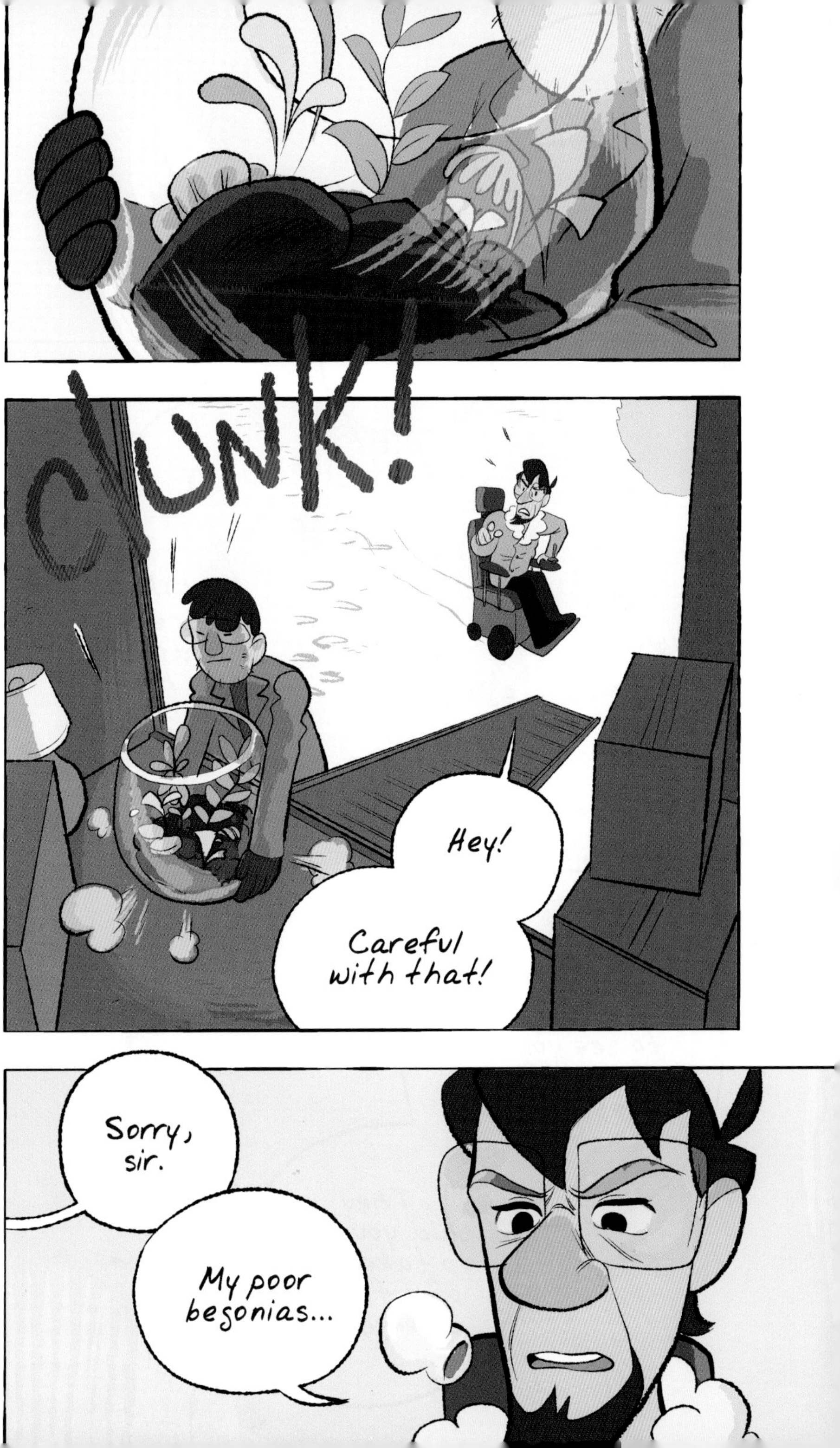
CHUNK!
Hey!
Careful with that!
Sorry, sir.
My poor begonias...

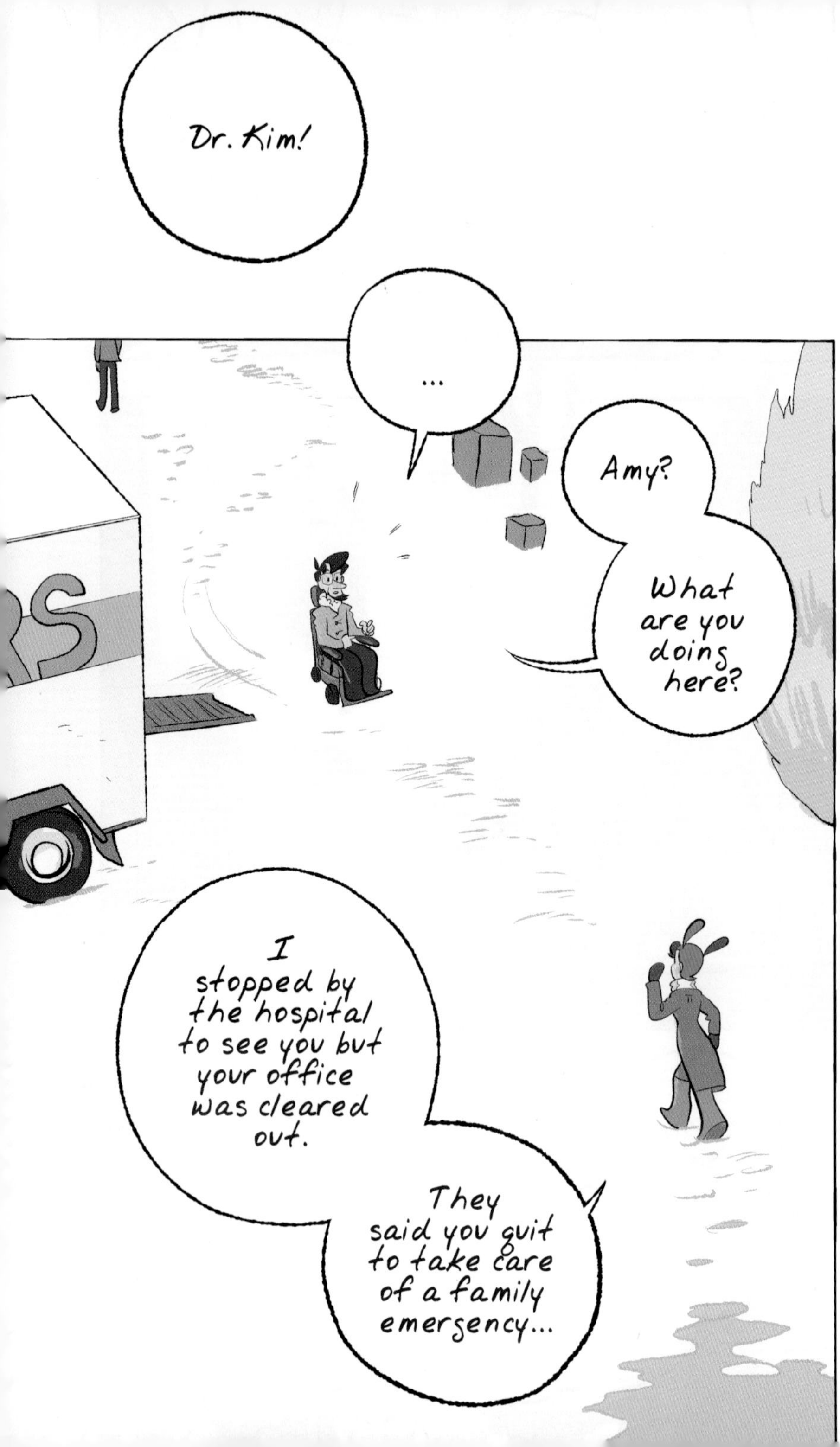
Dr. Kim!
...
Amy?
What are you doing here?
I stopped by the hospital to see you but your office was cleared out.
They said you quit to take care of a family emergency...

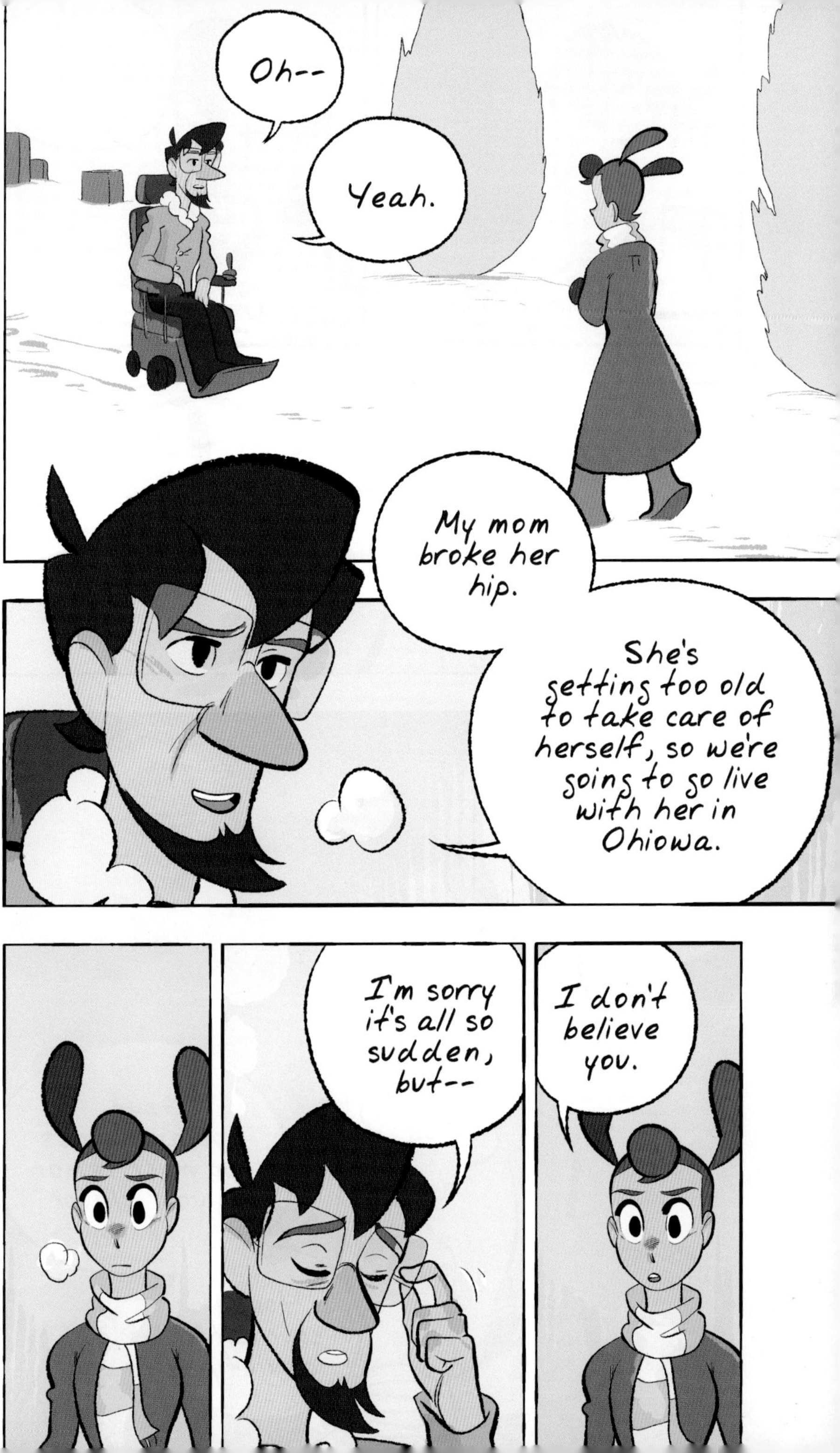
Oh--
Yeah.
My mom broke her hip.
She's getting too old to take care of herself, so we're going to go live with her in Ohiowa.
I'm sorry it's all so sudden, but--
I don't believe you.

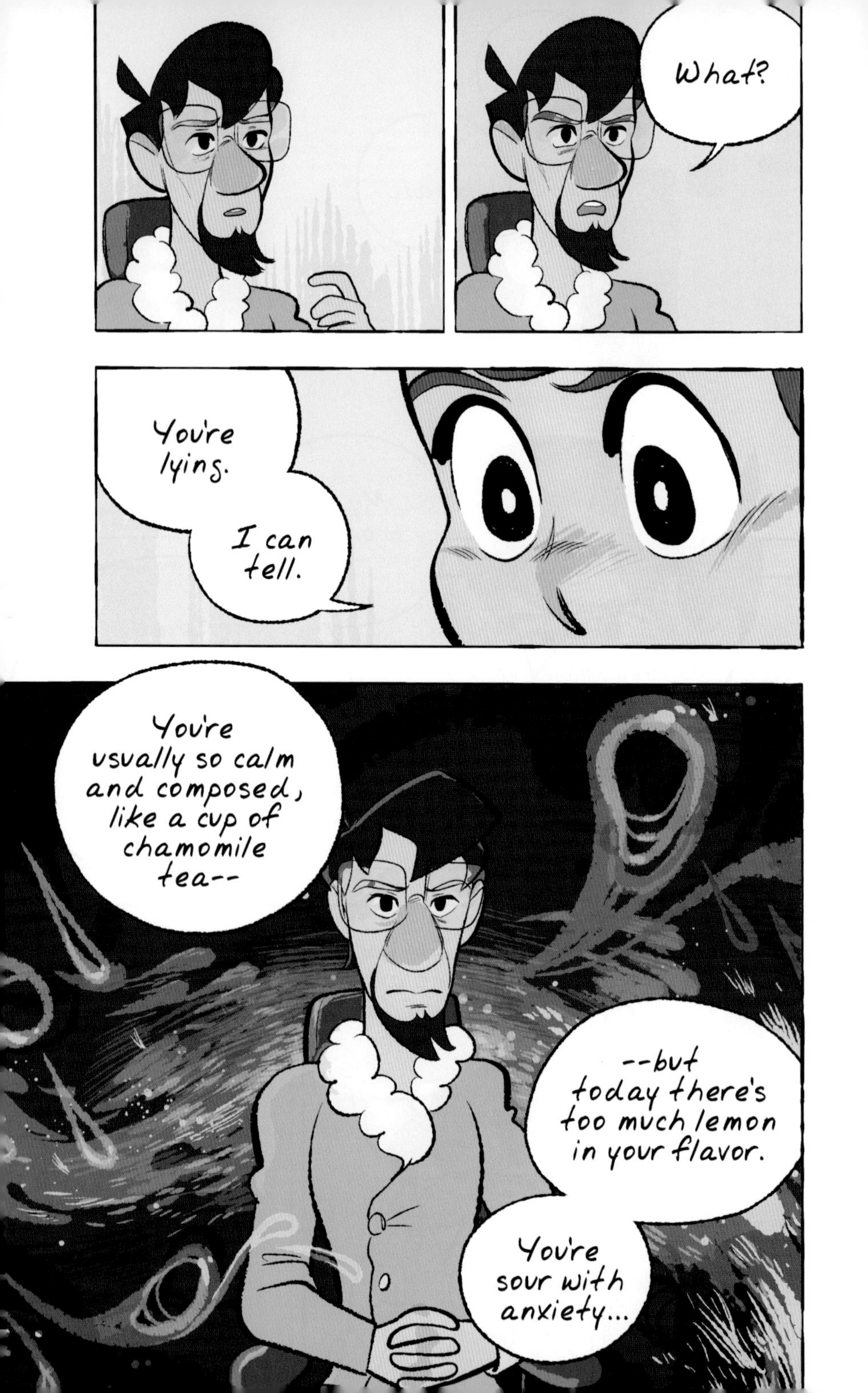
What?
You're lying.
I can tell.
You're usually so calm and composed, like a cup of chamomile tea--
--but today there's too much lemon in your flavor.
You're sour with anxiety...

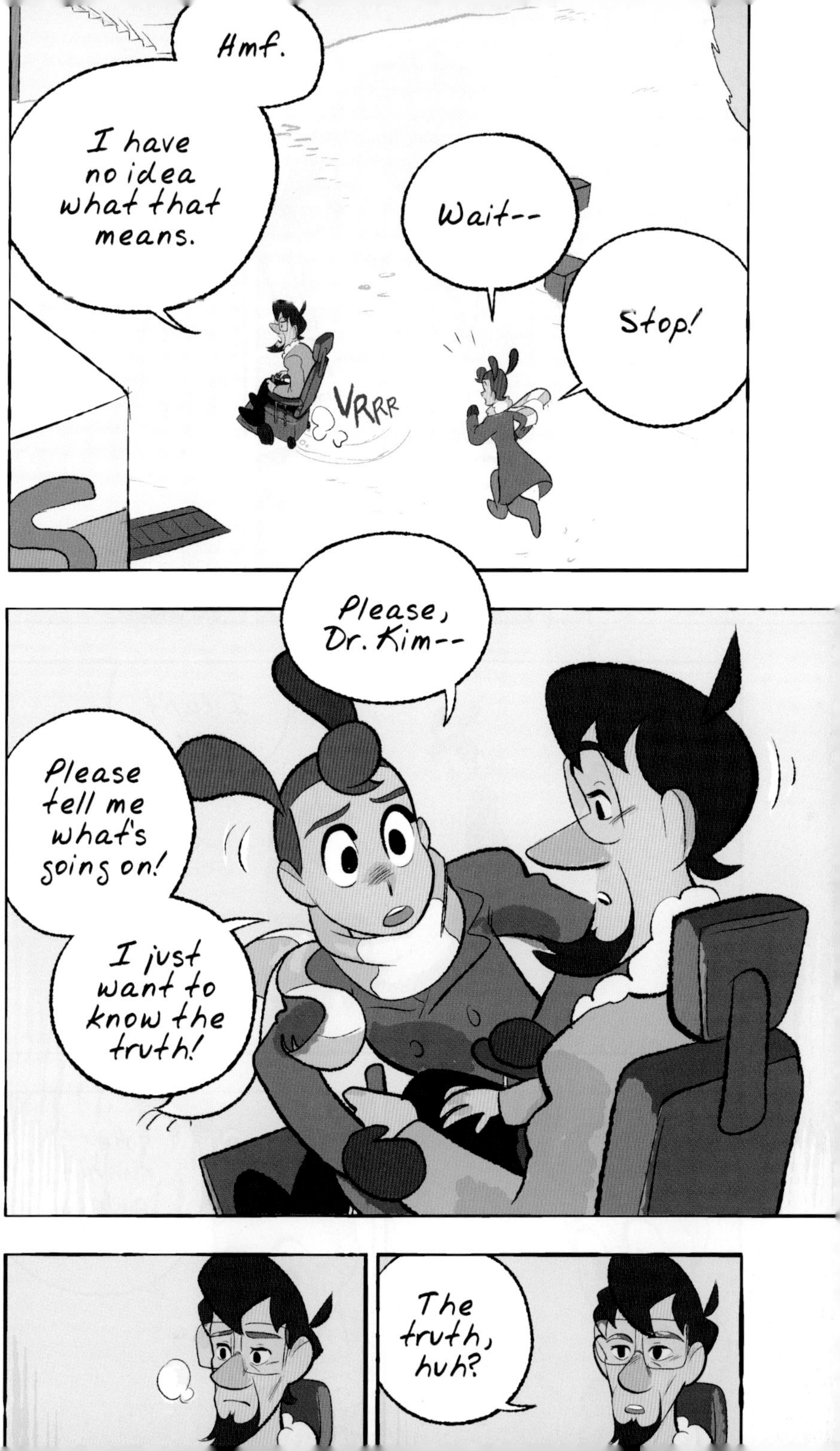
Hmf.
I have no idea what that means.
Wait--
Stop!
VRRR
Please, Dr. Kim--
Please tell me what's going on!
I just want to know the truth!
The truth, huh?

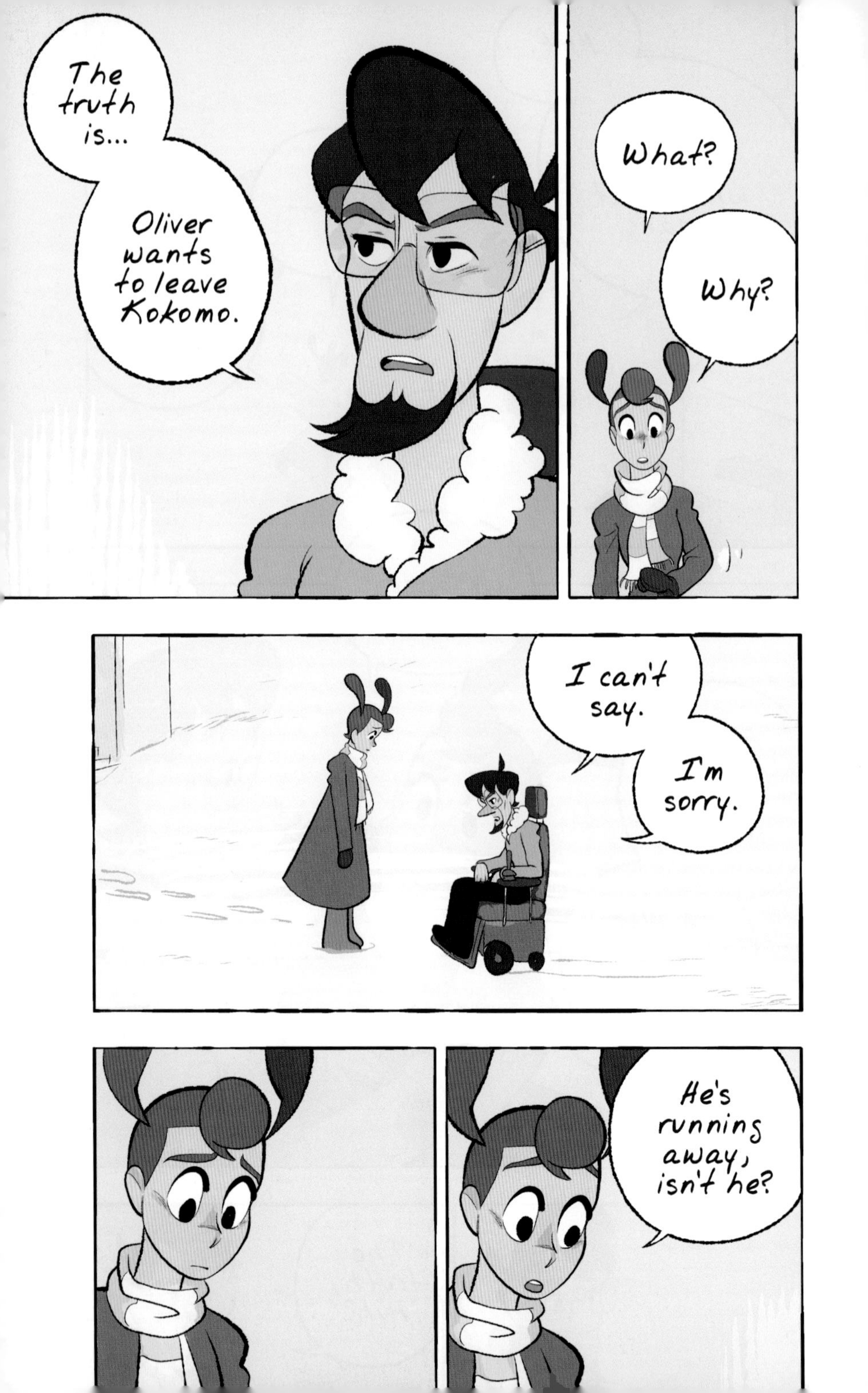

The truth is...
Oliver wants to leave Kokomo.
What?
Why?
I can't say.
I'm sorry.
He's running away, isn't he?

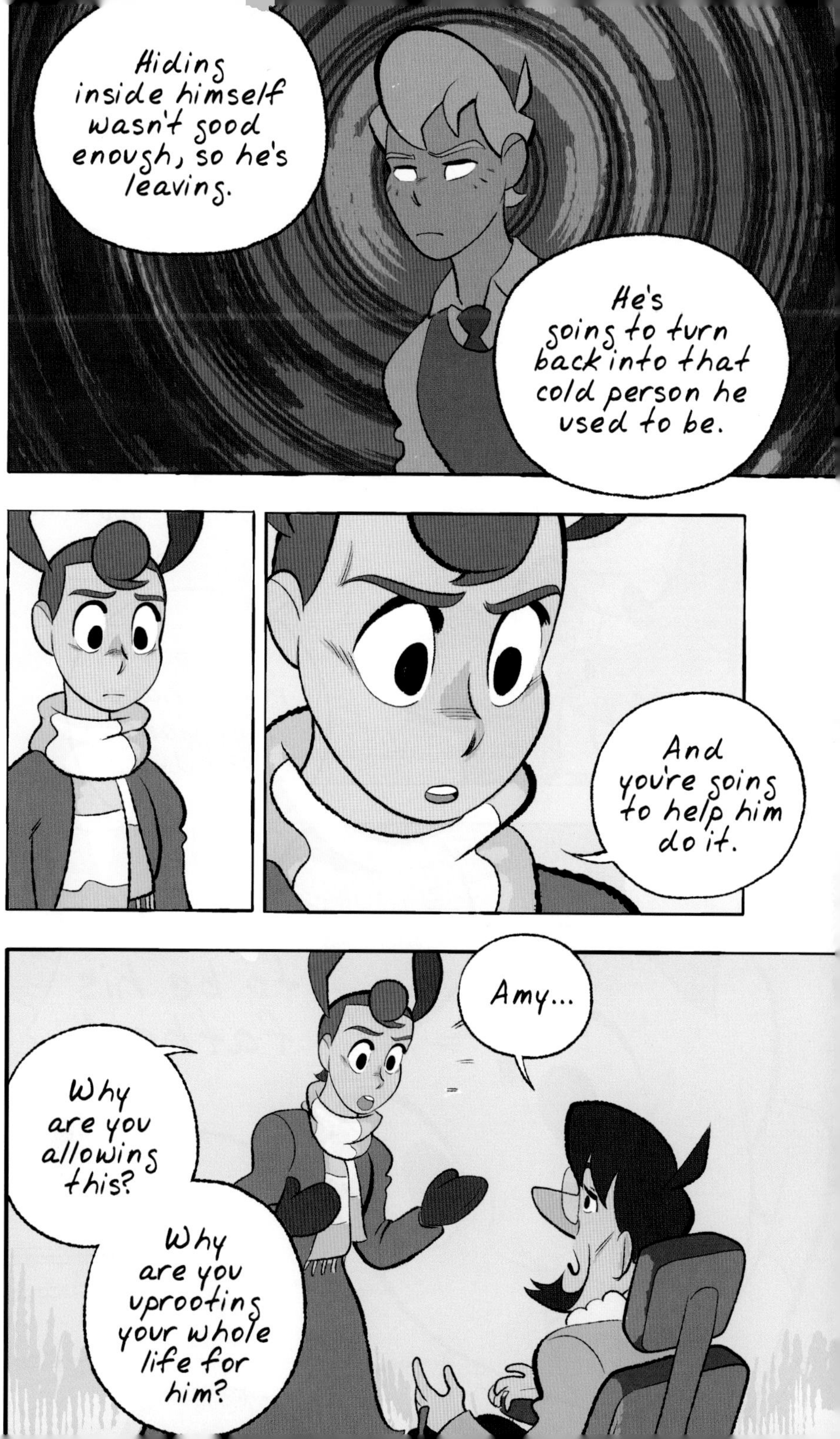
Hiding inside himself wasn't good enough, so he's leaving.
He's going to turn back into that cold person he used to be.
And you're going to help him do it.
Amy...
Why are you allowing this?
Why are you uprooting your whole life for him?

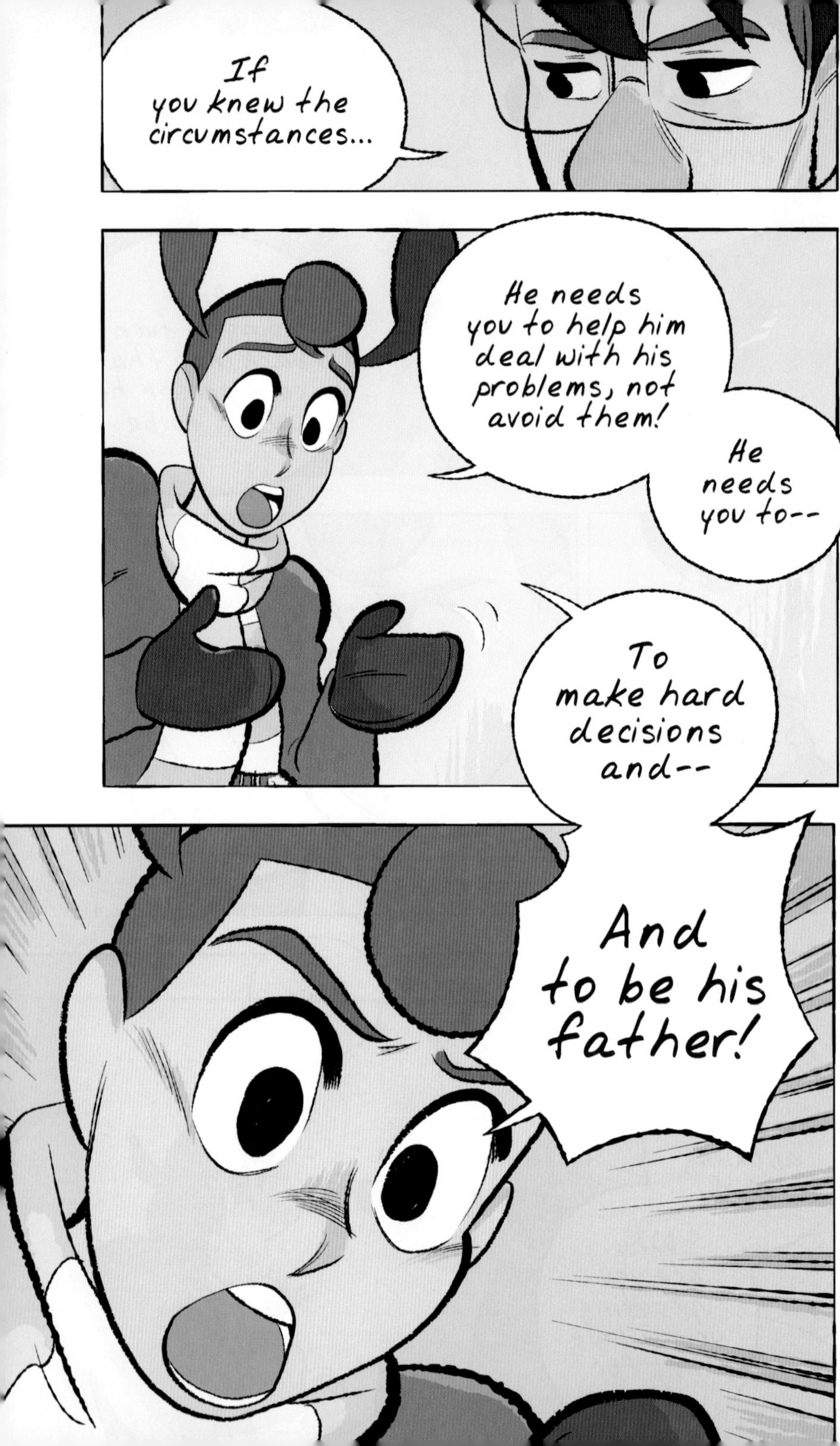
If you knew the circumstances...
He needs you to help him deal with his problems, not avoid them!
He needs you to--
To make hard decisions and--
And to be his father!

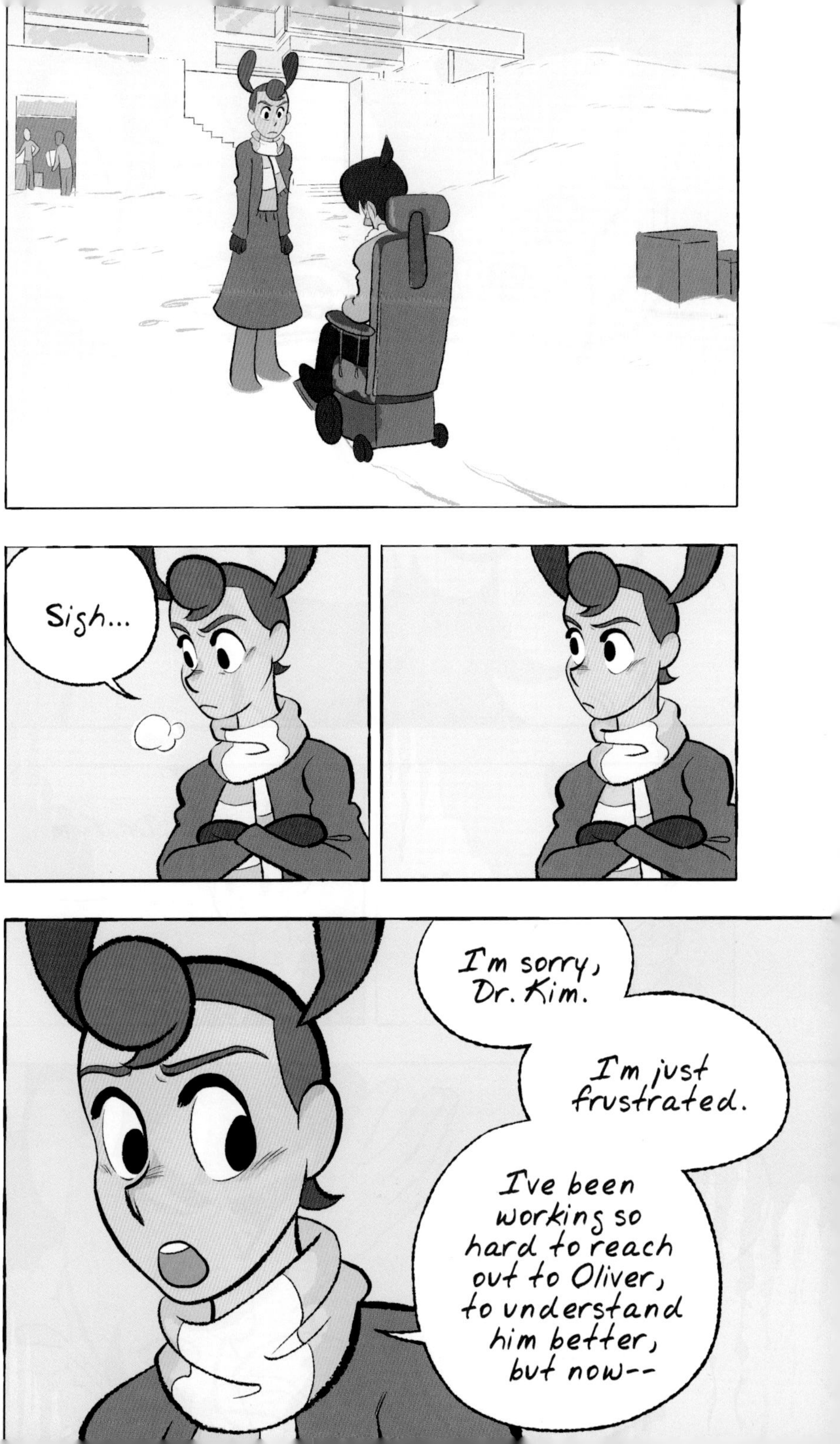
Sigh...
I'm sorry, Dr. Kim.
I'm just frustrated.
I've been working so hard to reach out to Oliver, to understand him better, but now--

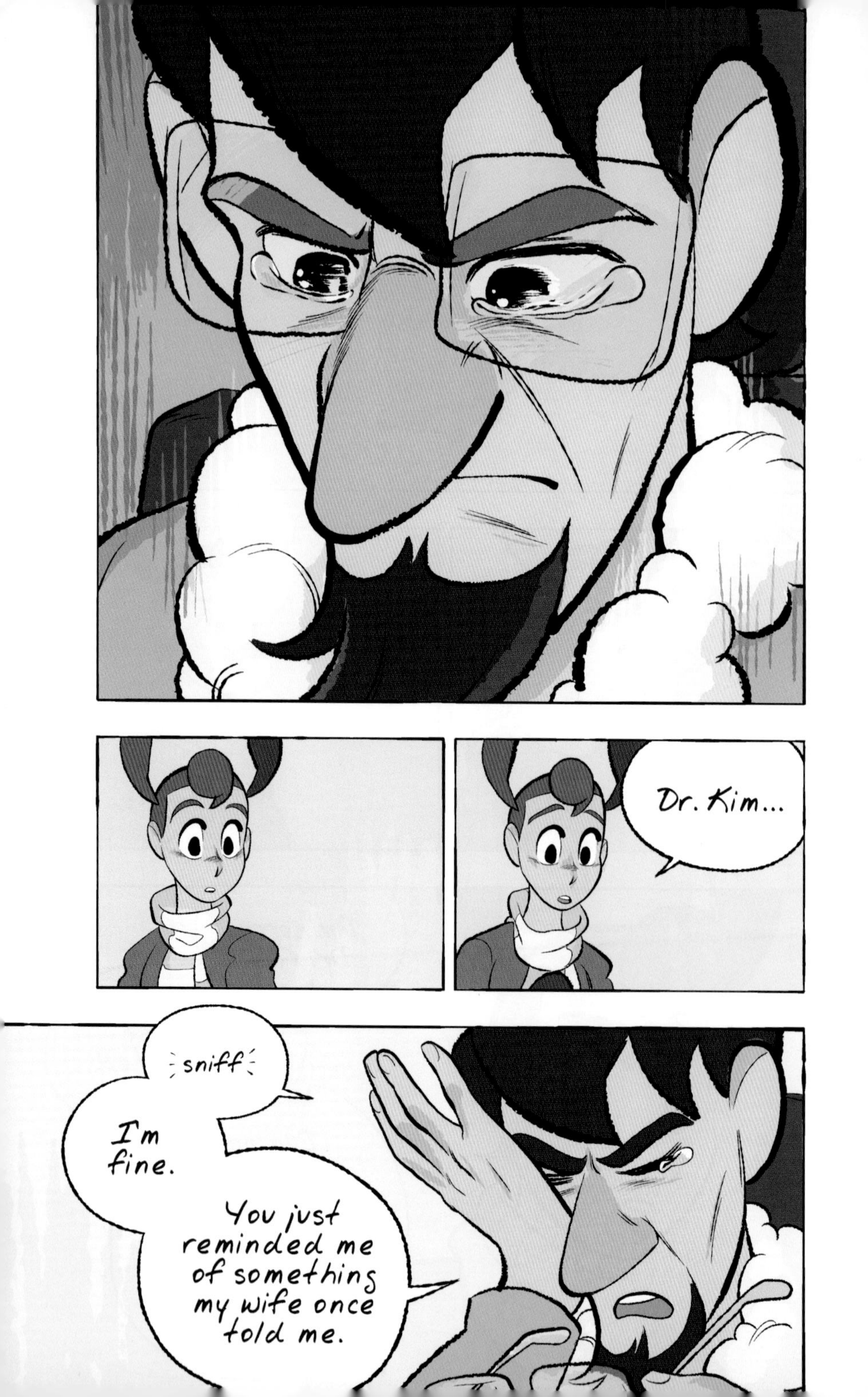

Dr. Kim...
sniff
I'm fine.
You just reminded me of somethins my wife once told me.

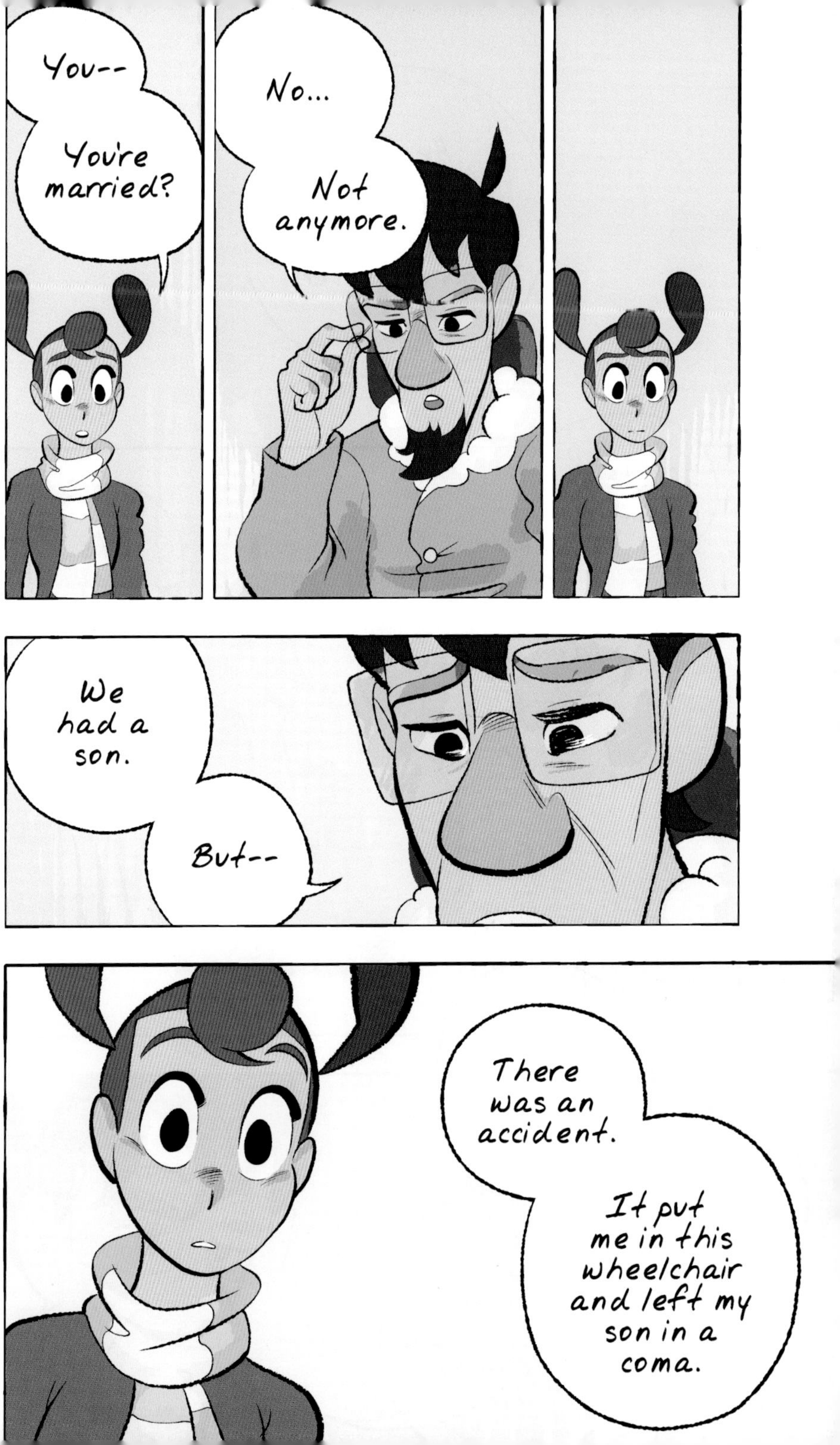
You--
You're married?
No...
Not anymore.
We had a son.
But--
There was an accident.
It put me in this wheelchair and left my son in a coma.

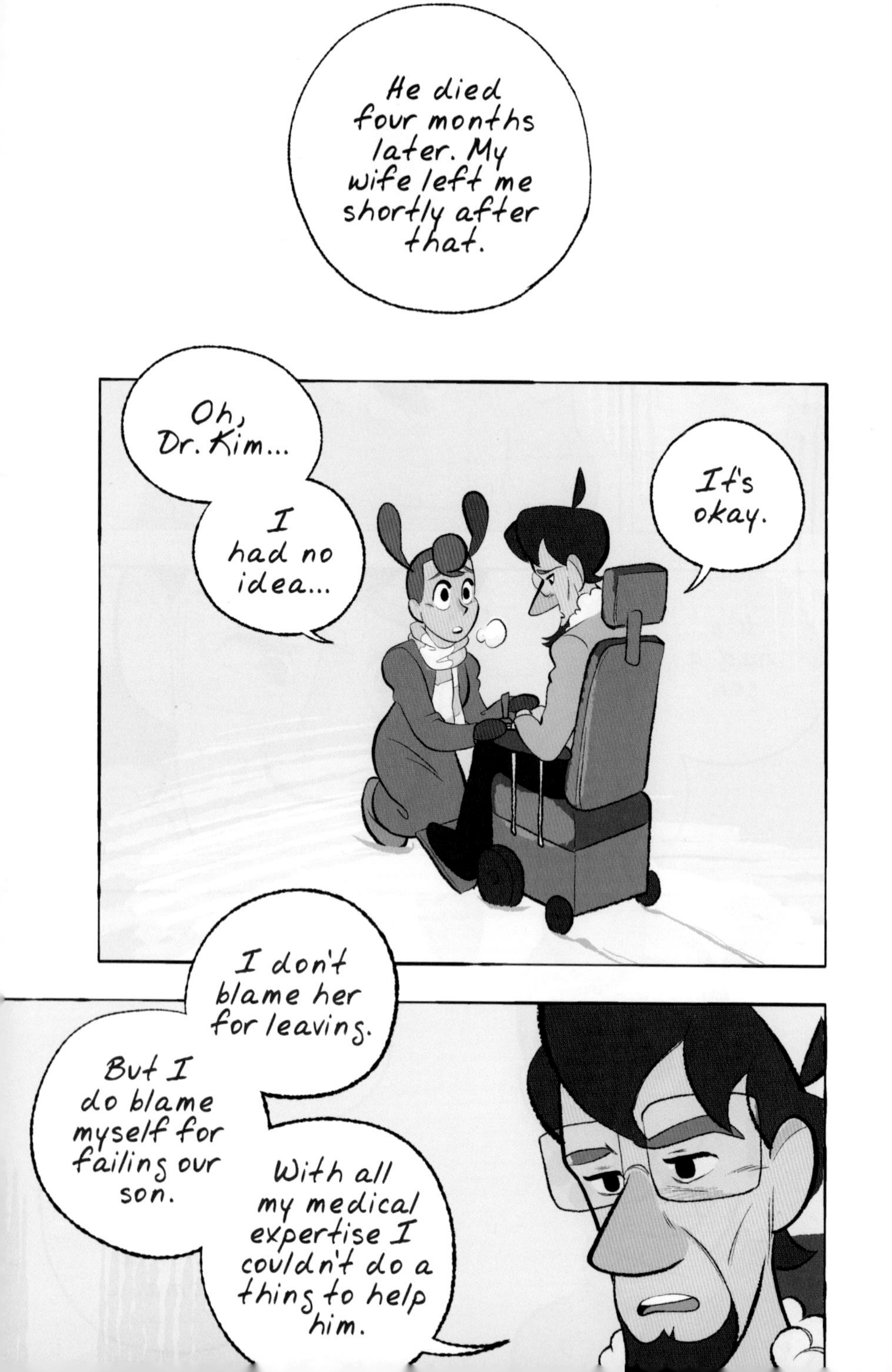
He died four months later. My wife left me shortly after that.
Oh, Dr. Kim...
I had no idea...
It's okay.
I don't blame her for leaving.
But I do blame myself for failing our son.
With all my medical expertise I couldn't do a thing to help him.

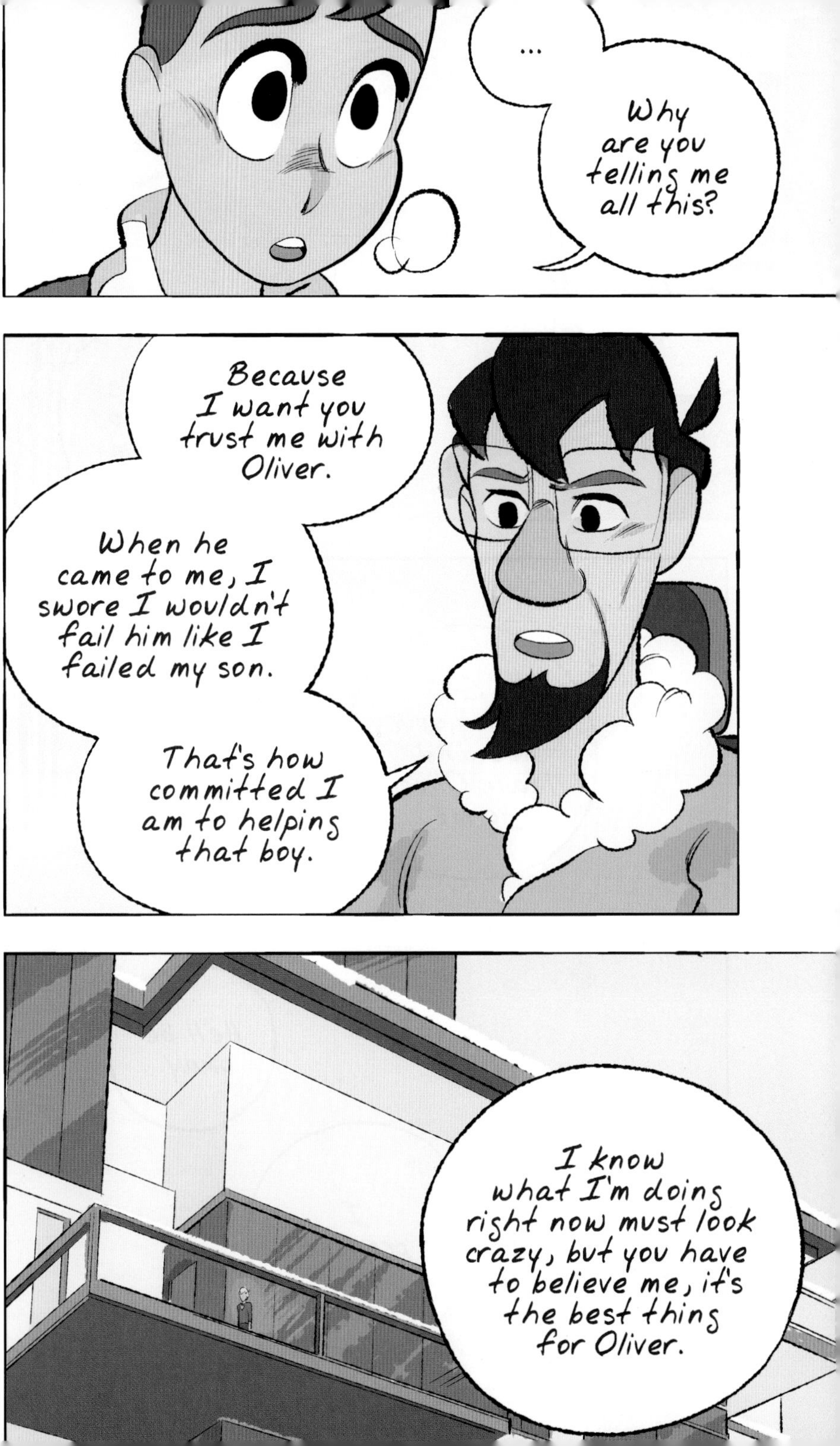
...
Why are you telling me all this?
Because I want you trust me with Oliver.
When he came to me, I swore I wouldn't fail him like I failed my son.
That's how committed I am to helping that boy.
I know what I'm doing right now must look crazy, but you have to believe me, it's the best thing for Oliver.

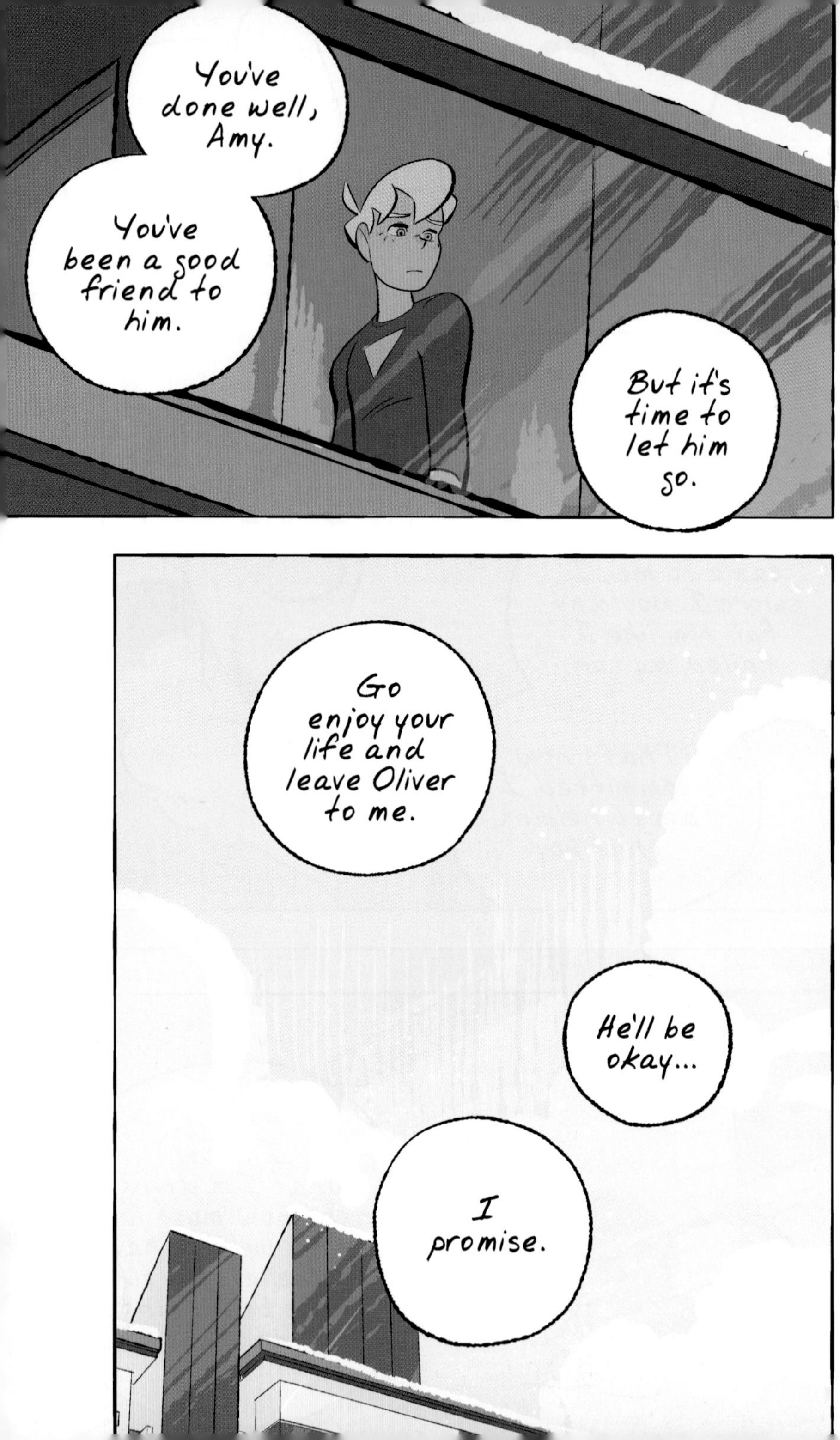
You've done well, Amy.
You've been a good friend to him.
But it's time to let him go.
Go enjoy your life and leave Oliver to me.
He'll be okay...
I promise.

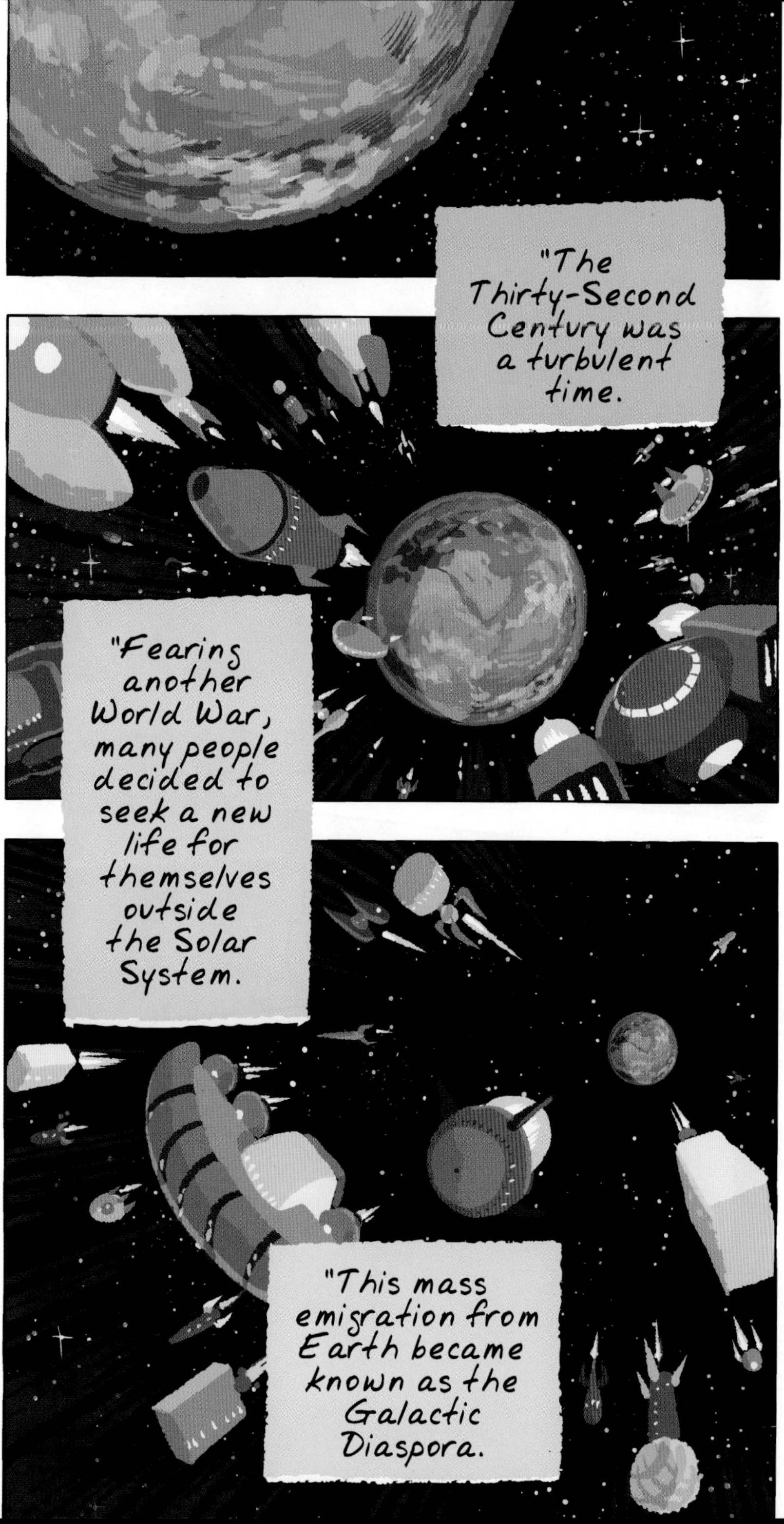
"The Thirty-Second Century was a turbulent time.
"Fearing another World War, many people decided to seek a new life for themselves outside the Solar System.
"This mass emigration from Earth became known as the Galactic Diaspora.

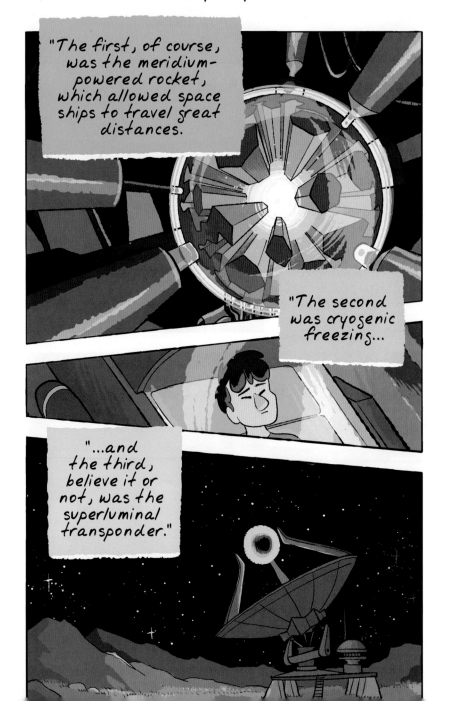

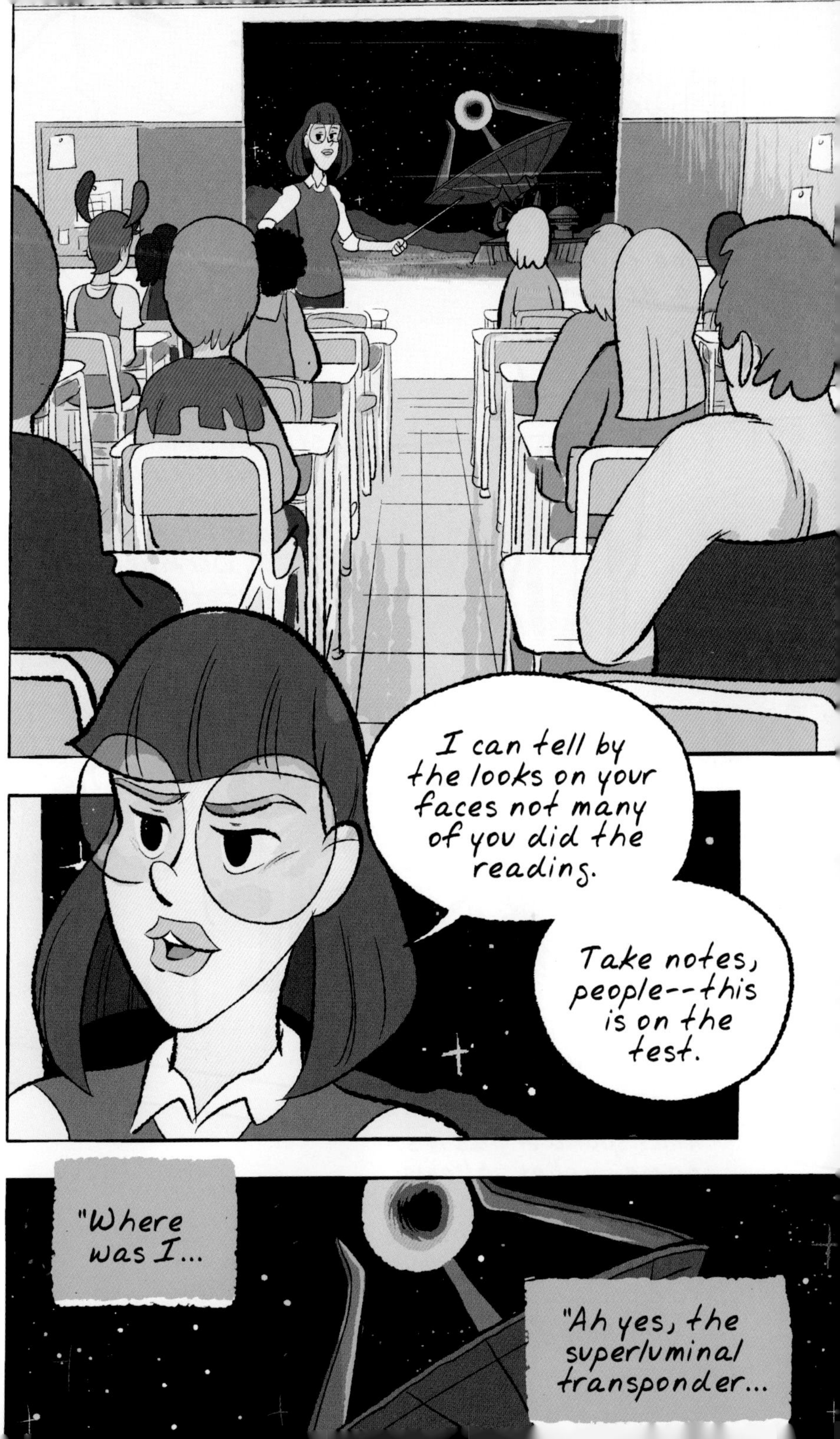
I can tell by the looks on your faces not many of you did the readings.
Take notes, people--this is on the test.
"Where was I...
"Ah yes, the superluminal transponder...

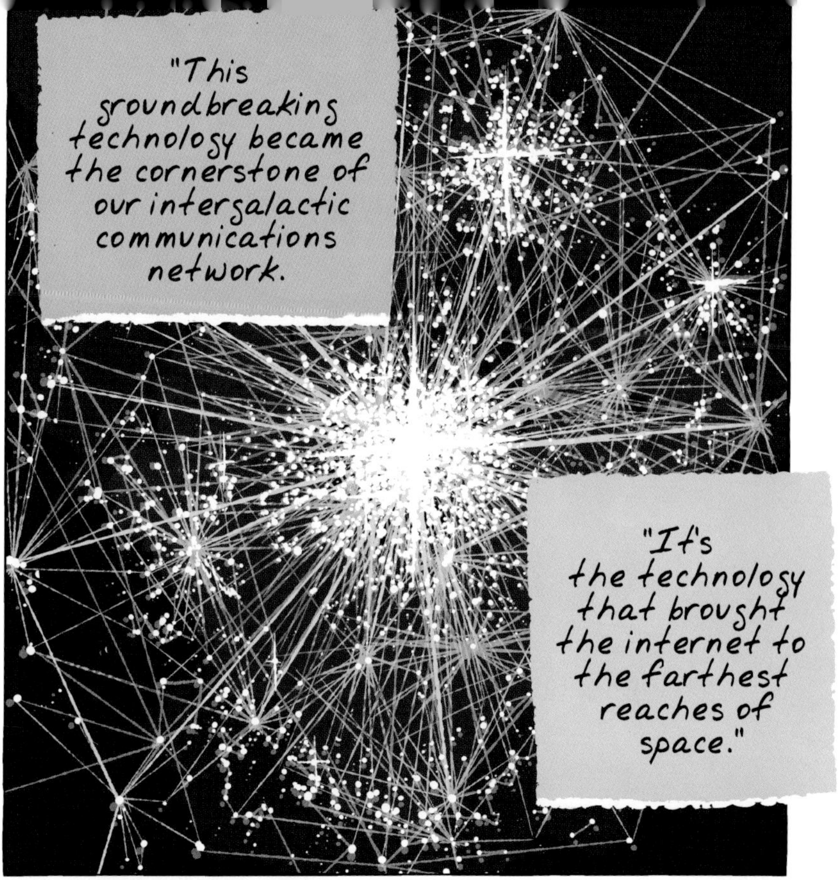
"This groundbreaking technology became the cornerstone of our intergalactic communications network.
"It's the technology that brought the internet to the farthest reaches of space."

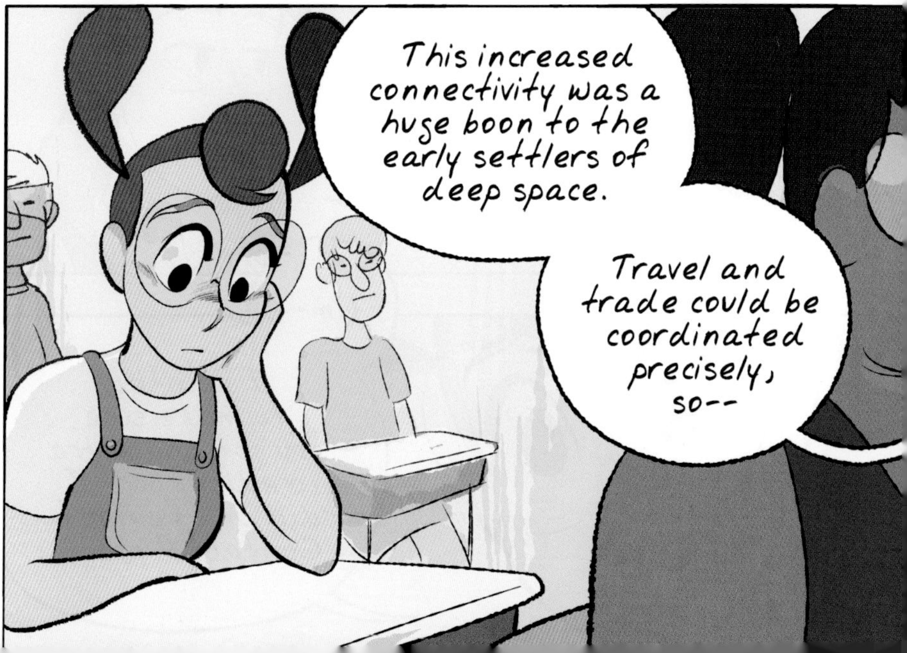
This increased connectivity was a huge boon to the early settlers of deep space.
Travel and trade could be coordinated precisely, so--

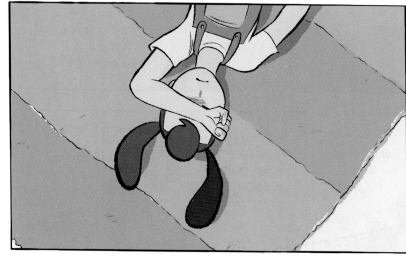

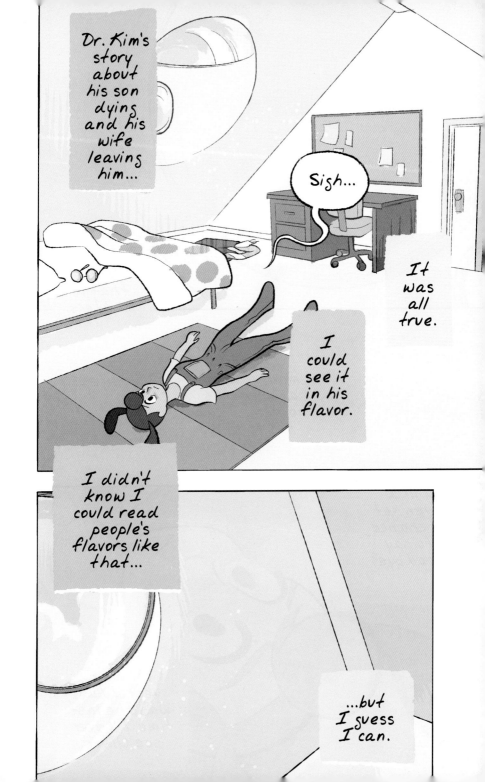

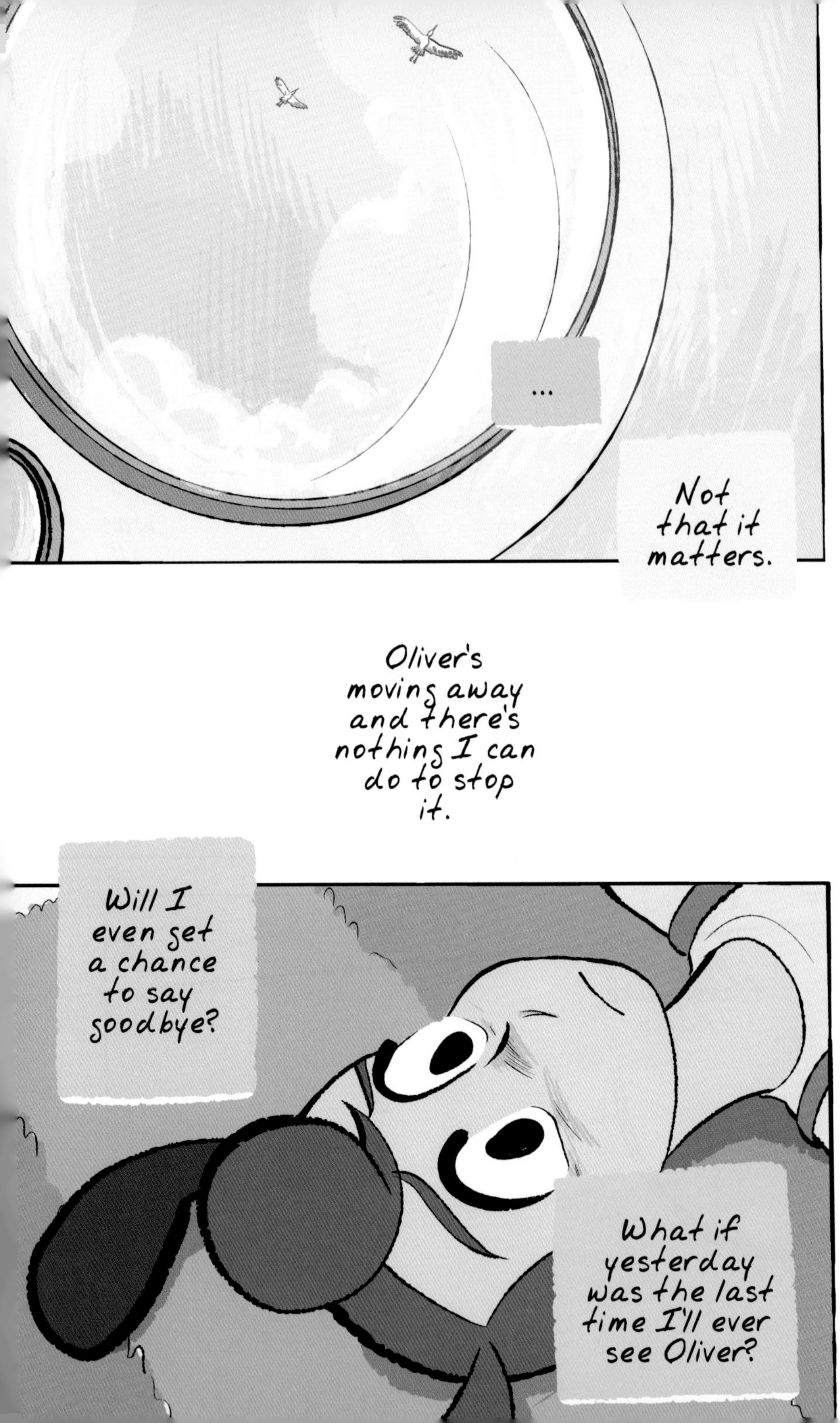
...
Not that it matters.
Oliver's moving away and there's nothing I can do to stop it.
Will I even get a chance to say goodbye?
What if yesterday was the last time I'll ever see Oliver?

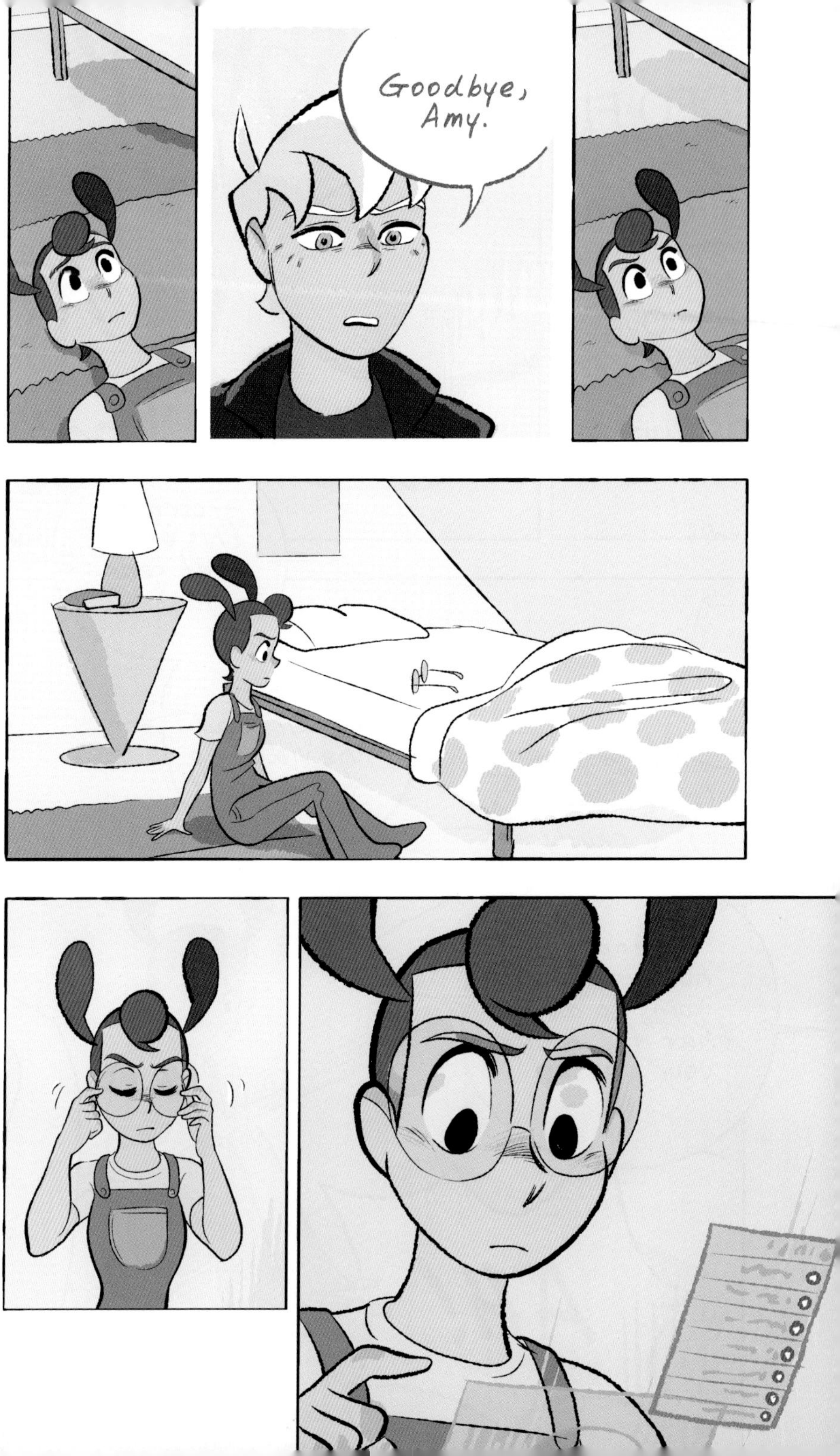
Goodbye, Amy.

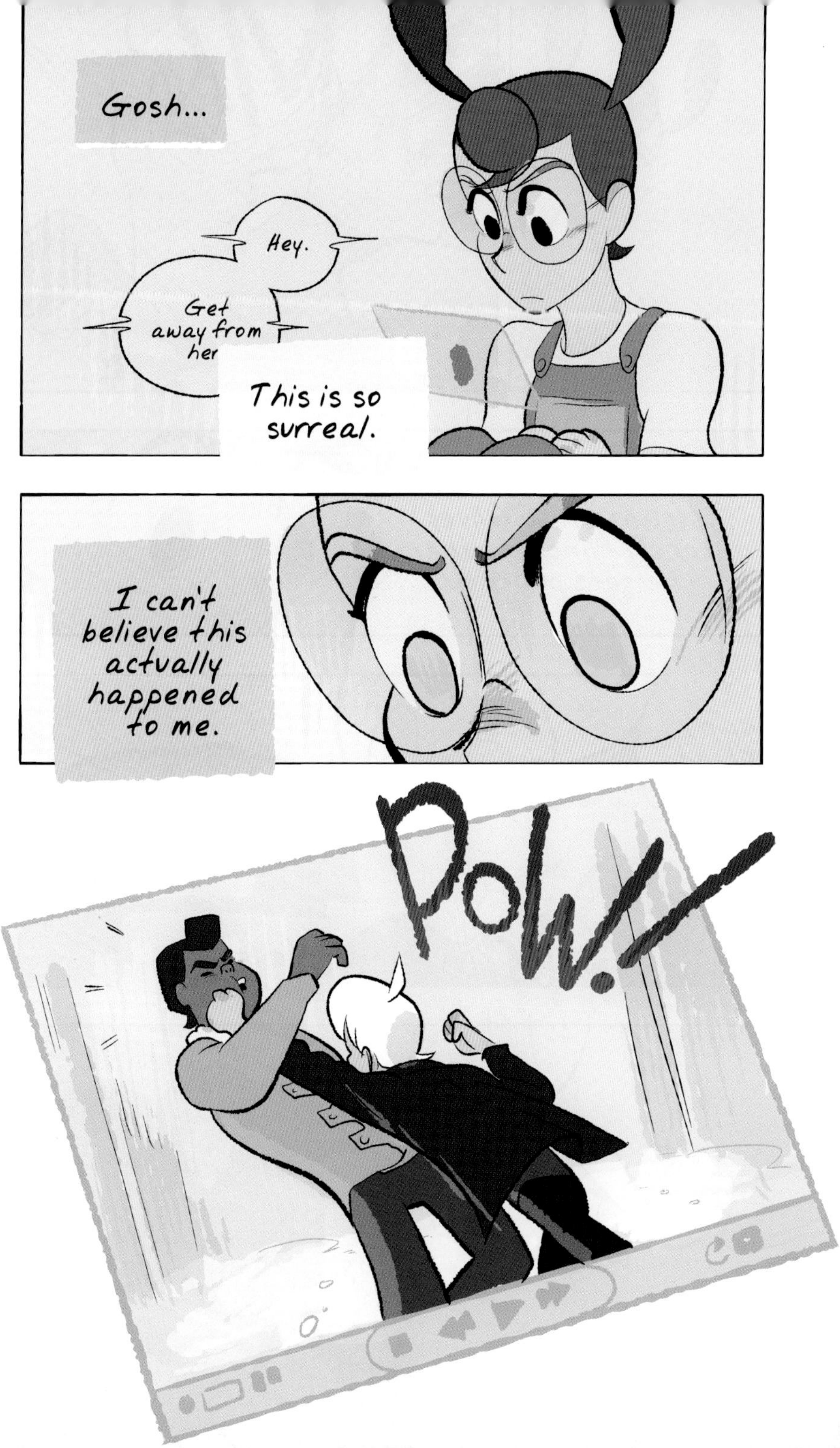
Gosh...
Hey.
Get away from her
This is so surreal.
I can't believe this actually happened to me.
POW!!

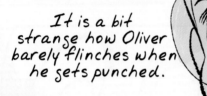

It is a bit strange how Oliver barely flinches when he gets punched.

I mean, look at him...

No scratches...

No bruises...

He's not even breathing hard.

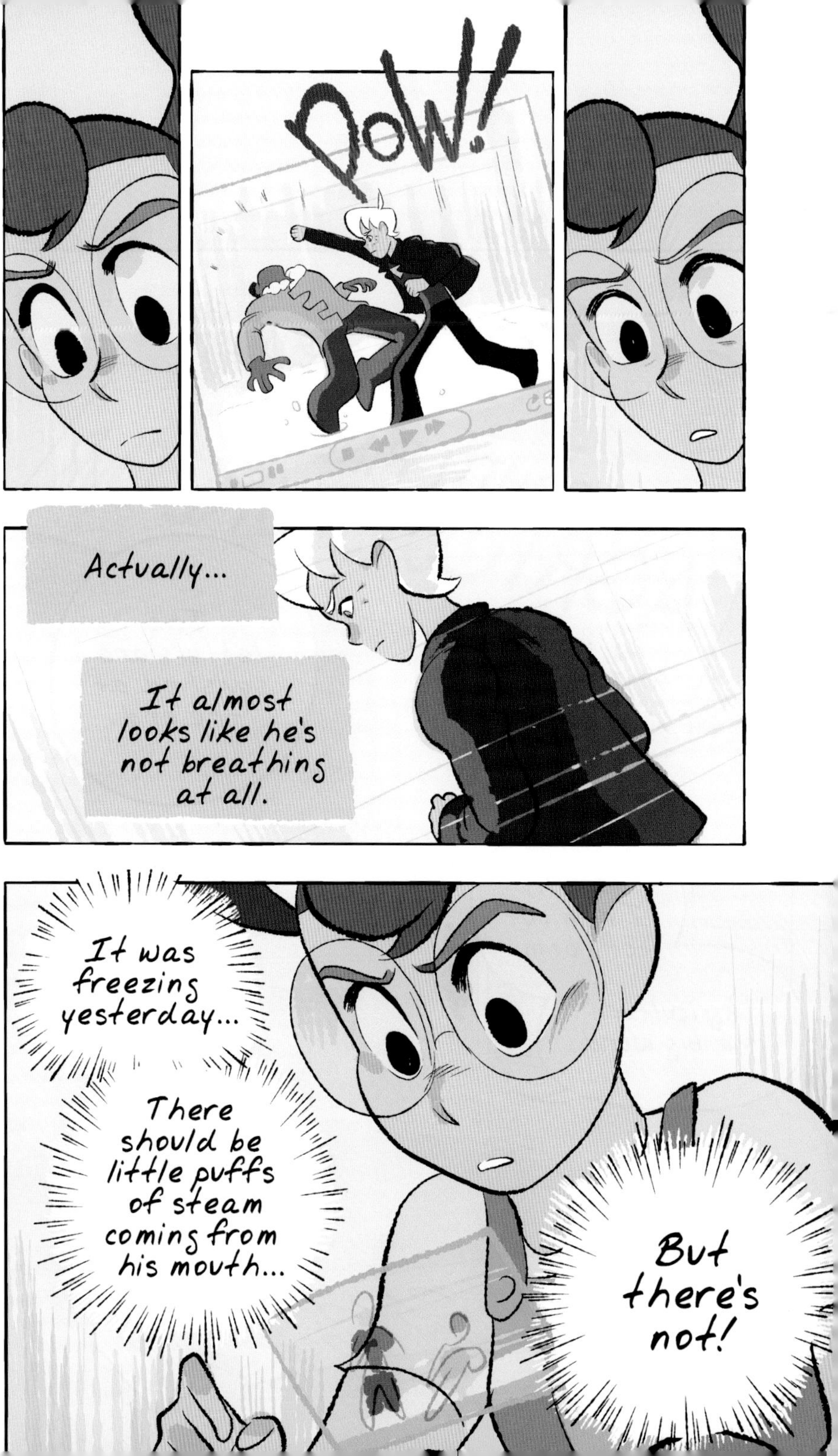
POW!!
Actually...
It almost looks like he's not breathing at all.
It was freezing yesterday...
There should be little puffs of steam coming from his mouth...
But there's not!

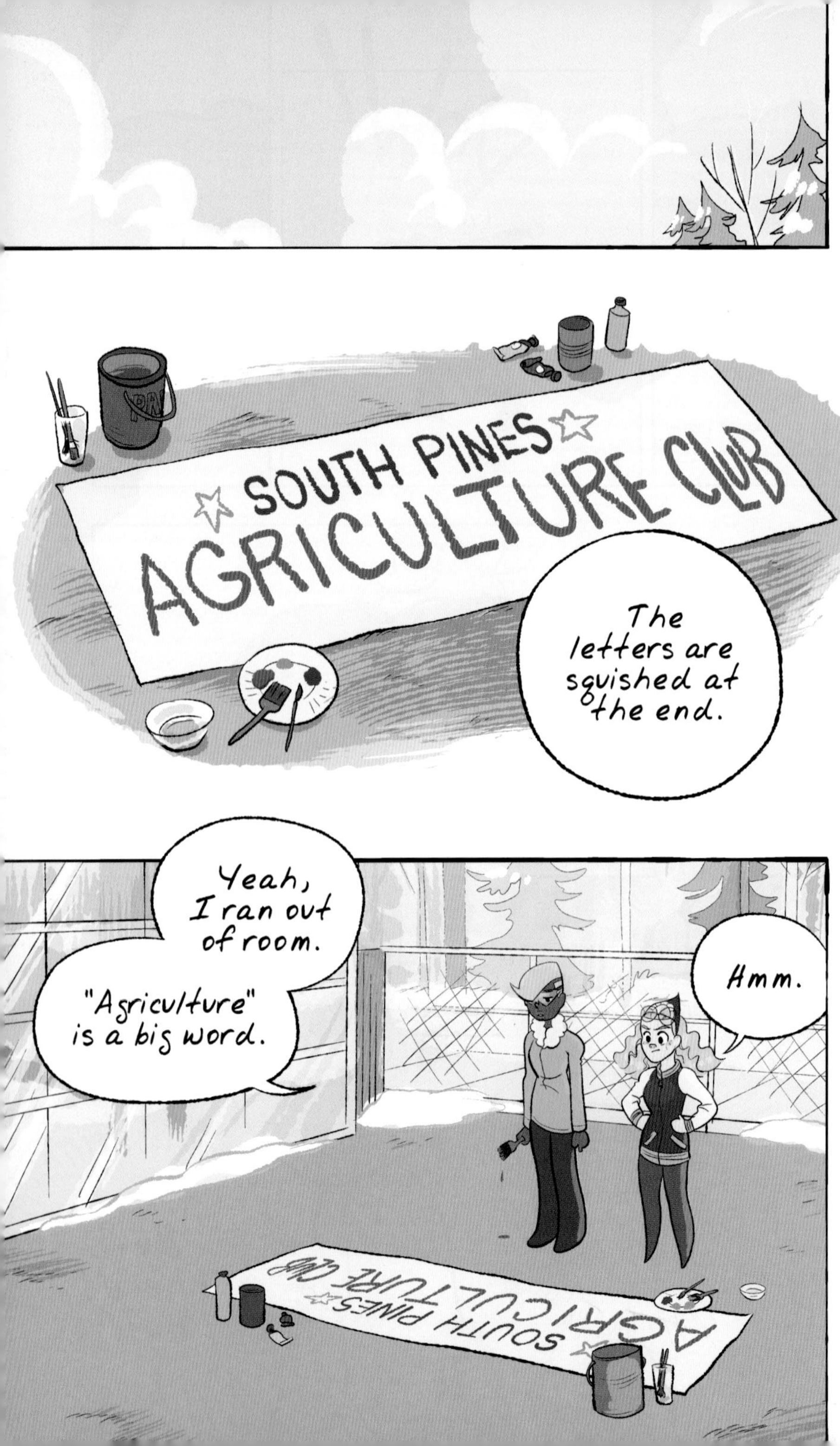
SOUTH PINES
AGRICULTURE CLUB
The letters are squished at the end.
Yeah, I ran out of room.
"Agriculture" is a big word.
Hmm.

They're on your--

I know!

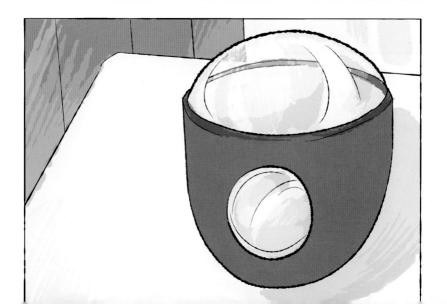

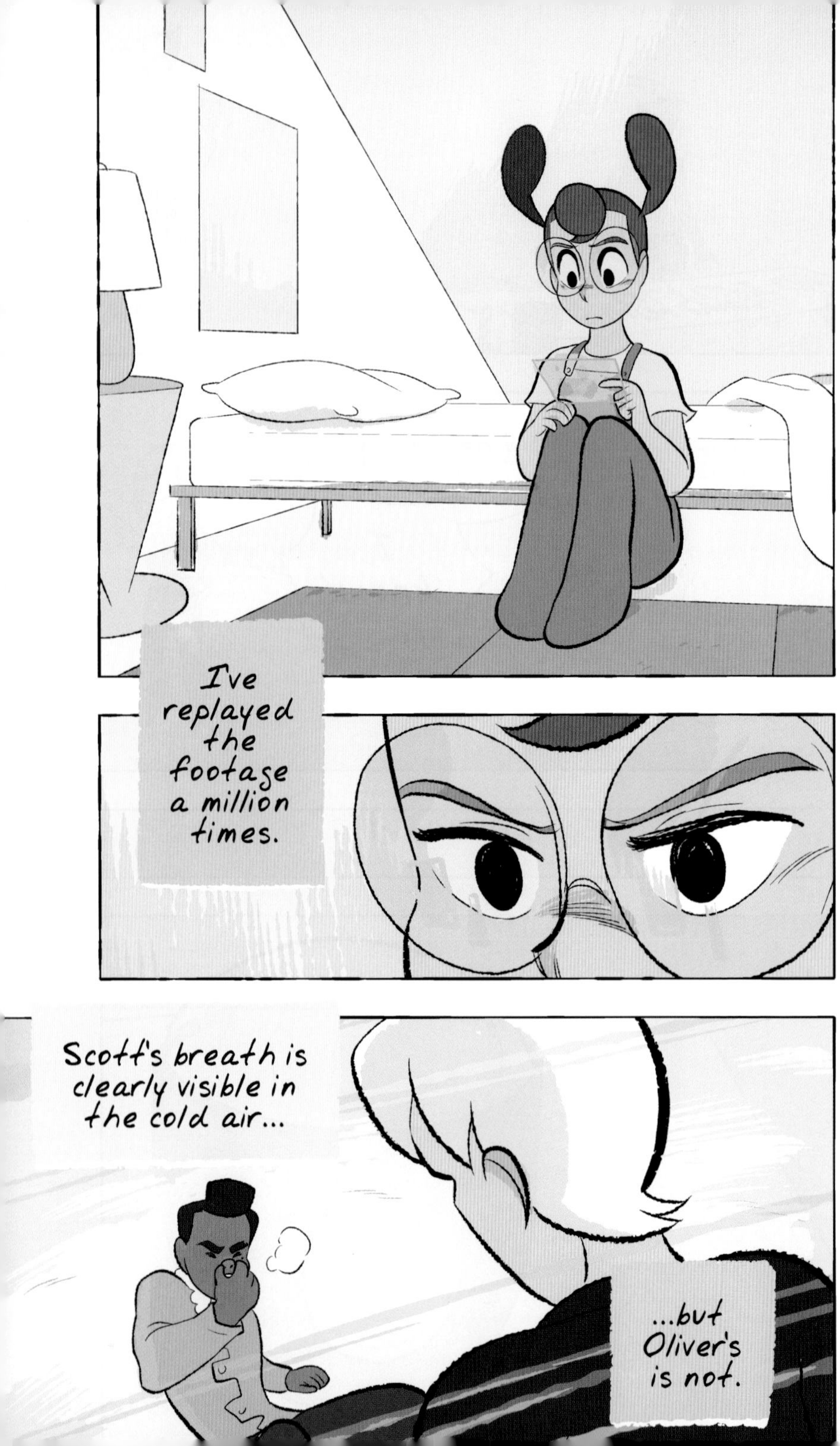
I've replayed the footage a million times.
Scott's breath is clearly visible in the cold air...
...but Oliver's is not.

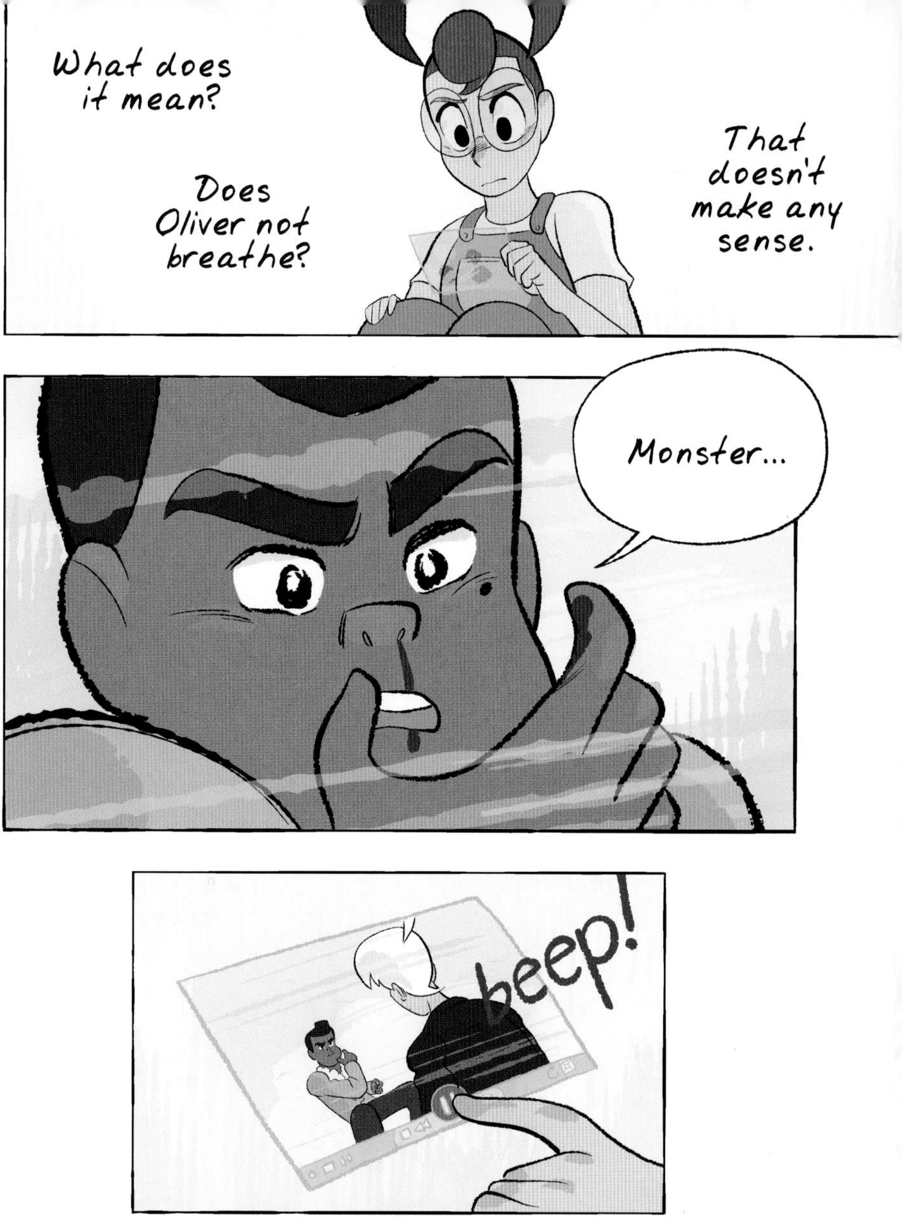
What does it mean?
Does Oliver not breathe?
That doesn't make any sense.
Monster...
beep!

No, Oliver is not a monster.

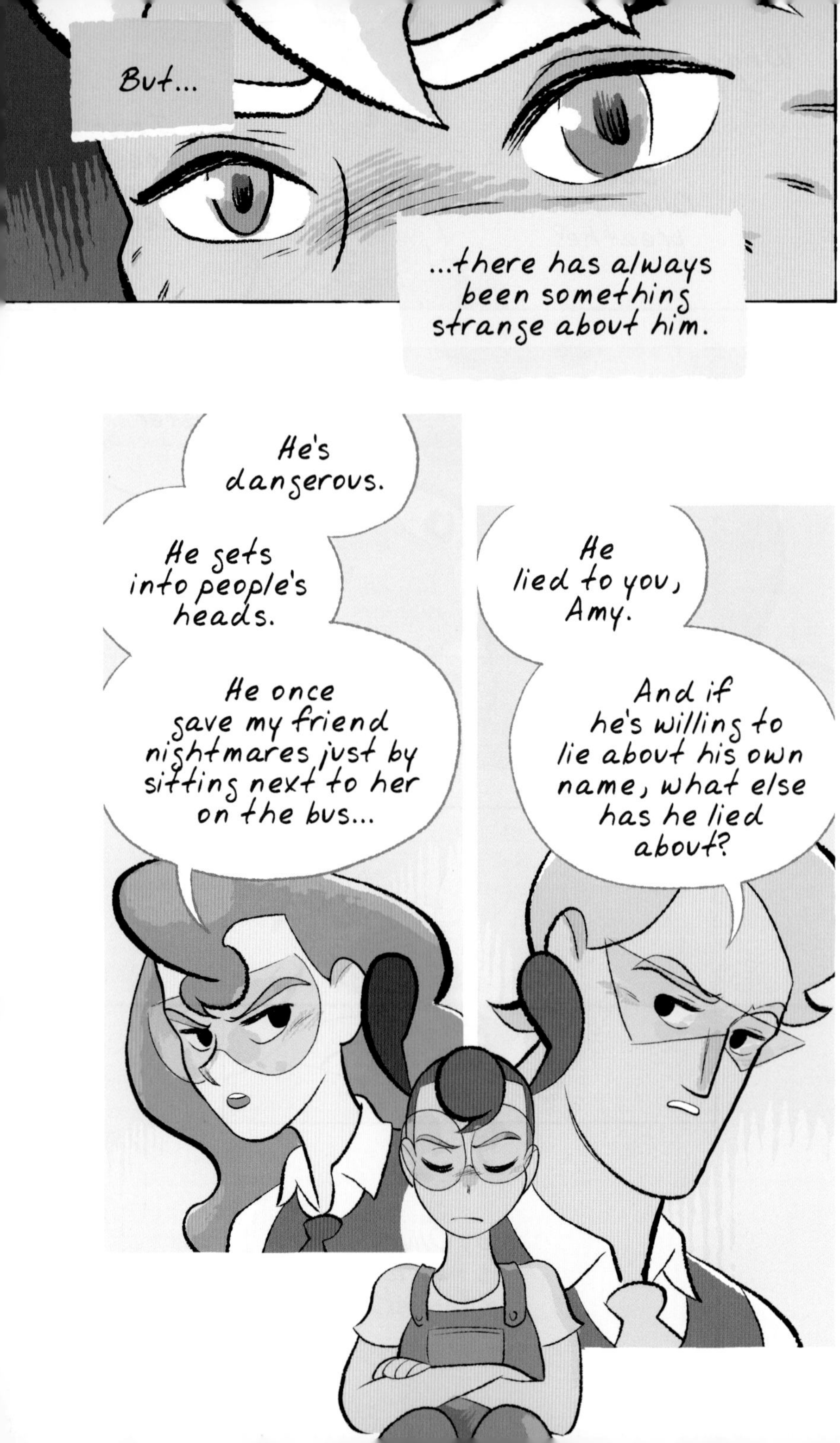
But...
...there has always been something strange about him.
He's dangerous.
He gets into people's heads.
He once gave my friend nightmares just by sitting next to her on the bus...
He lied to you, Amy.
And if he's willing to lie about his own name, what else has he lied about?

No.

Oliver's not a liar.

And he's not dangerous.

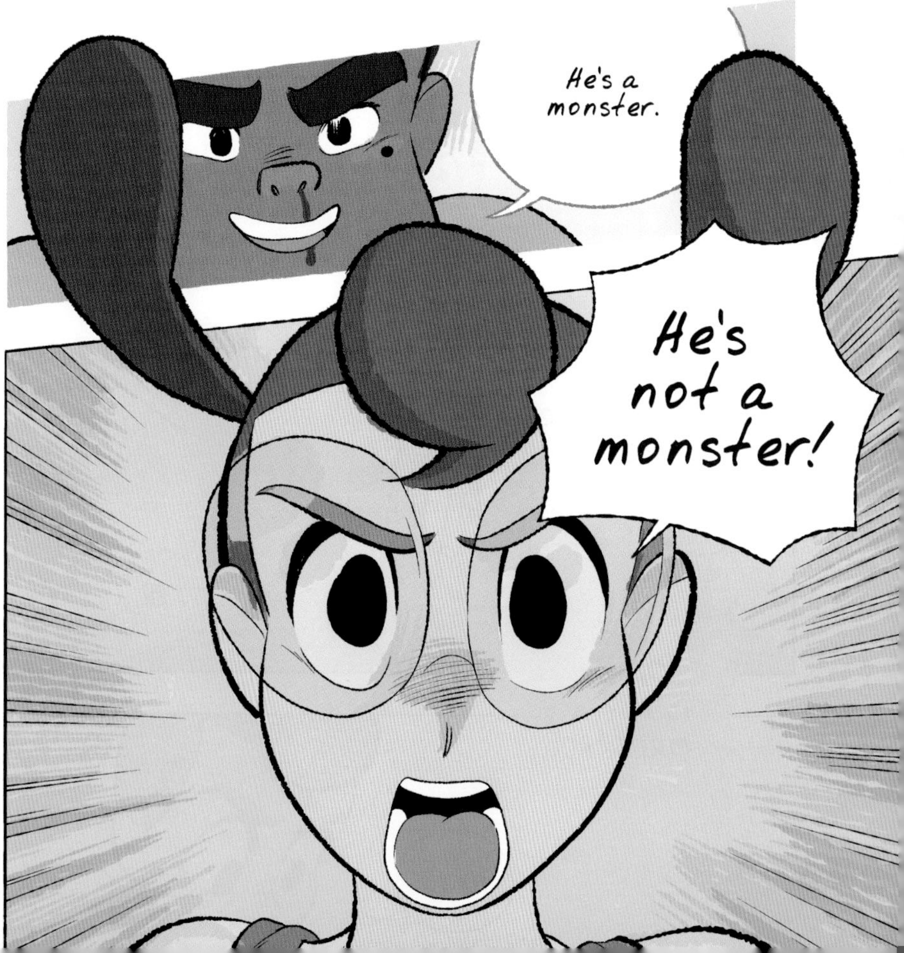
He's a monster.
He's not a monster!

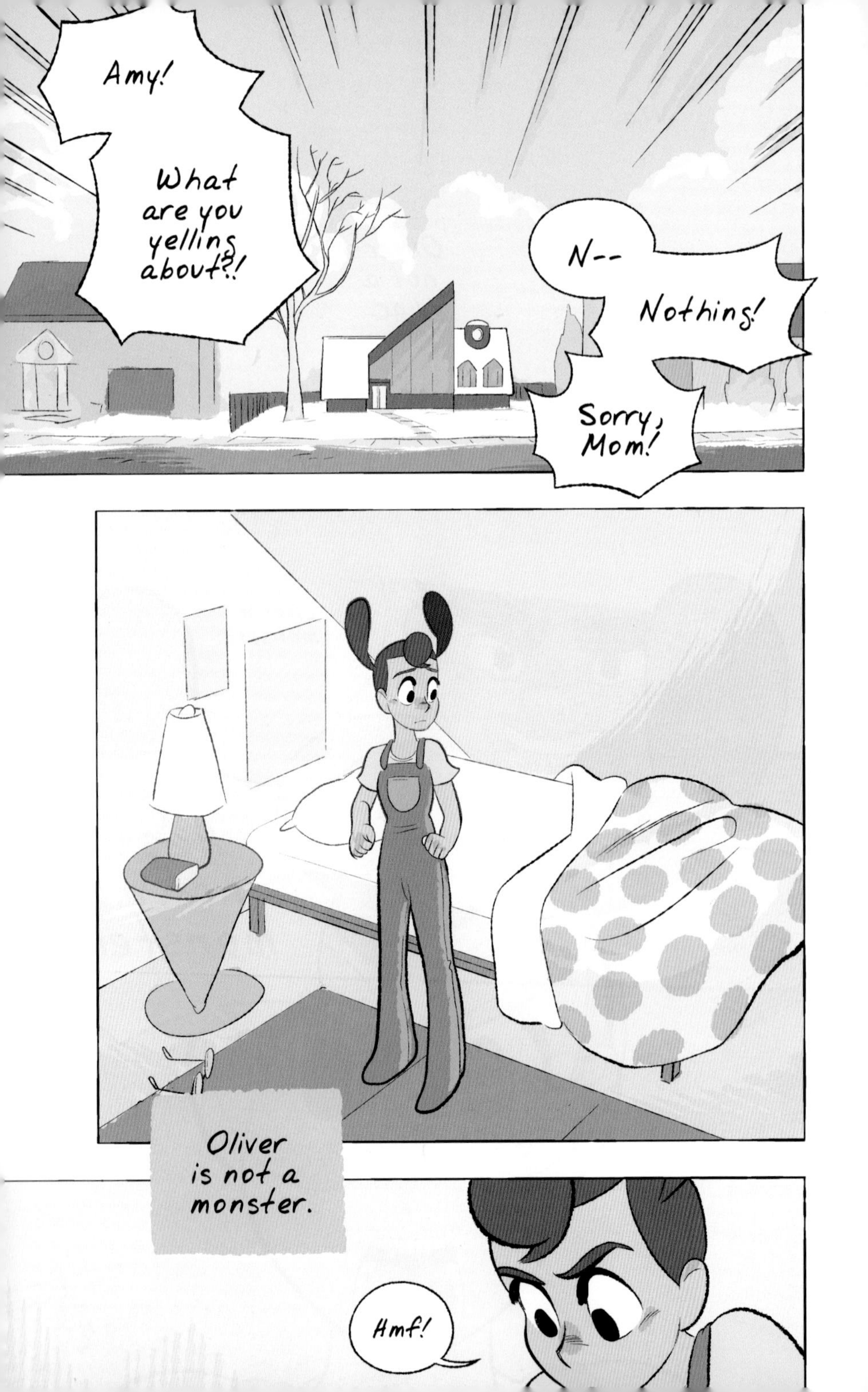

Amy!
What are you yelling about?!
N--
Nothing!
Sorry, Mom!
Oliver is not a monster.
Hmf!

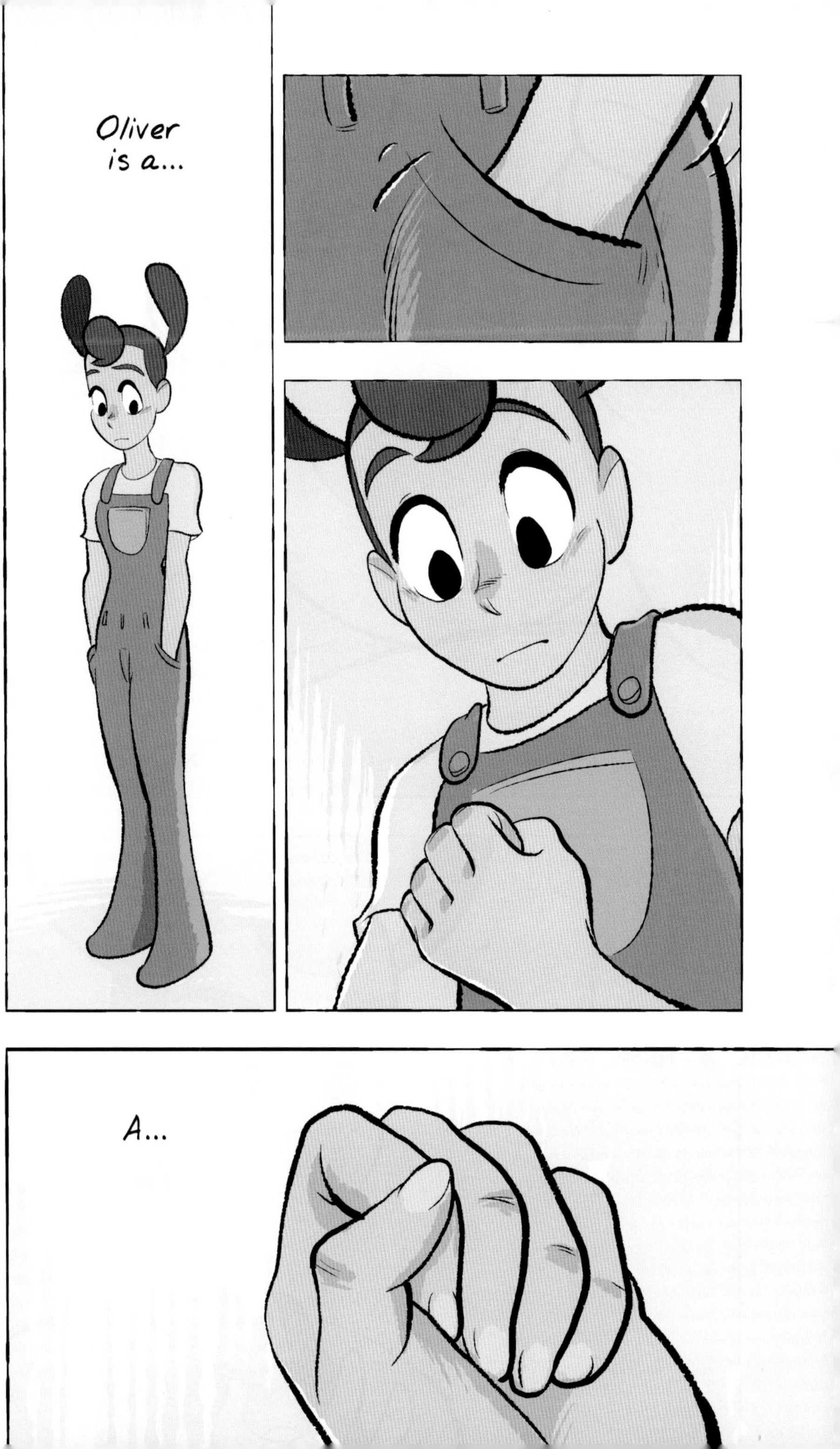
Oliver
is a...
A...

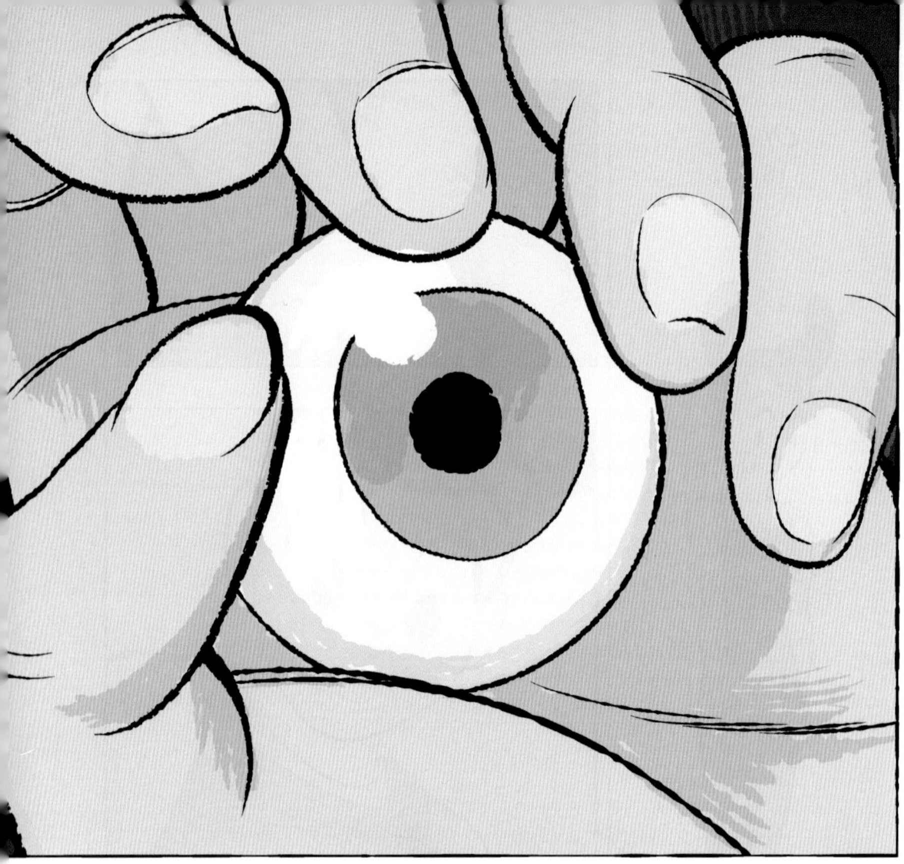

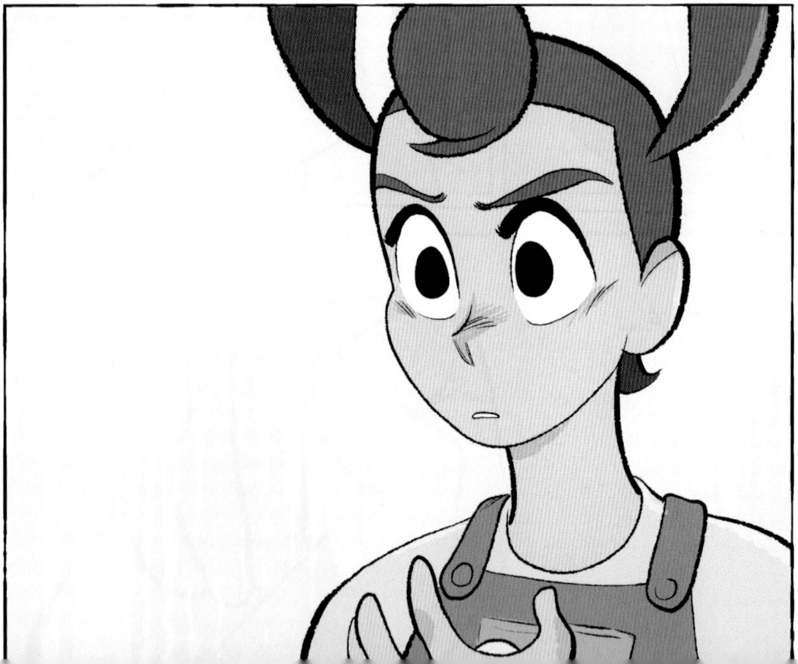

Unless, of course,
Oliver doesn't need
to breathe...

Unless,
of course,
Oliver is a...

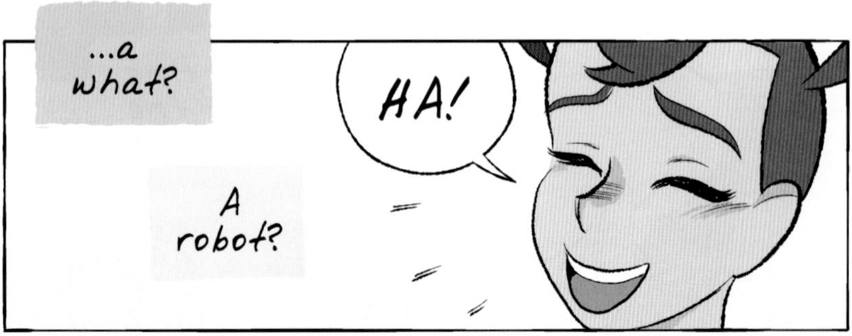
...a what?
HA!
A robot?

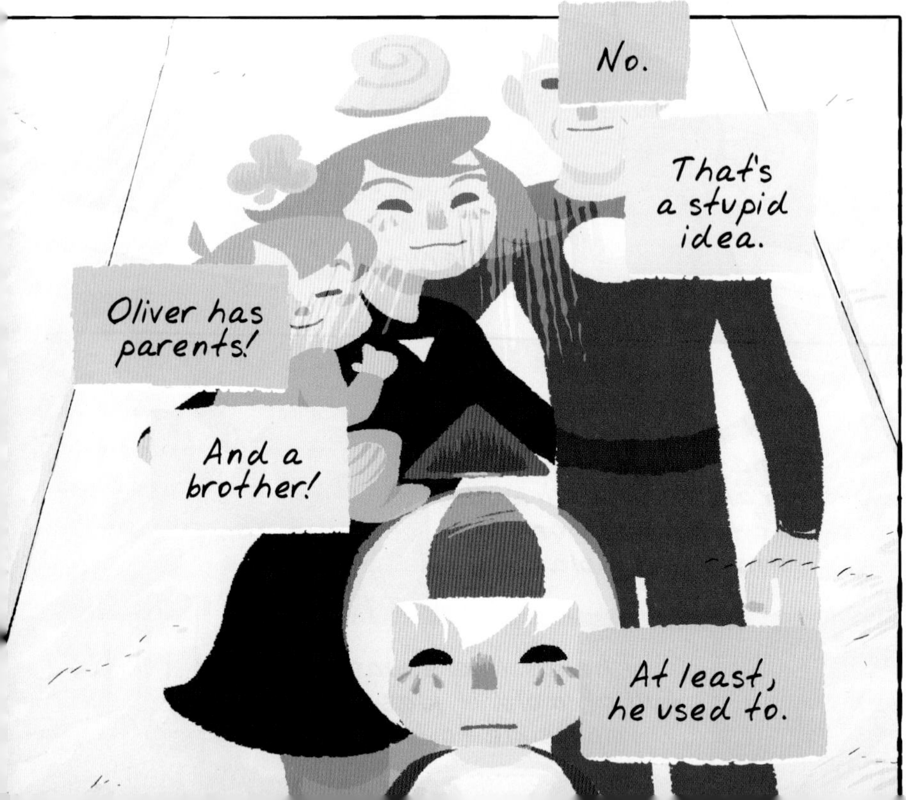
No.
That's a stupid idea.
Oliver has parents!
And a brother!
At least, he used to.

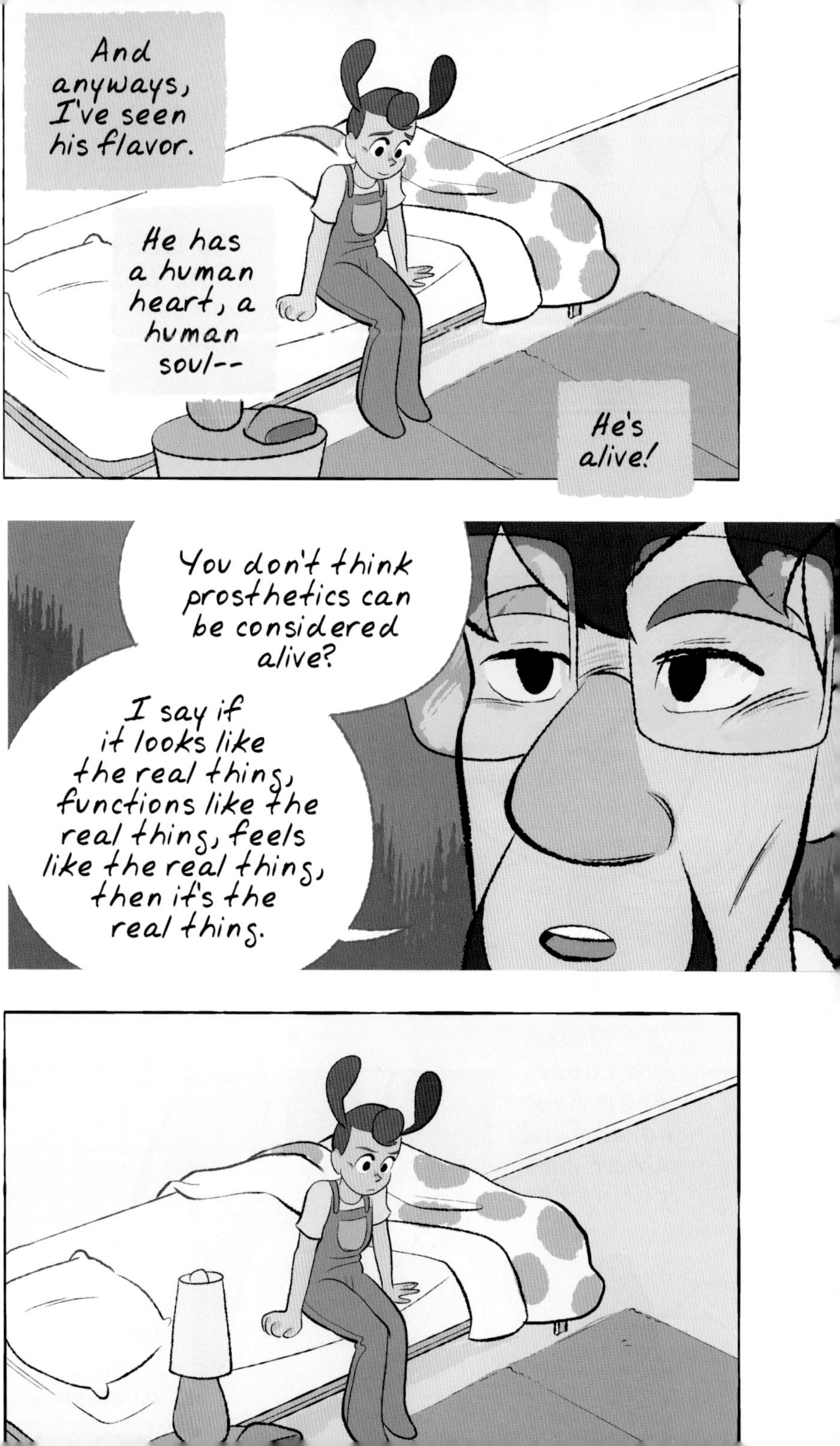
And anyways, I've seen his flavor.
He has a human heart, a human soul--
He's alive!
You don't think prosthetics can be considered alive?
I say if it looks like the real thing, functions like the real thing, feels like the real thing, then it's the real thing.

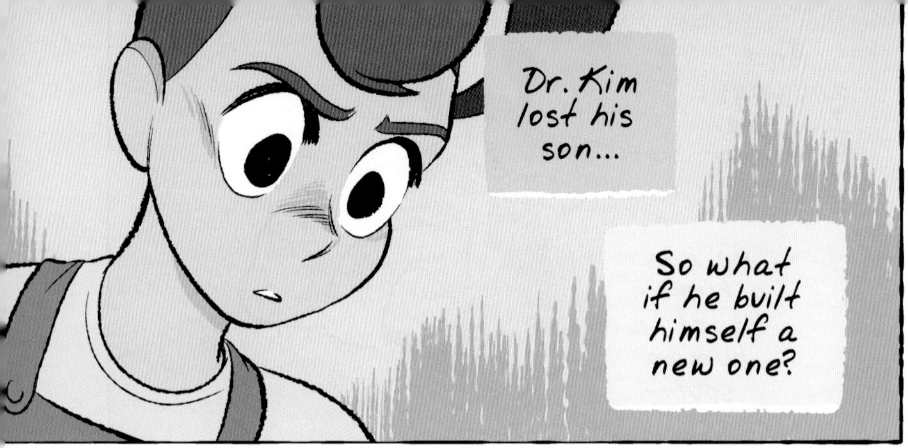
Dr. Kim lost his son...
So what if he built himself a new one?

No.

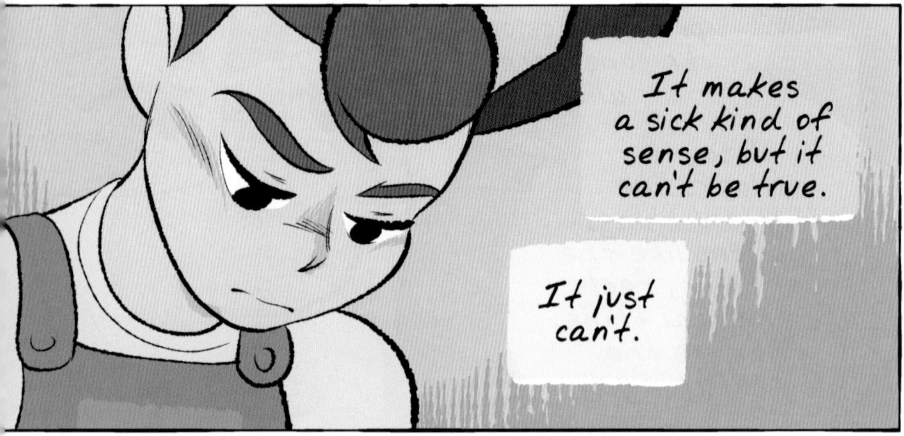
It makes a sick kind of sense, but it can't be true.
It just can't.

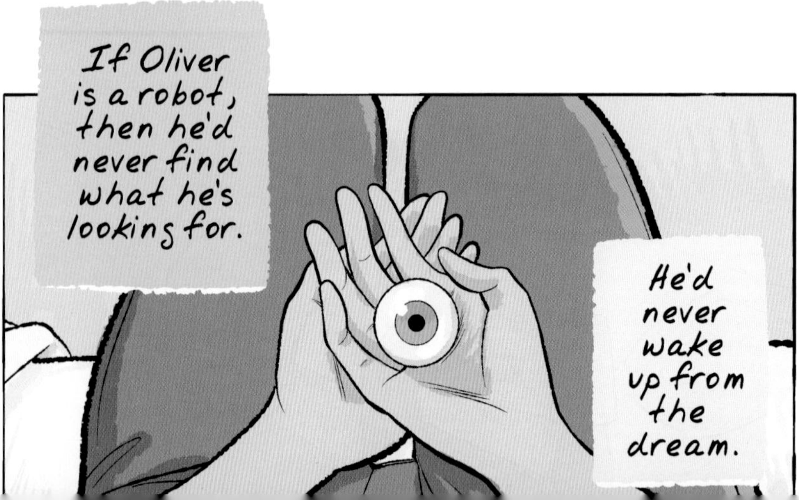
If Oliver is a robot, then he'd never find what he's looking for.
He'd never wake up from the dream.

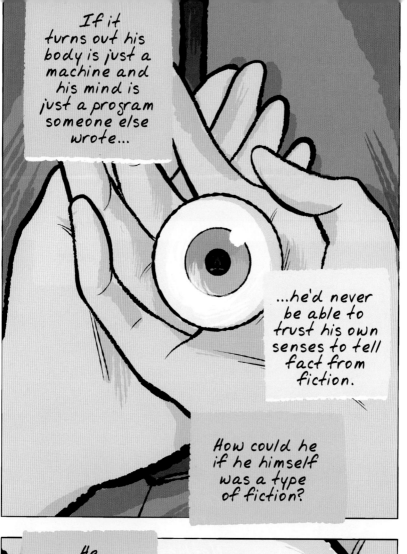

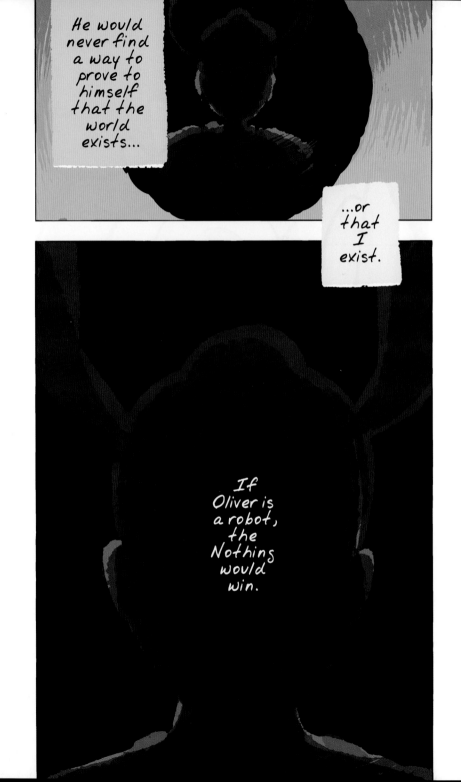

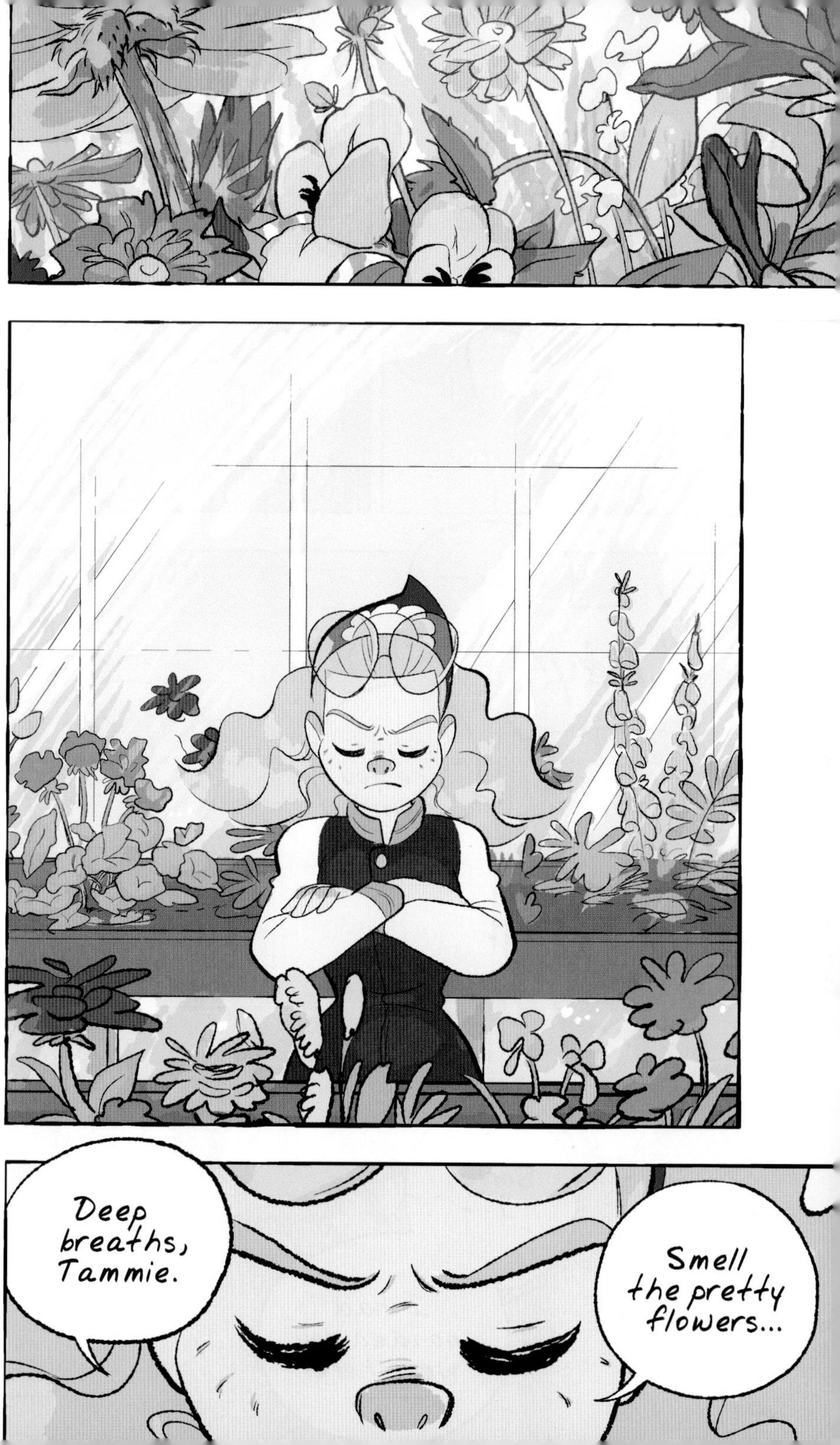
Deep breaths, Tammie.
Smell the pretty flowers...

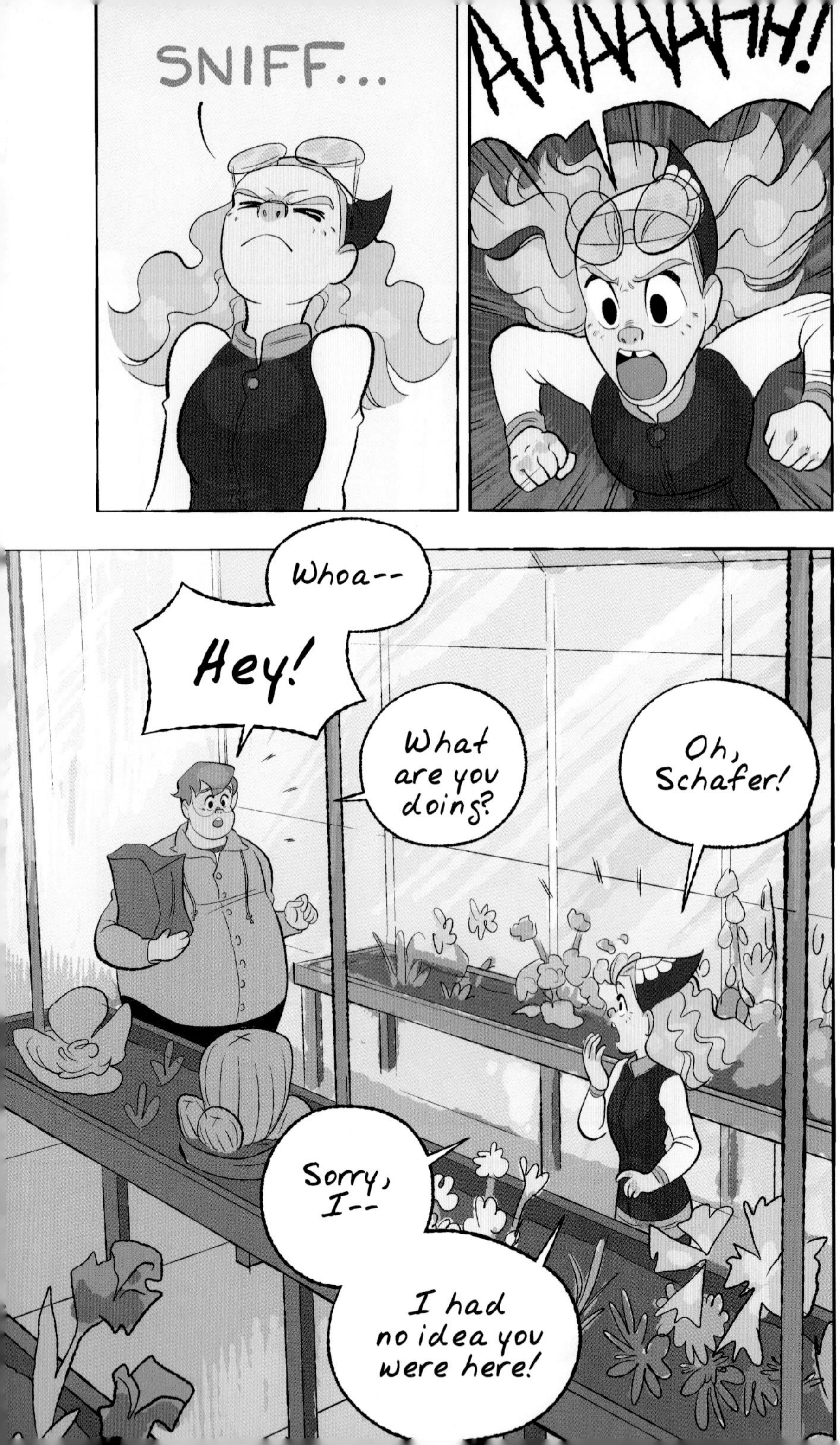
SNIFF...
AAAAAHH!
Whoa--
Hey!
What are you doing?
Oh, Schafer!
Sorry, I--
I had no idea you were here!

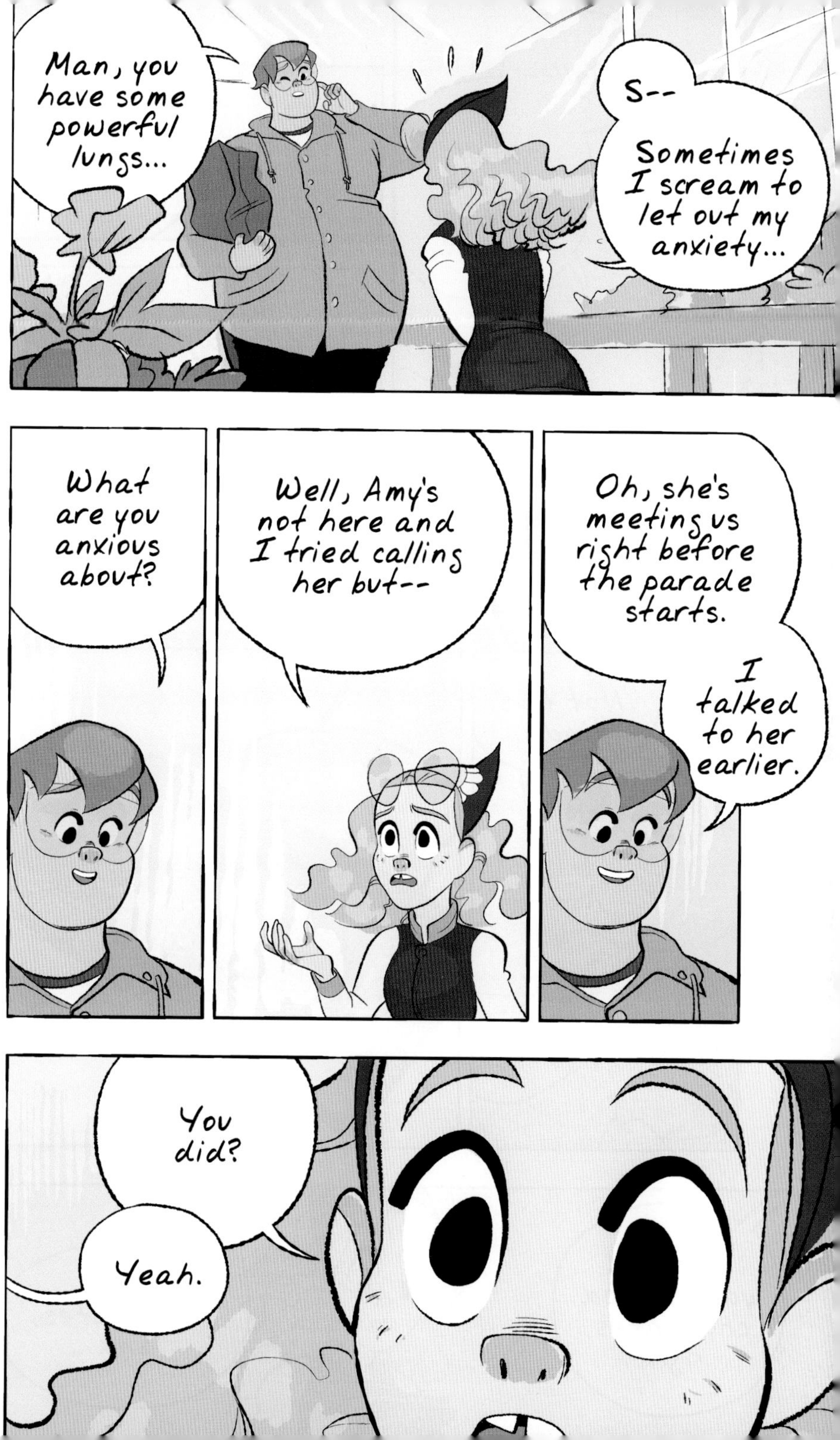
Man, you have some powerful lungs...
S--
Sometimes I scream to let out my anxiety...
What are you anxious about?
Well, Amy's not here and I tried calling her but--
Oh, she's meeting us right before the parade starts.
I talked to her earlier.
You did?
Yeah.

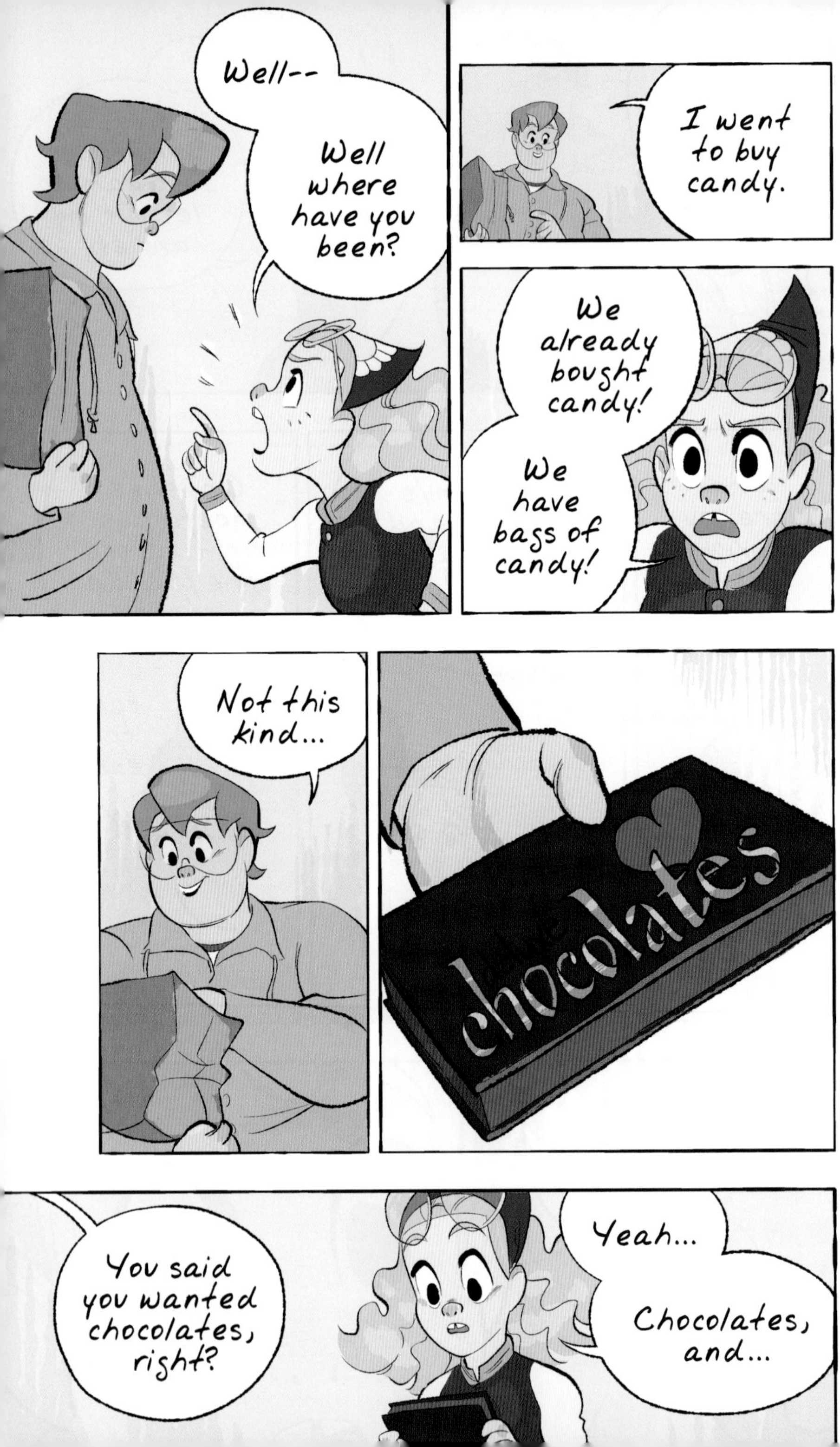
Well--
Well where have you been?
I went to buy candy.
We already bought candy!
We have bags of candy!
Not this kind...
chocolates
You said you wanted chocolates, right?
Yeah...
Chocolates, and...

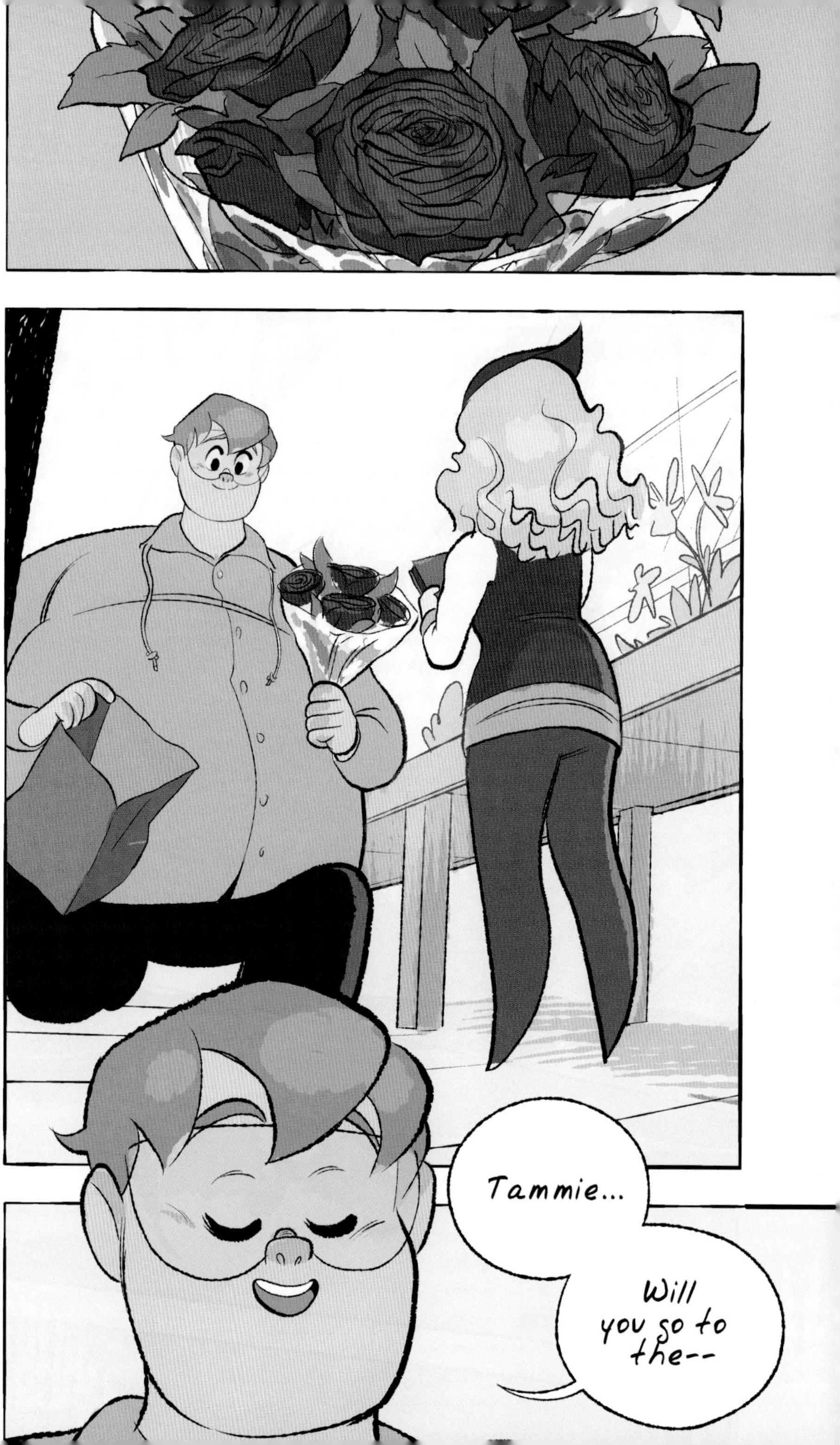
Tammie...
Will you go to the--

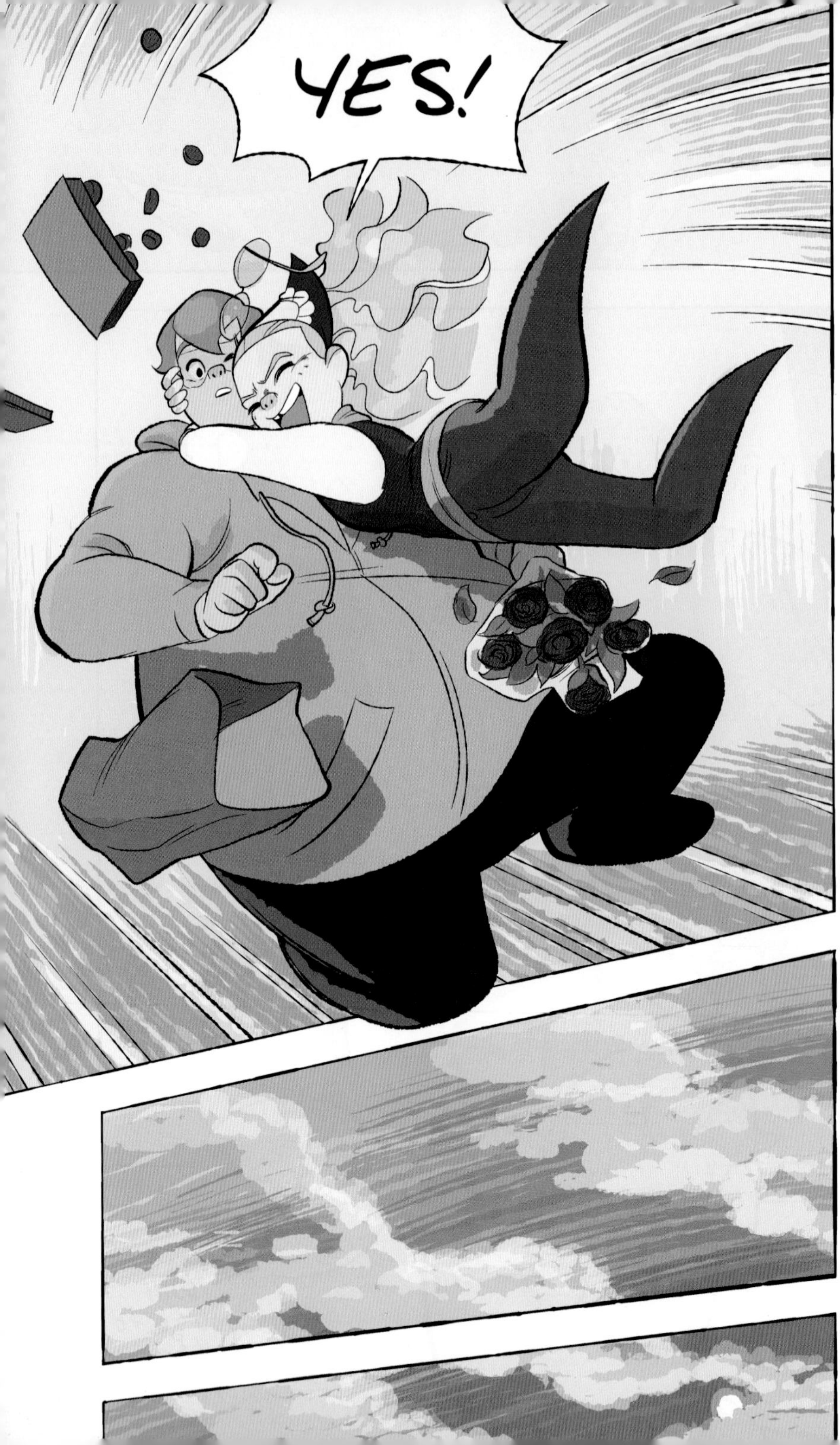
YES!

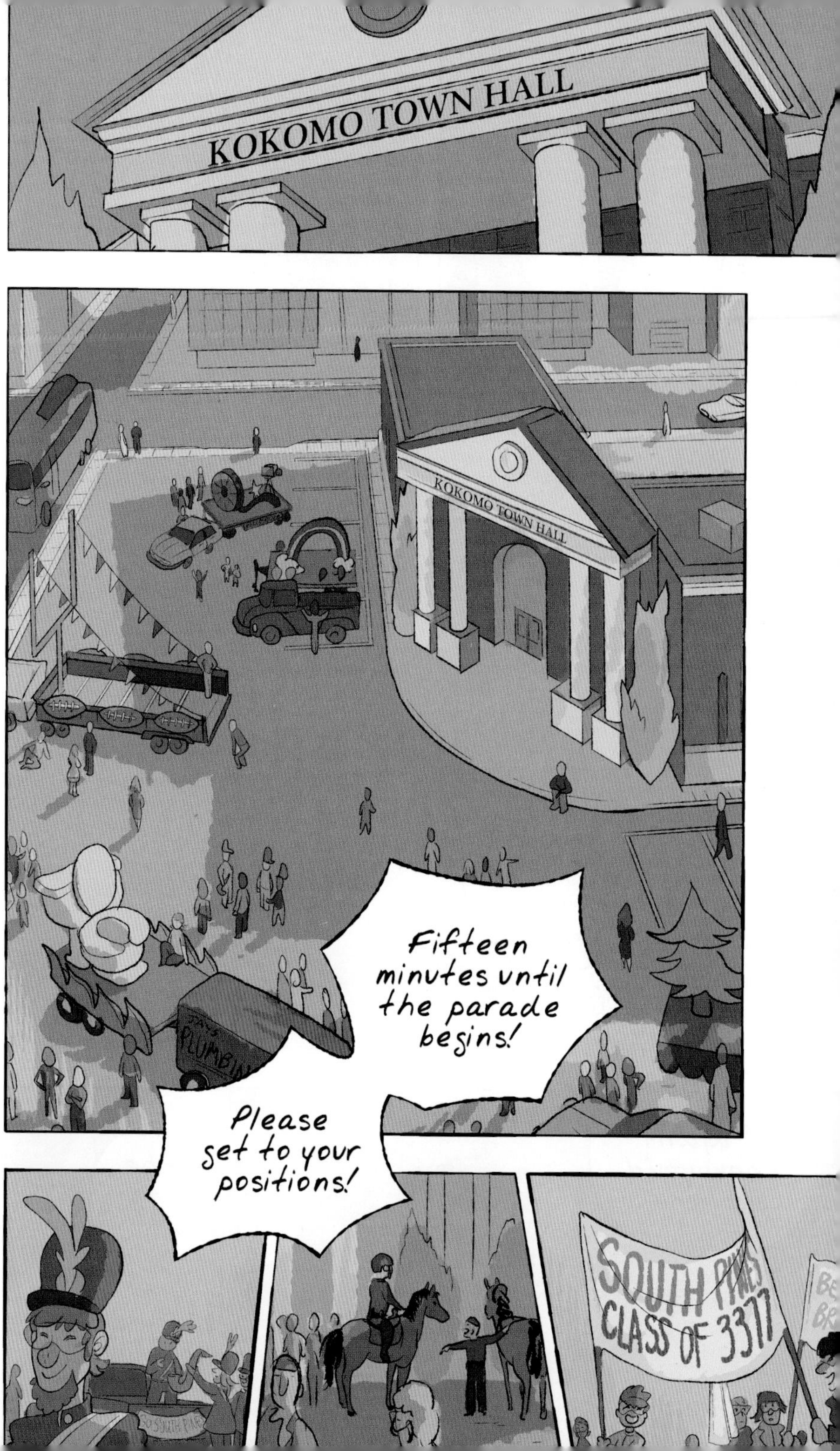
KOKOMO TOWN HALL
KOKOMO TOWN HALL
Fifteen minutes until the parade begins!
Please set to your positions!
SOUTH PINES CLASS OF 3377

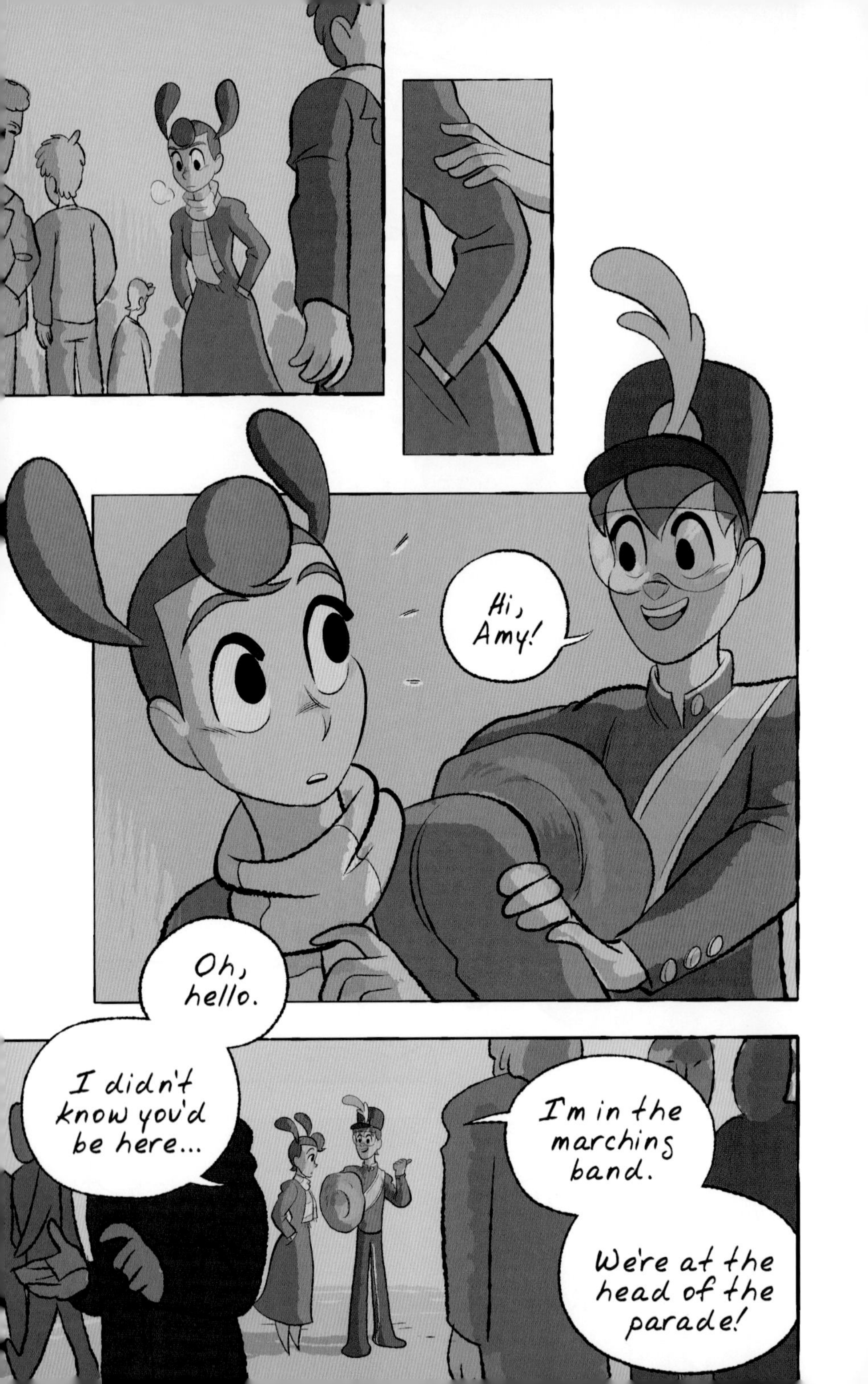
Hi, Amy!
Oh, hello.
I didn't know you'd be here...
I'm in the marching band.
We're at the head of the parade!

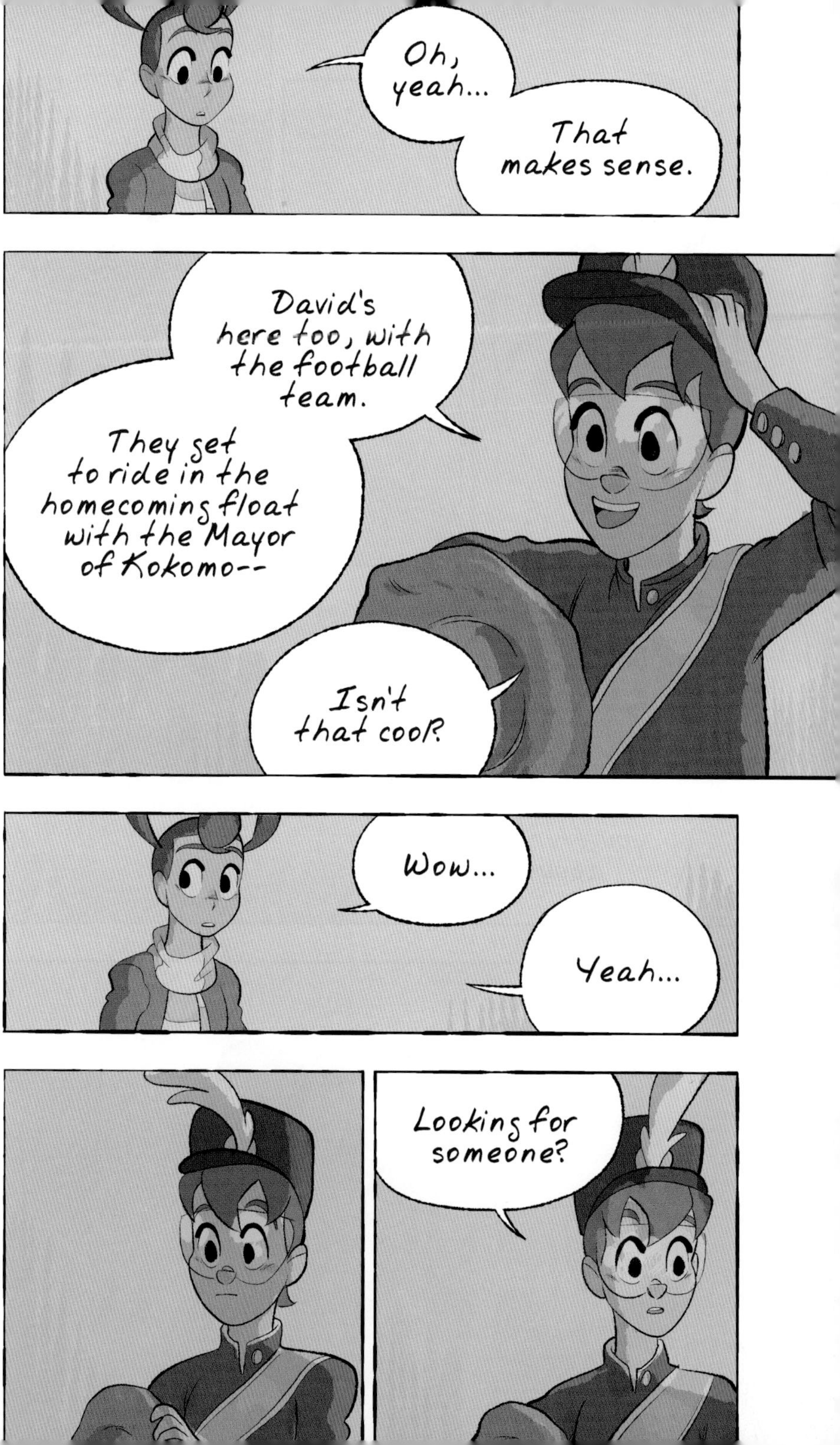
Oh, yeah...
That makes sense.
David's here too, with the football team.
They set to ride in the homecoming float with the Mayor of Kokomo--
Isn't that cool?
Wow...
Yeah...
Looking for someone?

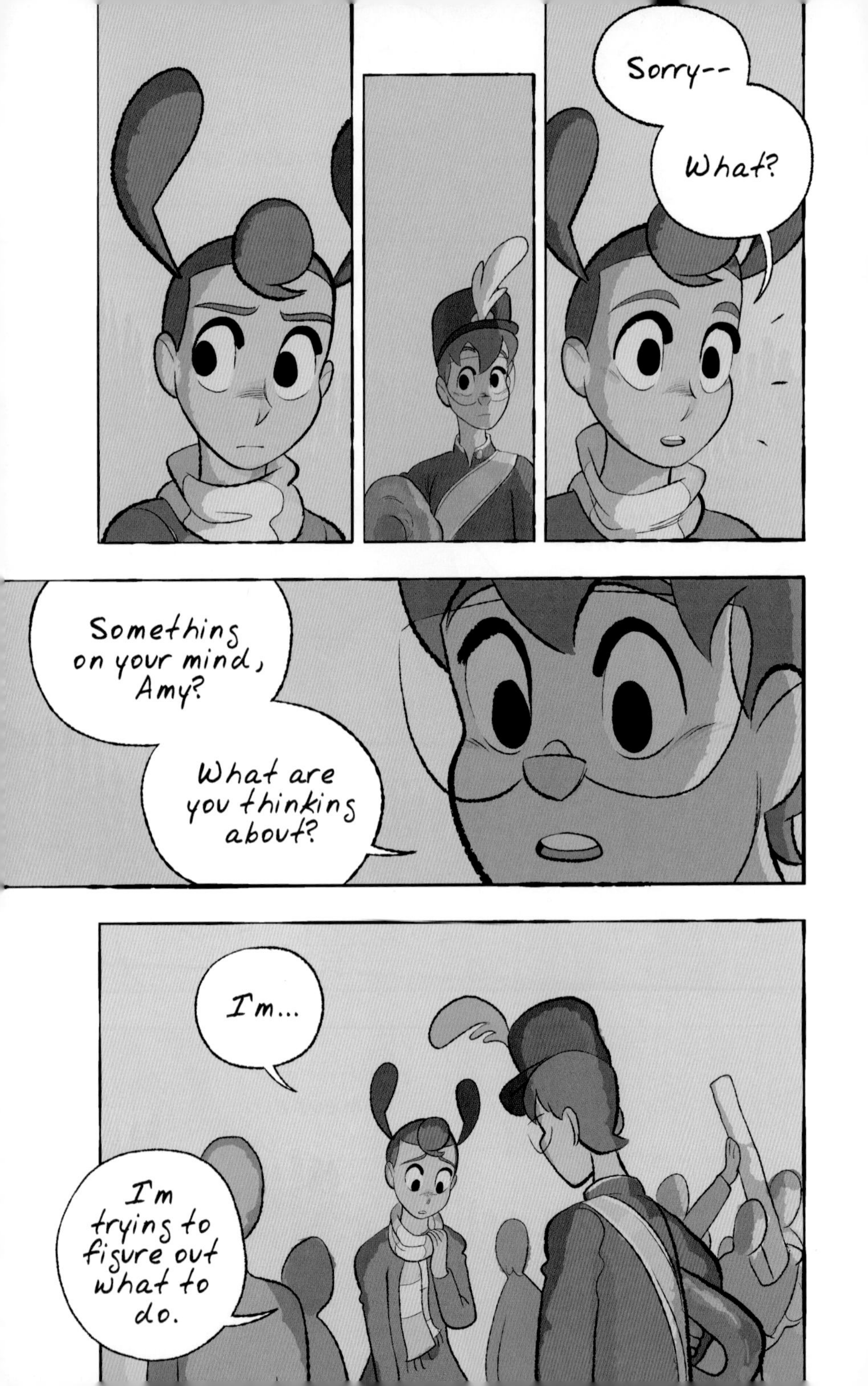
Sorry--
What?
Something on your mind, Amy?
What are you thinking about?
I'm...
I'm trying to figure out what to do.

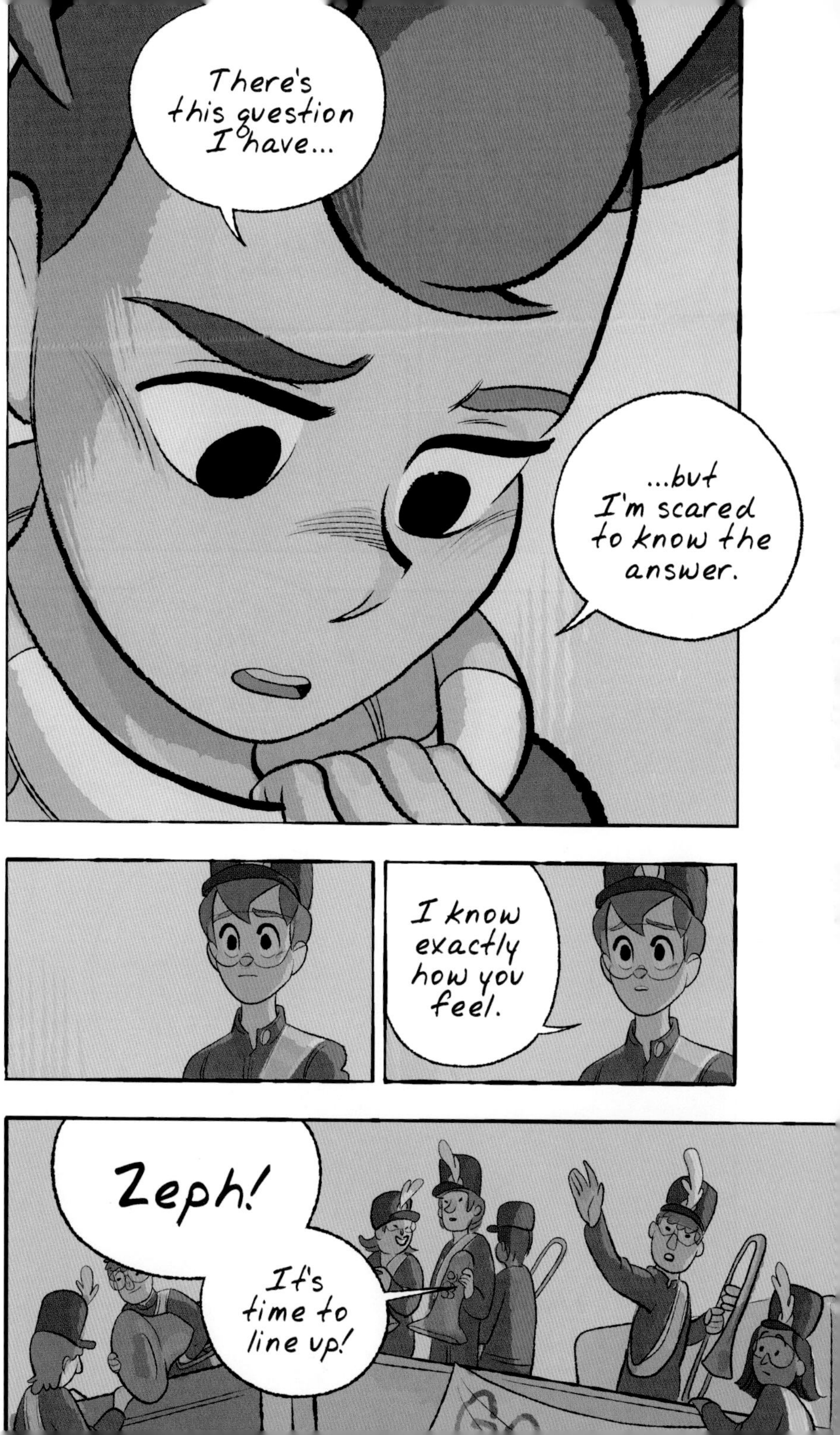
There's this question I have...
...but I'm scared to know the answer.
I know exactly how you feel.
Zeph!
It's time to line up!

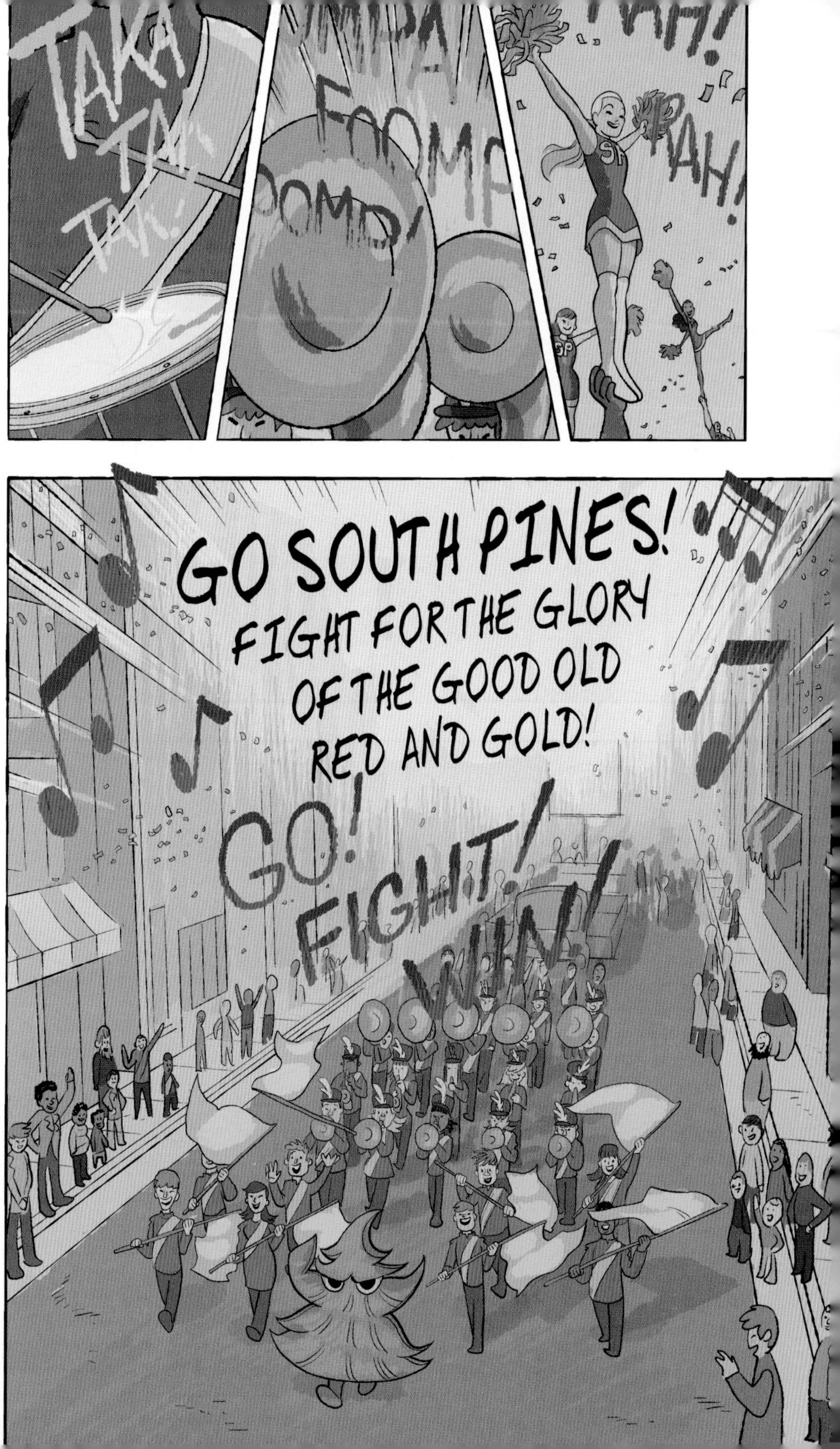
FOOMP
OOMP!
RAH!
GO SOUTH PINES!
FIGHT FOR THE GLORY
OF THE GOOD OLD
RED AND GOLD!
GO!
FIGHT!
WIN!

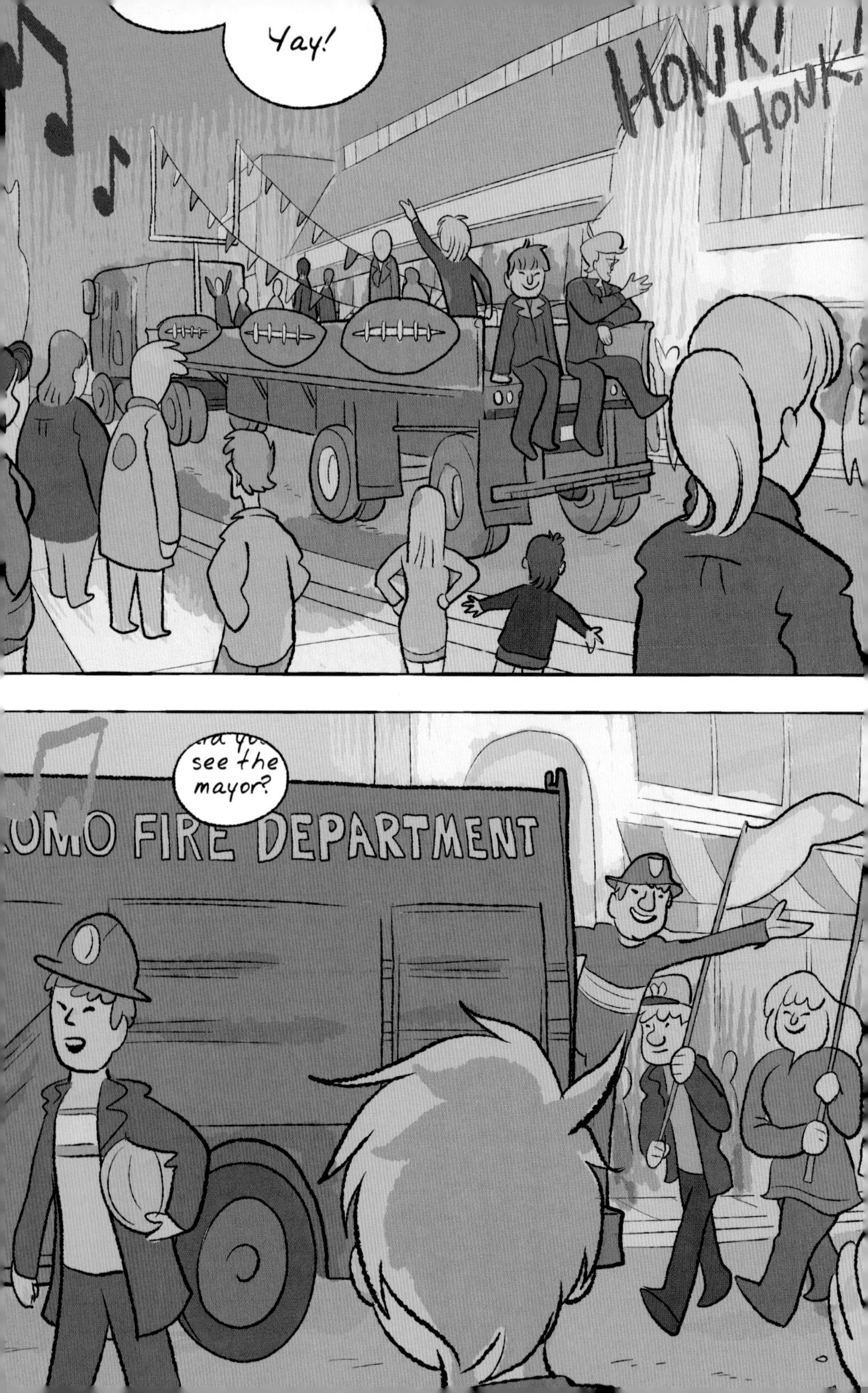
Yay!
HONK! HONK!
see the mayor?
FIRE DEPARTMENT

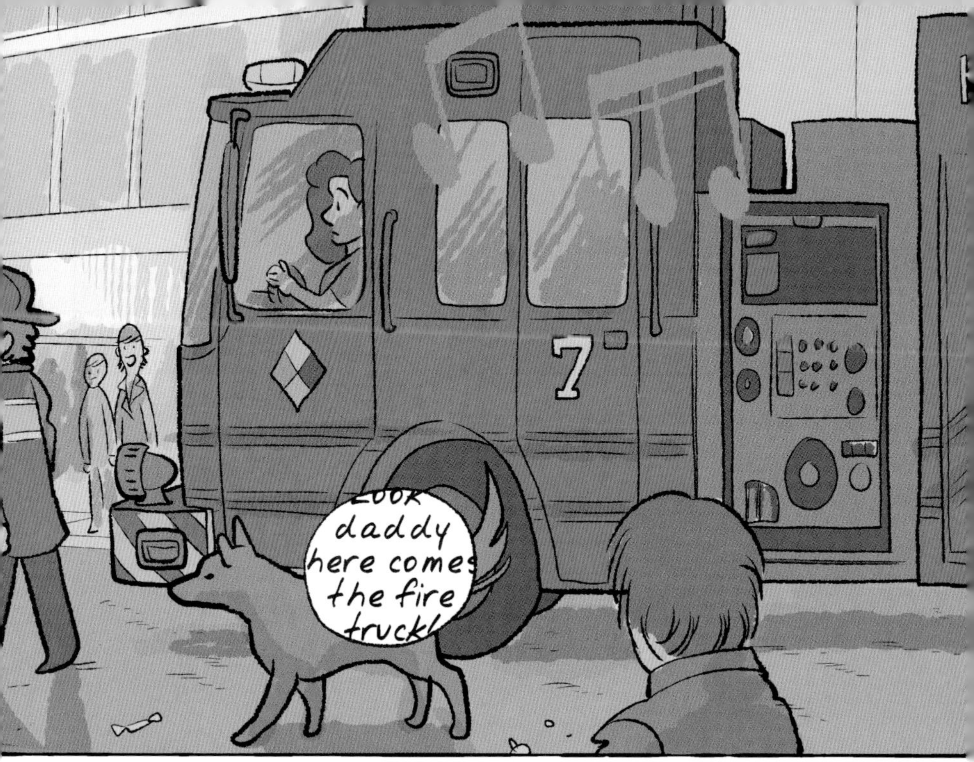
daddy here comes the fire truck!

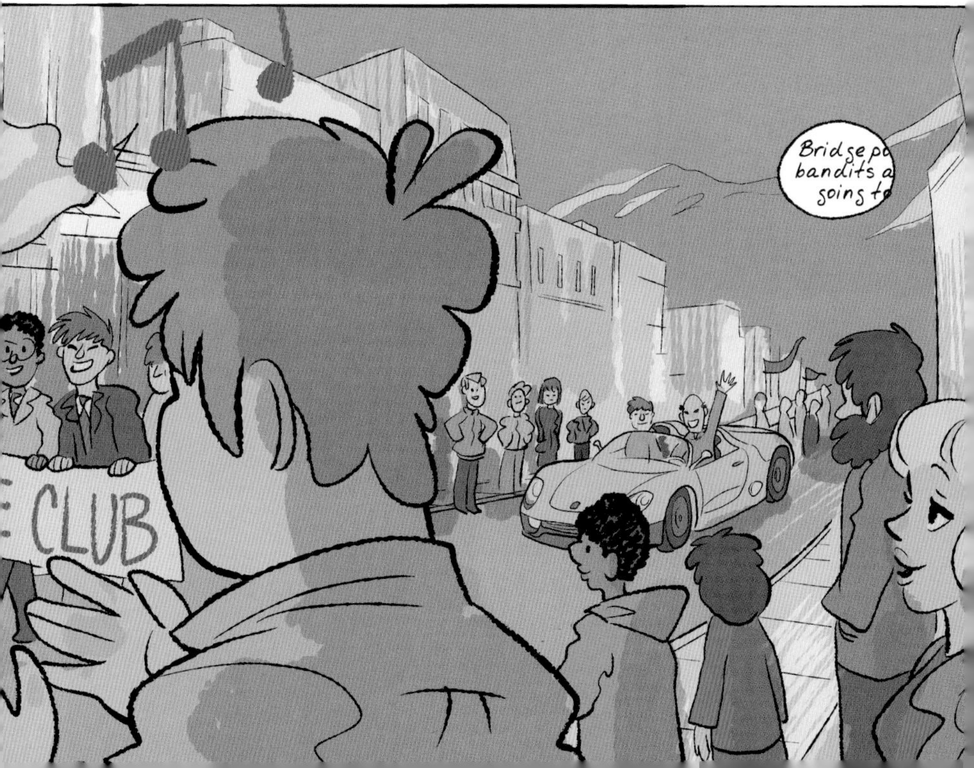
CLUB
bandits

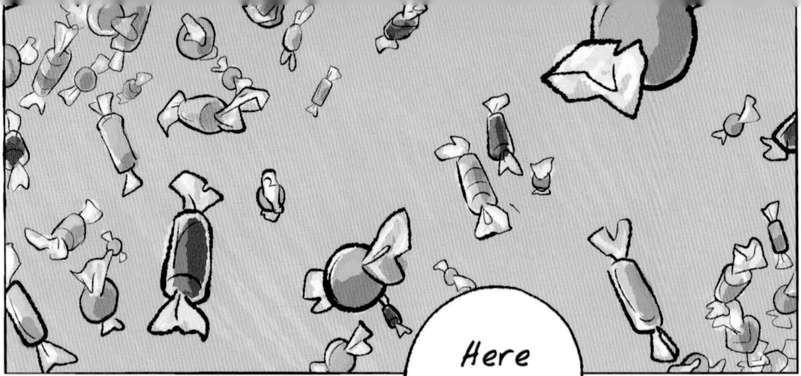

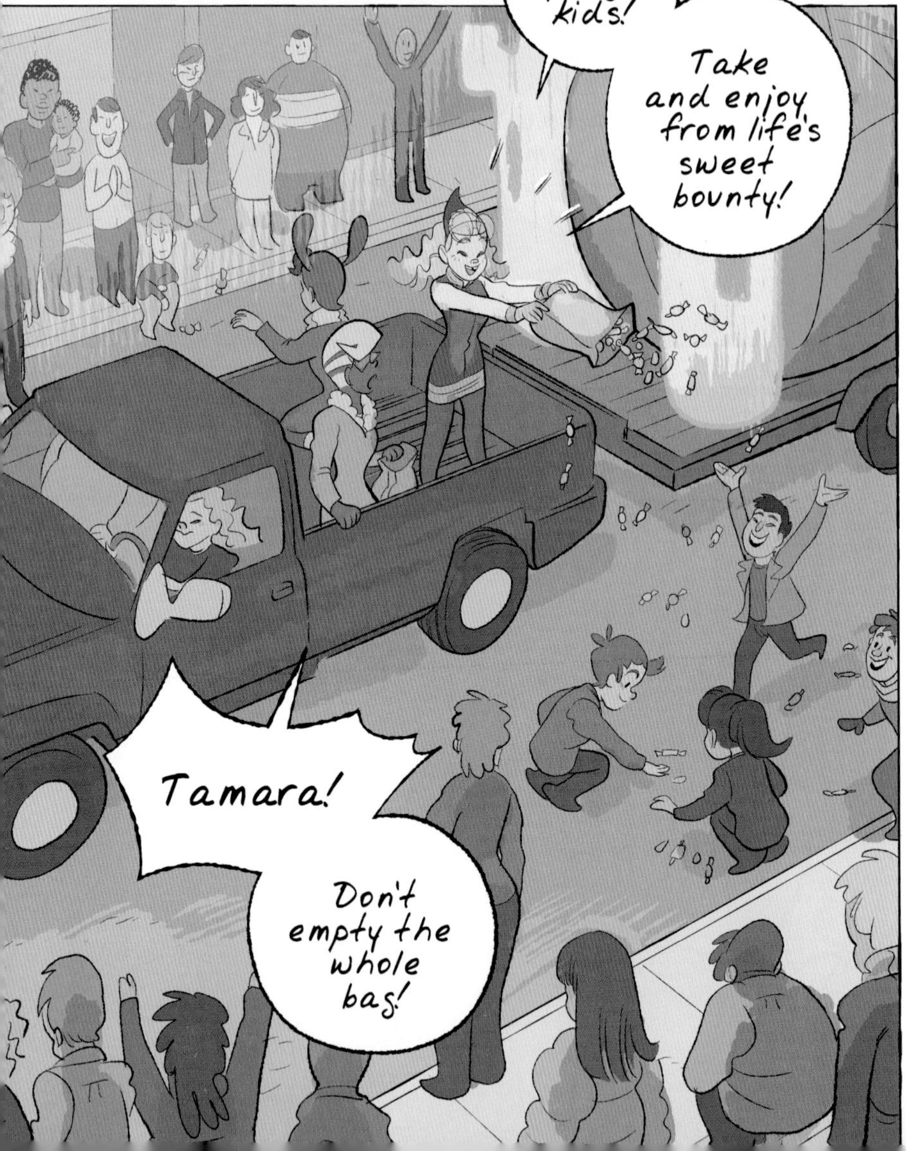
Here you go, kids!
Take and enjoy from life's sweet bounty!
Tamara!
Don't empty the whole bag!

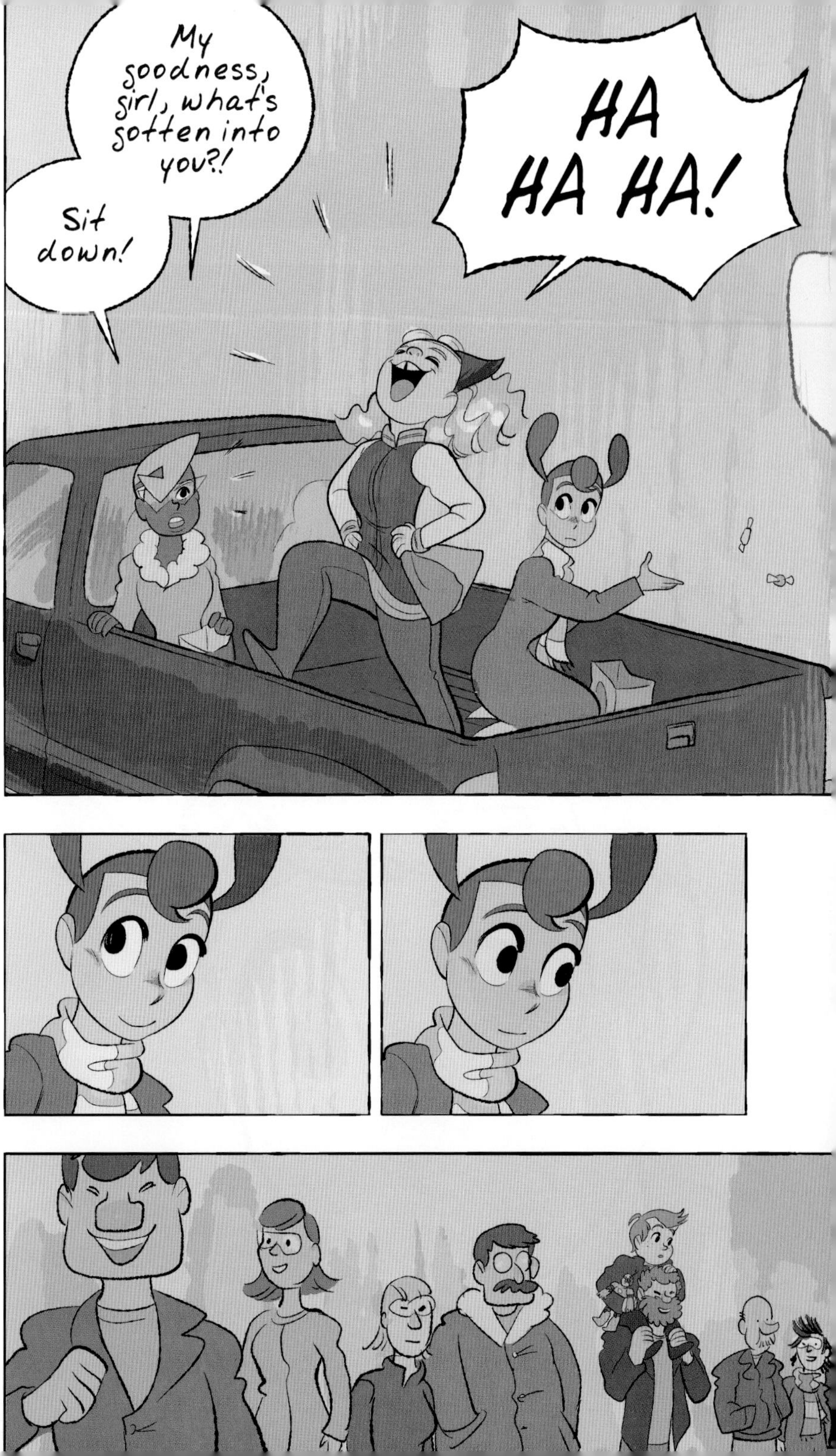
My goodness, girl, what's gotten into you?!
Sit down!
HA HA HA!

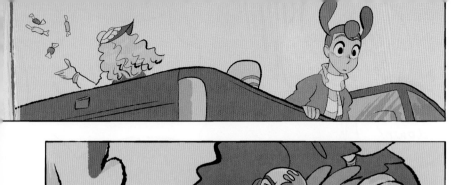

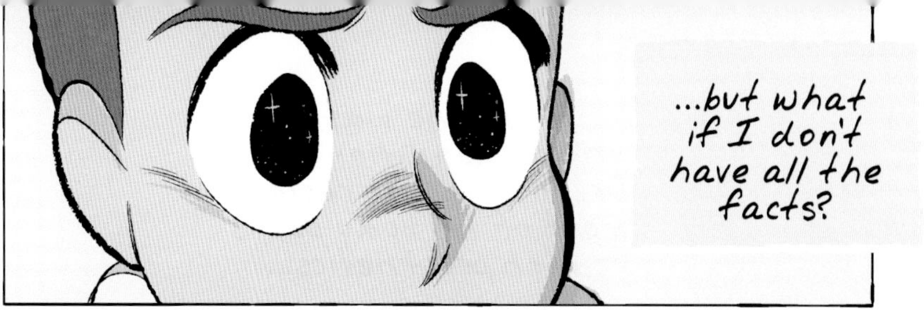
...but what if I don't have all the facts?

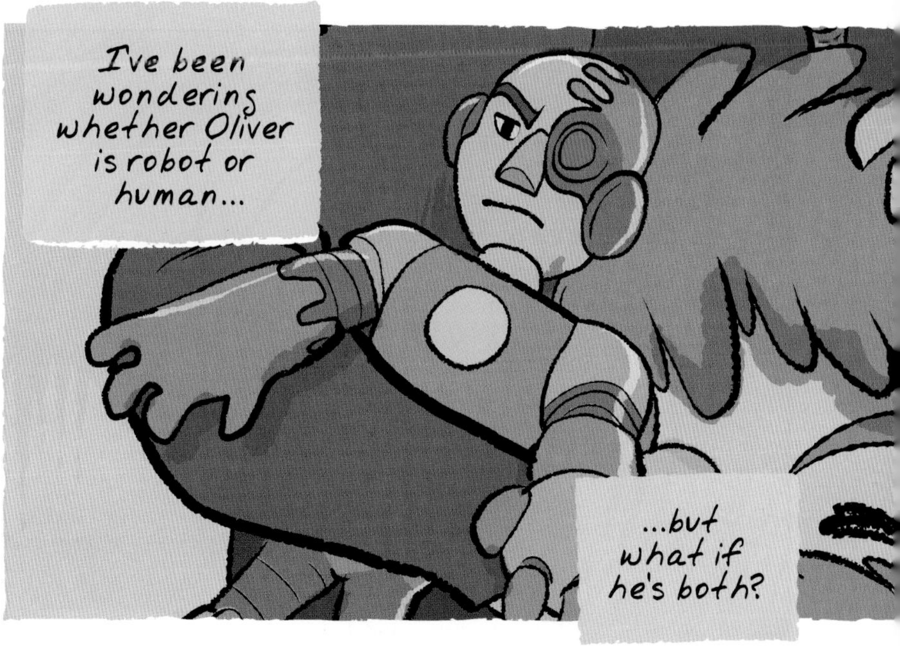
I've been wondering whether Oliver is robot or human...
...but what if he's both?

Suppose Oliver was hurt in the car accident that killed his family...

Perhaps he was taken to the hospital where Dr. Kim worked...

Maybe he was in critical condition and Dr. Kim had to replace most of his body parts with prosthetics...

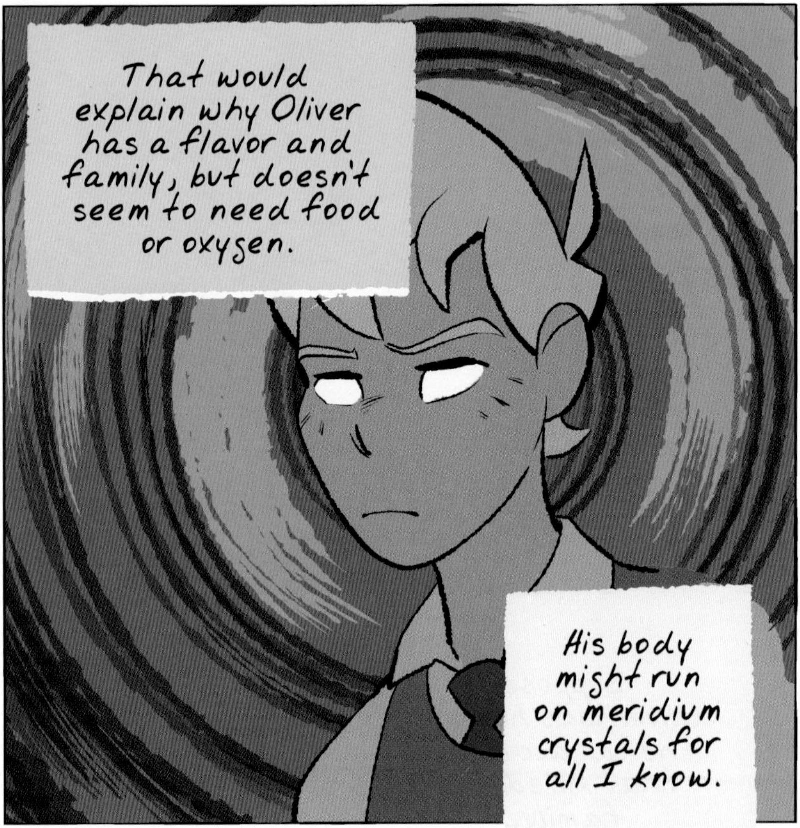
That would explain why Oliver has a flavor and family, but doesn't seem to need food or oxygen.
His body might run on meridium crystals for all I know.

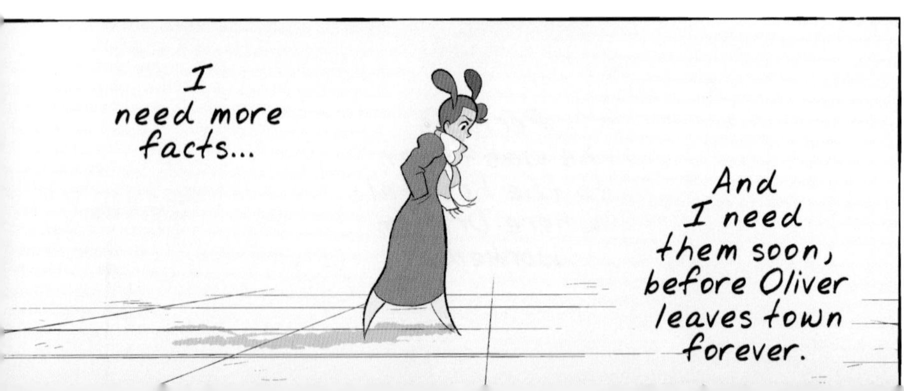
I need more facts...
And I need them soon, before Oliver leaves town forever.

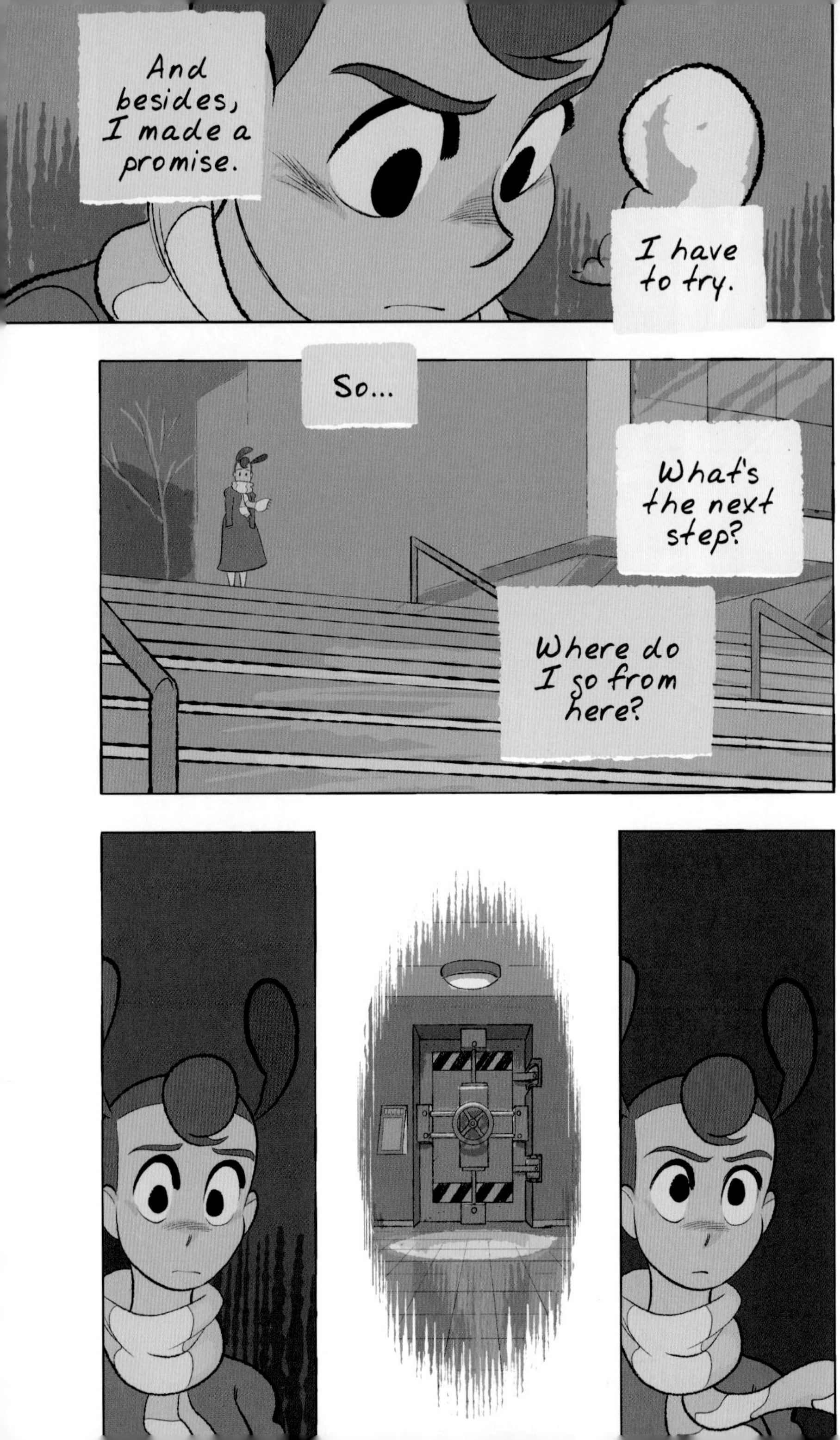
And besides, I made a promise.
I have to try.
So...
What's the next step?
Where do I go from here?

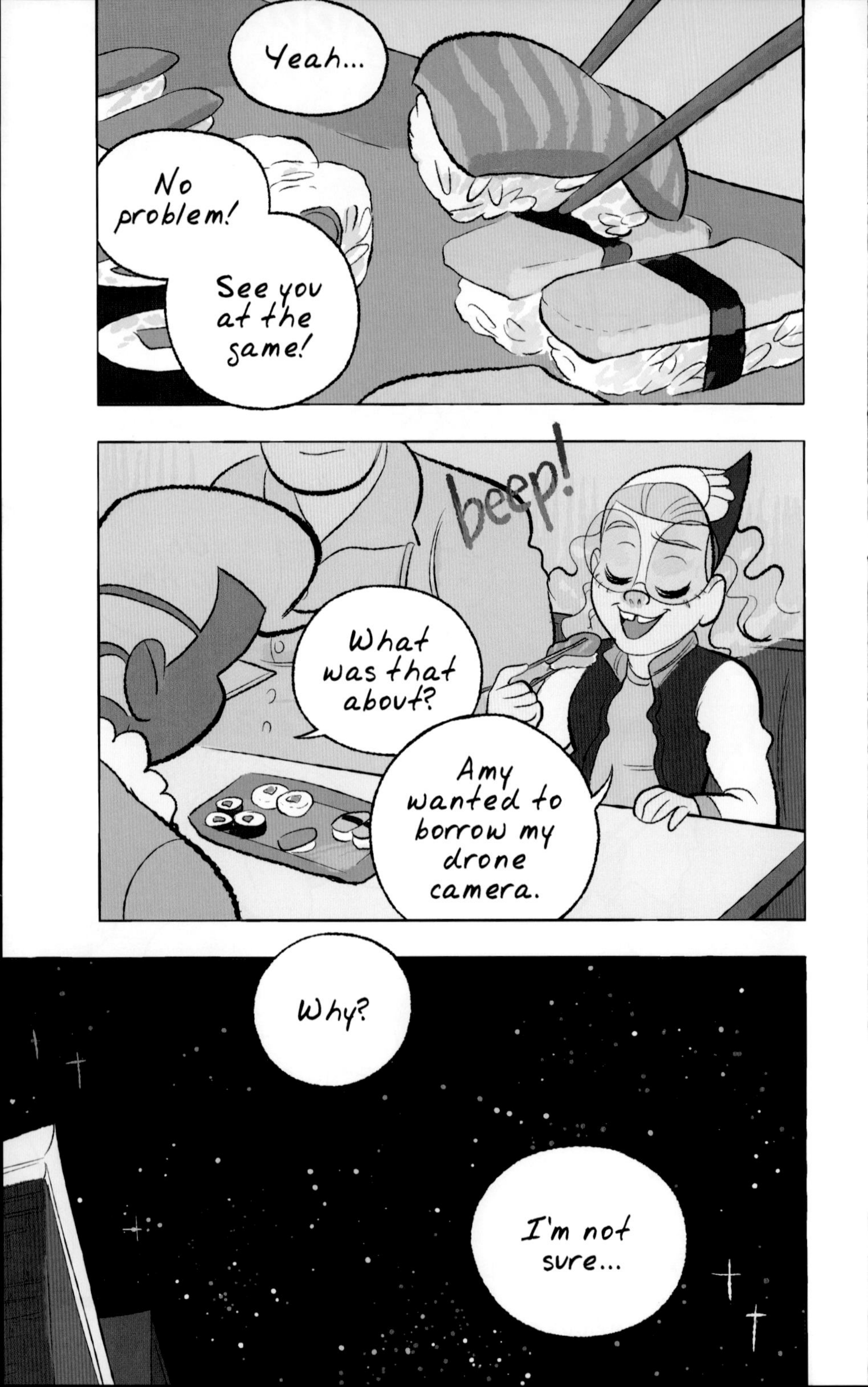

Yeah...
No problem!
See you at the game!
beep!
What was that about?
Amy wanted to borrow my drone camera.
Why?
I'm not sure...

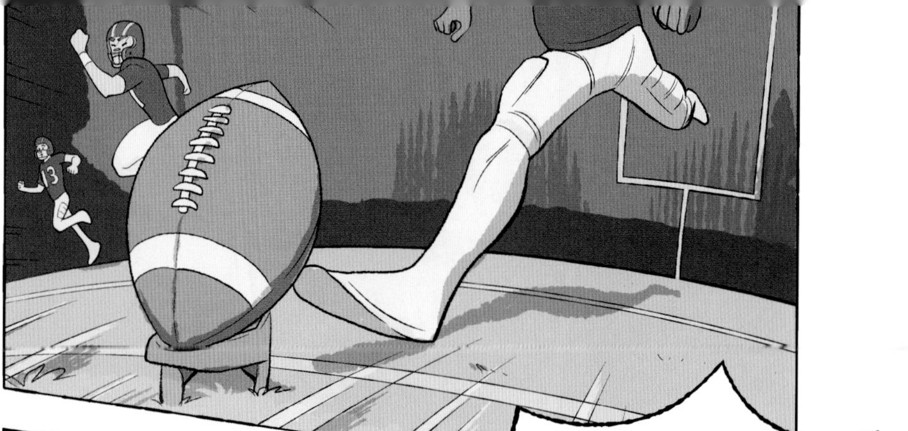

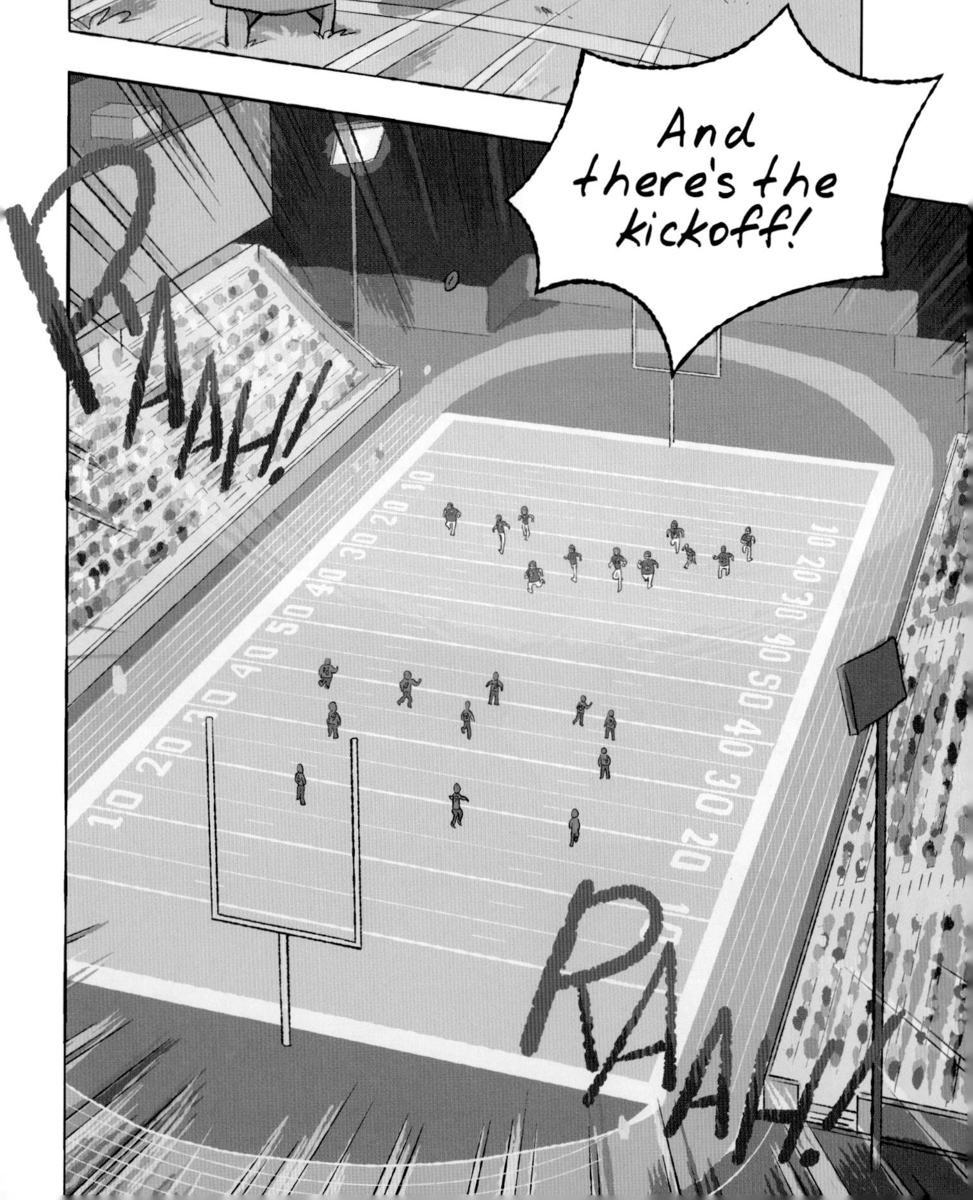
And there's the kickoff!
RAAH!
RAAH!

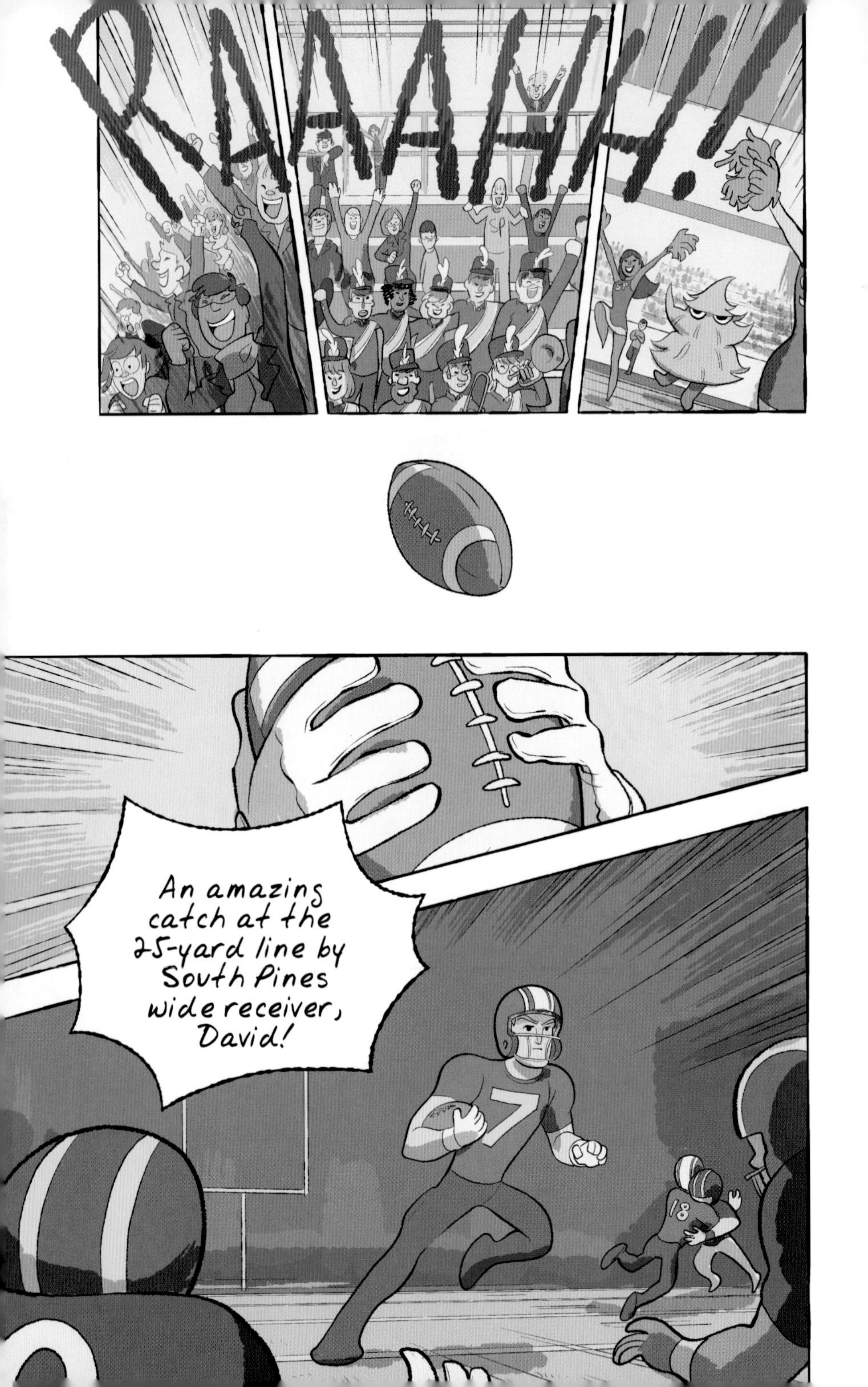
RAAAHH!!
An amazing catch at the 25-yard line by South Pines wide receiver, David!

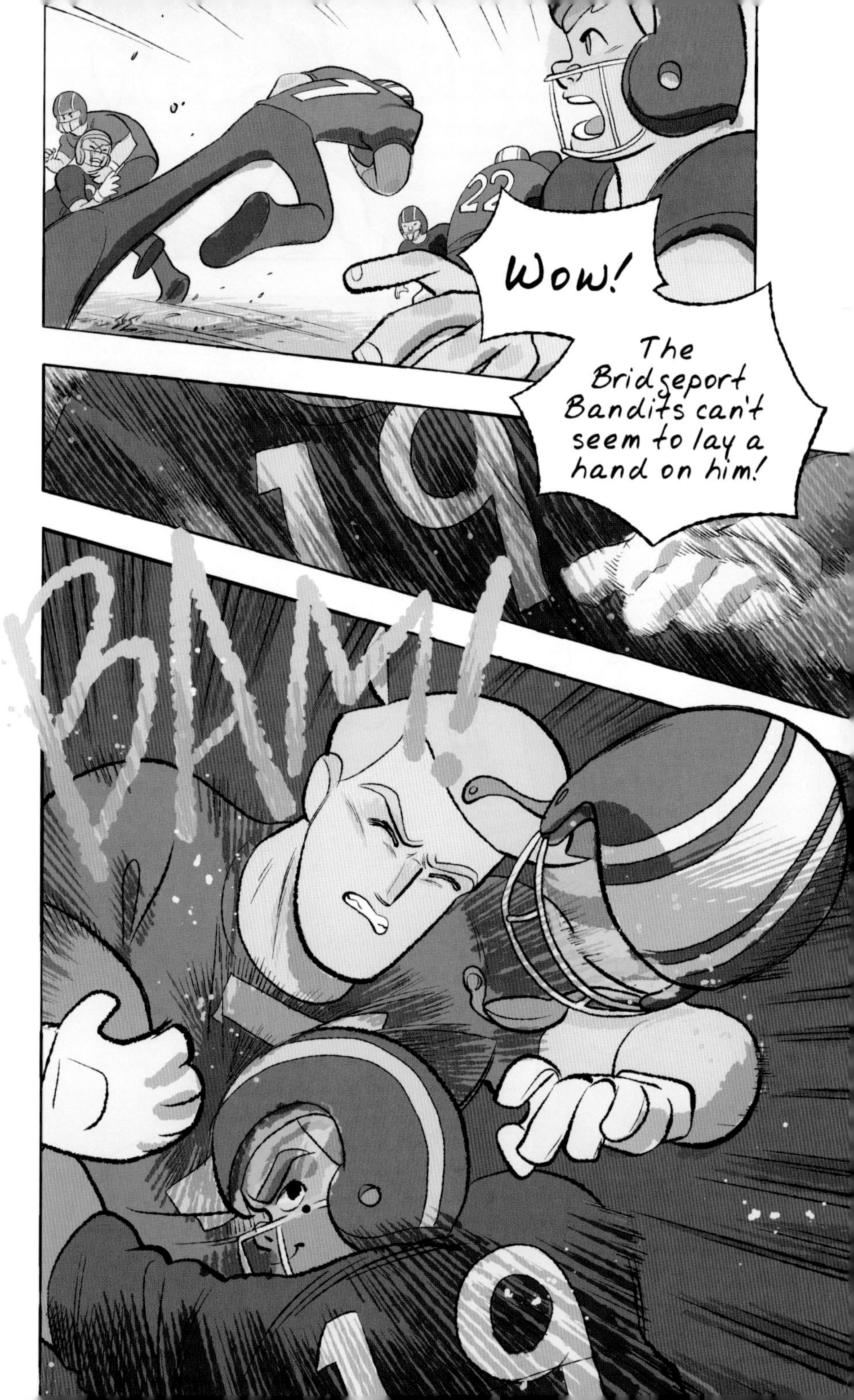
Wow!
The Bridgeport Bandits can't seem to lay a hand on him!
BAM!

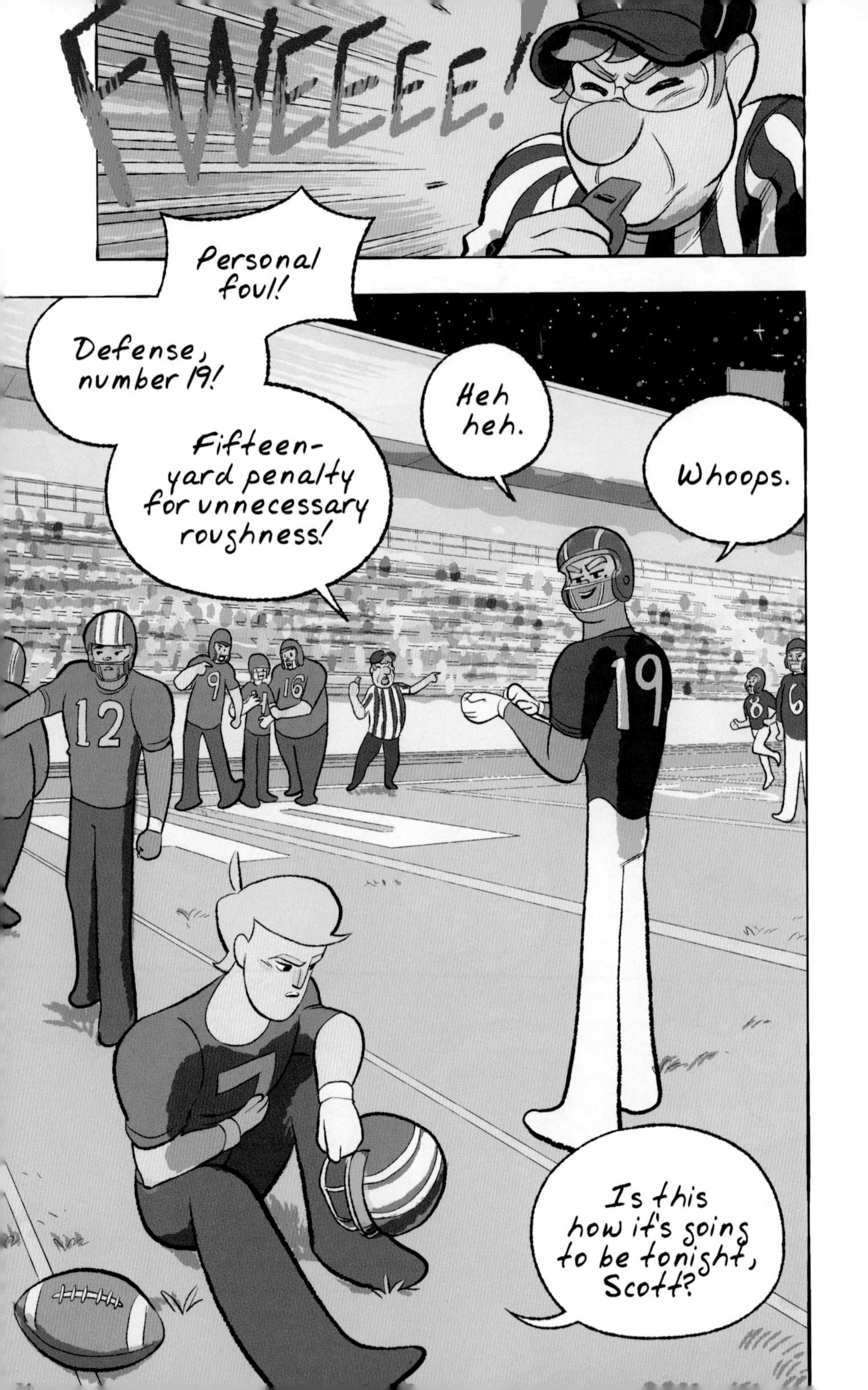
FWEEEE!
Personal foul!
Defense, number 19!
Fifteen-yard penalty for unnecessary roughness!
Heh heh.
Whoops.
Is this how it's going to be tonight, Scott?

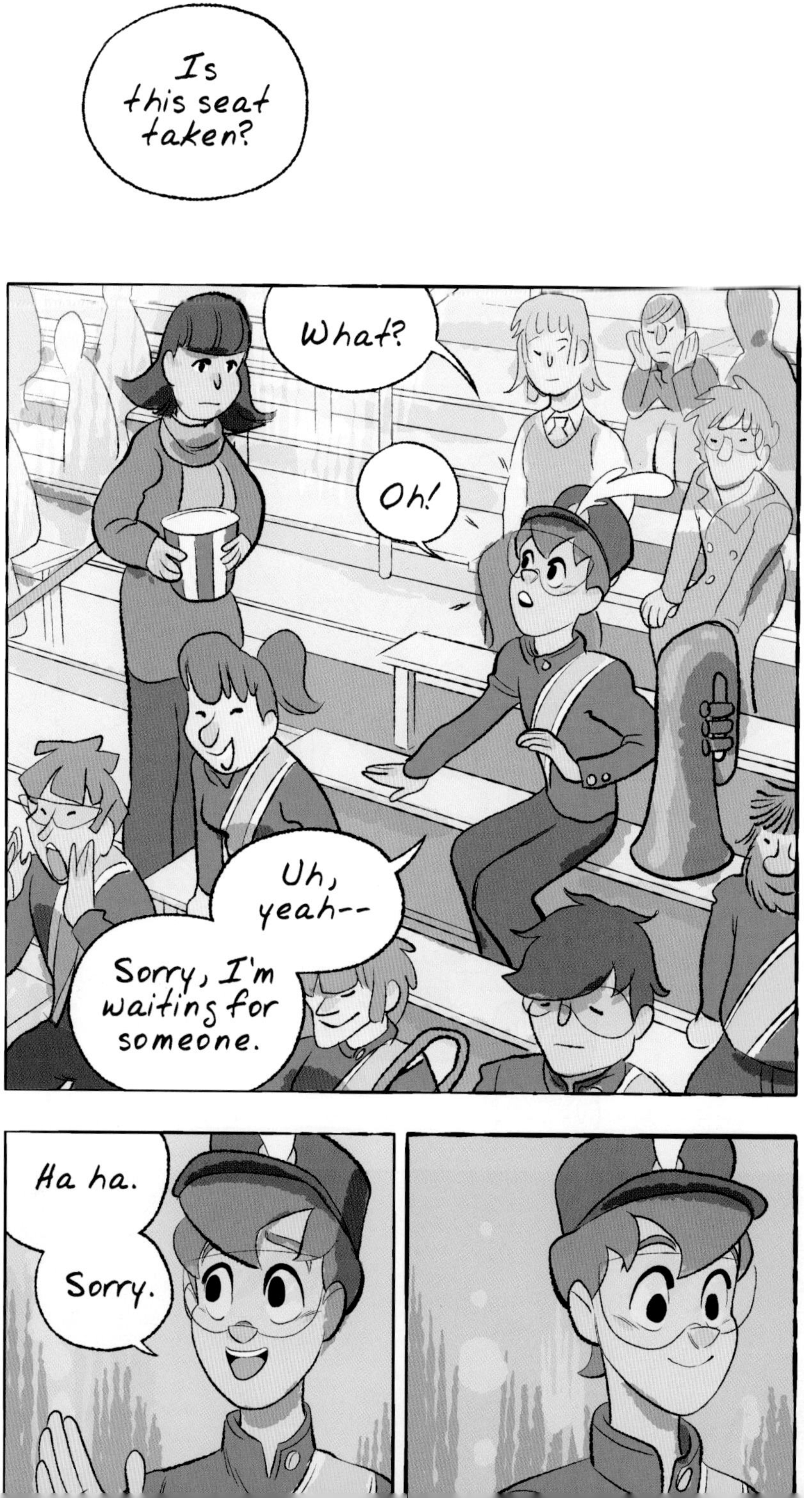
Is this seat taken?
What?
Oh!
Uh, yeah--
Sorry, I'm waiting for someone.
Ha ha.
Sorry.

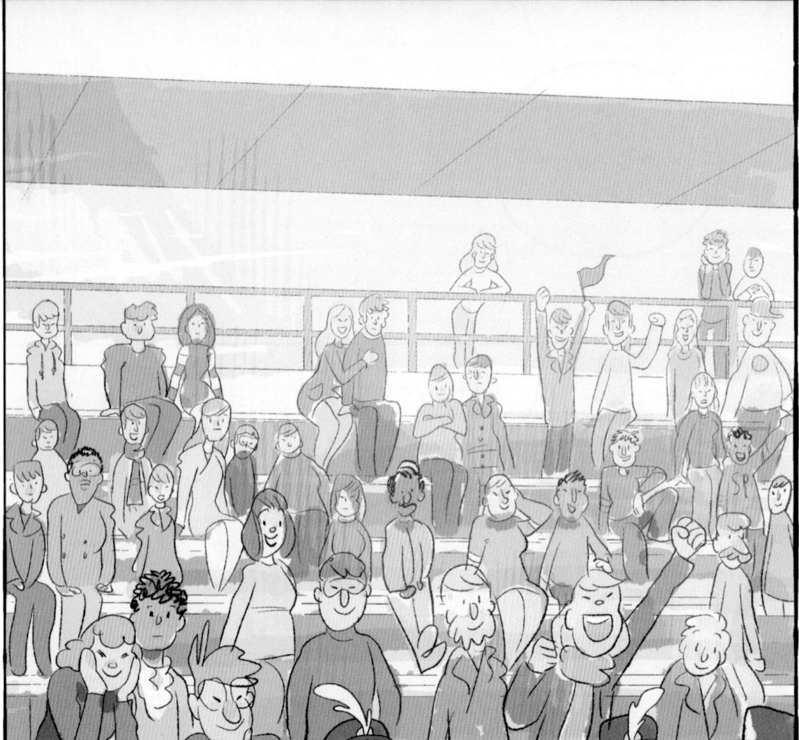

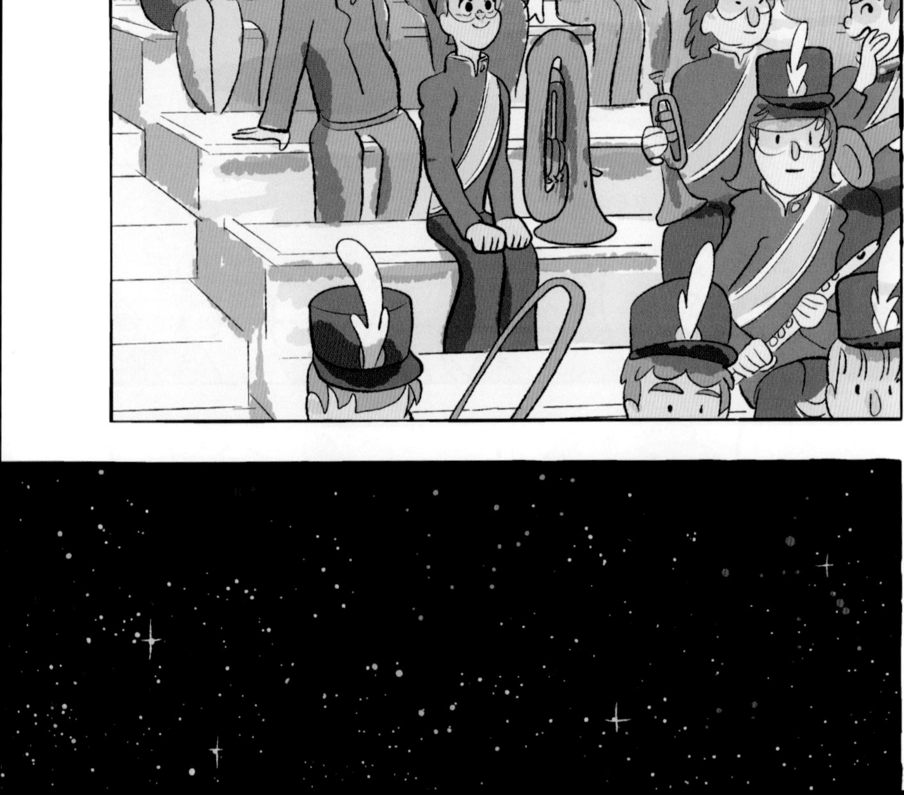

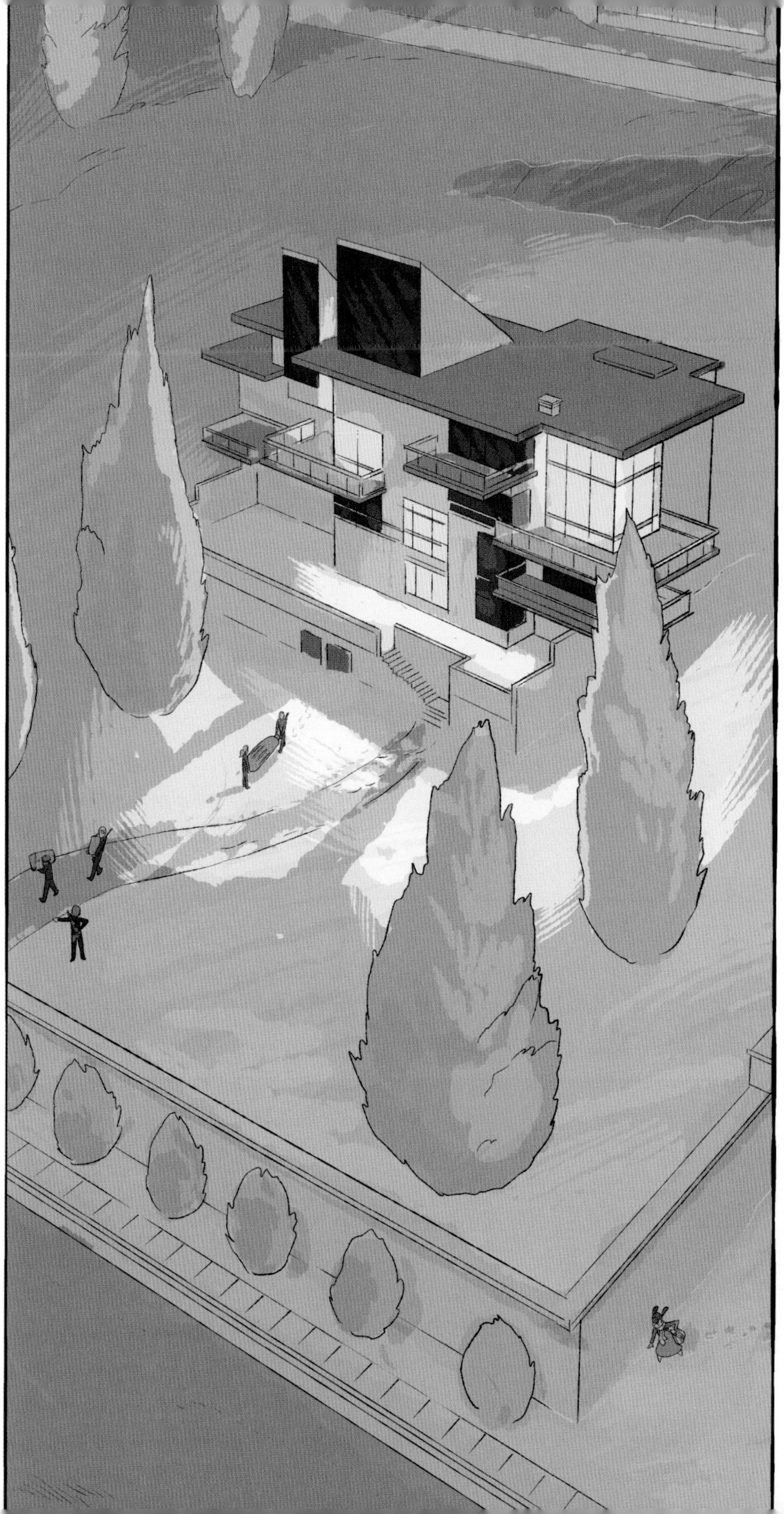

This is a crazy, stupid plan.

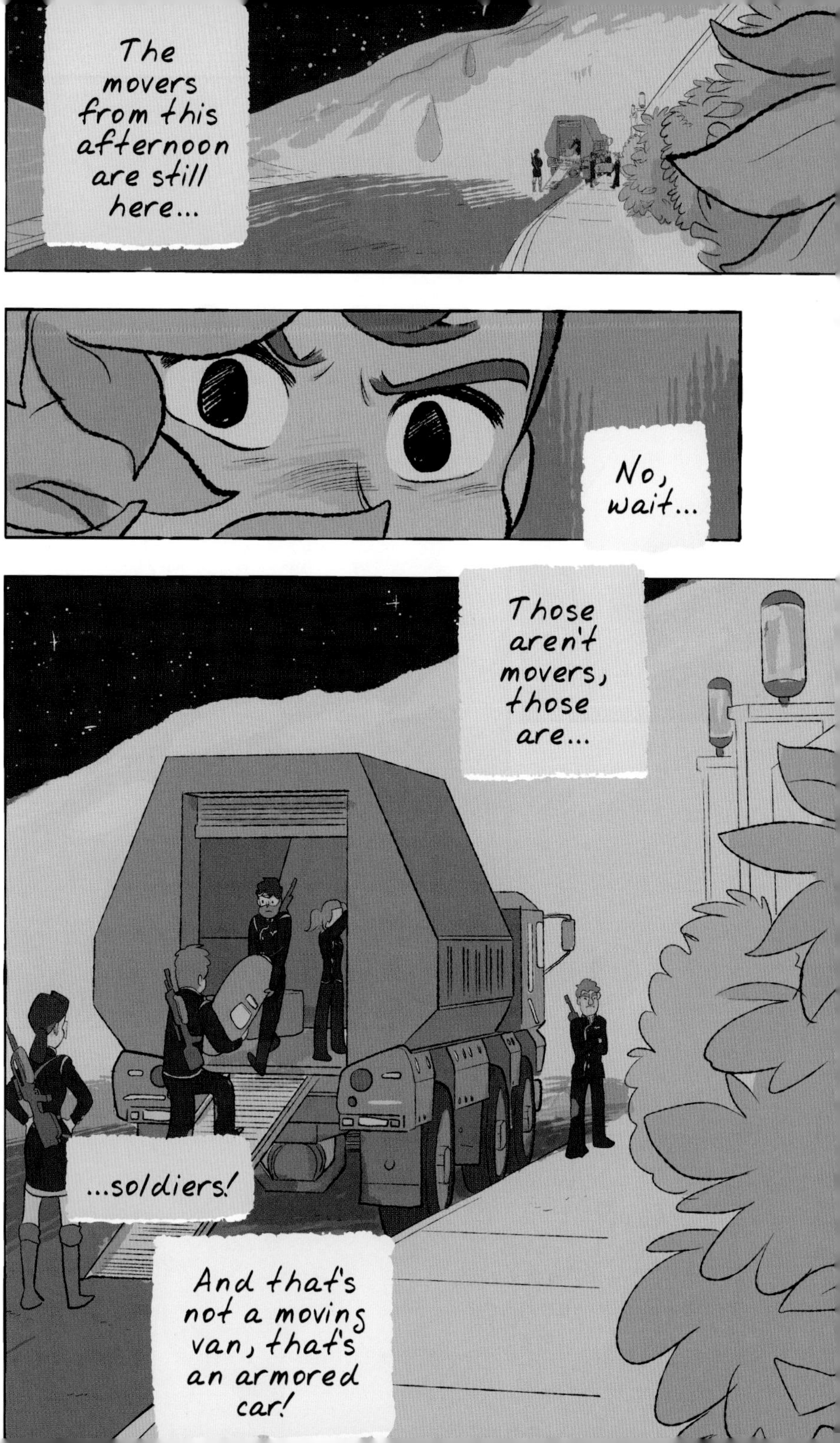
The movers from this afternoon are still here...
No, wait...
Those aren't movers, those are...
...soldiers!
And that's not a movins van, that's an armored car!

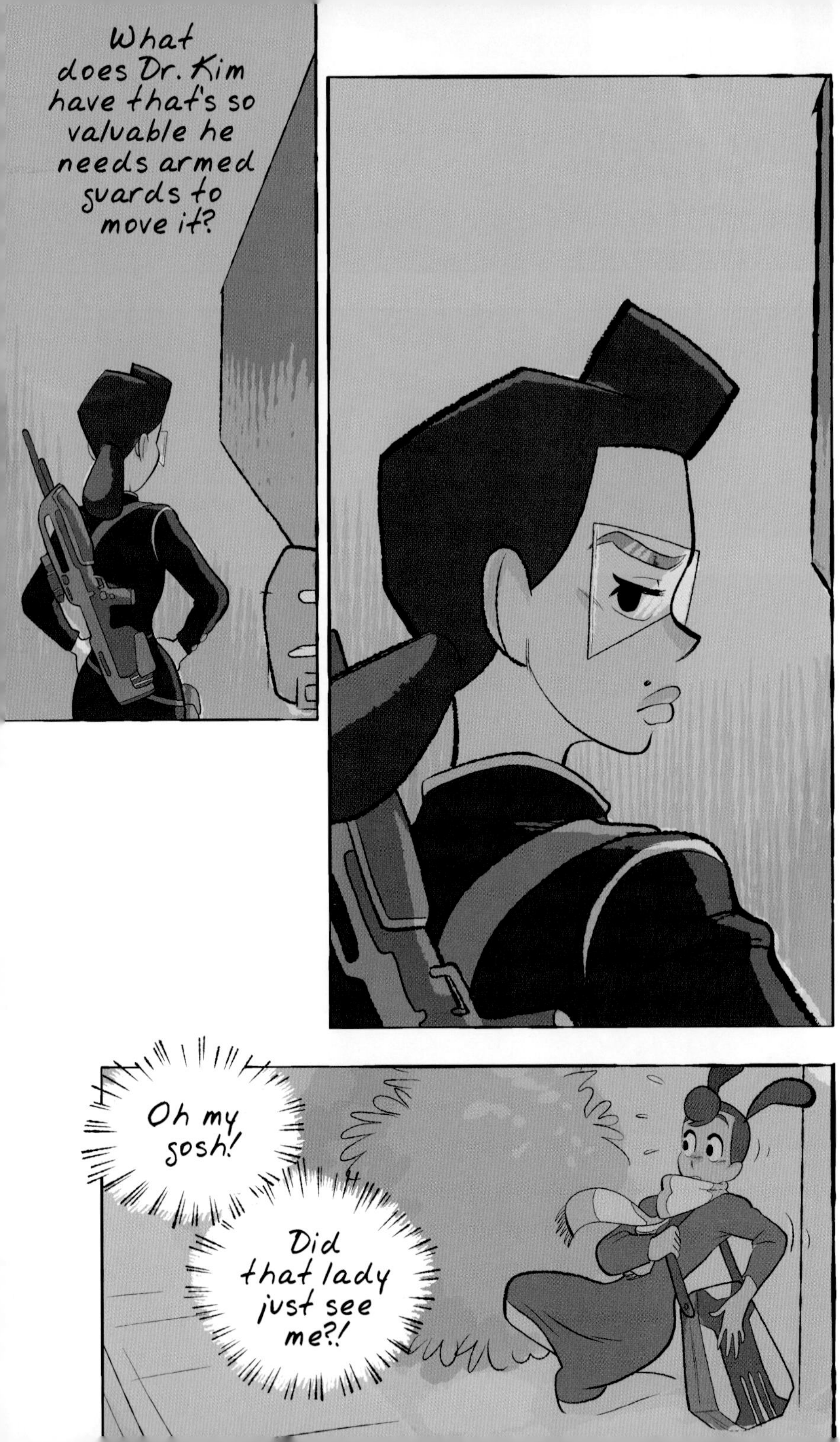
What does Dr. Kim have that's so valuable he needs armed guards to move it?
Oh my gosh!
Did that lady just see me?!

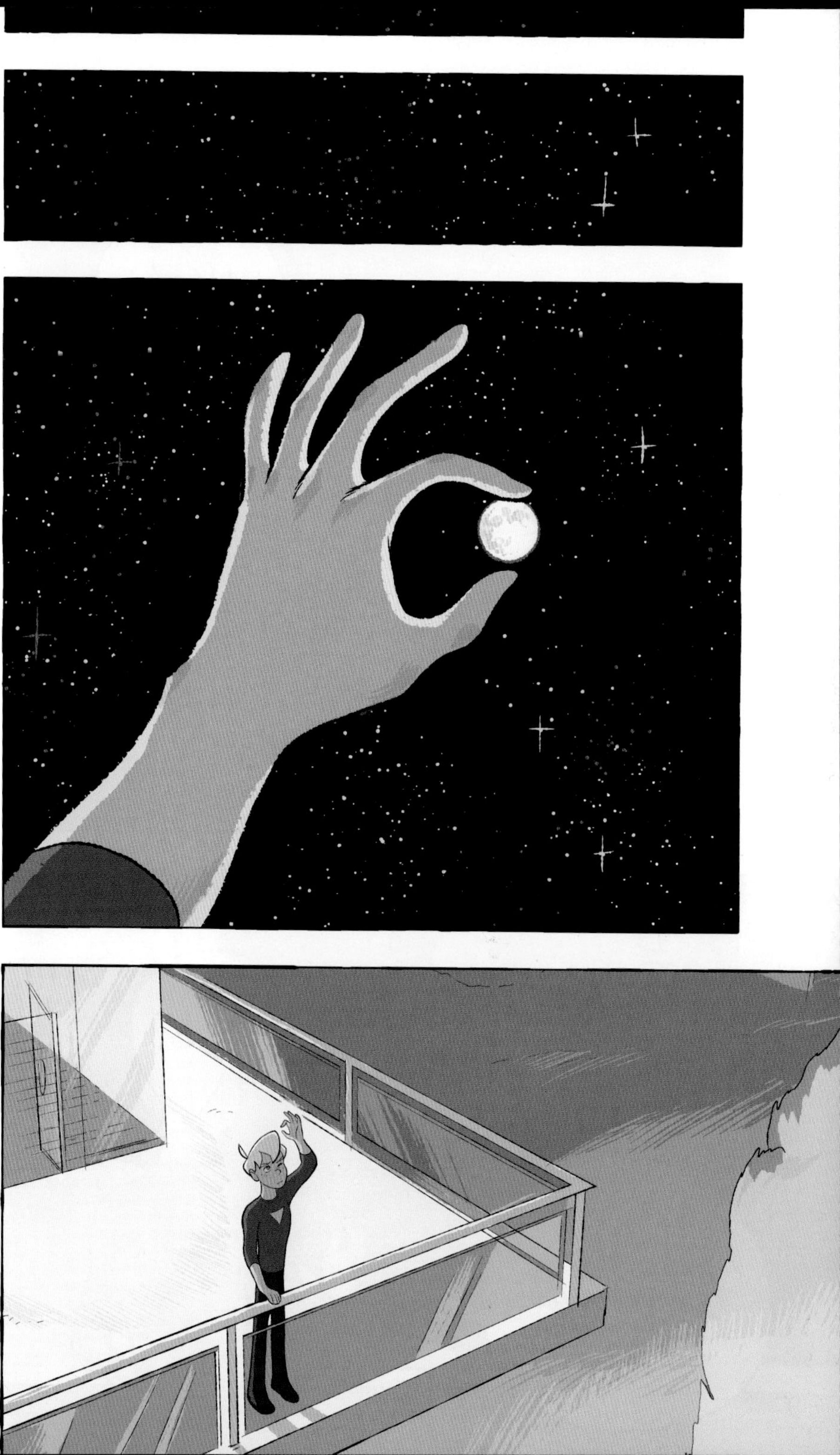

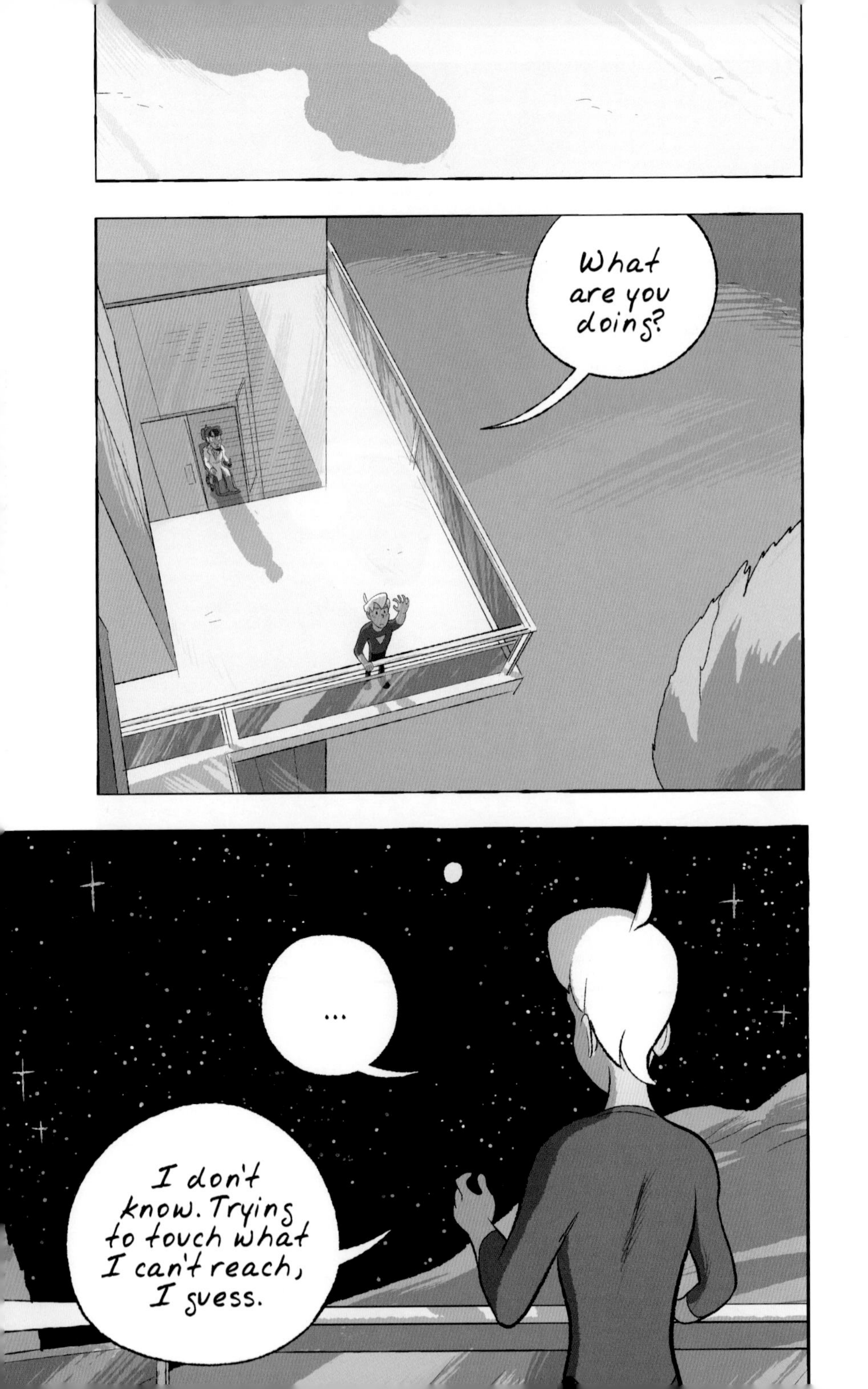
What are you doing?
...
I don't know. Trying to touch what I can't reach, I guess.

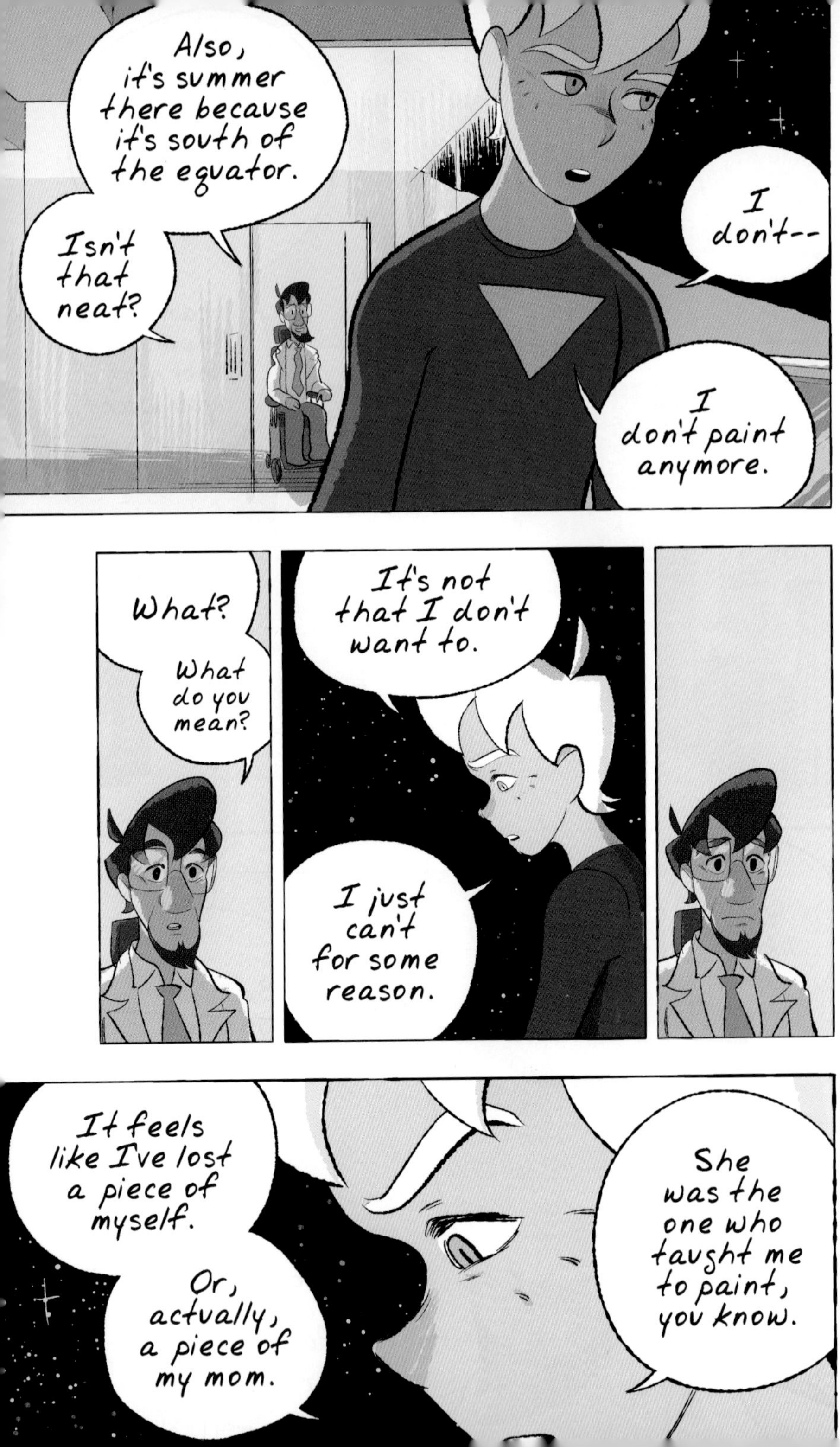
Also, it's summer there because it's south of the equator.
Isn't that neat?
I don't--
I don't paint anymore.
What?
What do you mean?
It's not that I don't want to.
I just can't for some reason.
It feels like I've lost a piece of myself.
Or, actually, a piece of my mom.
She was the one who taught me to paint, you know.

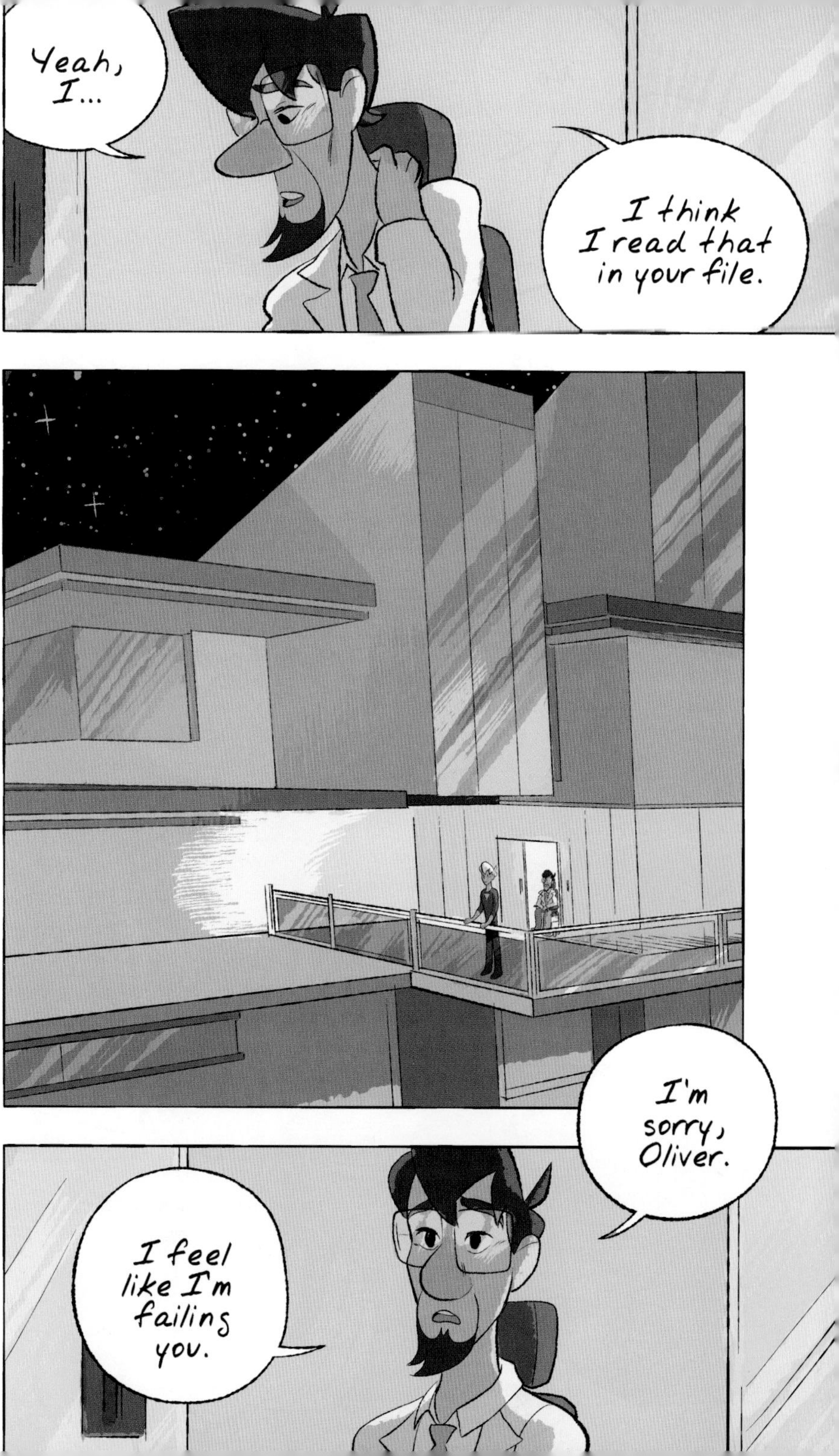
Yeah, I...
I think I read that in your file.
I'm sorry, Oliver.
I feel like I'm failing you.

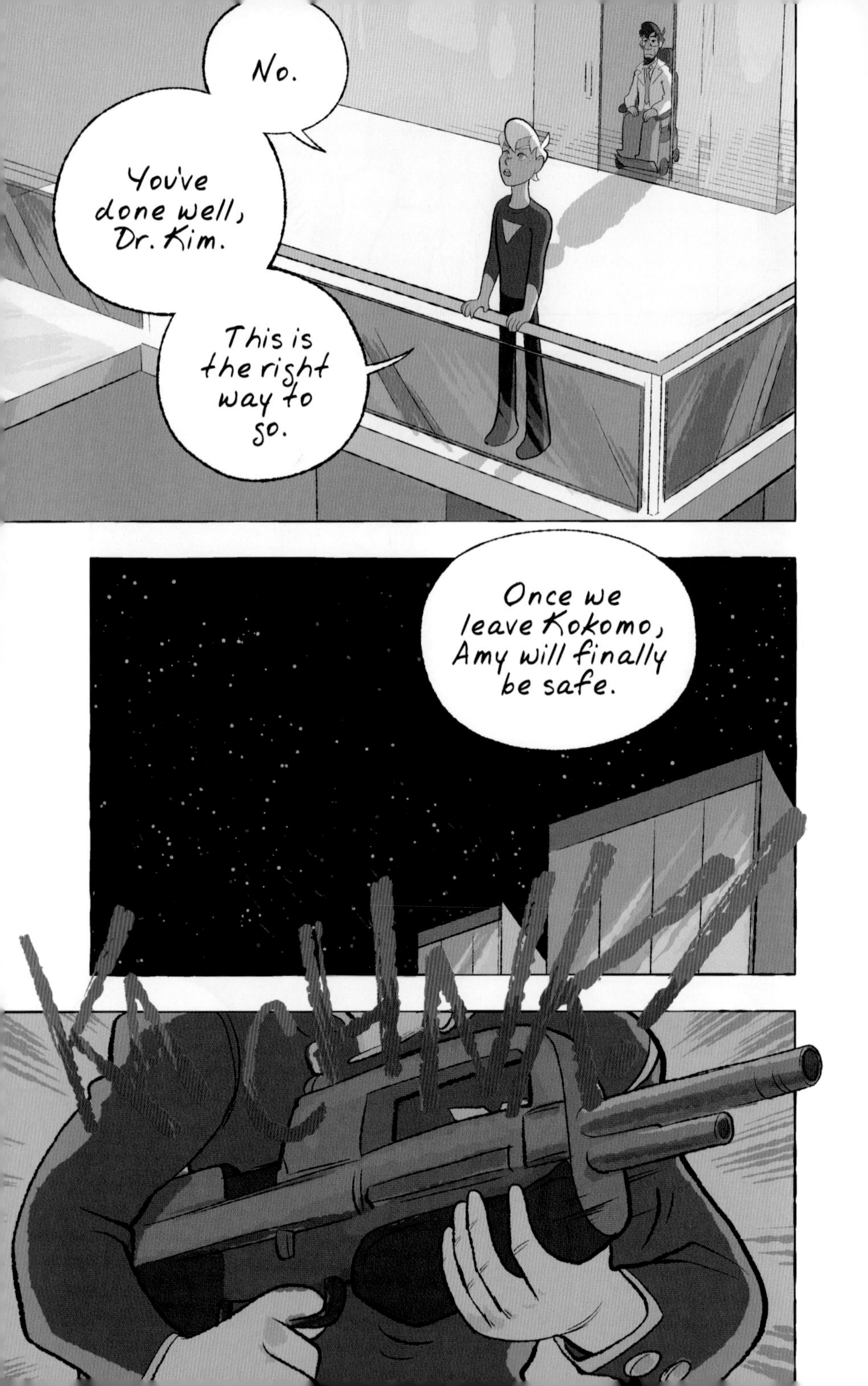
No.
You've done well, Dr. Kim.
This is the right way to go.
Once we leave Kokomo, Amy will finally be safe.

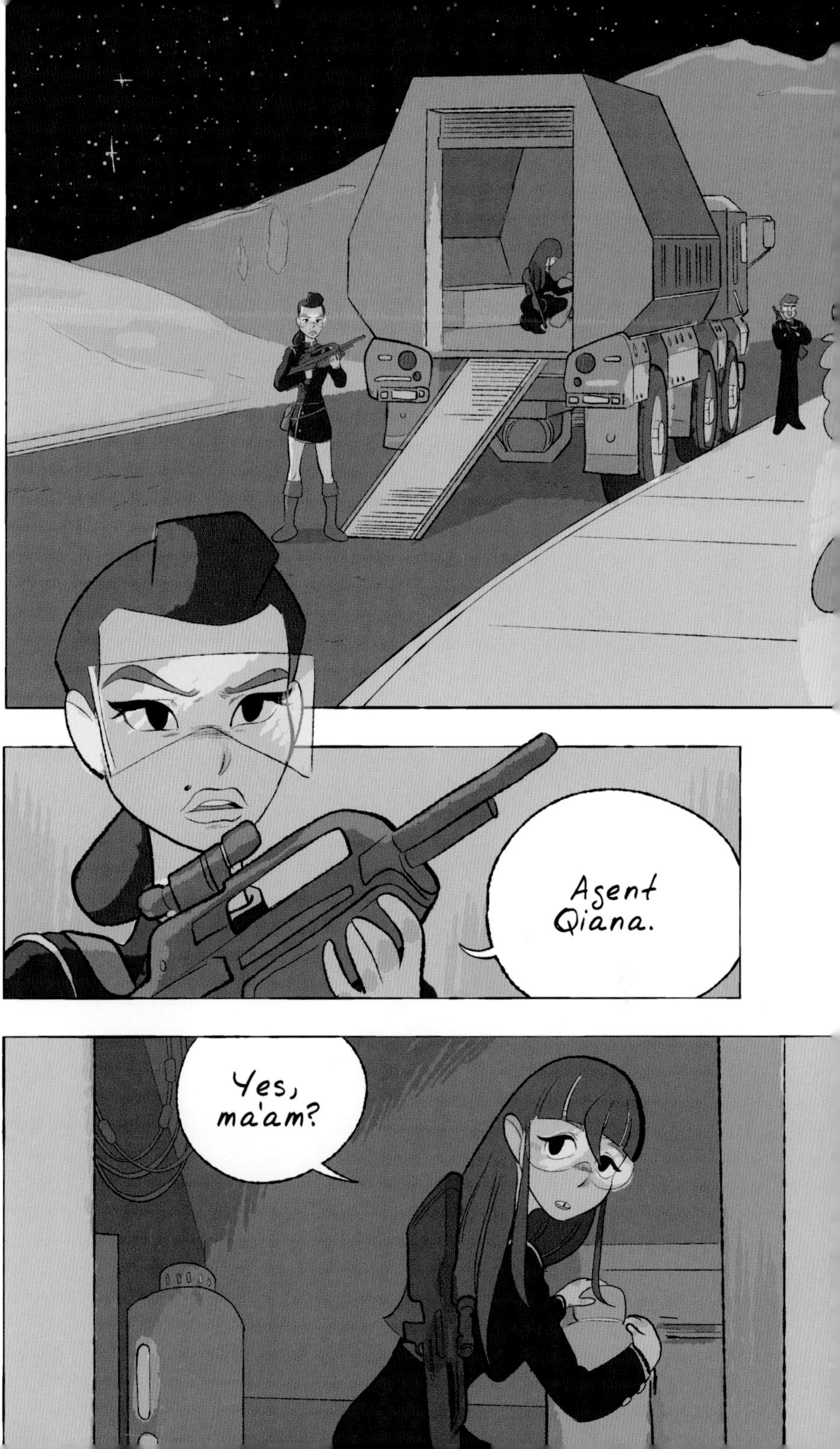
Agent Qiana.
Yes, ma'am?

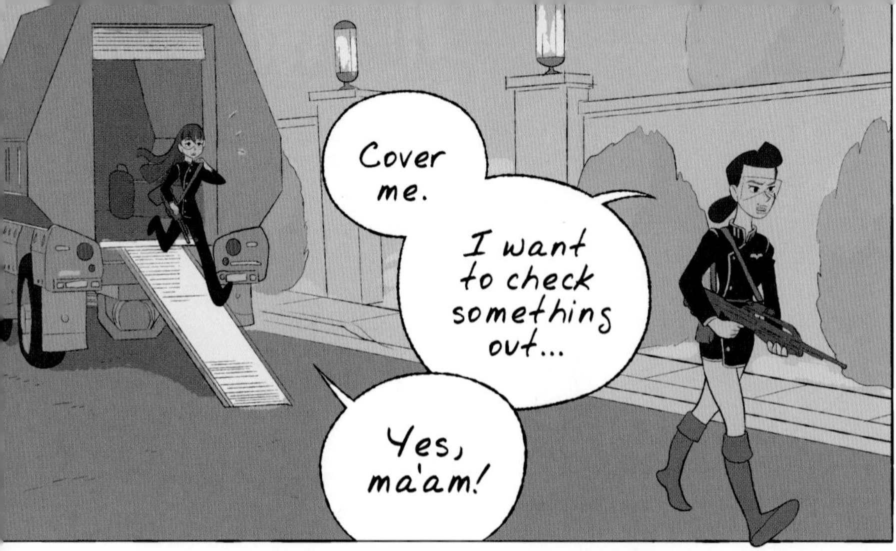
Cover me.
I want to check somethins out...
Yes, ma'am!

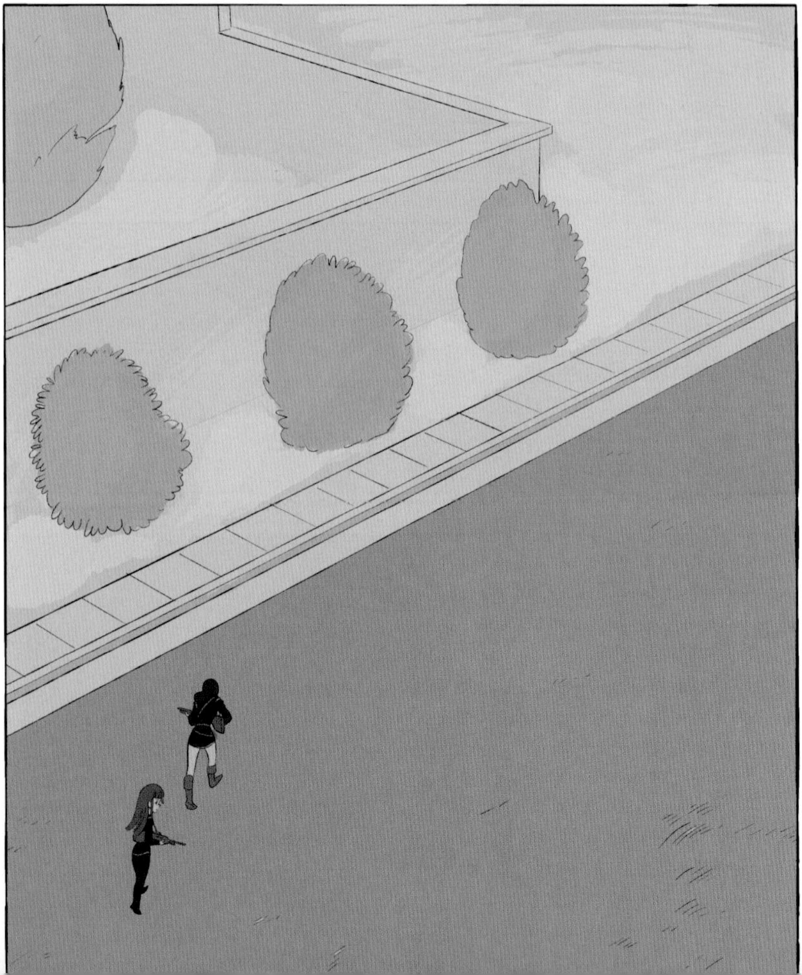

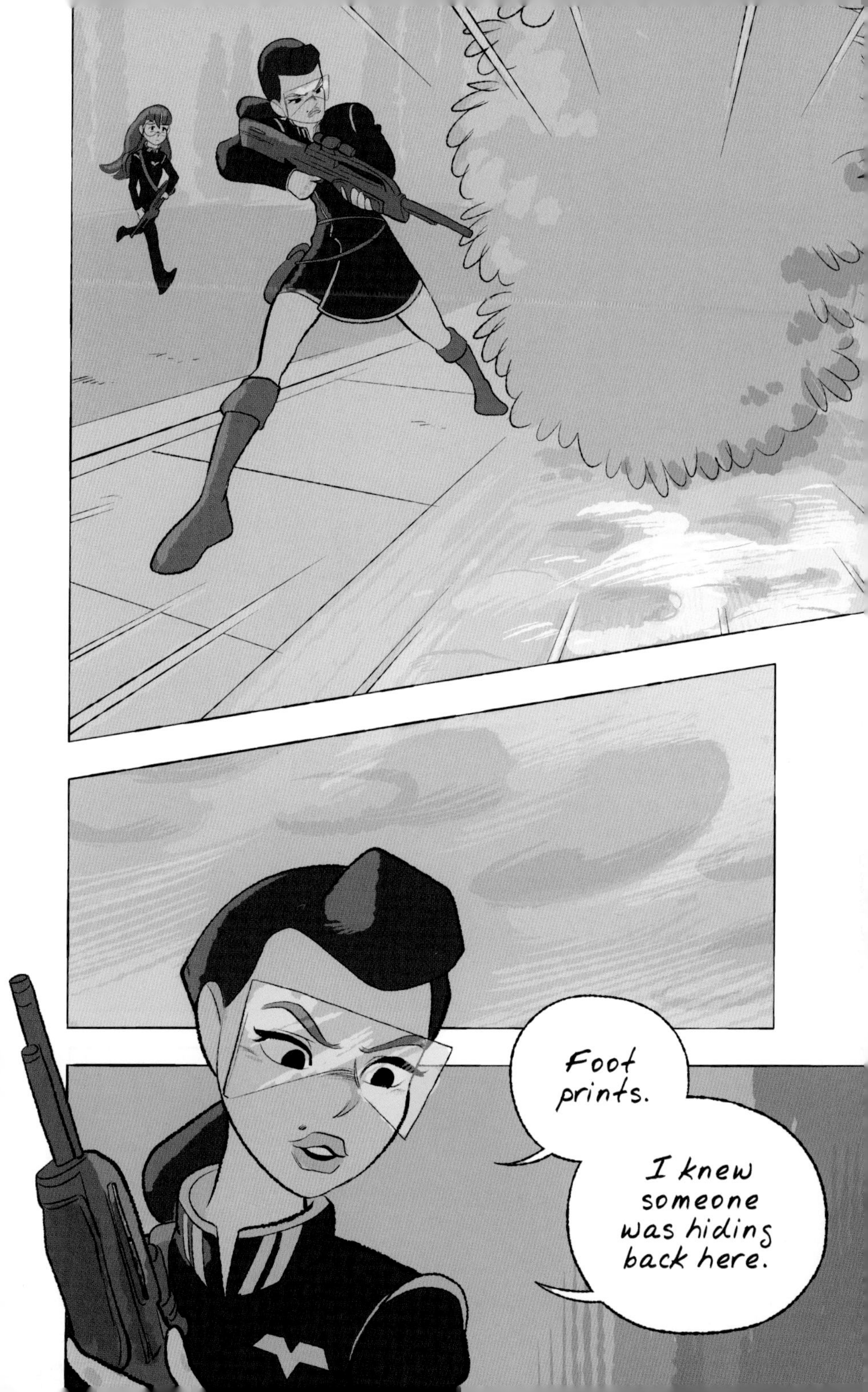
Foot prints.
I knew someone was hiding back here.

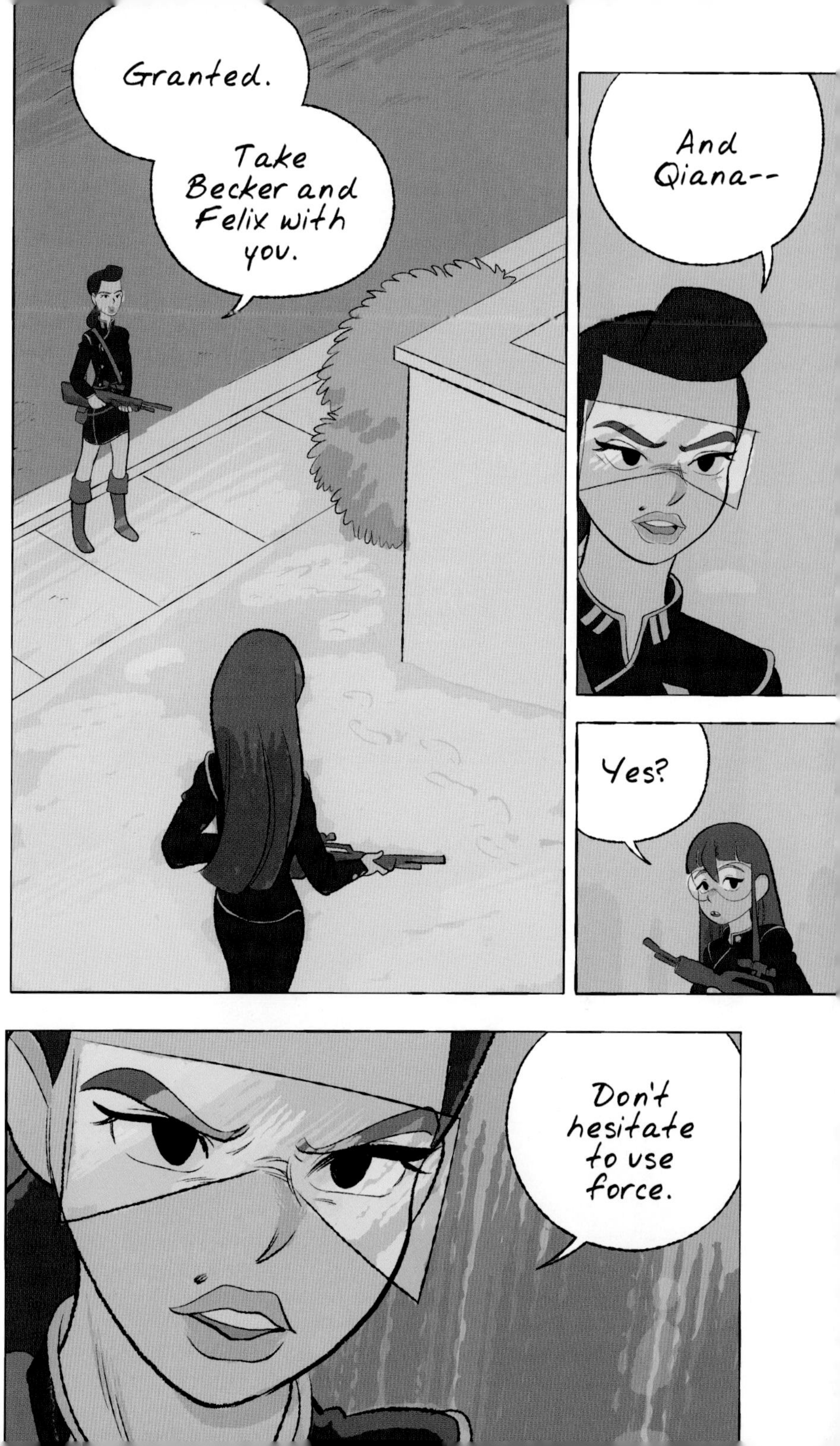
Granted.
Take Becker and Felix with you.
And Qiana--
Yes?
Don't hesitate to use force.

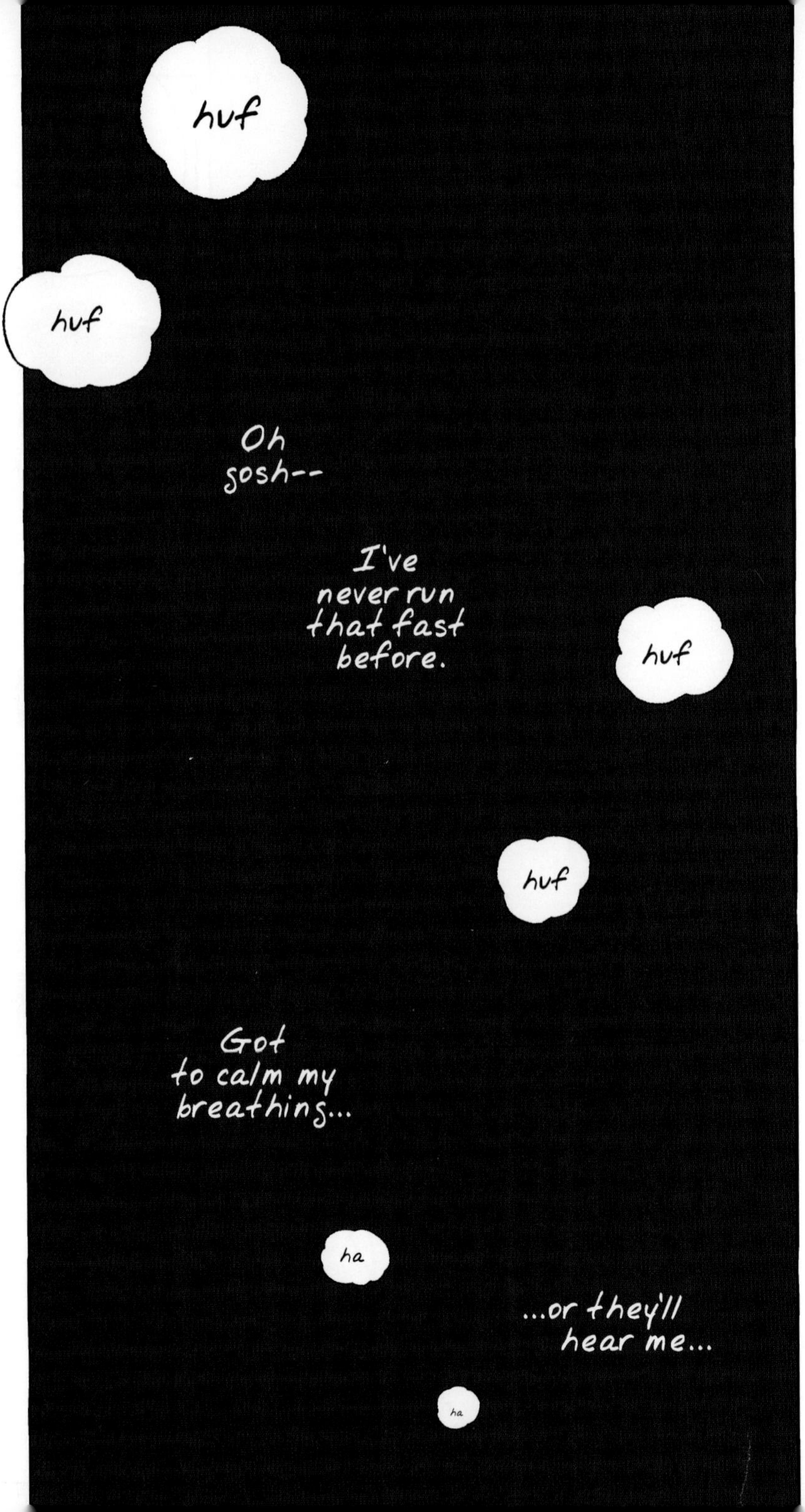
huf
huf
Oh gosh--
I've never run that fast before.
huf
huf
Got to calm my breathing...
ha
...or they'll hear me...
ha

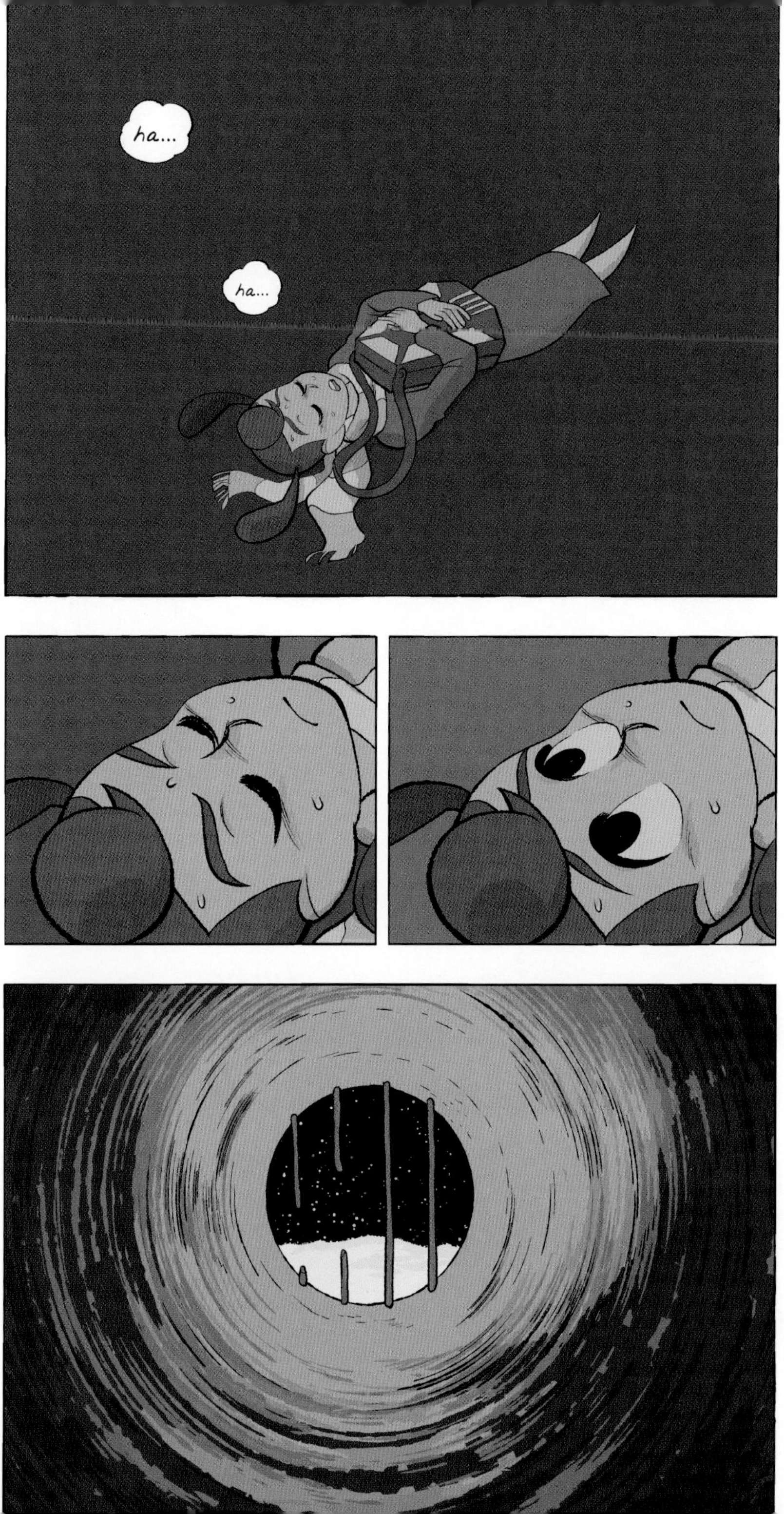
ha...
ha...

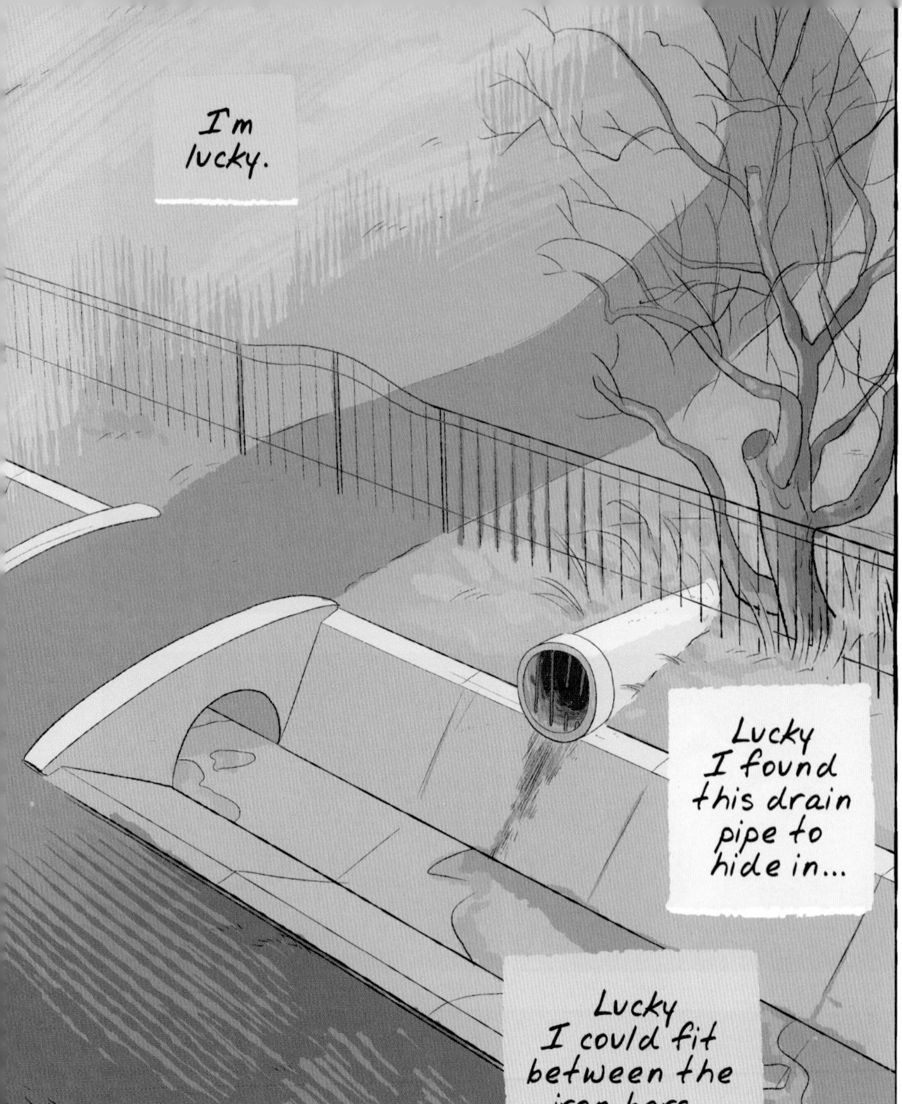
I'm lucky.
Lucky I found this drain pipe to hide in...
Lucky I could fit between the iron bars...

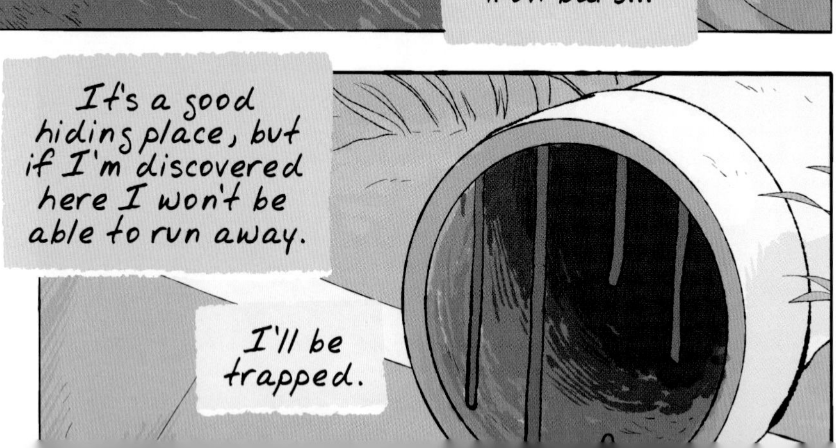
It's a good hiding place, but if I'm discovered here I won't be able to run away.
I'll be trapped.

I need to get out of here,
but I don't want to get shot.

Maybe that's my fear talking.
Soldiers don't shoot civilians, right?

That woman with the piercing gaze--
she would shoot someone if given the chance.
I could tell.

There was poison in her flavor.

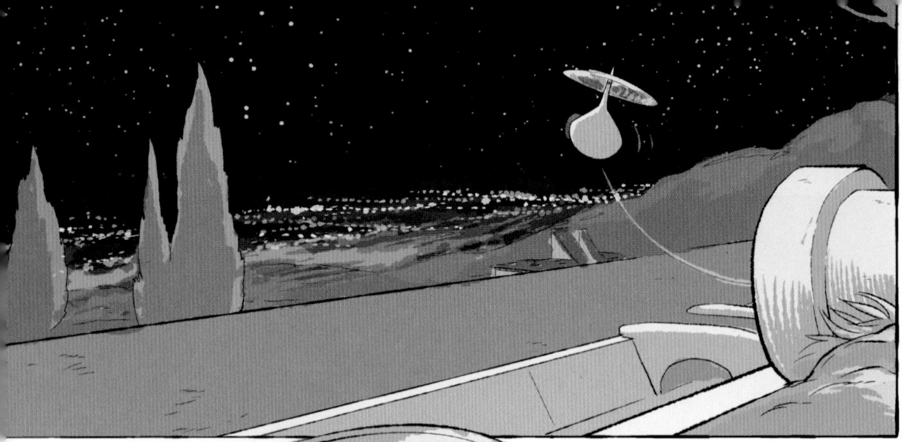

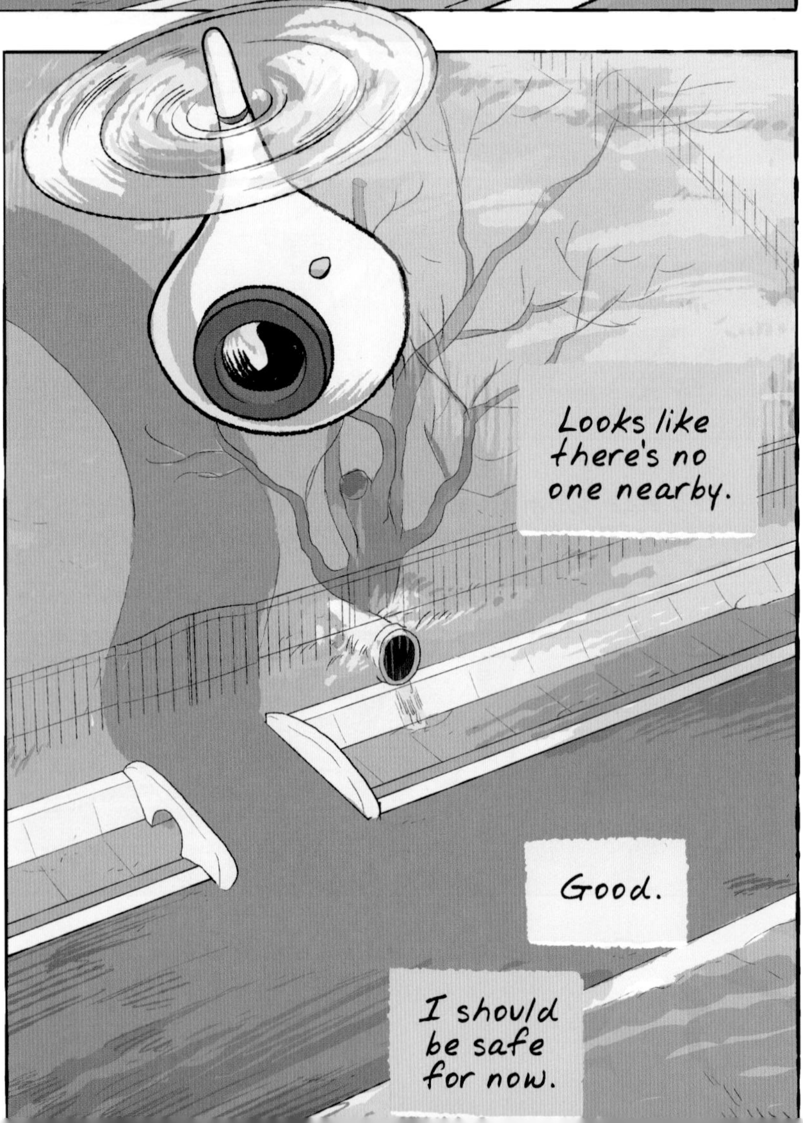
Looks like there's no one nearby.
Good.
I should be safe for now.

Almost.

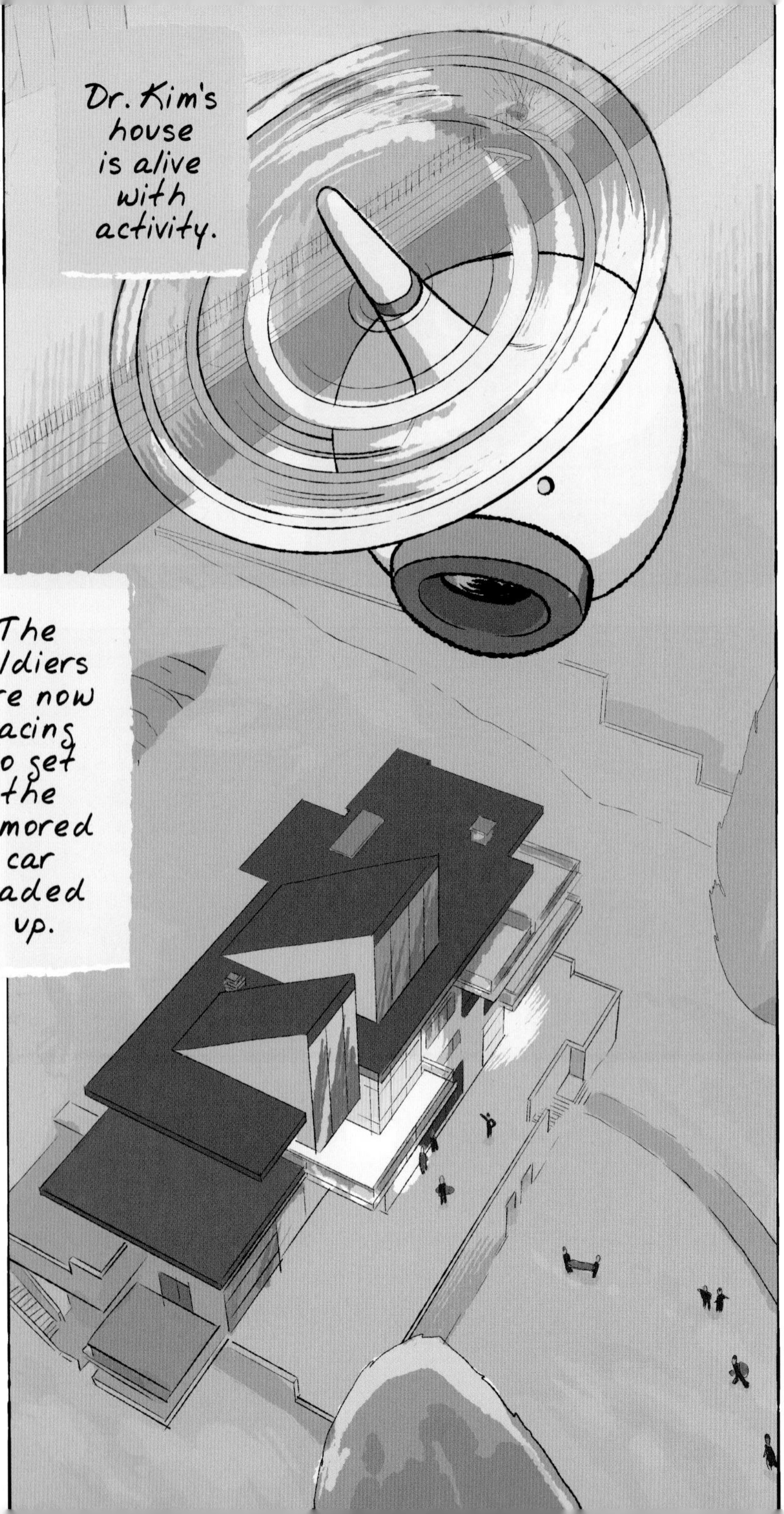
Dr. Kim's house is alive with activity.
The soldiers are now racing to get the armored car loaded up.

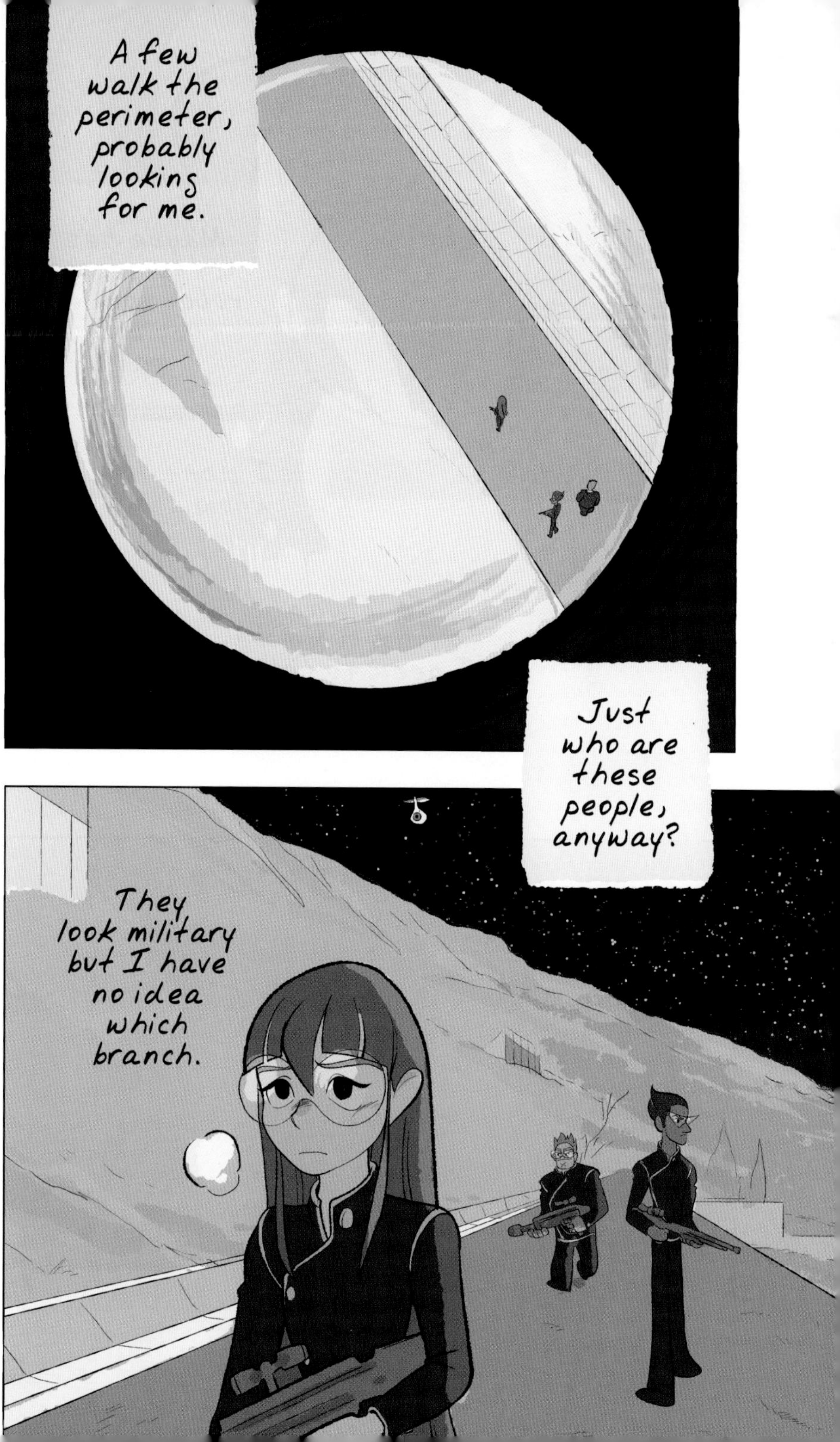
A few walk the perimeter, probably looking for me.
Just who are these people, anyway?
They look military but I have no idea which branch.

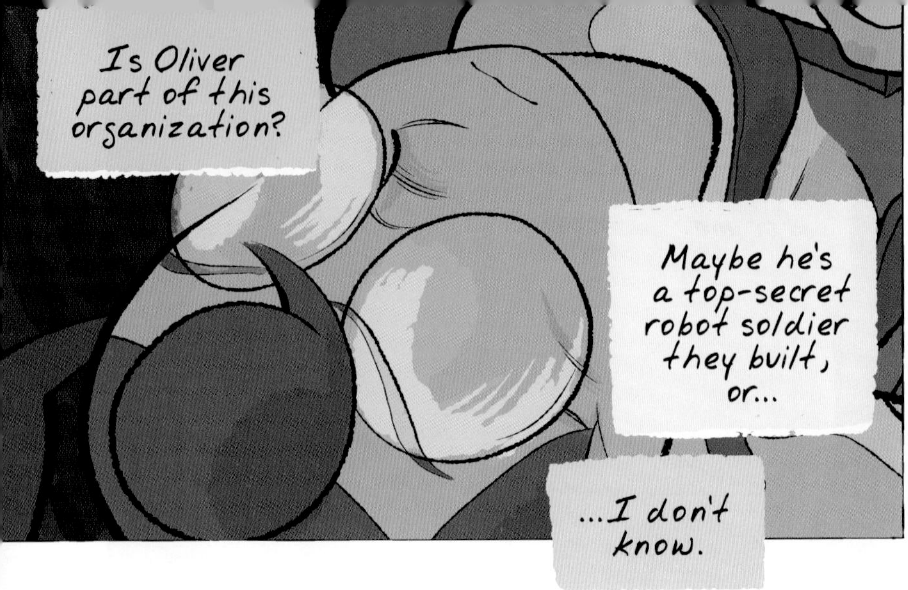
Is Oliver part of this organization?
Maybe he's a top-secret robot soldier they built, or...
...I don't know.

If I want to find out more, I need to follow through with my plan.

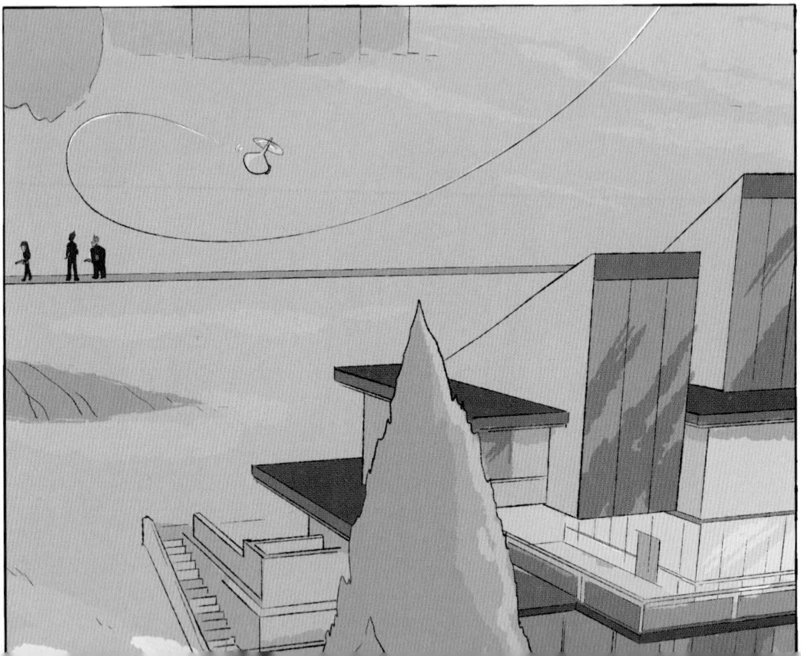

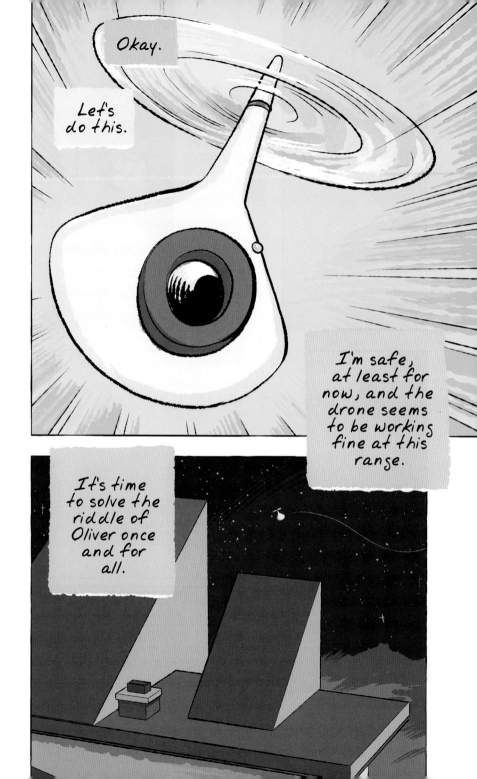

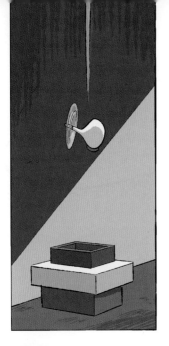

Hopefully Oliver's fireplace isn't lit right now.

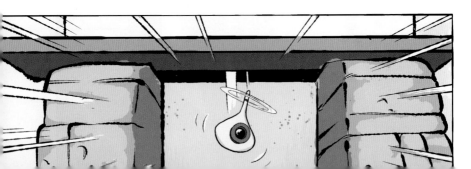

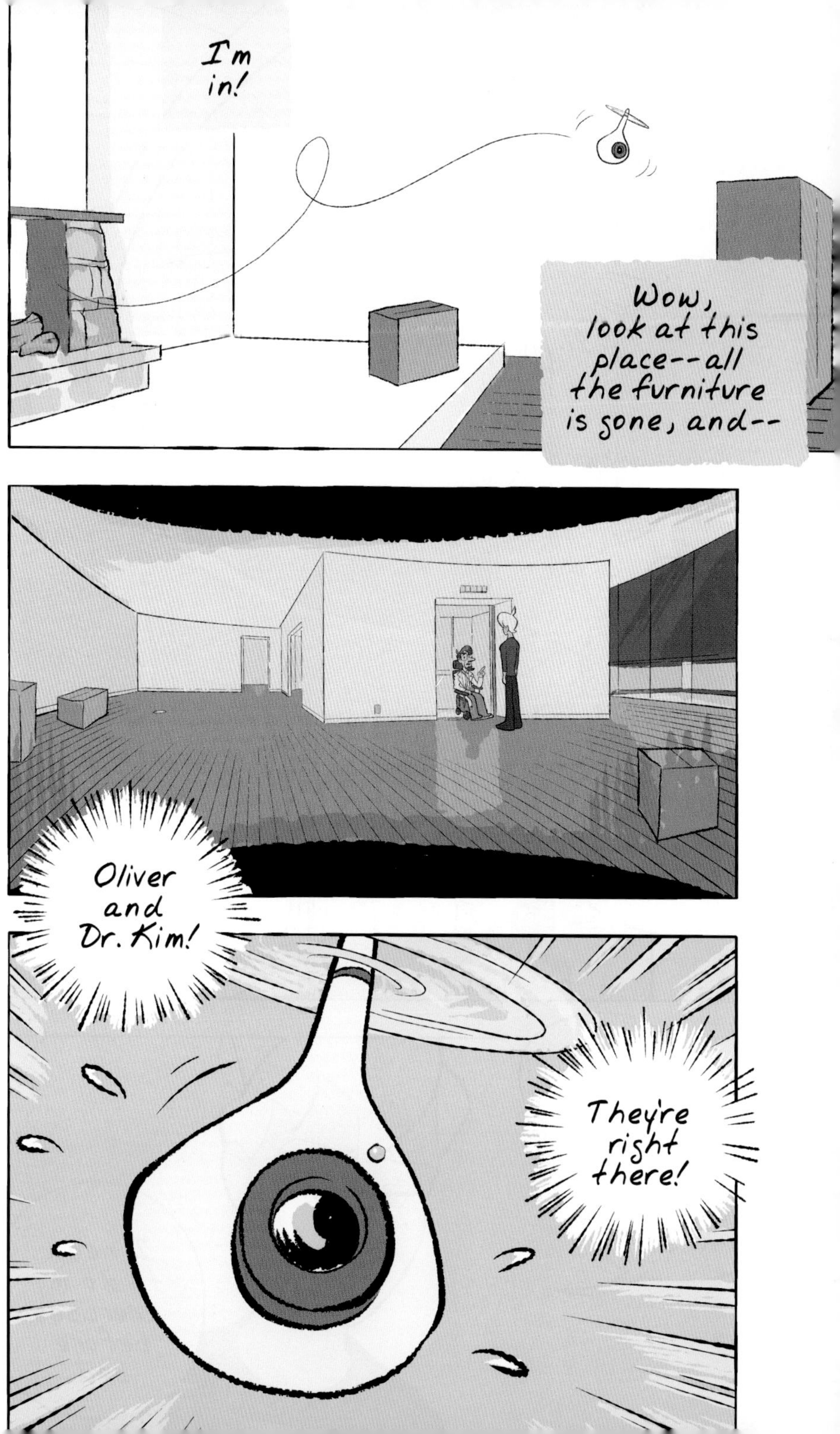
I'm in!
Wow, look at this place--all the furniture is gone, and--
Oliver and Dr. Kim!
They're right there!

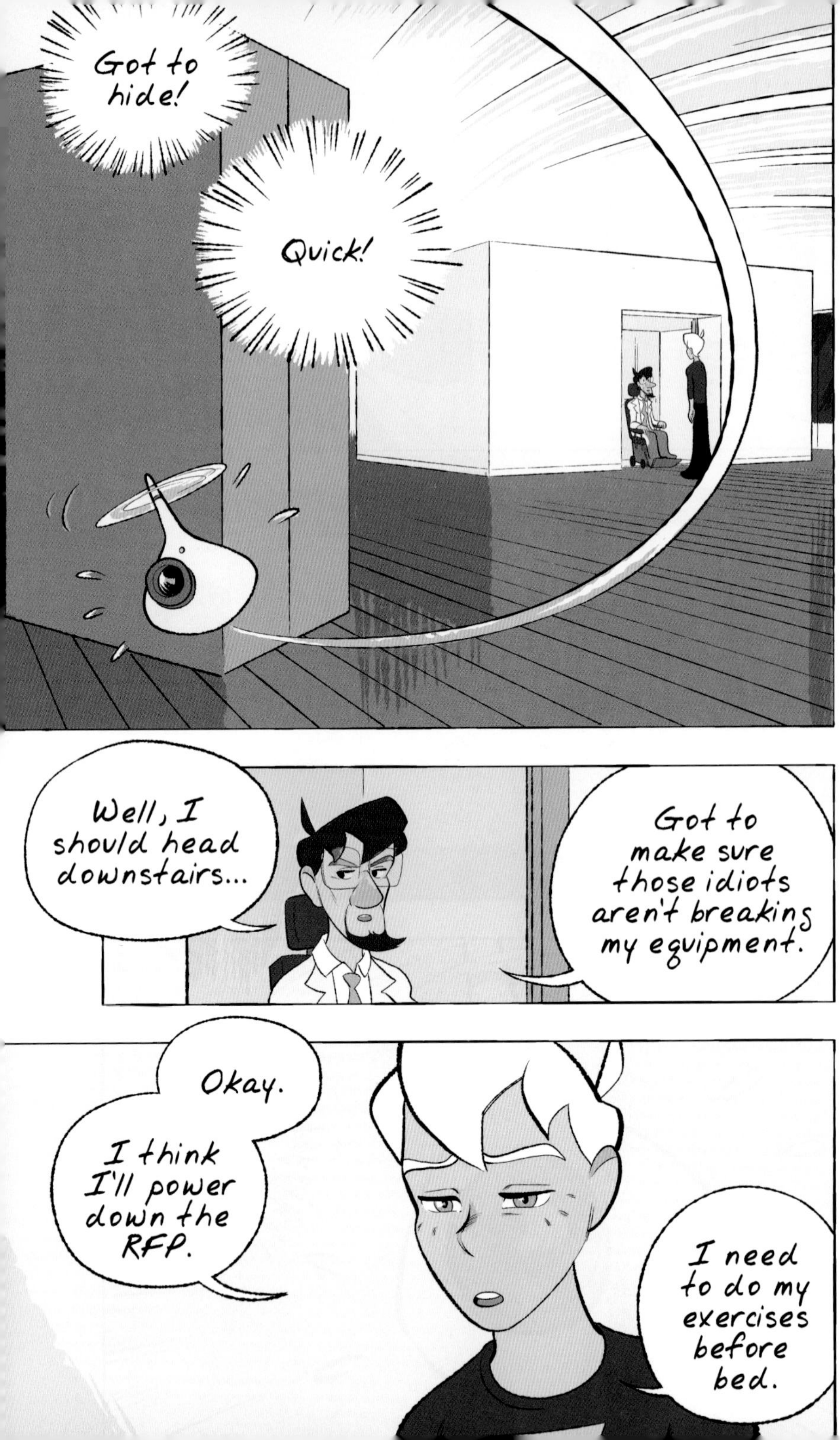
Got to hide!
Quick!
Well, I should head downstairs...
Got to make sure those idiots aren't breaking my equipment.
Okay.
I think I'll power down the RFP.
I need to do my exercises before bed.

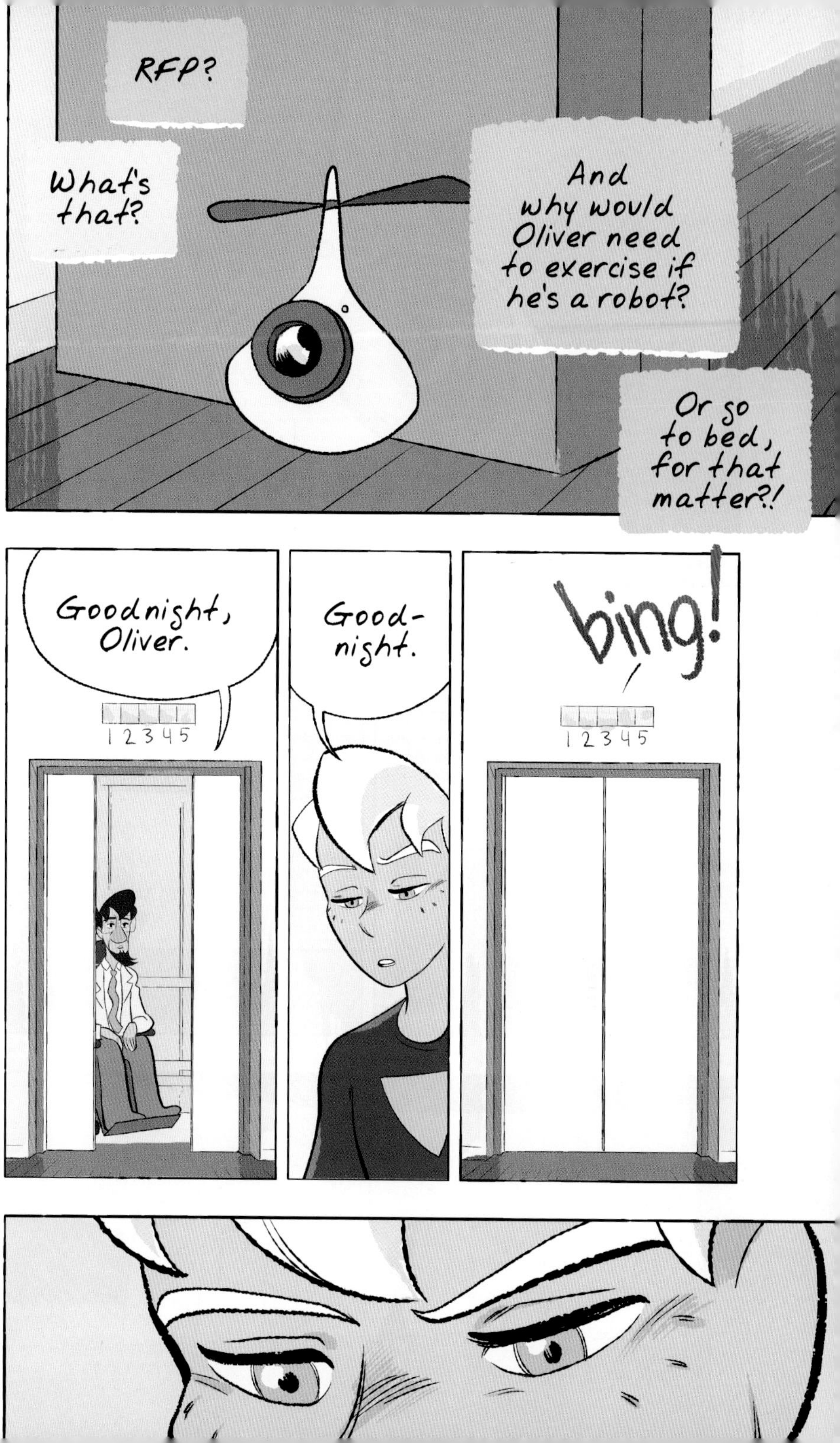
RFP?
What's that?
And why would Oliver need to exercise if he's a robot?
Or go to bed, for that matter?!
Goodnight, Oliver.
1 2 3 4 5
Good-night.
bing!
1 2 3 4 5

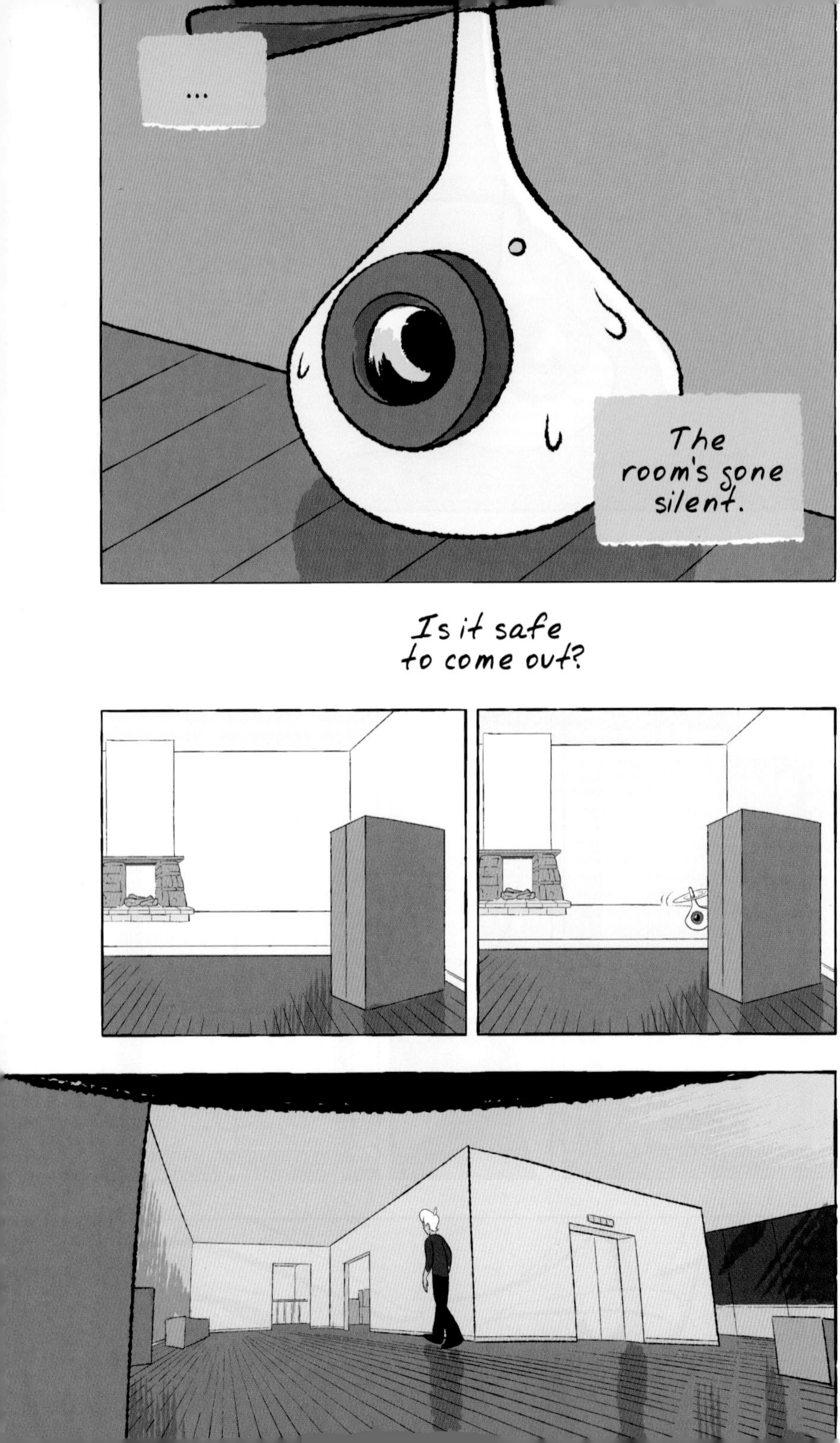
...
The room's gone silent.
Is it safe to come out?

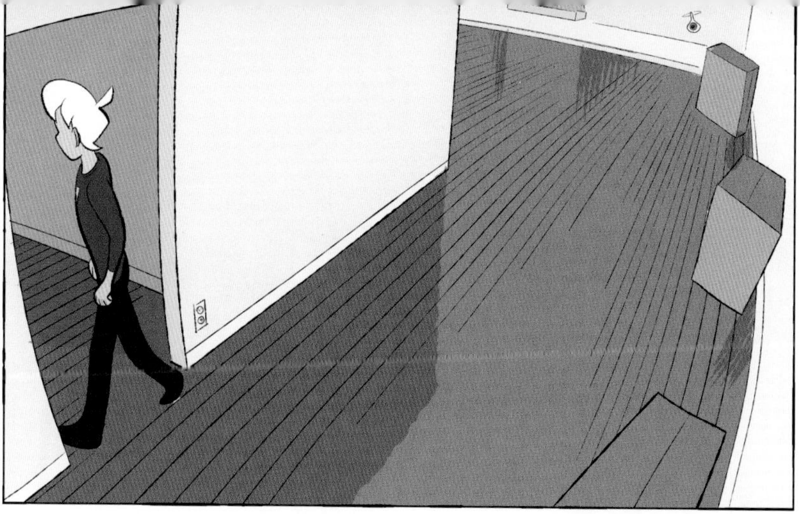
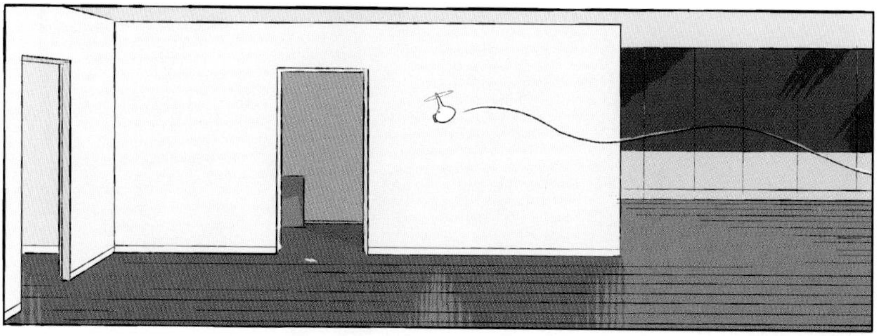
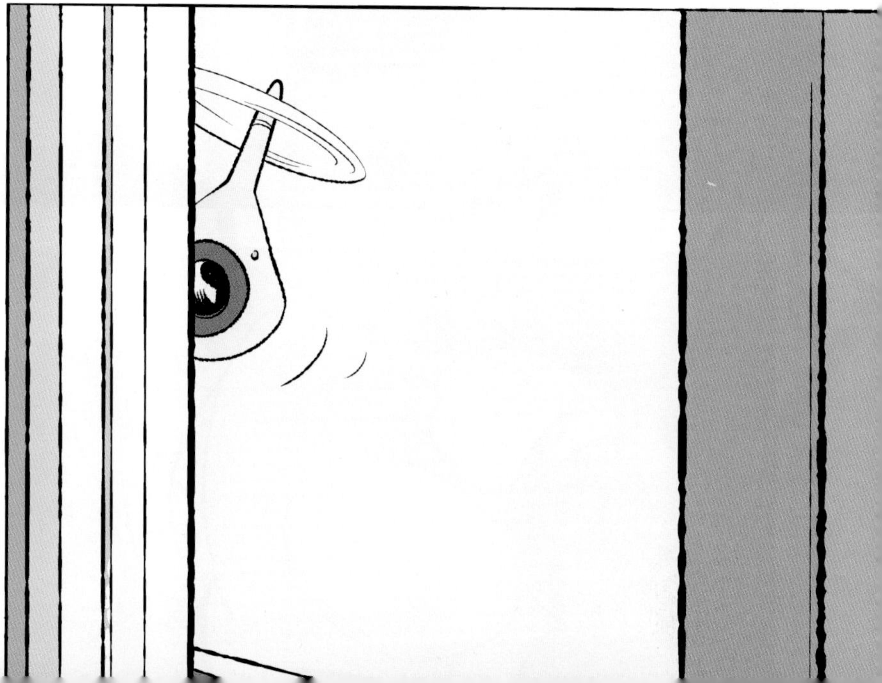

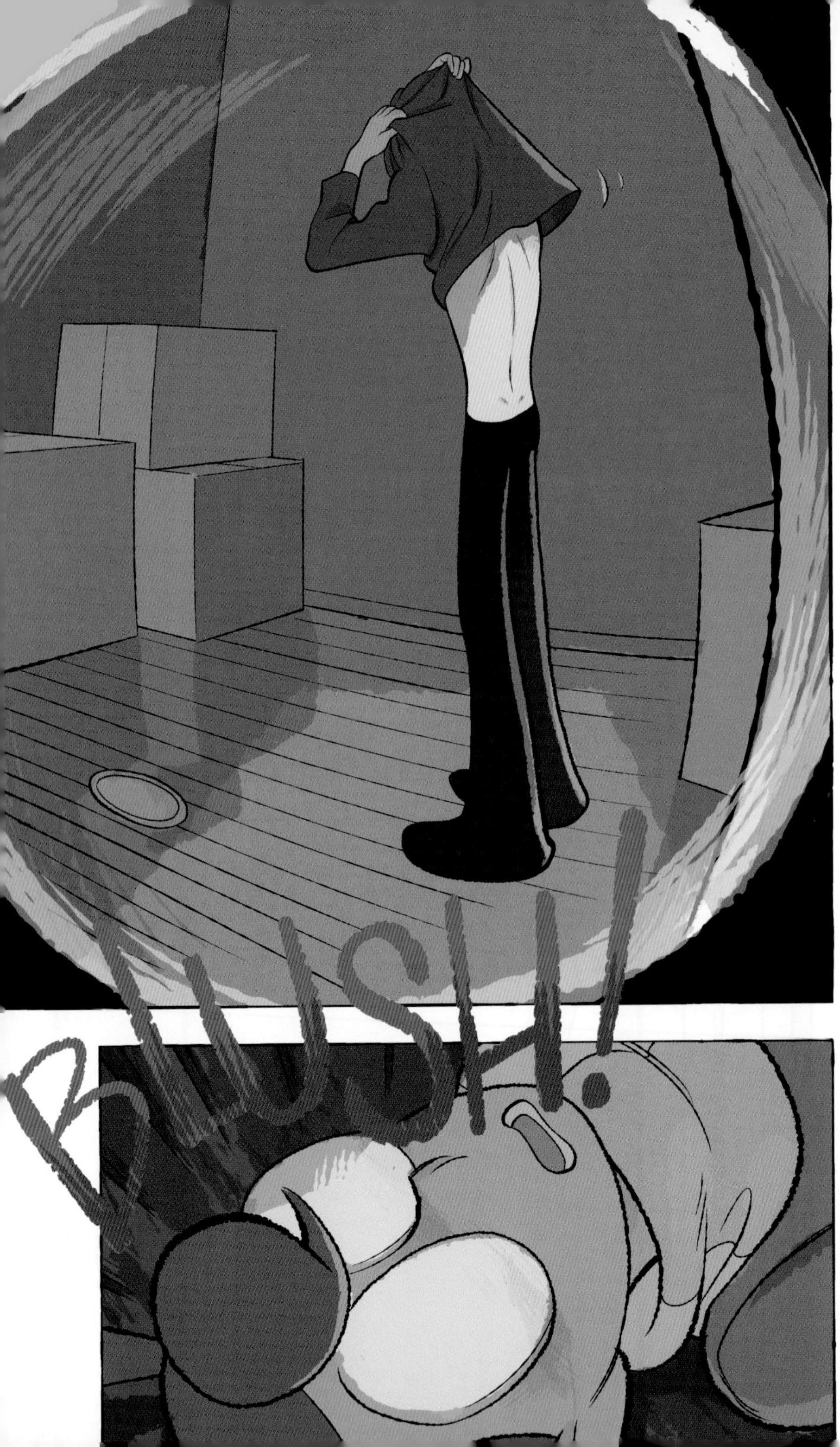
BLUSH!!

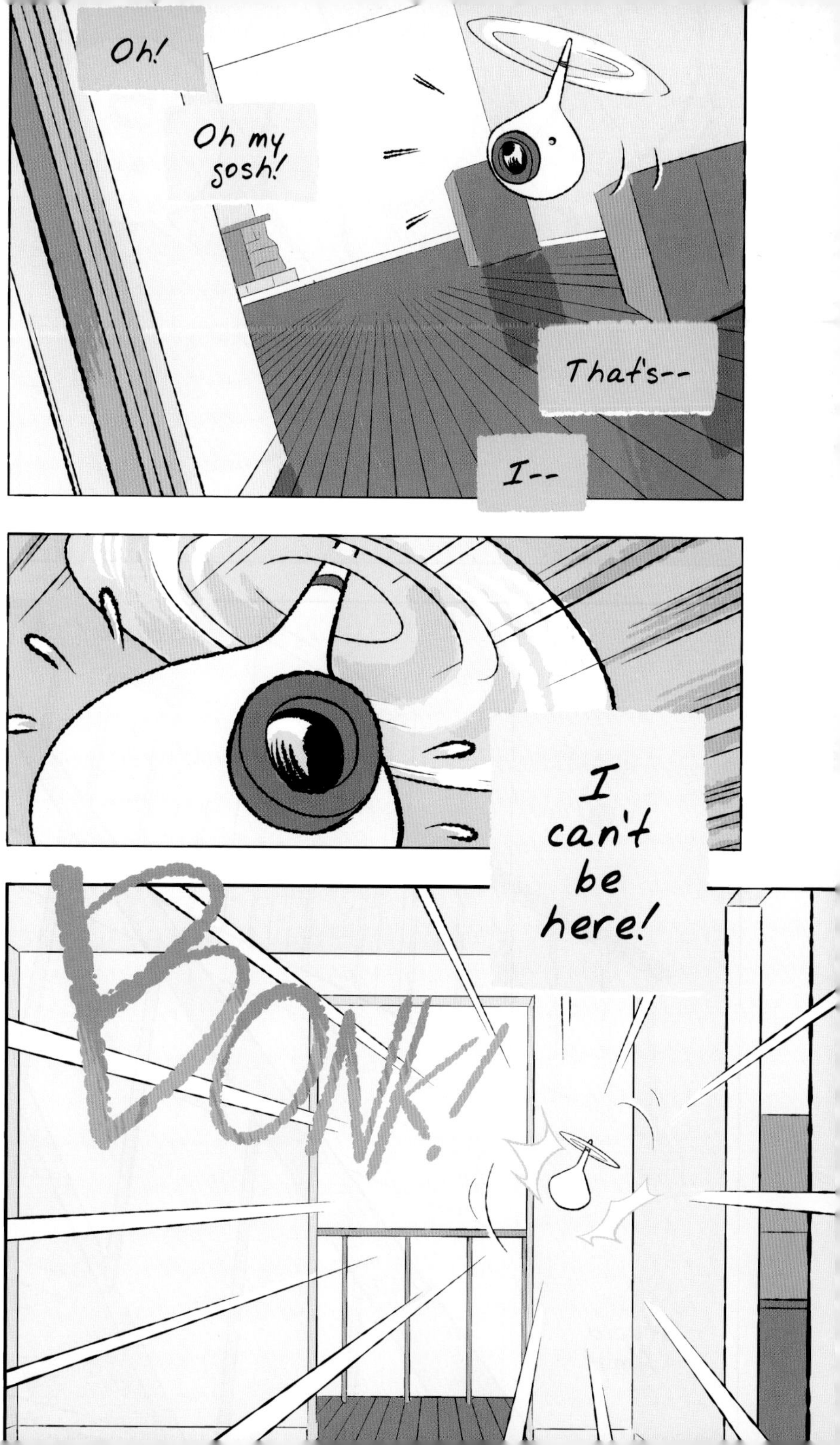
Oh!
Oh my gosh!
That's--
I--
I can't be here!
BONK!

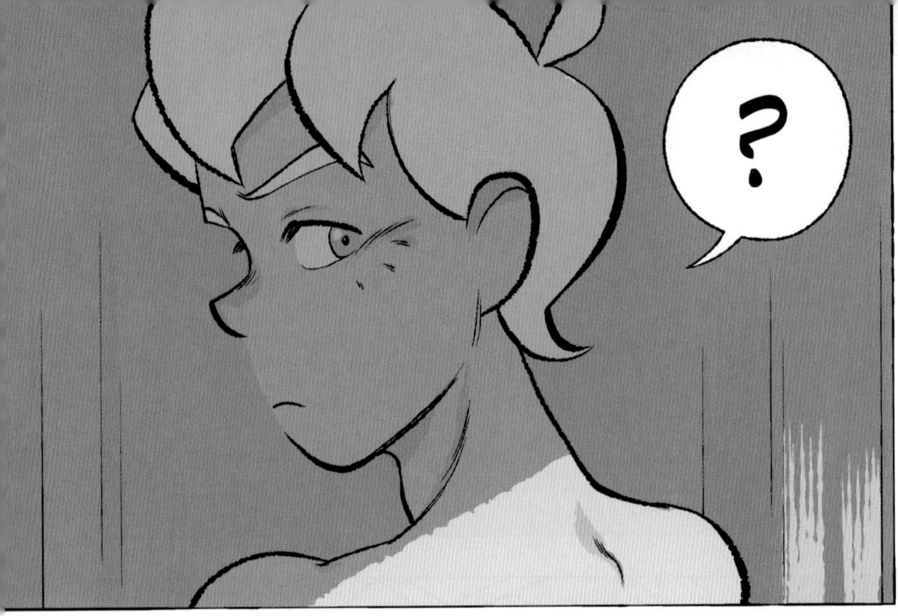
?

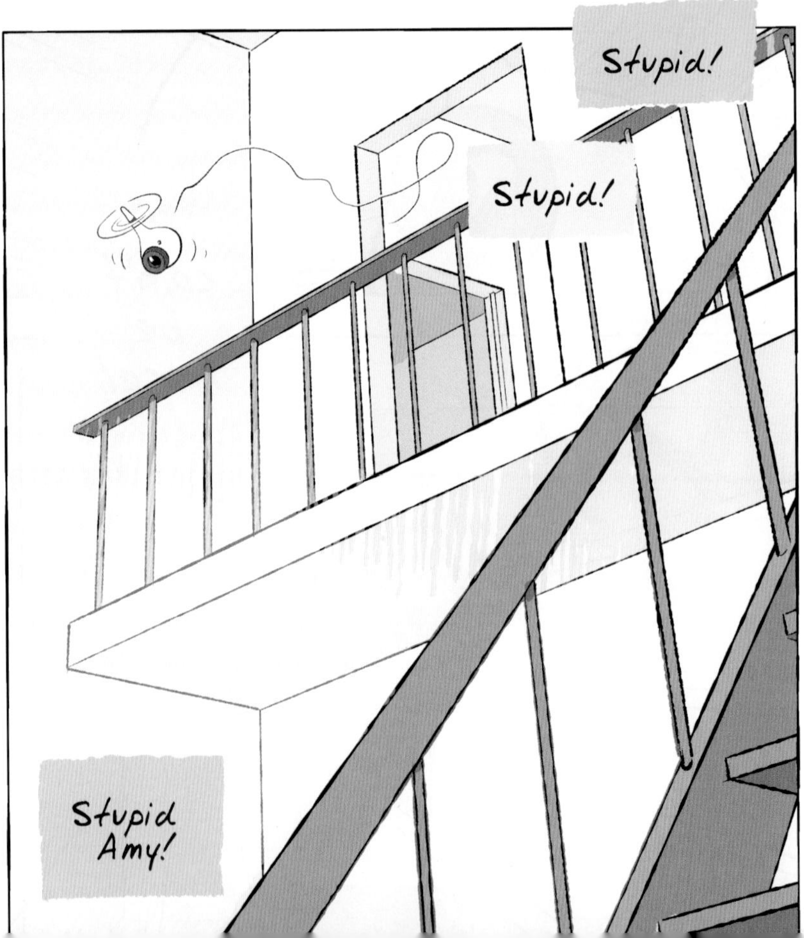
Stupid!
Stupid!
Stupid Amy!

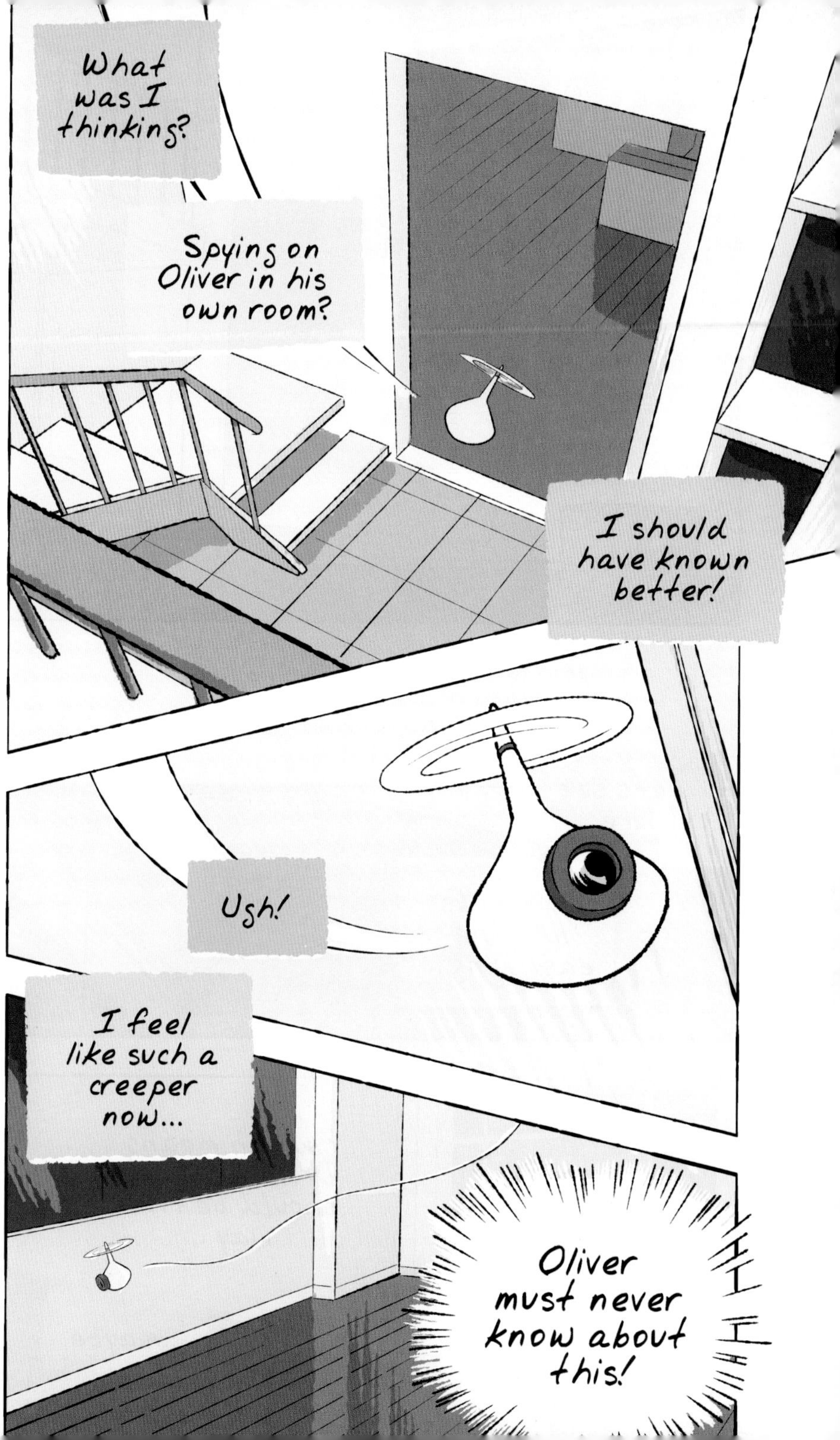
What was I thinking?
Spying on Oliver in his own room?
I should have known better!
Ugh!
I feel like such a creeper now...
Oliver must never know about this!

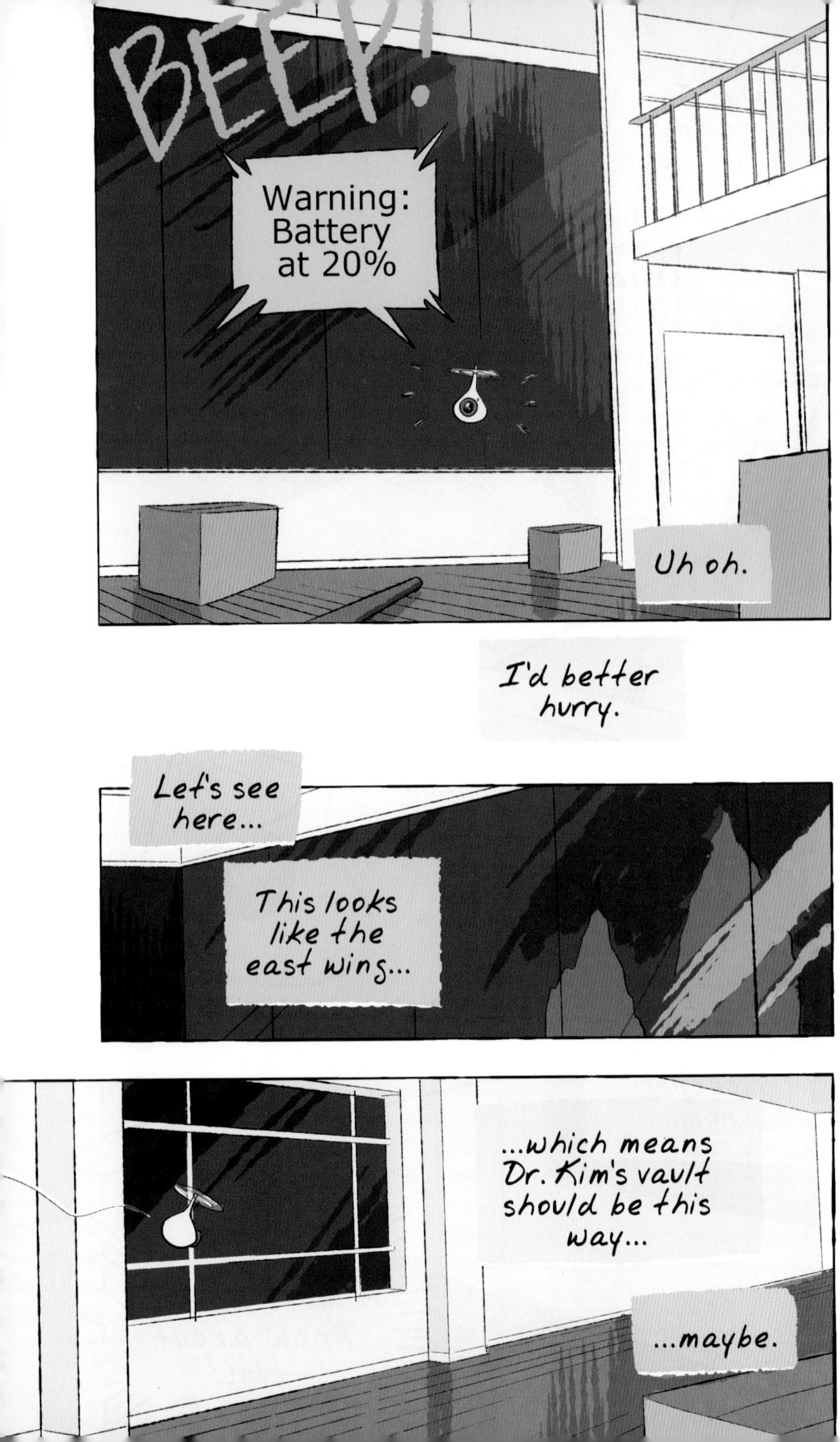
BEEP!
Warning: Battery at 20%
Uh oh.
I'd better hurry.
Let's see here...
This looks like the east wing...
...which means Dr. Kim's vault should be this way...
...maybe.

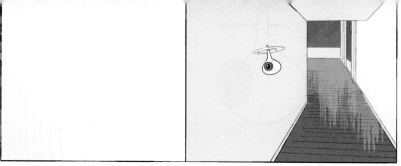

KLANG!

Careful, dude!

Whoops, ha ha.

Dr. Kim will skin us alive if there's even a scratch on this machine!

Whatever.

I'm not afraid of that old cripple...

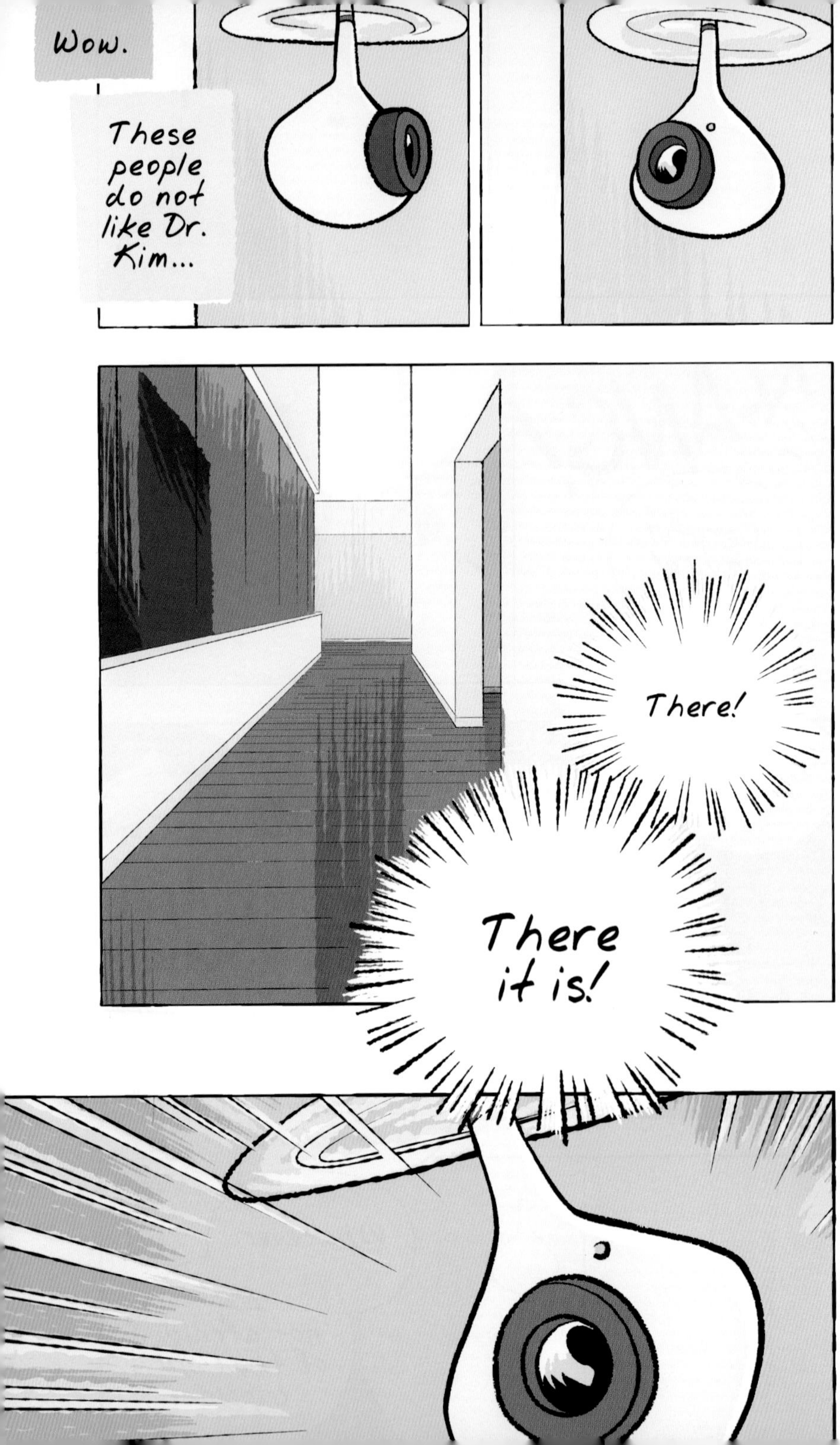
Wow.
These people do not like Dr. Kim...
There!
There it is!

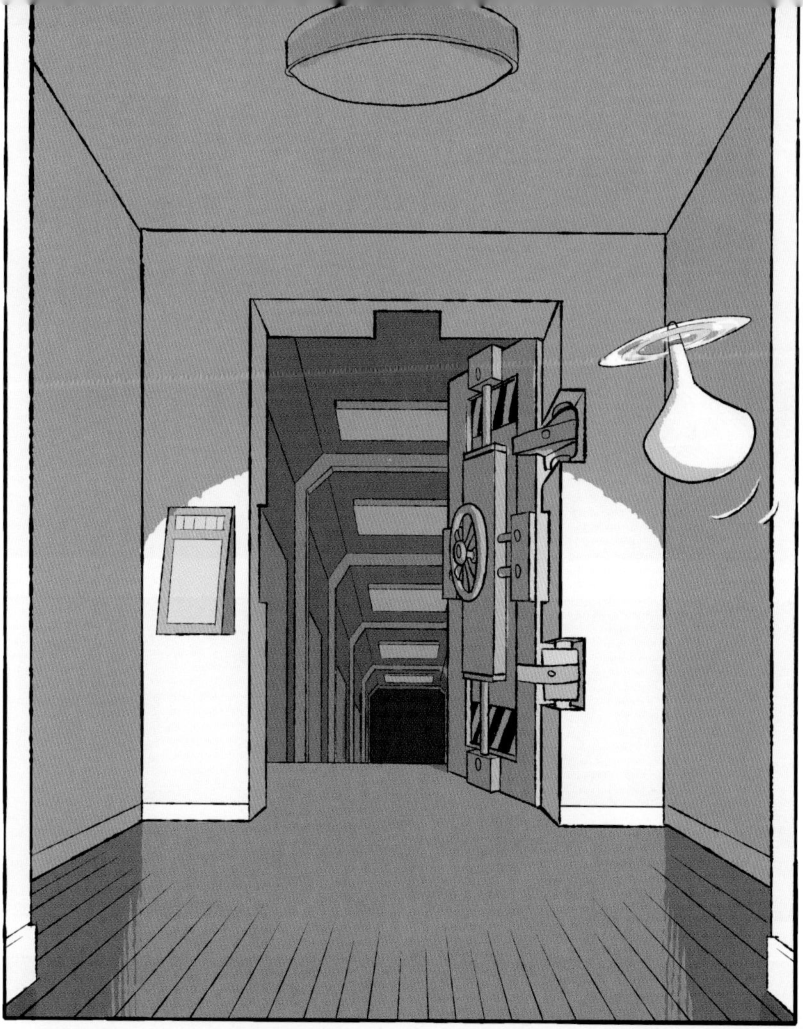
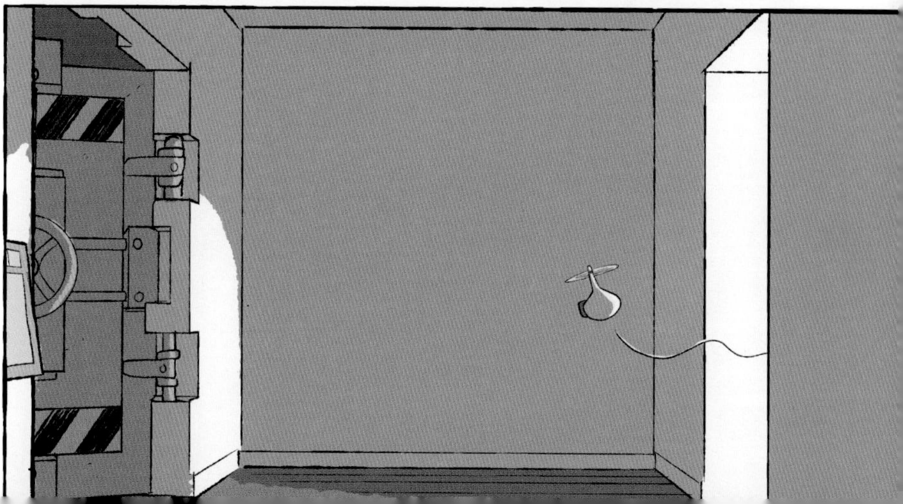

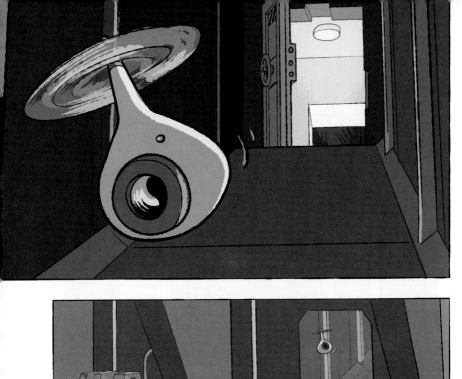

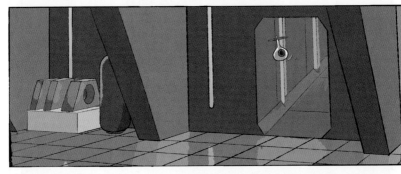

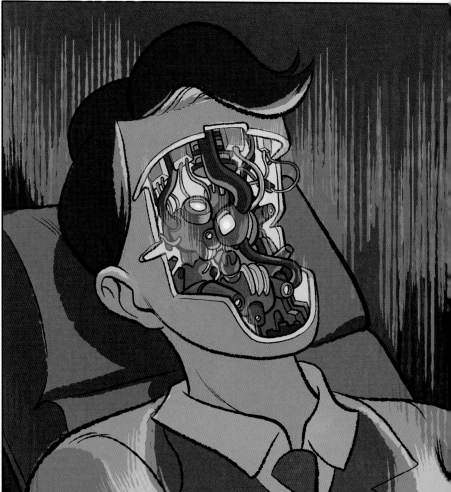

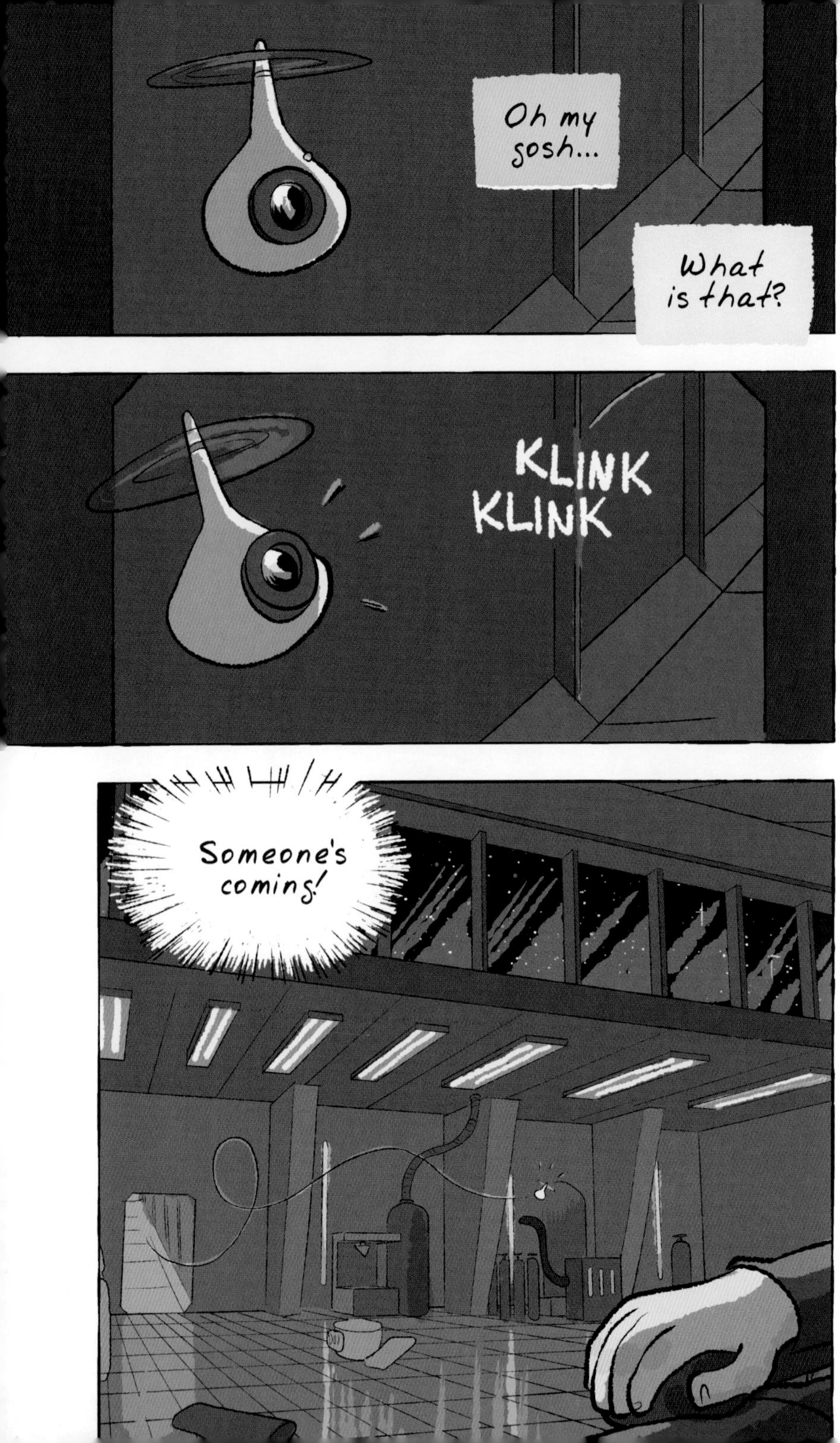
Oh my gosh...
What is that?
KLINK
KLINK
Someone's coming!

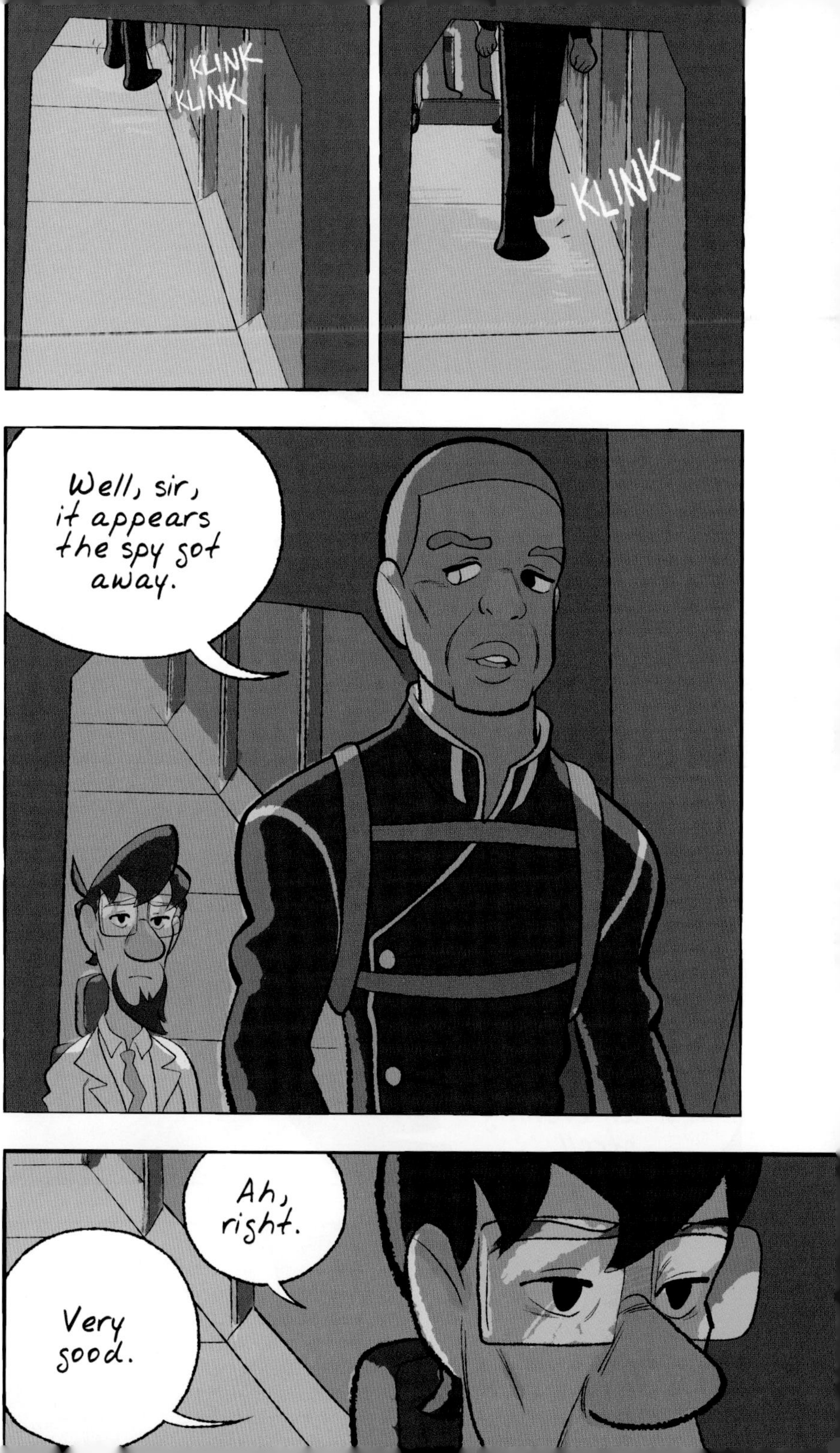
KLINK
KLINK
KLINK
Well, sir, it appears the spy got away.
Ah, right.
Very good.

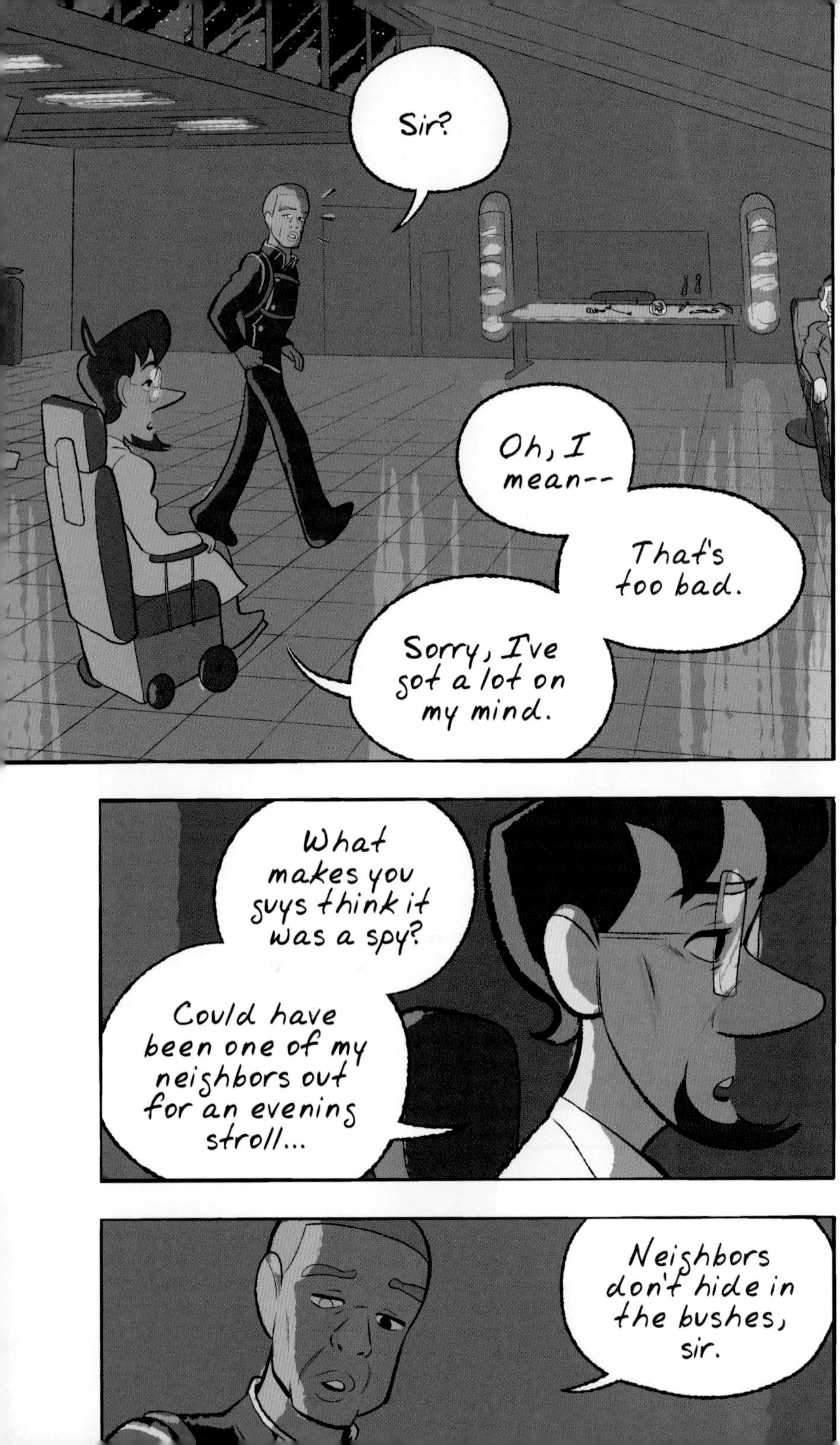
Sir?
Oh, I mean--
That's too bad.
Sorry, I've got a lot on my mind.
What makes you guys think it was a spy?
Could have been one of my neighbors out for an evening stroll...
Neighbors don't hide in the bushes, sir.

I'll so set a team ready to move it out to the transport.

Uh, right...

Thank you.

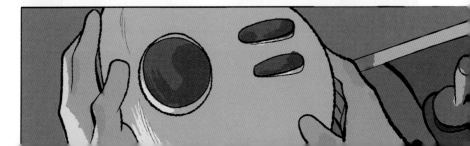

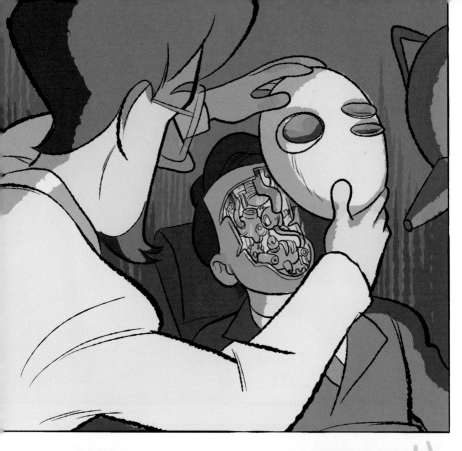

click!

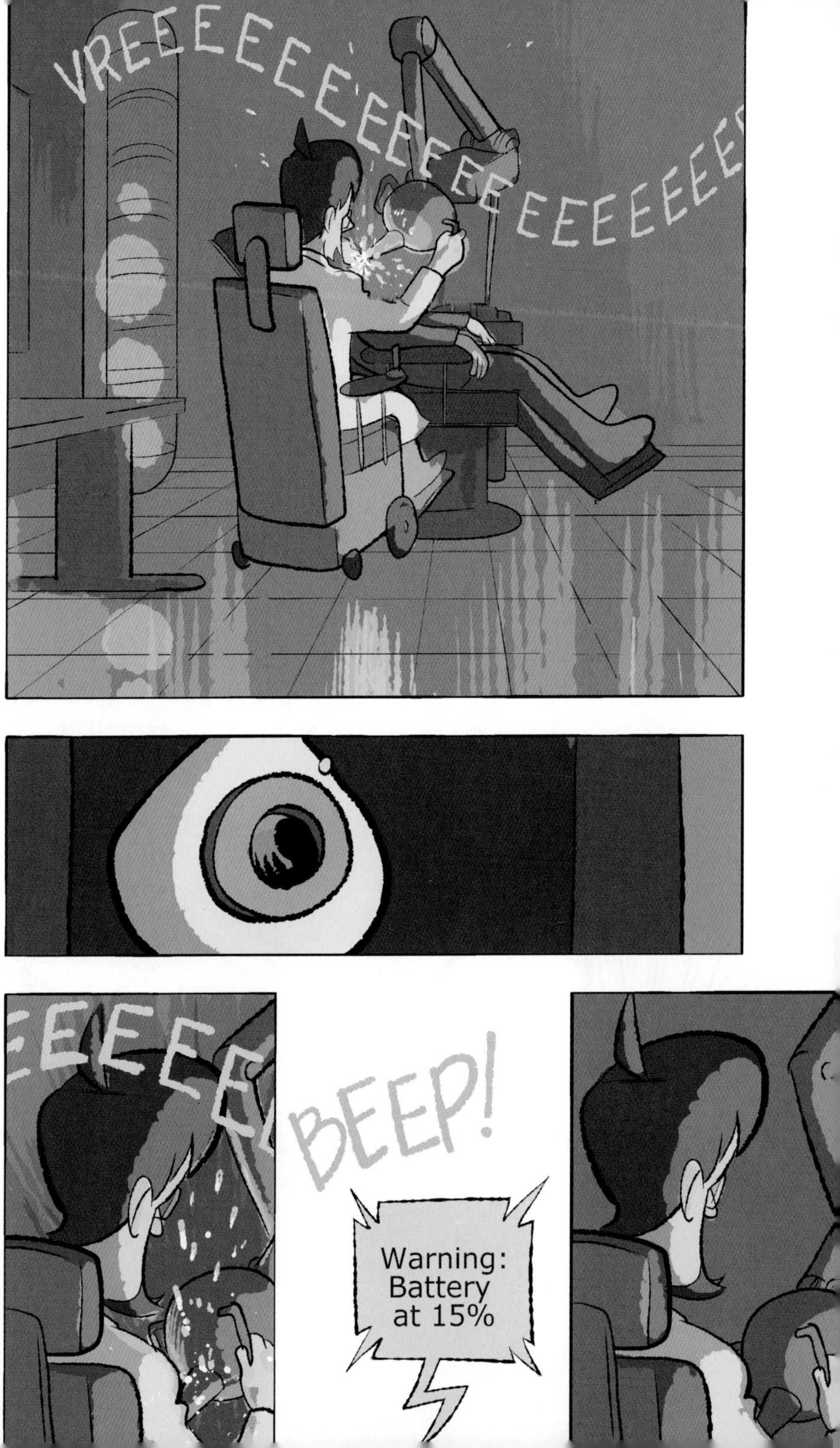
VREEEEEEEEEEEEEEEEEEEEE
EEEEEE
BEEP!
Warning: Battery at 15%

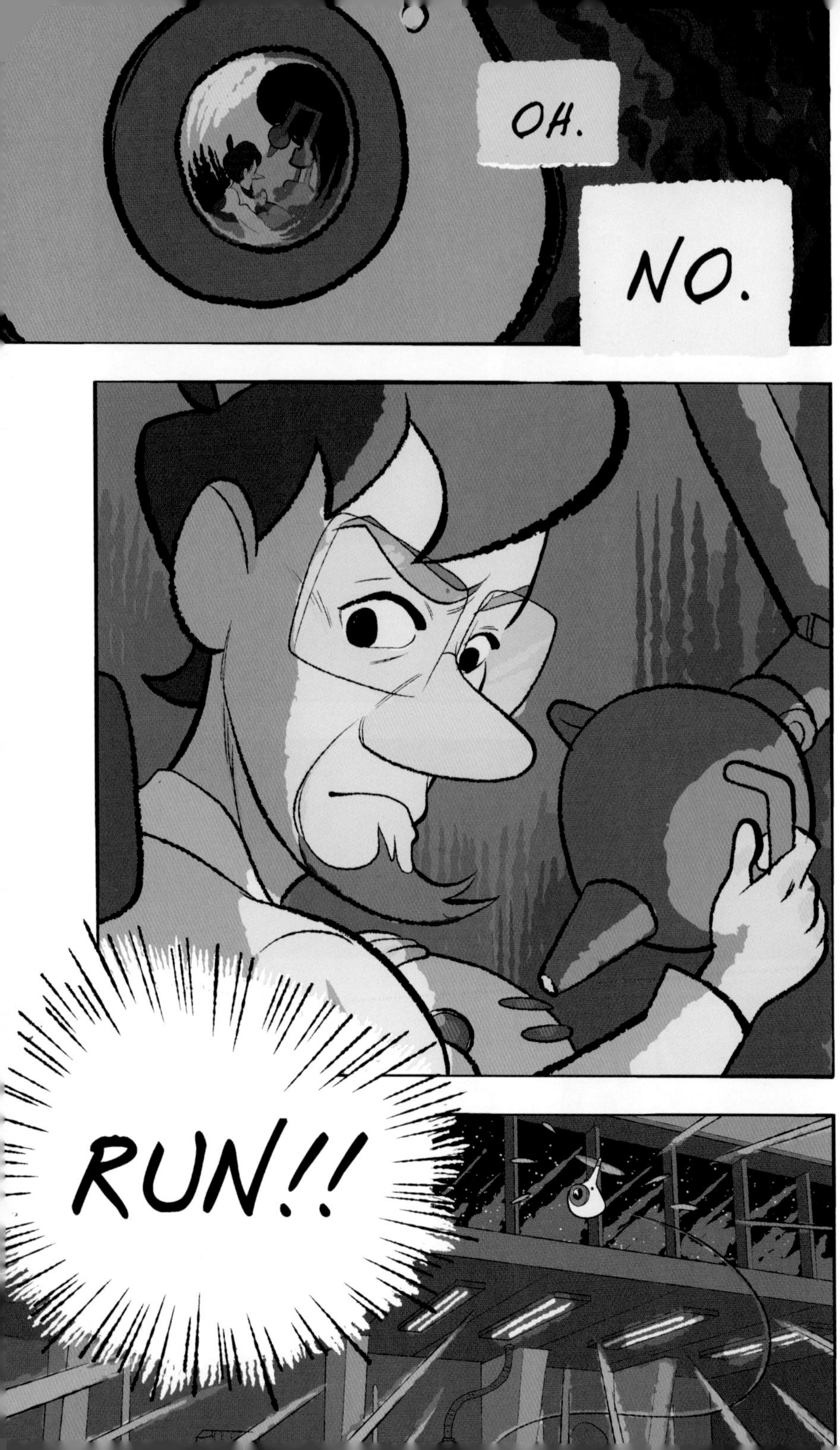
OH.
NO.
RUN!!

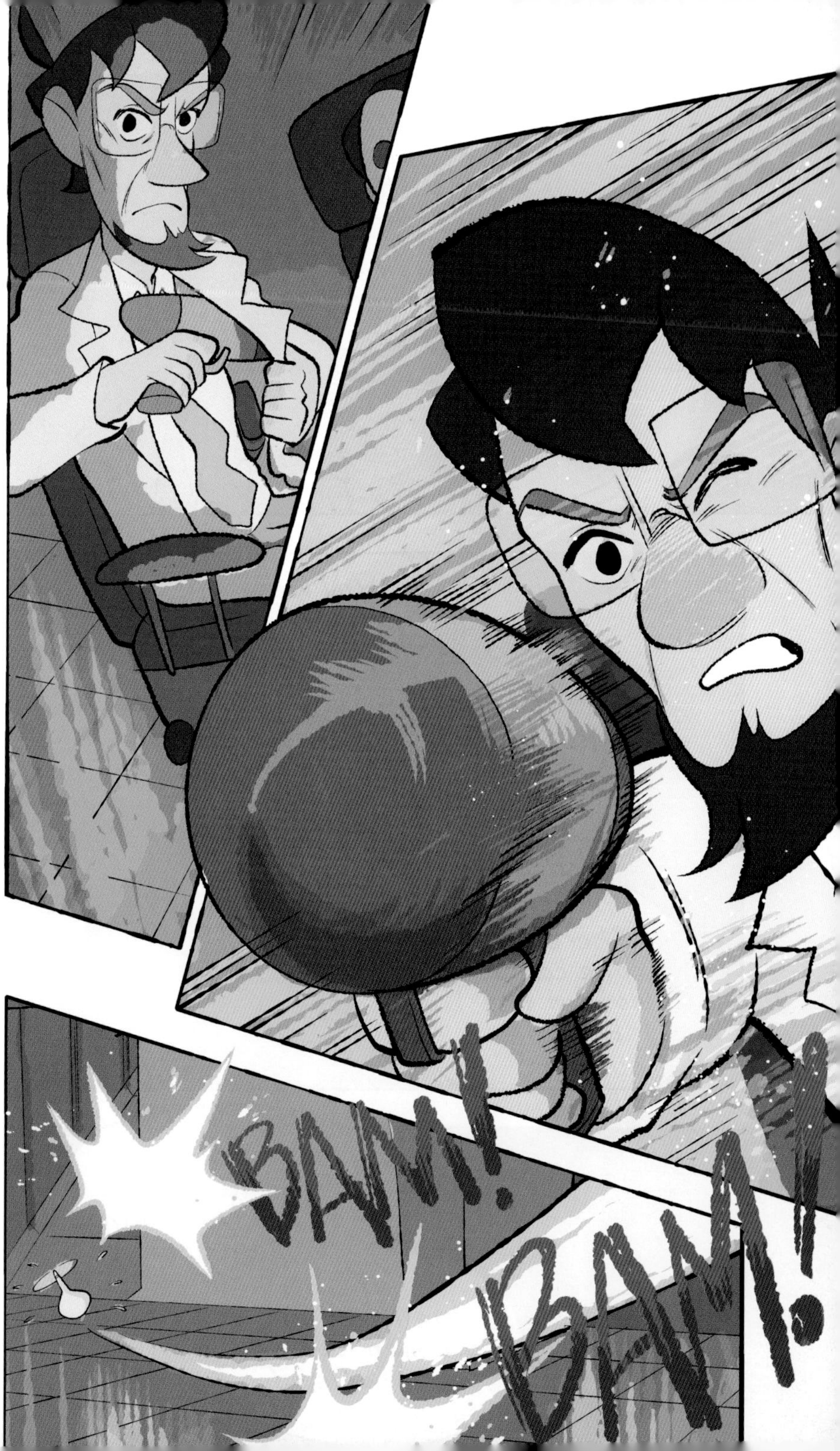
BAM!
BAM!

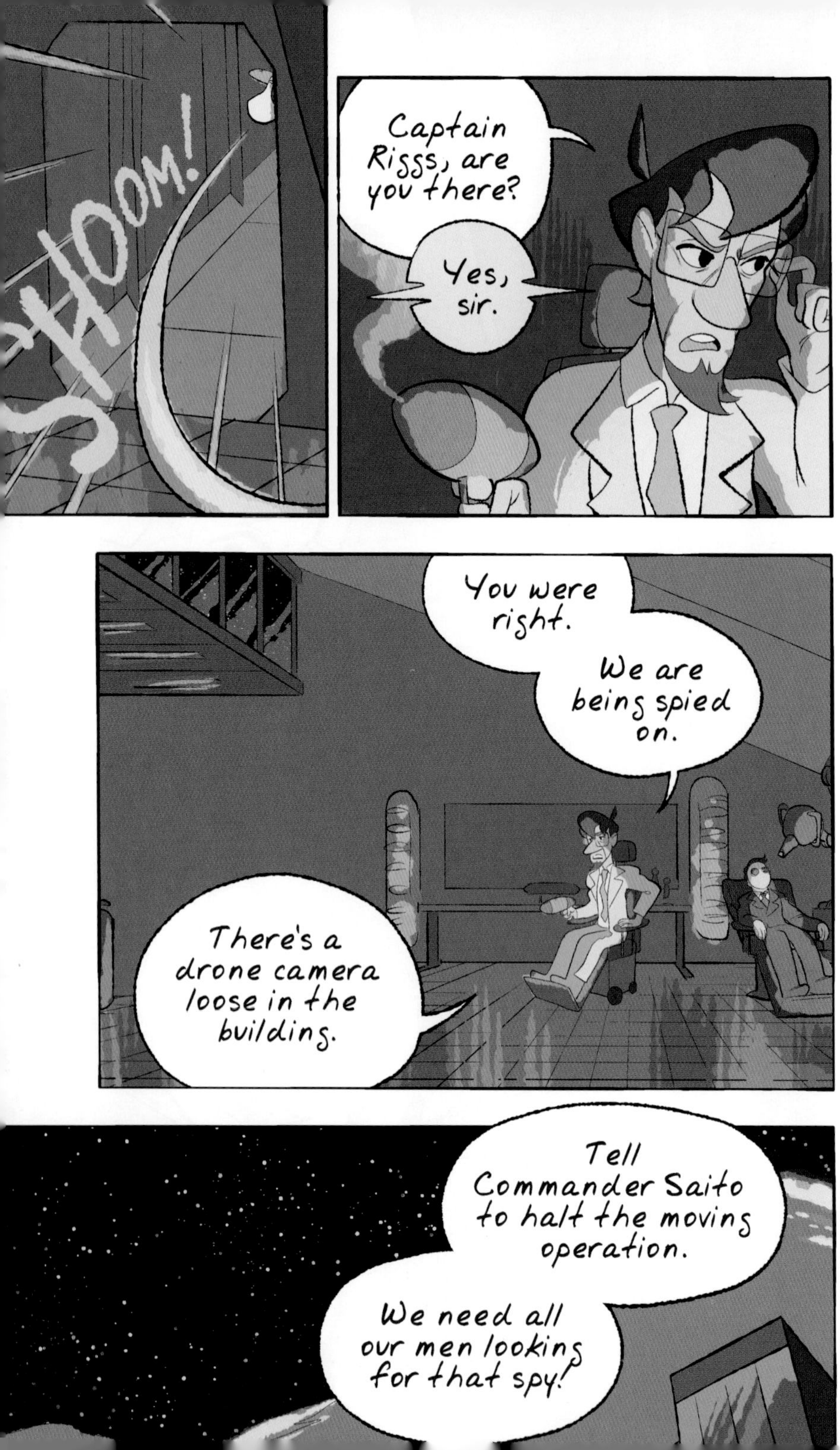
SHOOM!
Captain Risss, are you there?
Yes, sir.
You were right.
We are being spied on.
There's a drone camera loose in the buildings.
Tell Commander Saito to halt the moving operation.
We need all our men looking for that spy!

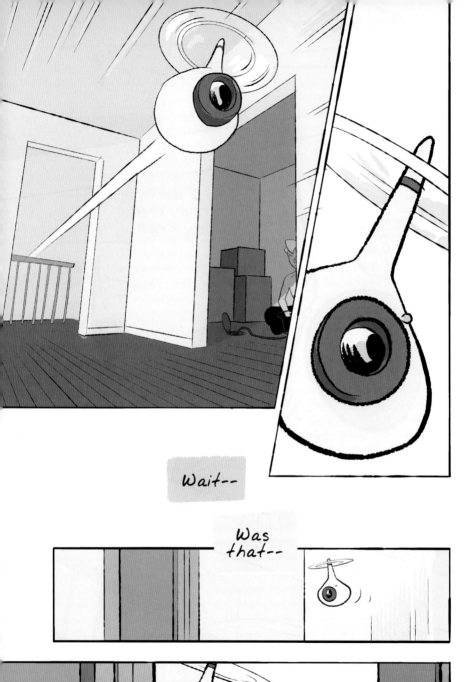

Wait--

Was that--

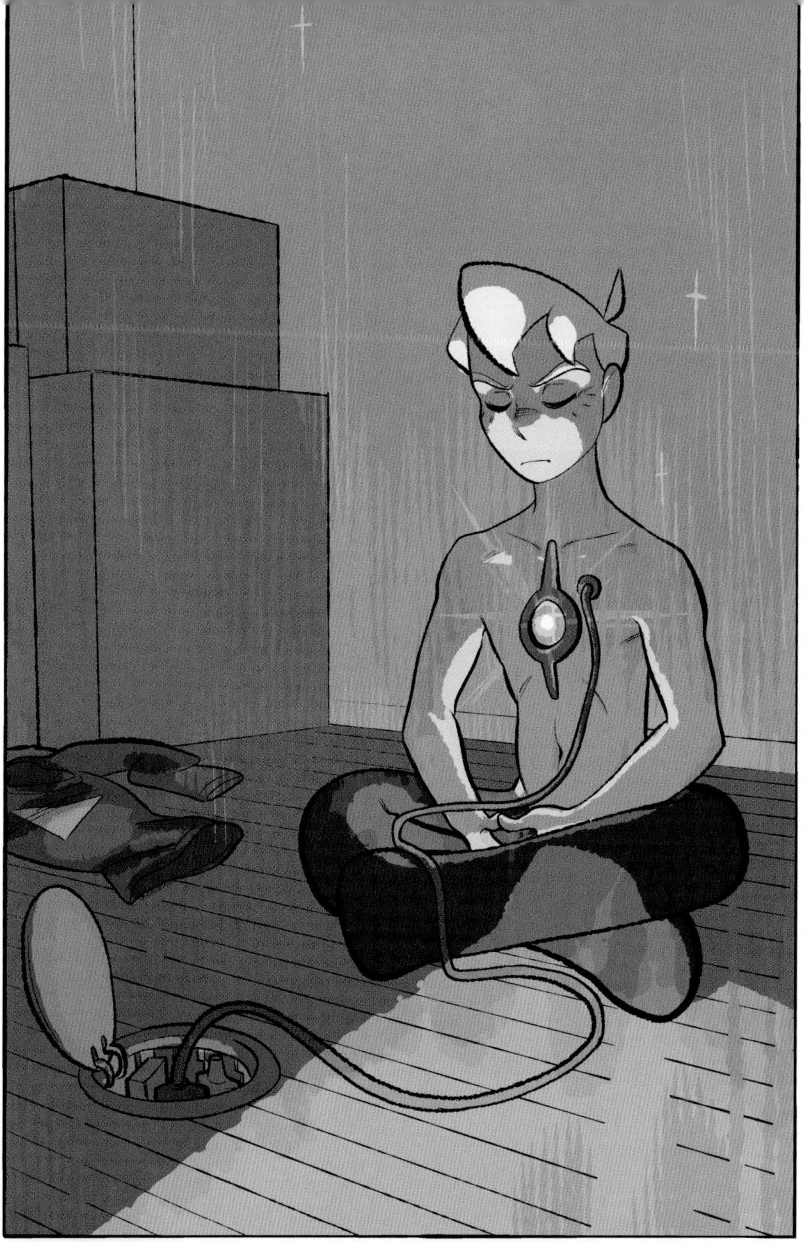
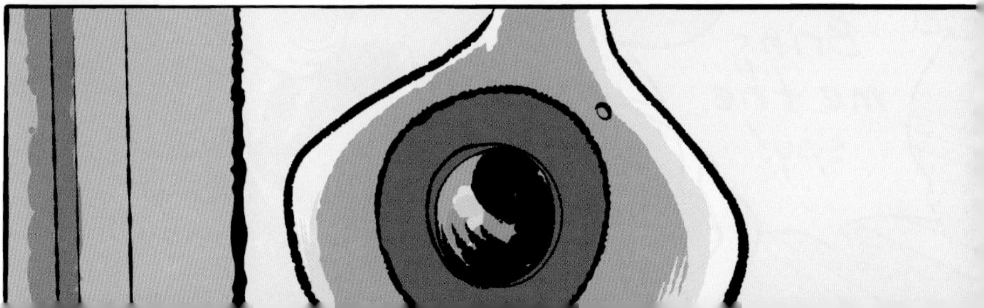

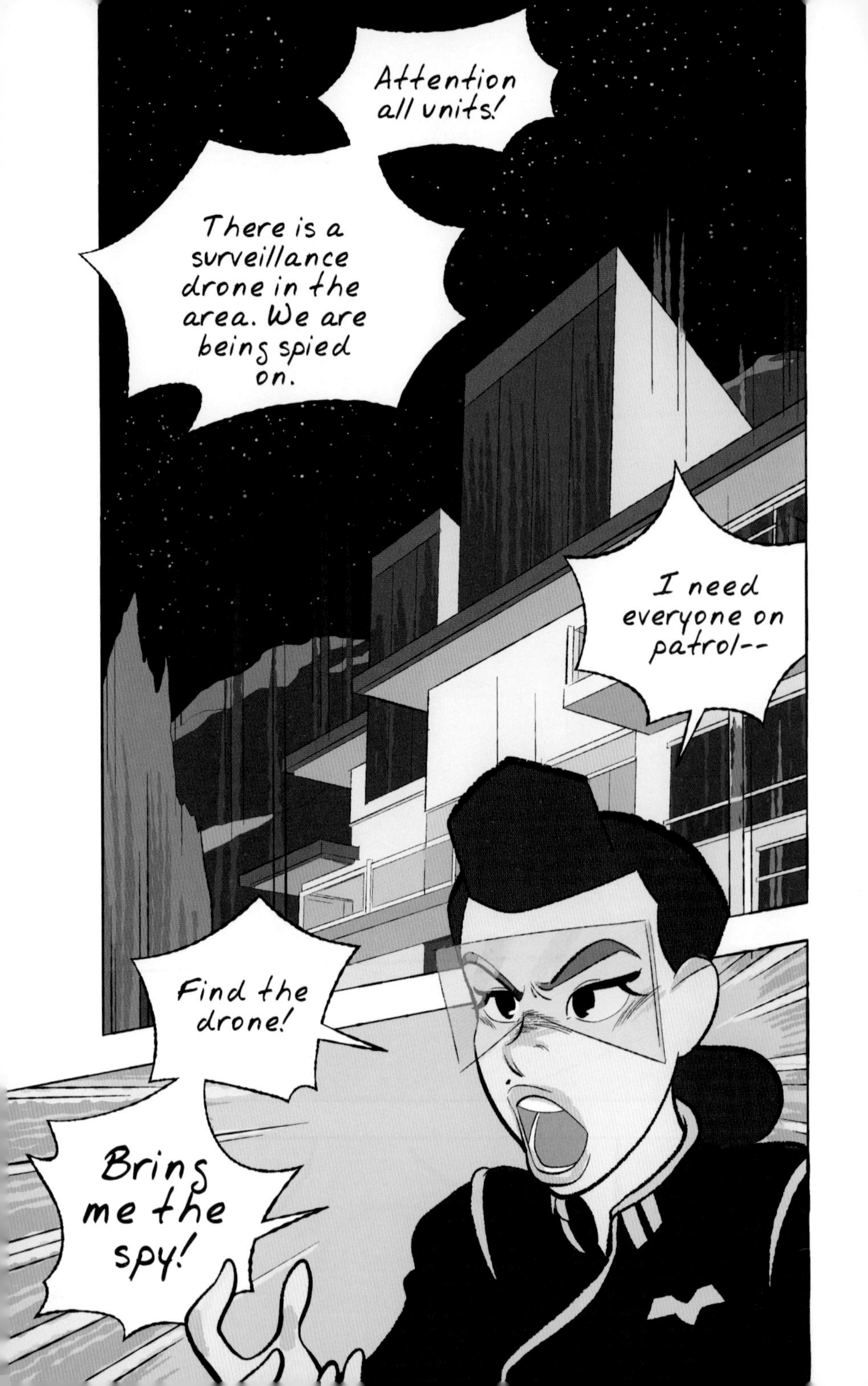
Attention all units!
There is a surveillance drone in the area. We are being spied on.
I need everyone on patrol--
Find the drone!
Bring me the spy!

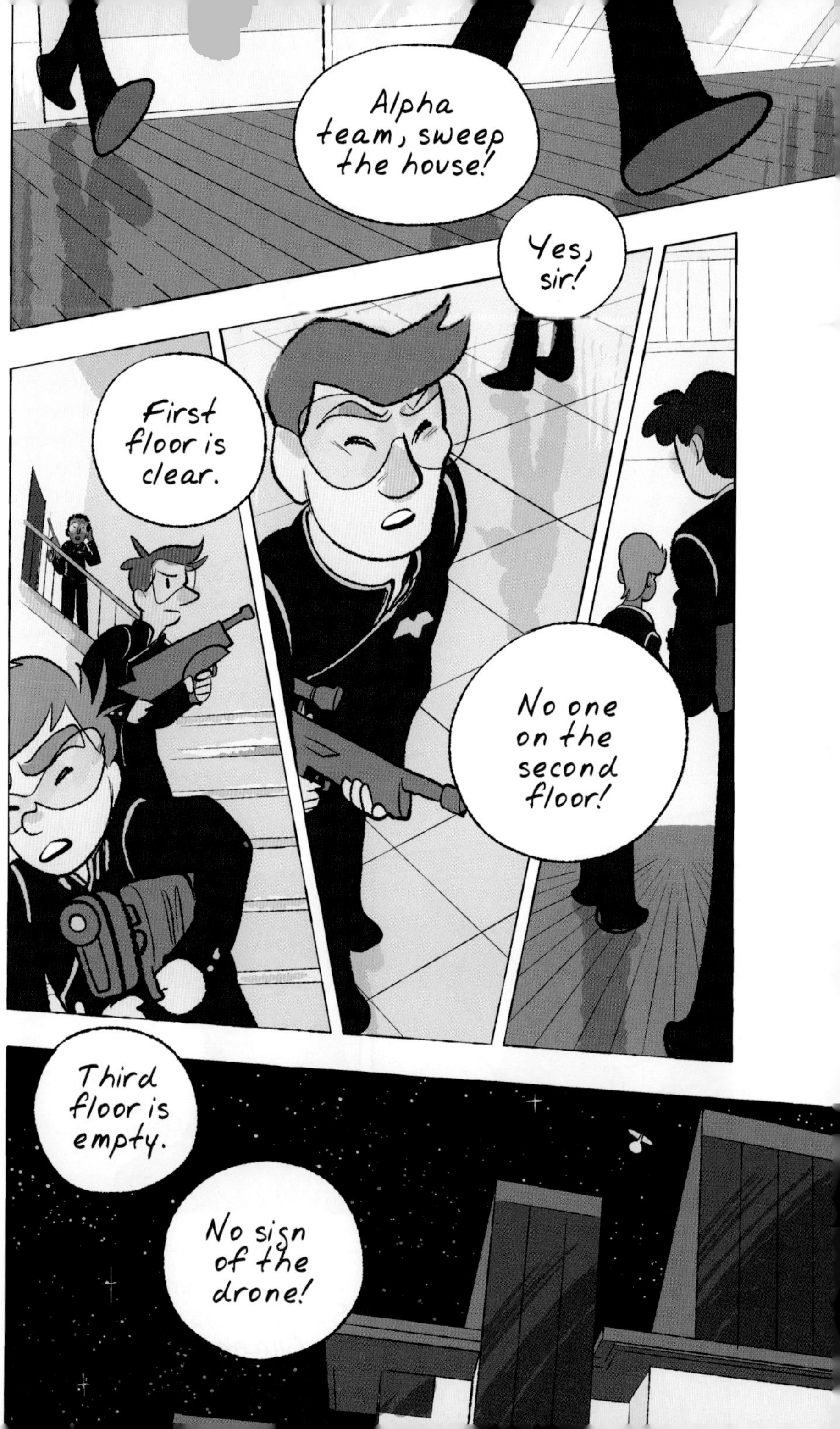
Alpha team, sweep the house!
Yes, sir!
First floor is clear.
No one on the second floor!
Third floor is empty.
No sign of the drone!

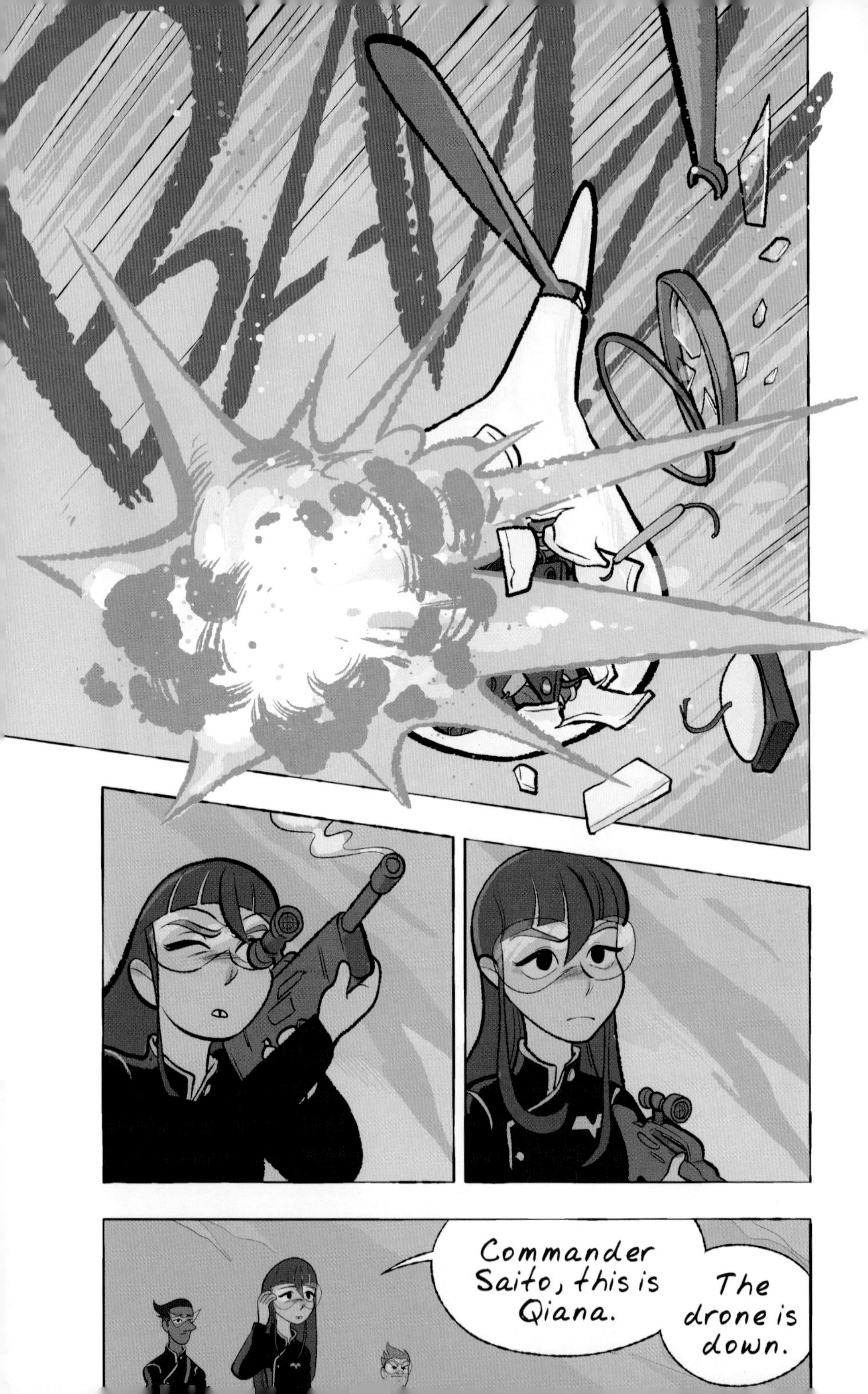
BLAM!
Commander Saito, this is Qiana.
The drone is down.

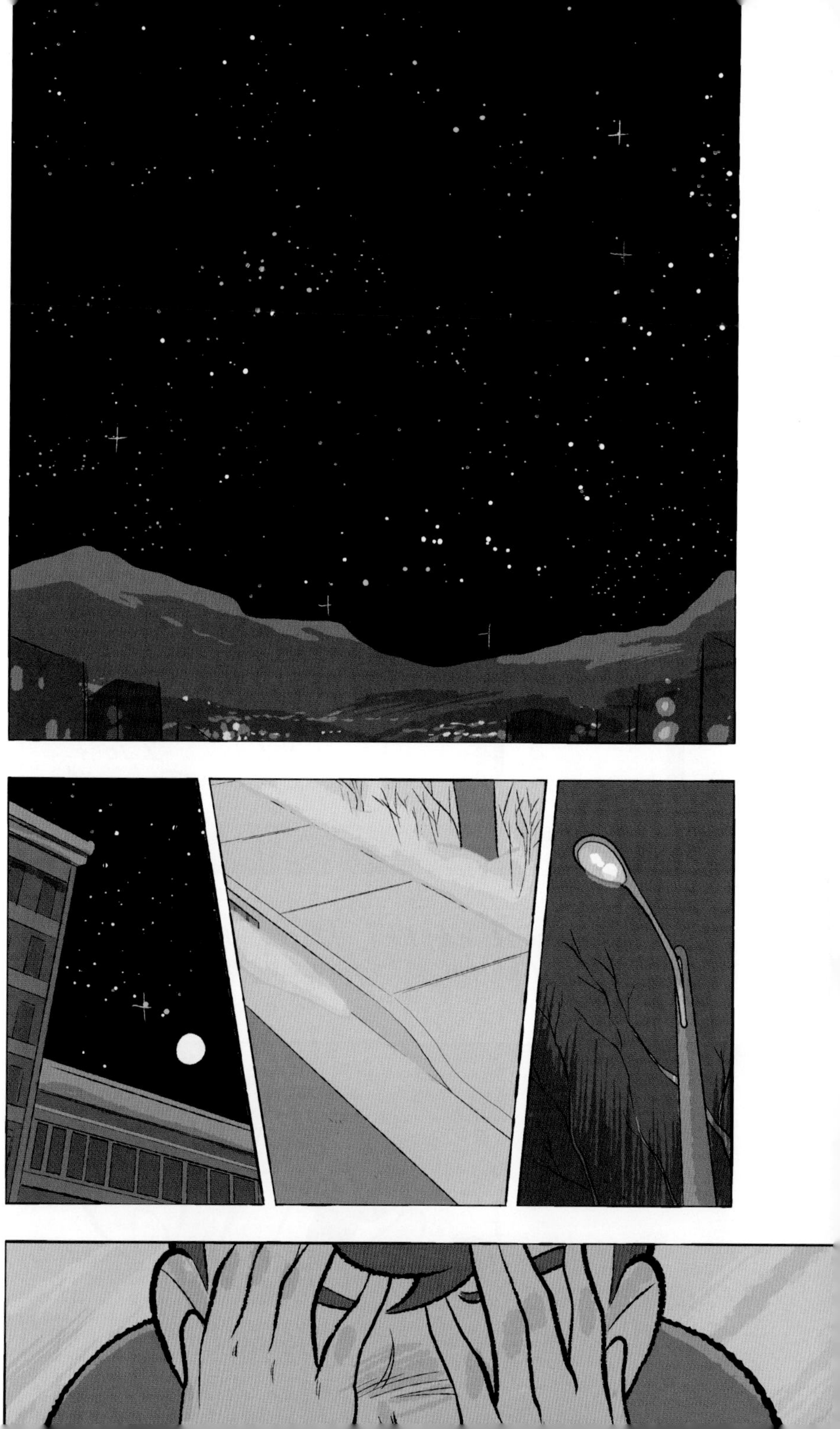

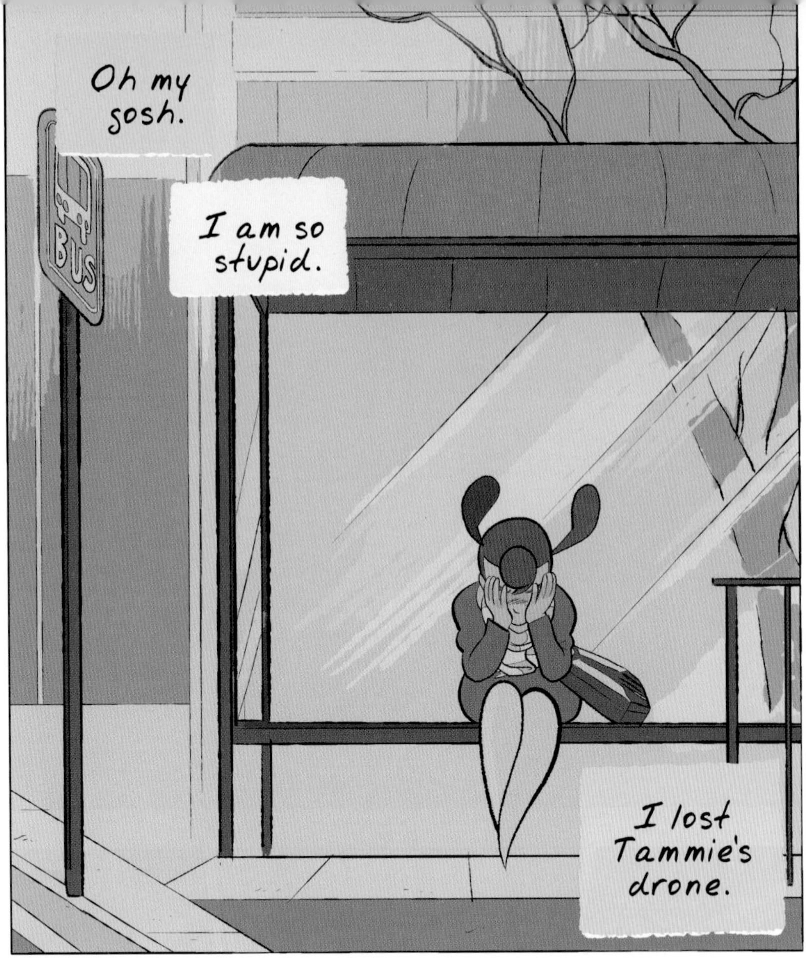
Oh my gosh.
BUS
I am so stupid.
I lost Tammie's drone.

It'll cost me, like, thirty weeks of allowance to pay her back.

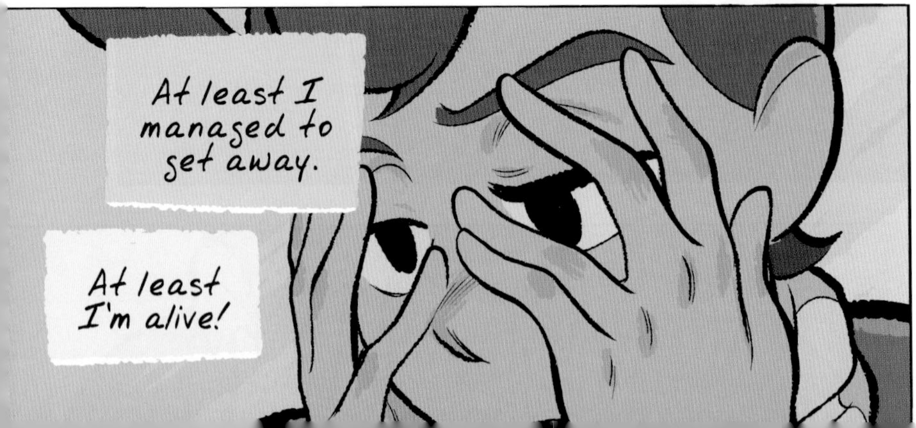
At least I managed to get away.
At least I'm alive!

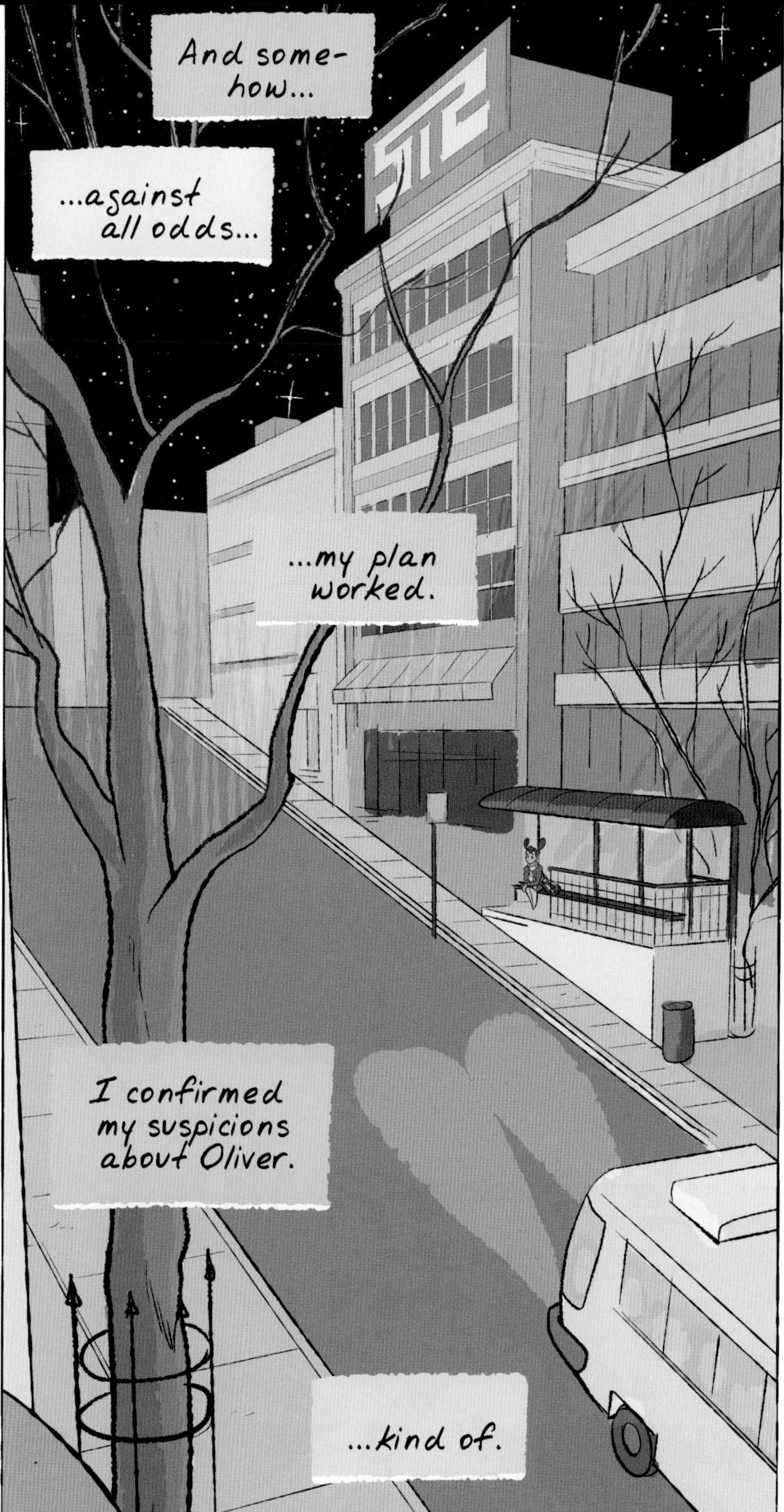
And some-how...
...against all odds...
...my plan worked.
I confirmed my suspicions about Oliver.
...kind of.

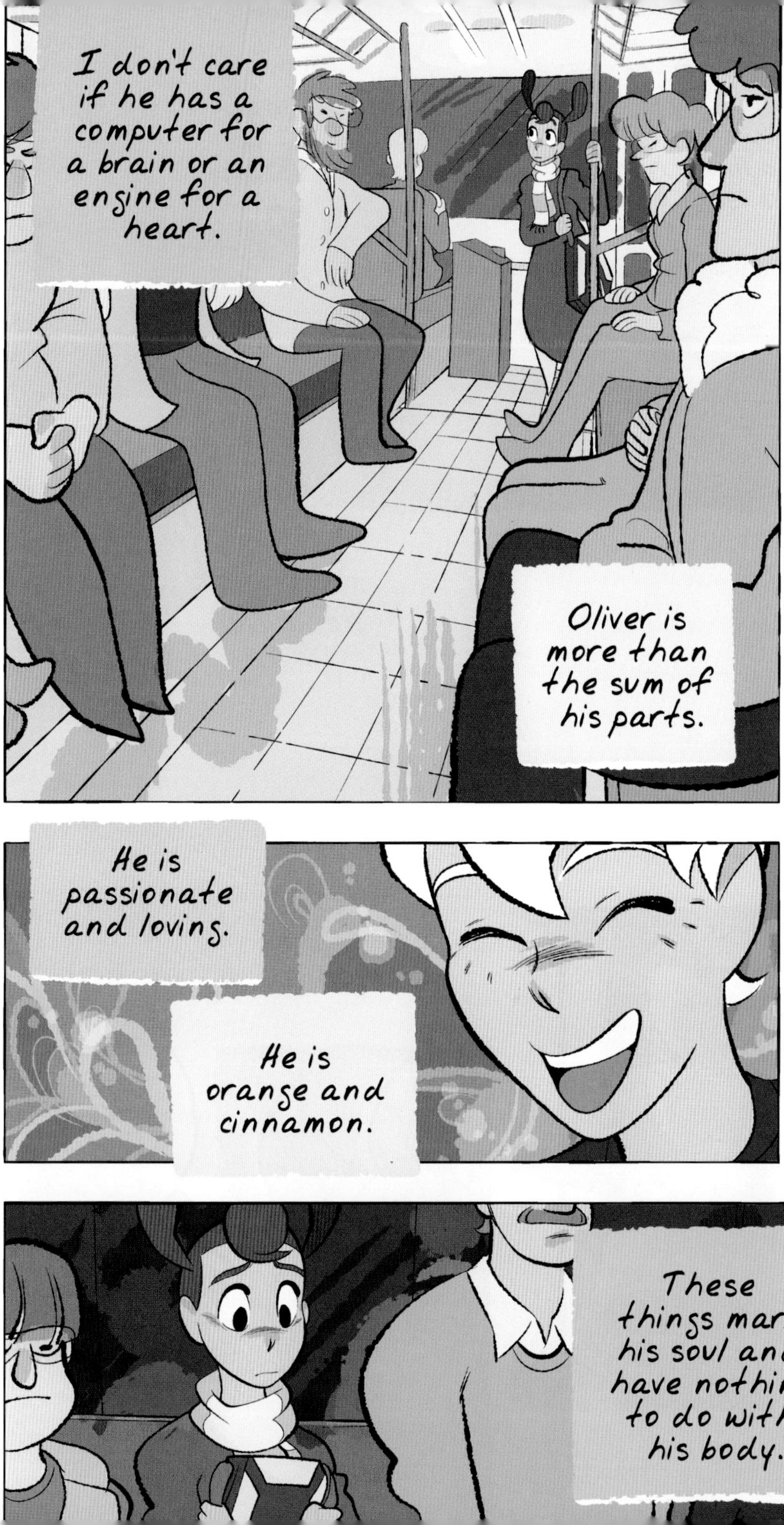
I don't care if he has a computer for a brain or an engine for a heart.
Oliver is more than the sum of his parts.
He is passionate and loving.
He is orange and cinnamon.
These things mark his soul and have nothing to do with his body.

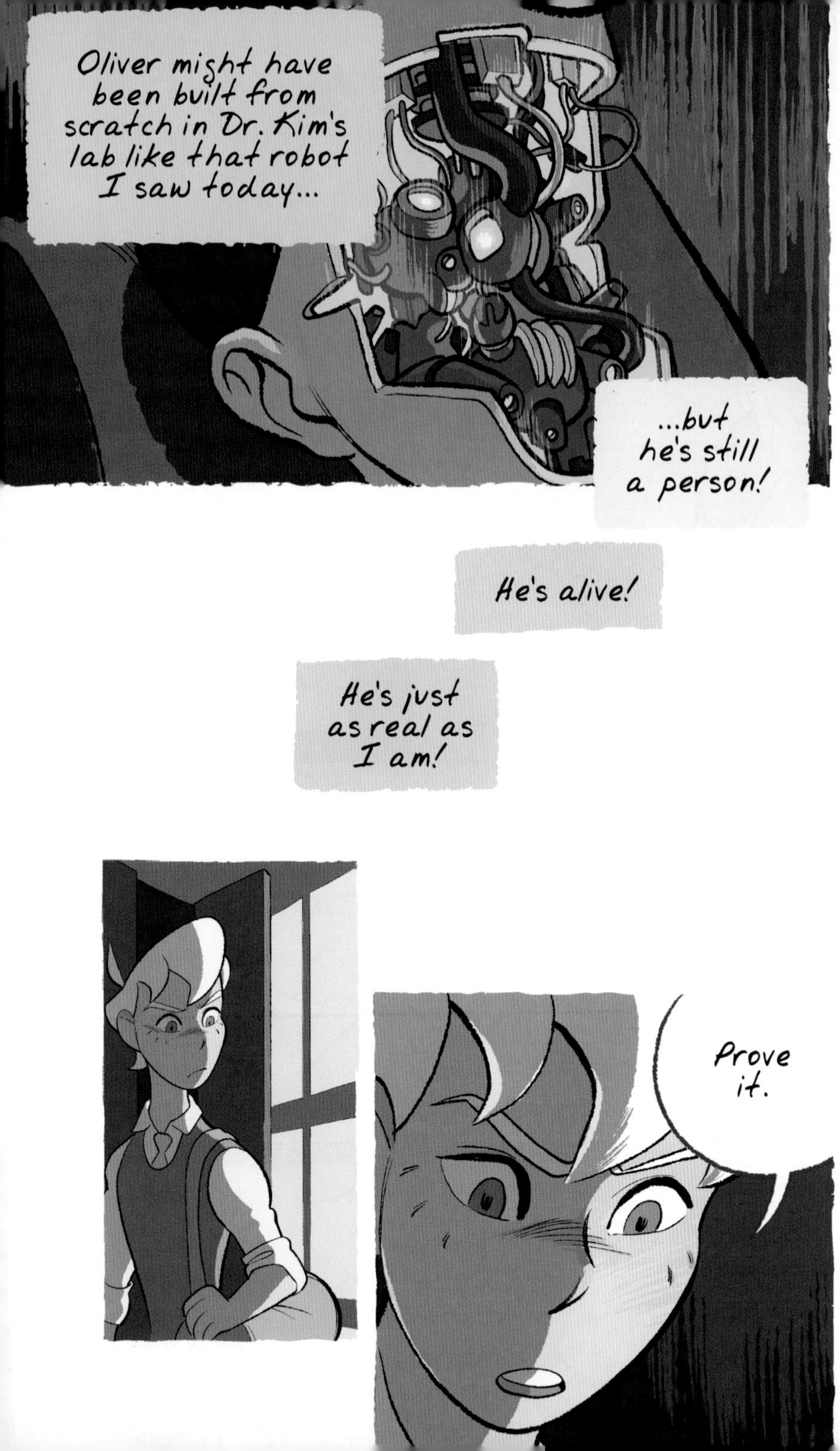
Oliver might have been built from scratch in Dr. Kim's lab like that robot I saw today...
...but he's still a person!
He's alive!
He's just as real as I am!
Prove it.

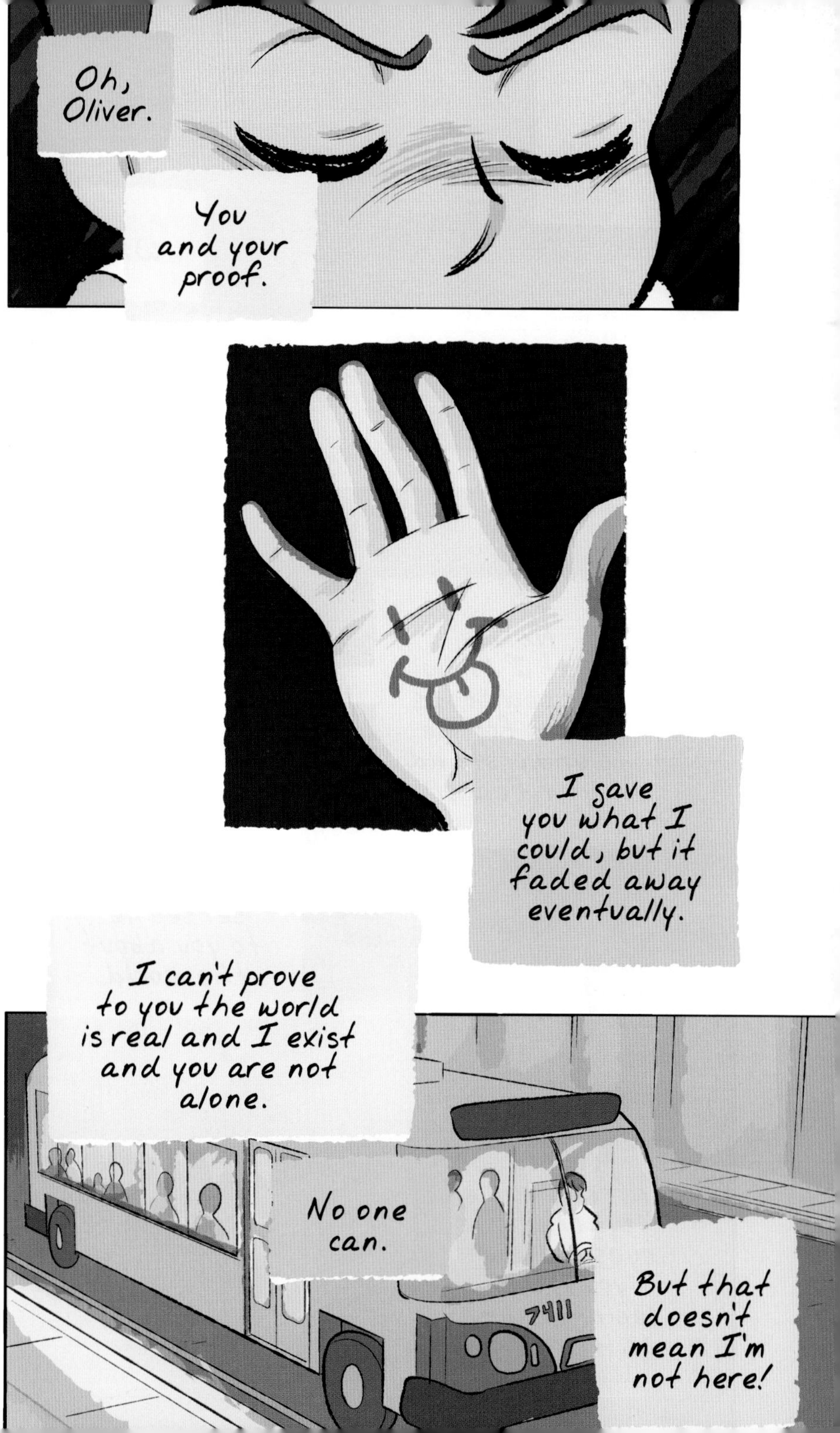
Oh, Oliver.
You and your proof.
I gave you what I could, but it faded away eventually.
I can't prove to you the world is real and I exist and you are not alone.
No one can.
7411
But that doesn't mean I'm not here!

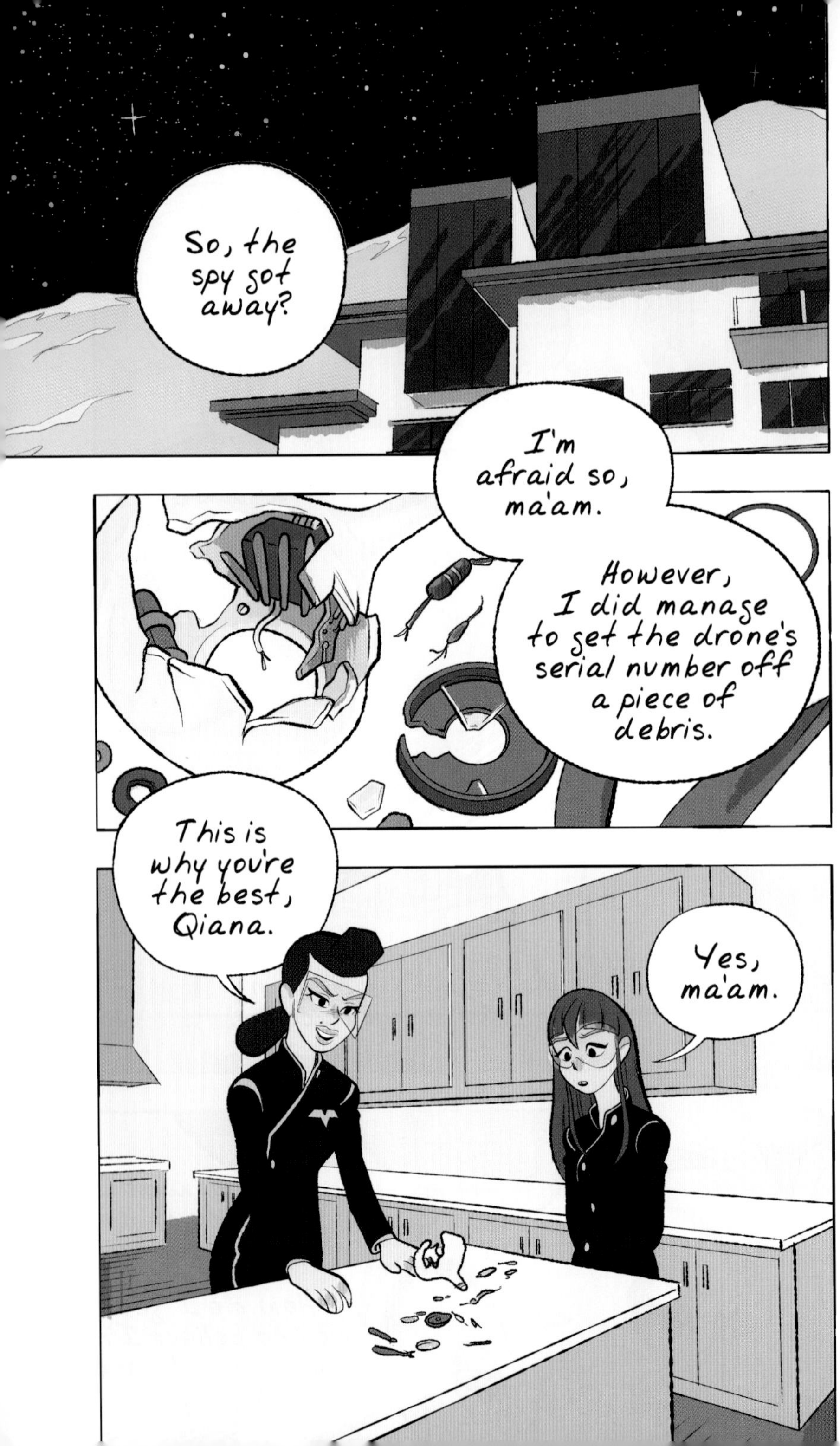
So, the spy got away?
I'm afraid so, ma'am.
However, I did manage to get the drone's serial number off a piece of debris.
This is why you're the best, Qiana.
Yes, ma'am.

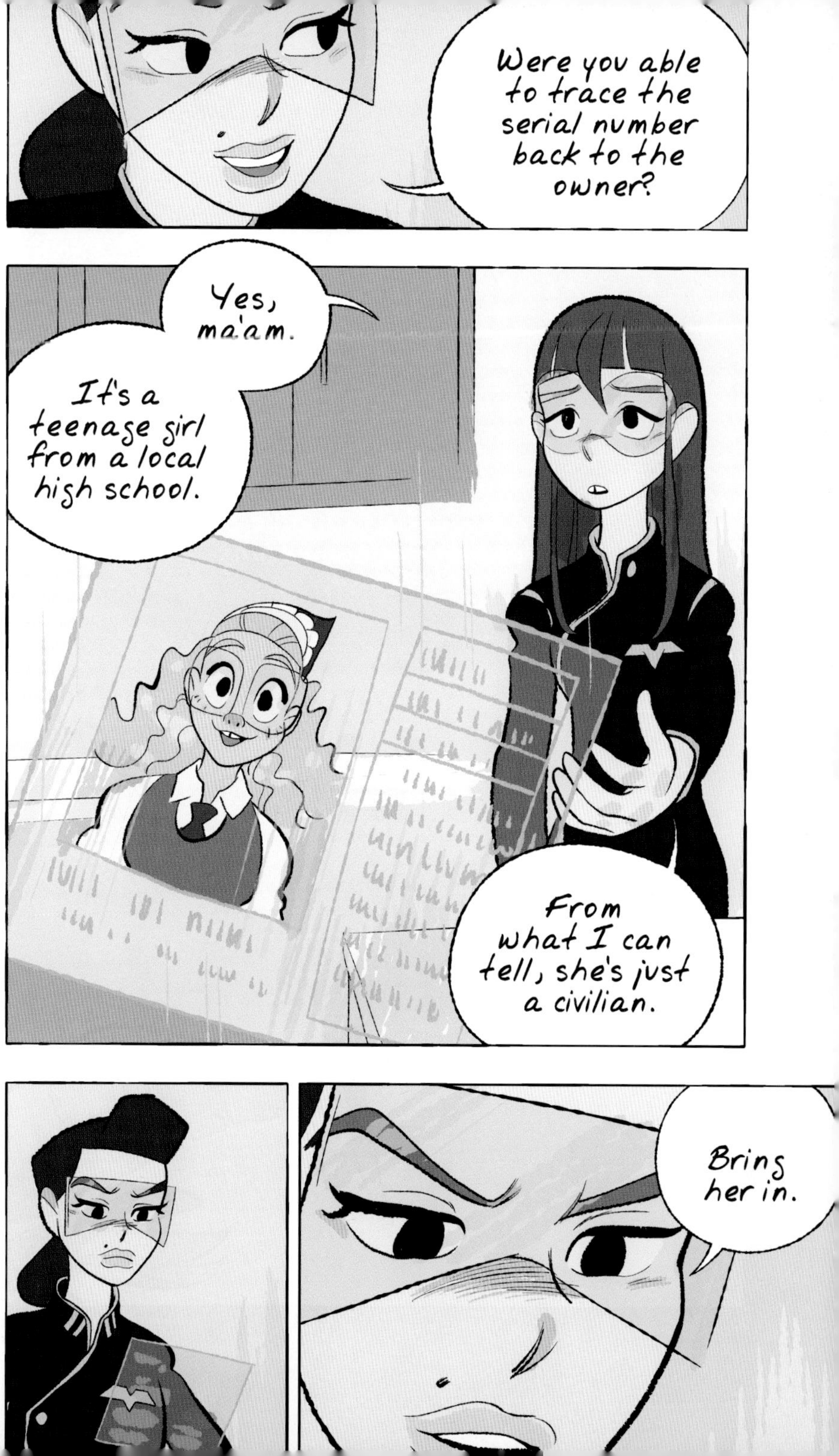
Were you able to trace the serial number back to the owner?
Yes, ma'am.
It's a teenage girl from a local high school.
From what I can tell, she's just a civilian.
Bring her in.

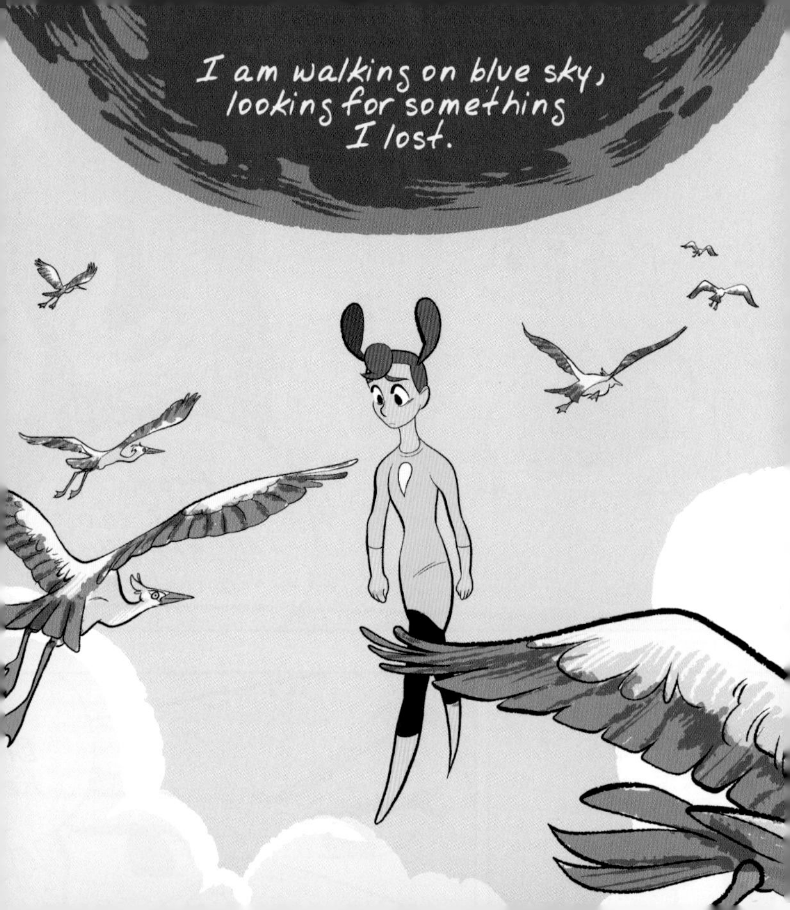
I am walking on blue sky, looking for something I lost.

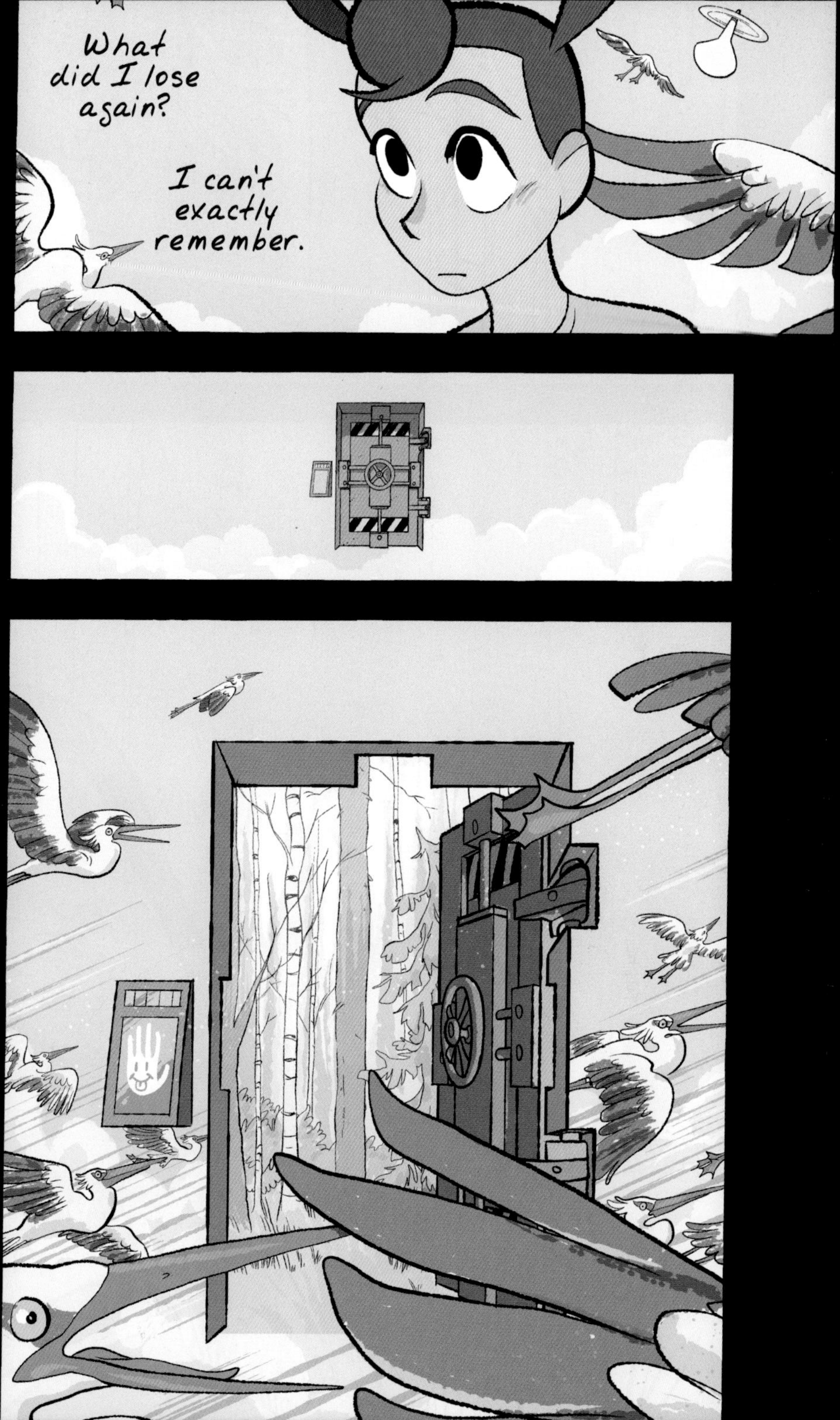
What did I lose again?
I can't exactly remember.

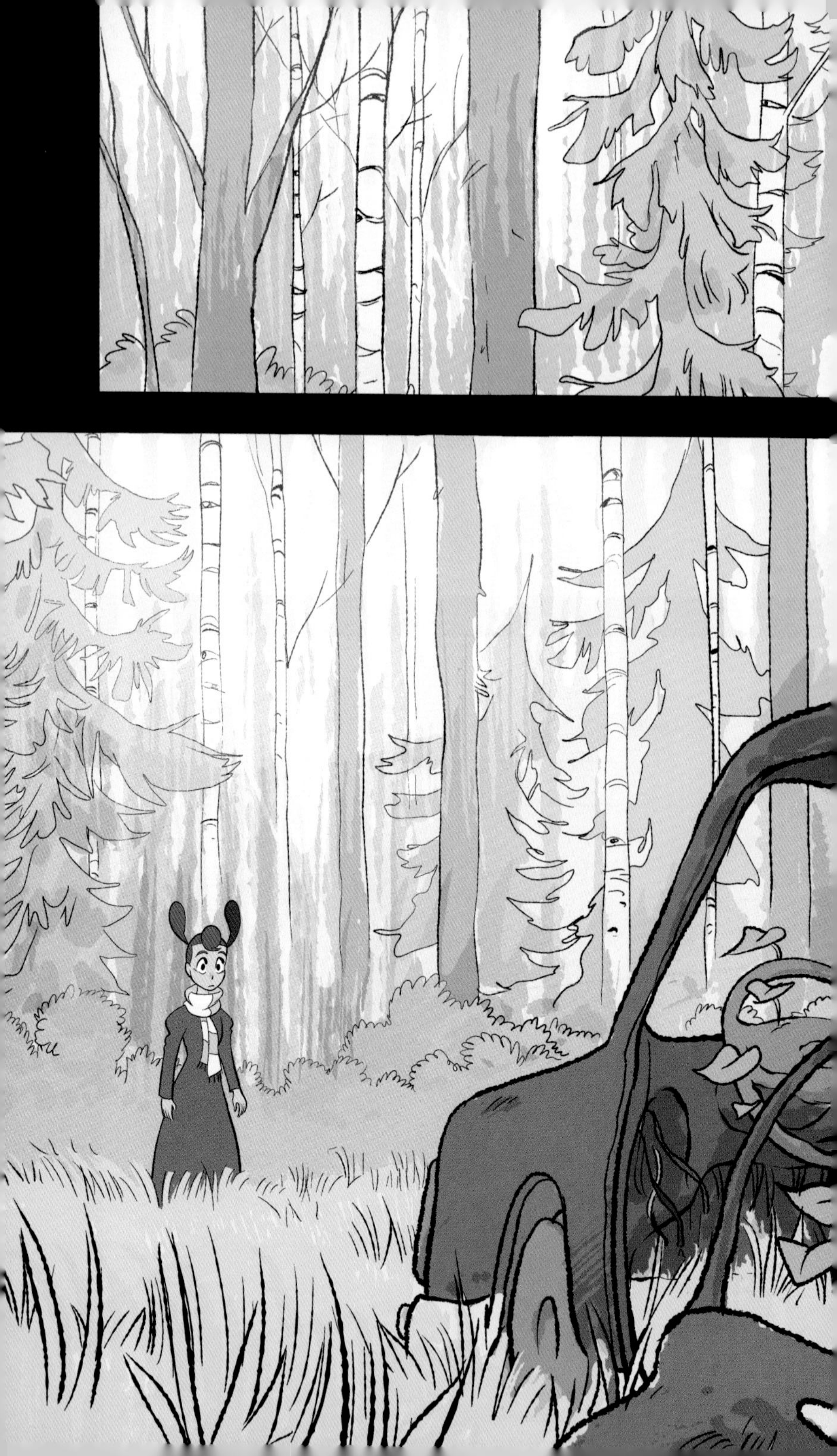

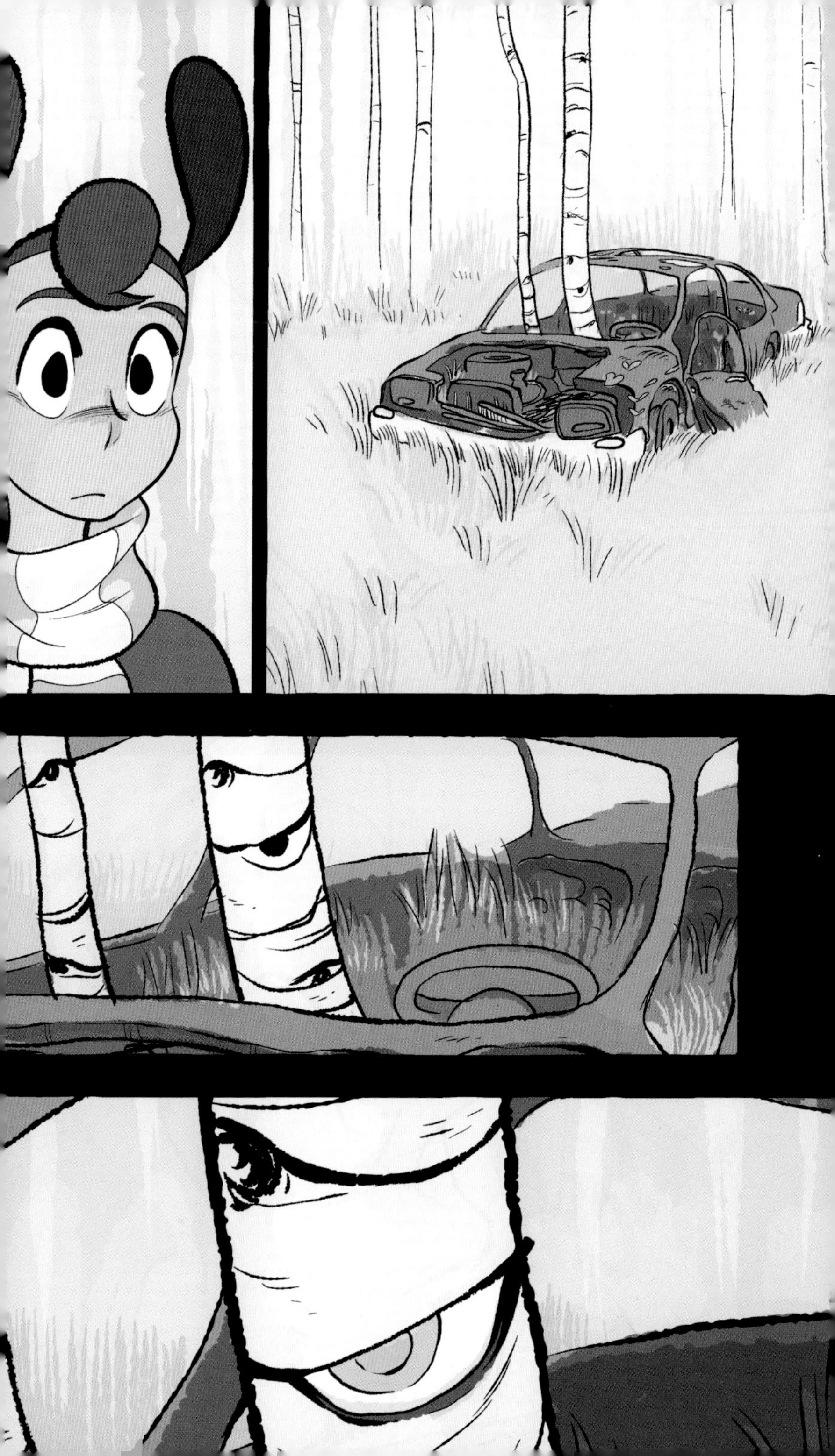

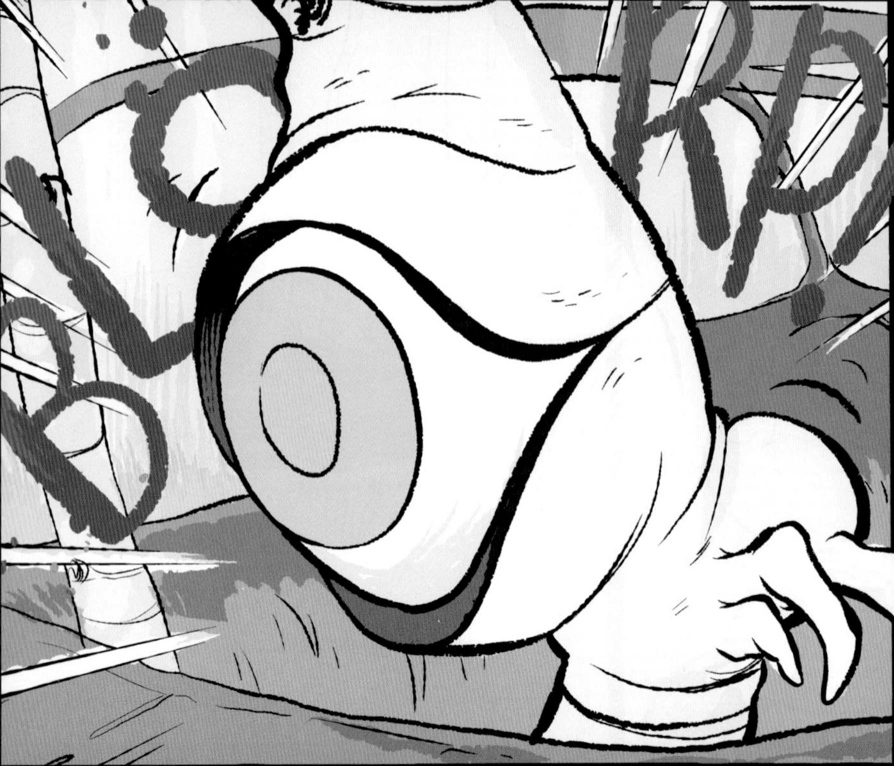
BLORP!

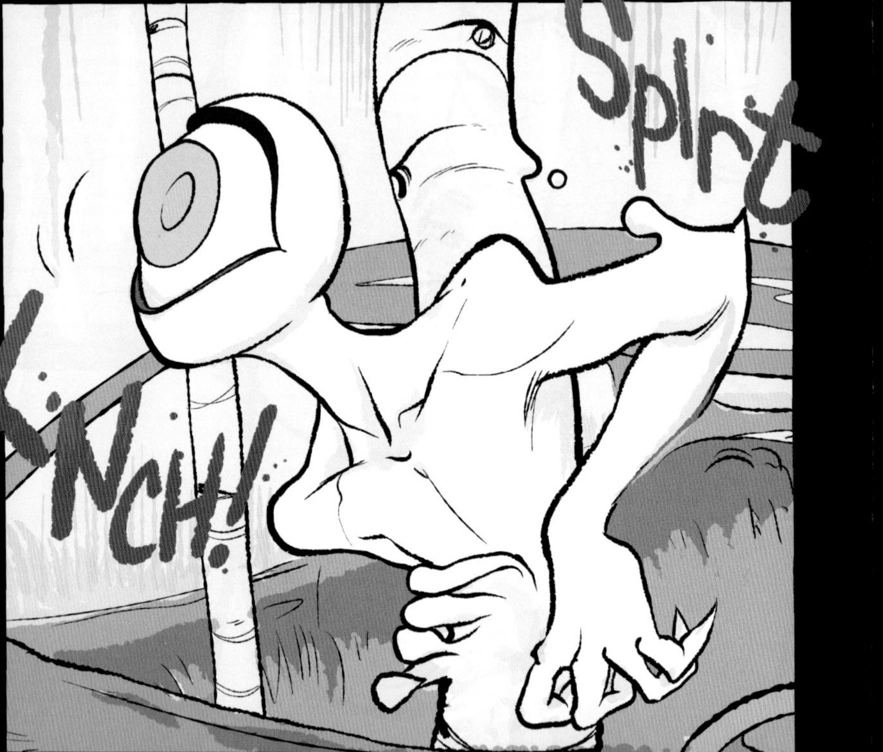
KNCH!
Splrt

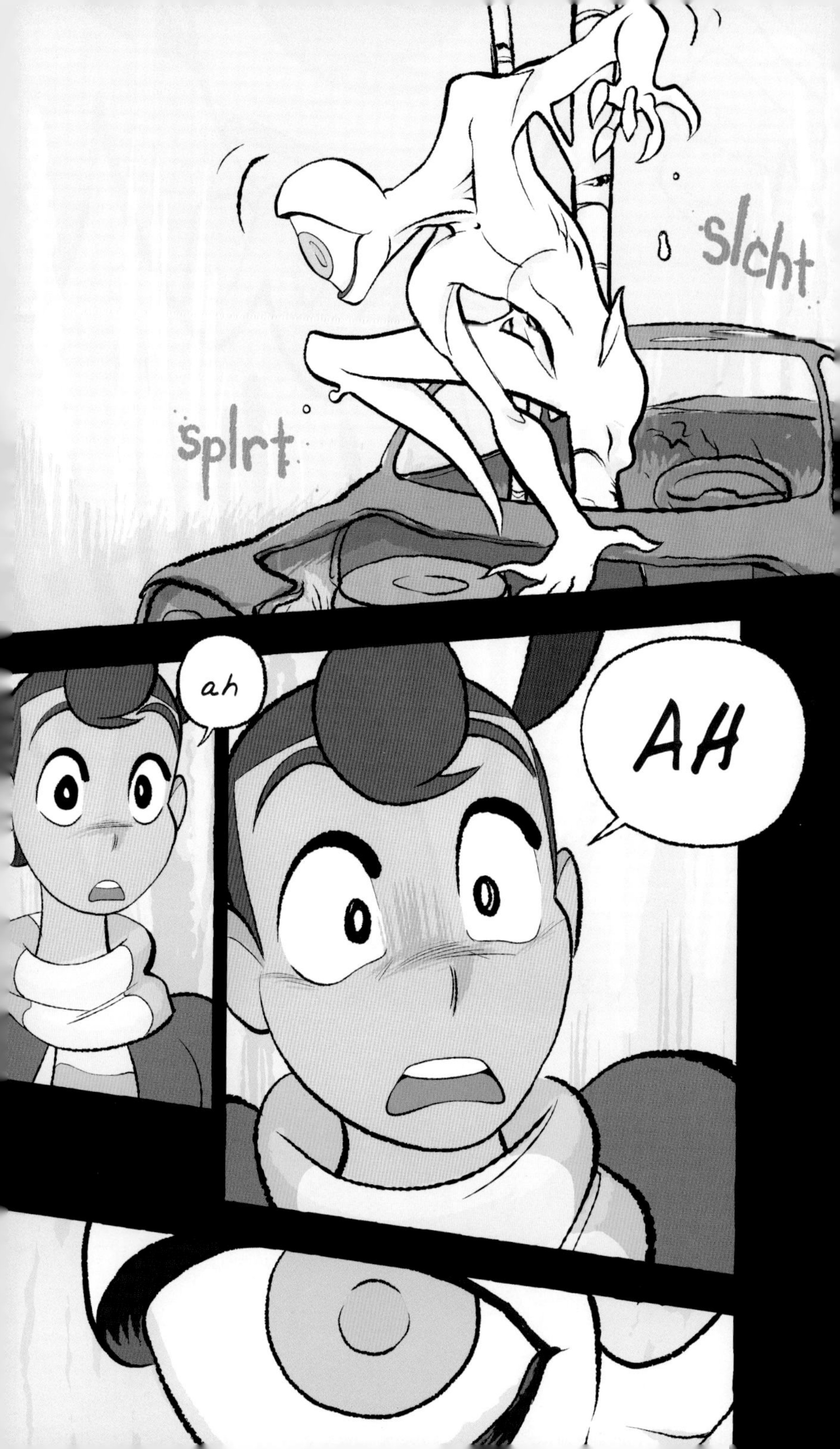
slcht
splrt
ah
AH

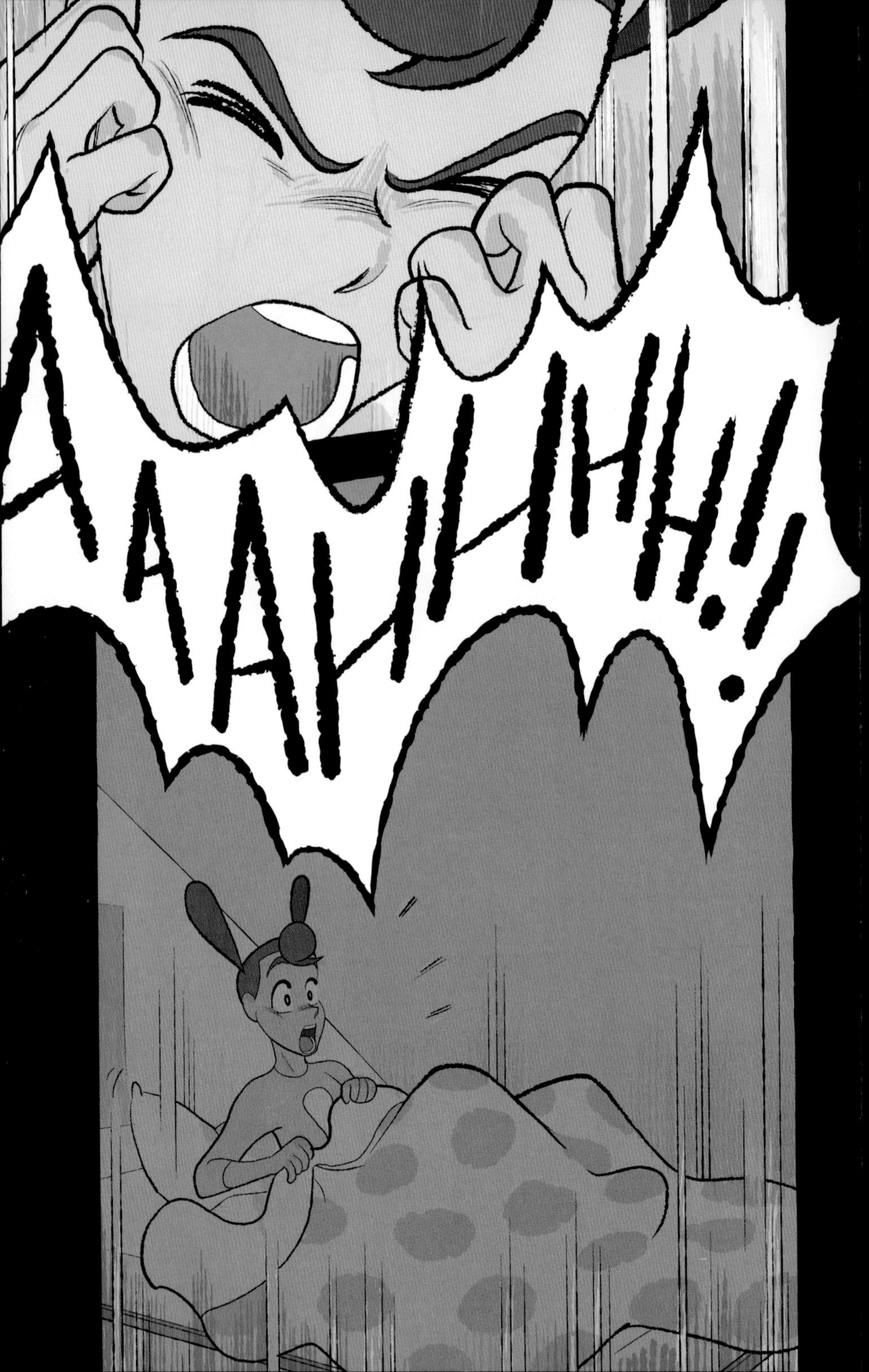
AAAHHHH!!

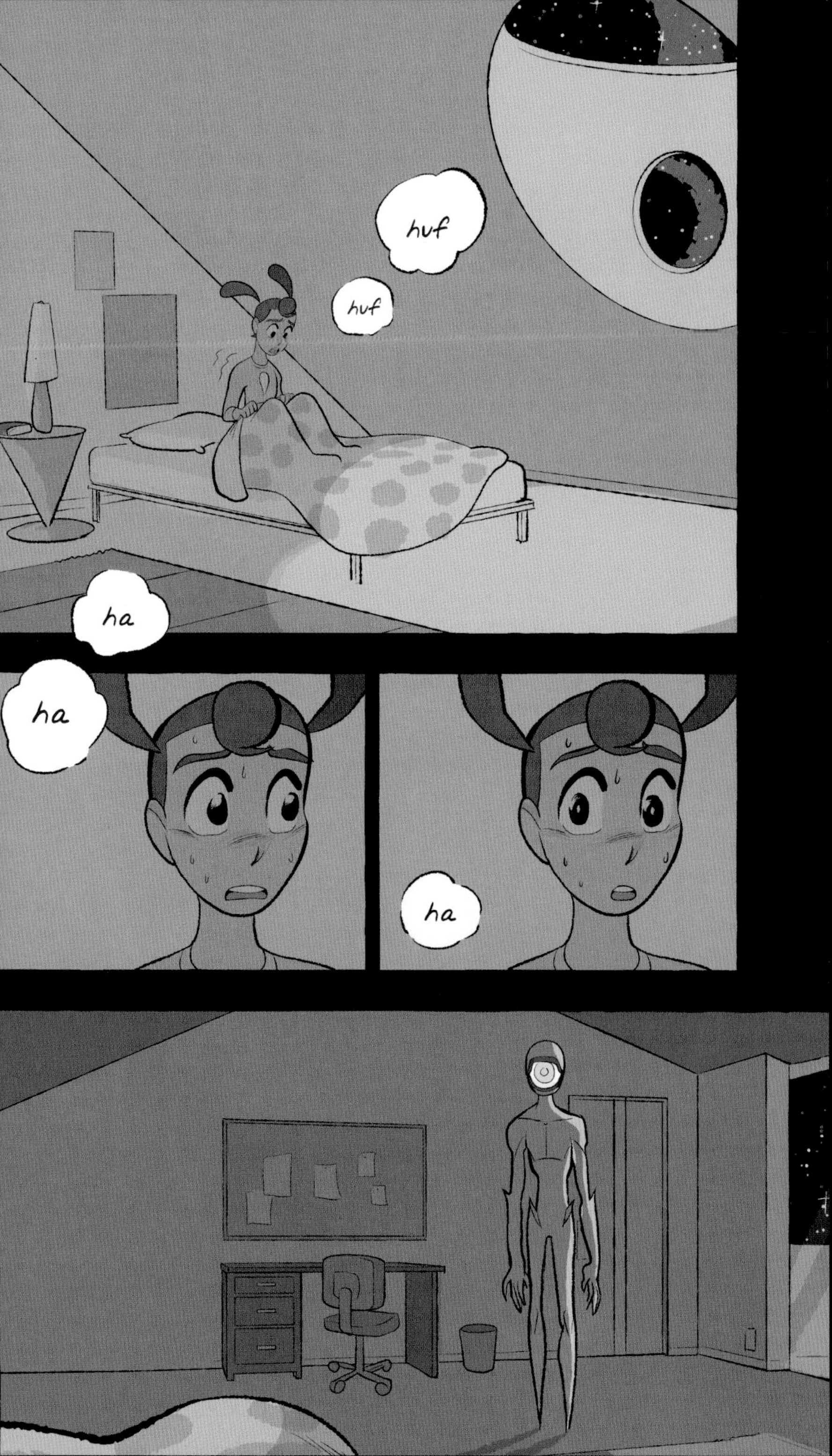
huf
huf
ha
ha
ha

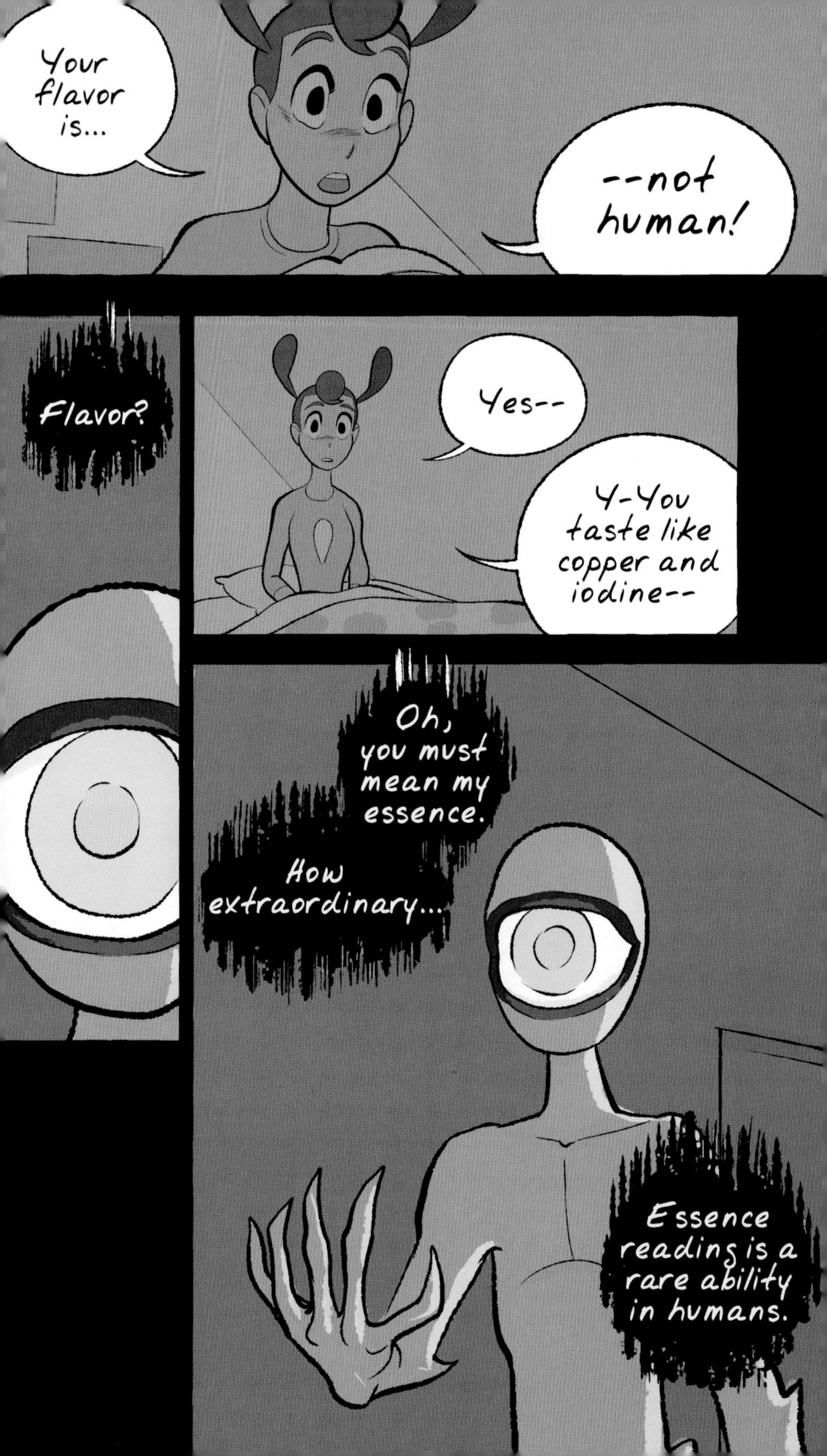
Your flavor is...
--not human!
Flavor?
Yes--
Y-You taste like copper and iodine--
Oh, you must mean my essence.
How extraordinary...
Essence reading is a rare ability in humans.

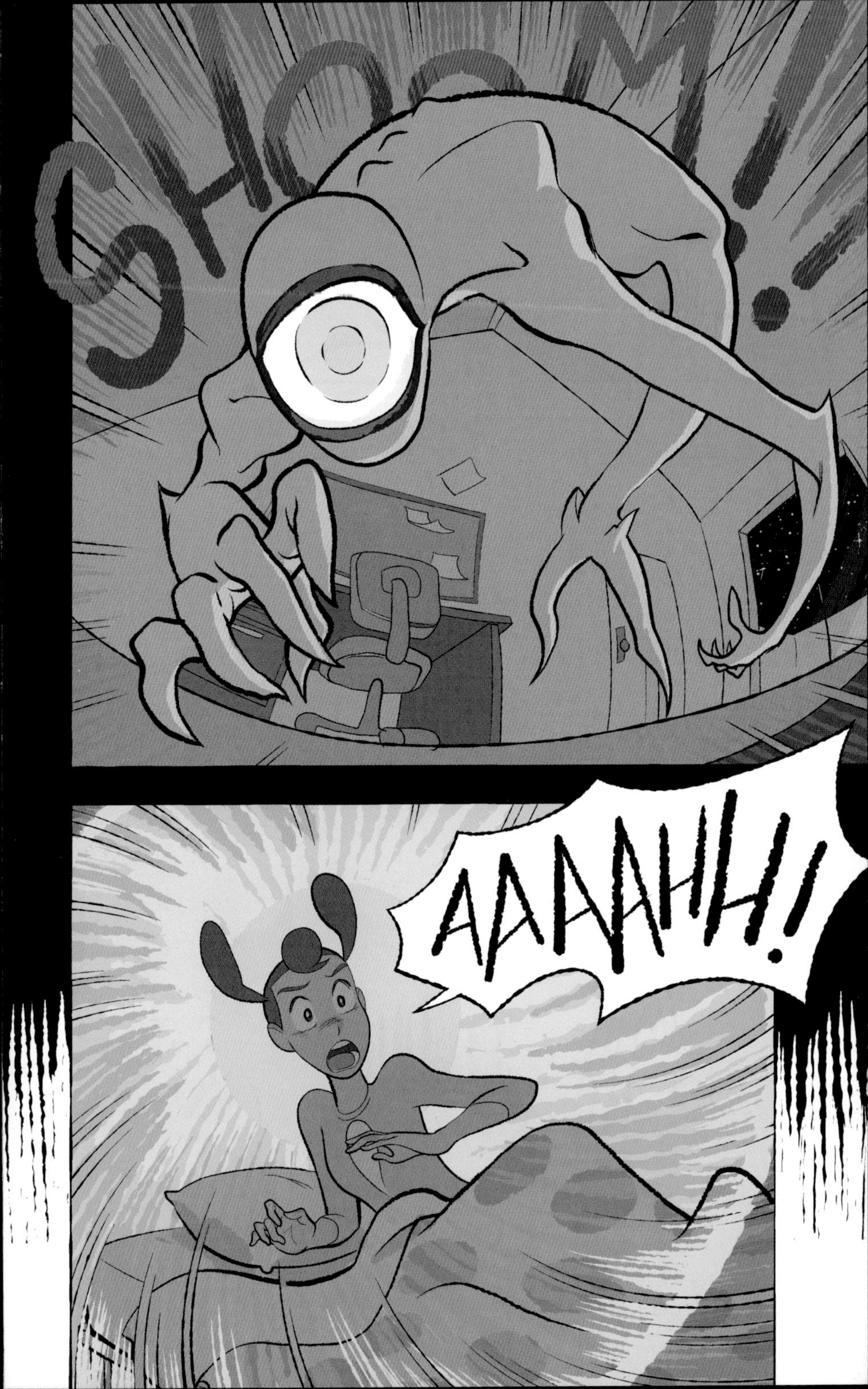
SHOOM!!
AAAAHH!

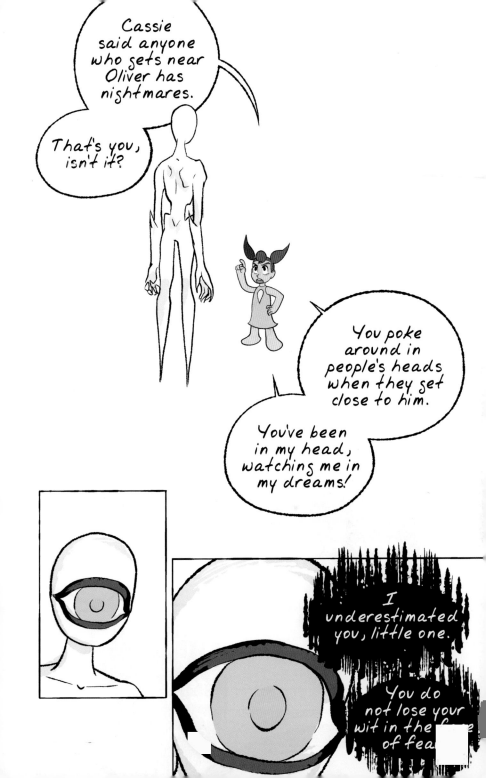

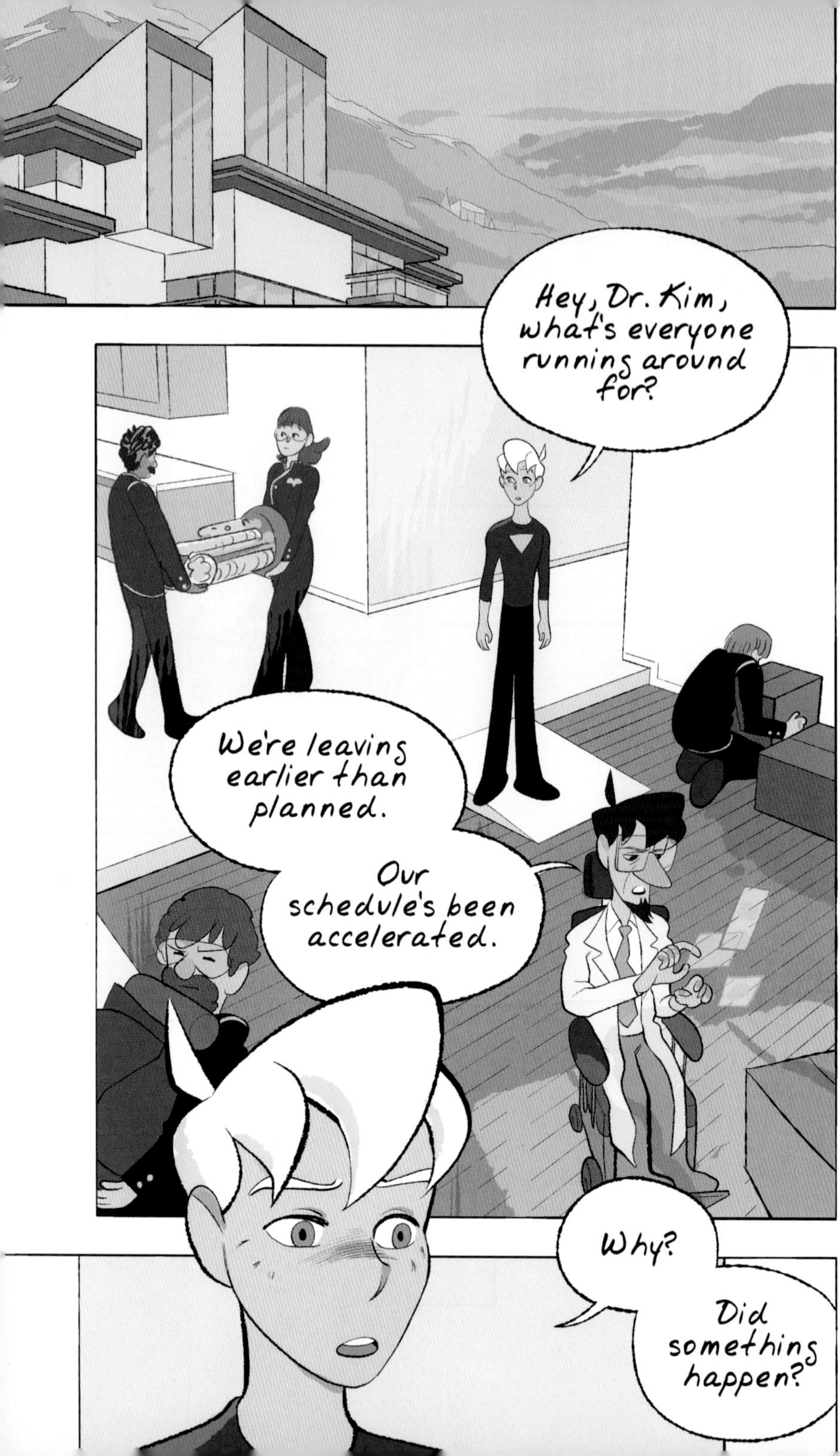
Hey, Dr. Kim, what's everyone running around for?
We're leaving earlier than planned.
Our schedule's been accelerated.
Why?
Did something happen?

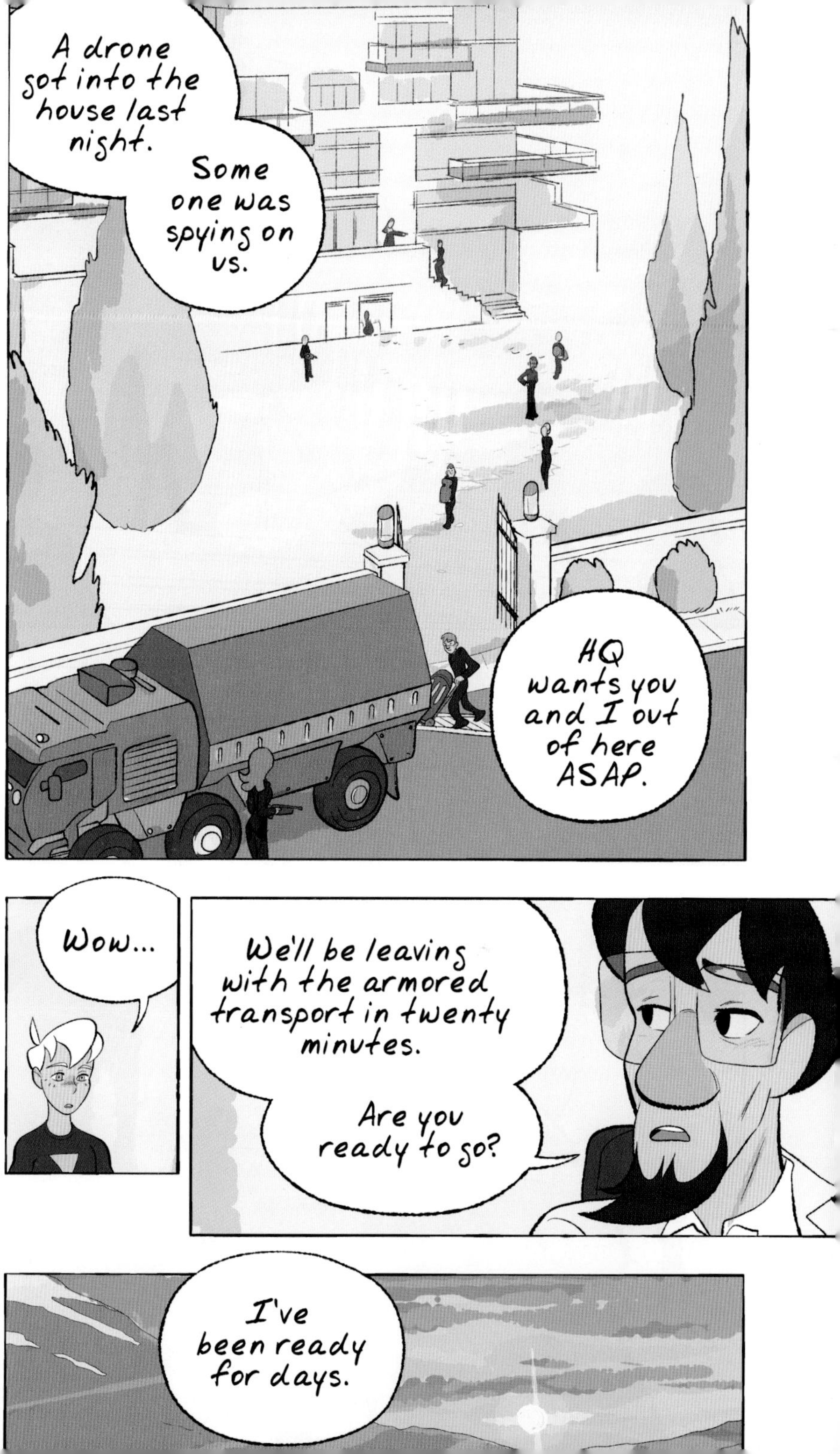
A drone got into the house last night.
Some one was spying on us.
HQ wants you and I out of here ASAP.
Wow...
We'll be leaving with the armored transport in twenty minutes.
Are you ready to go?
I've been ready for days.

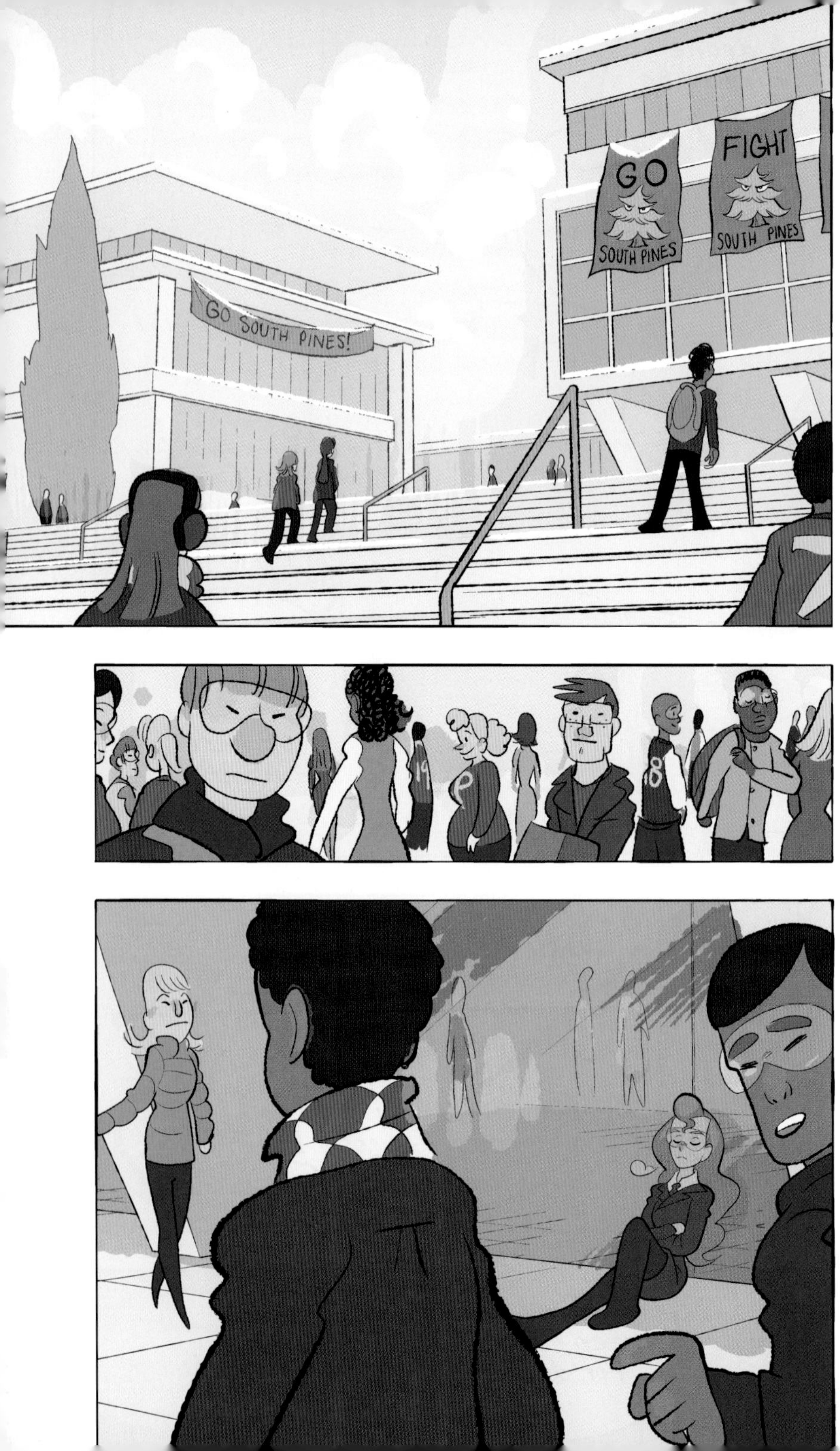
GO SOUTH PINES!
GO
SOUTH PINES
FIGHT
SOUTH PINES

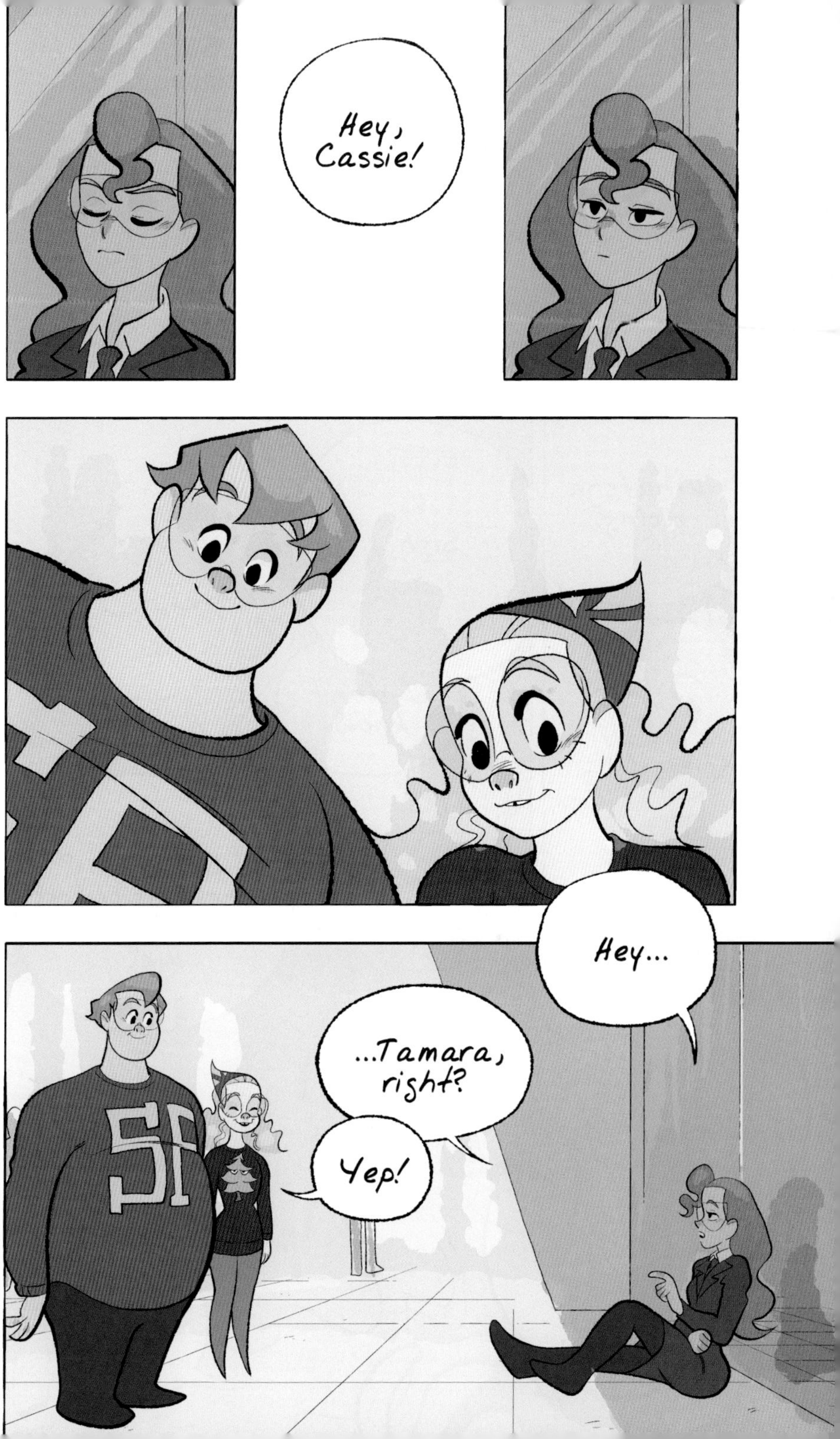
Hey, Cassie!
Hey...
...Tamara, right?
Yep!

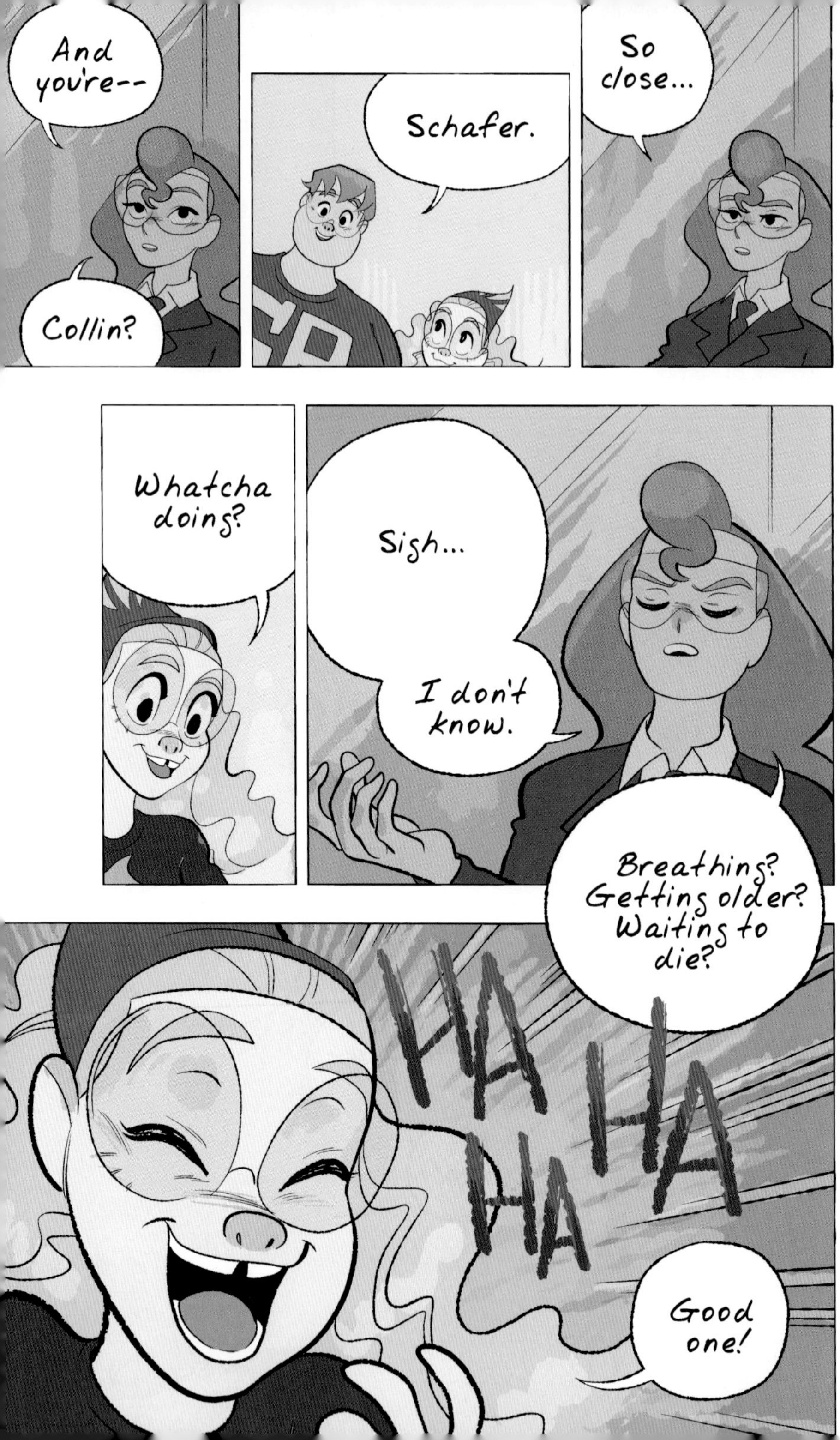
And you're--
Collin?
Schafer.
So close...
Whatcha doing?
Sigh...
I don't know.
Breathing? Getting older? Waiting to die?
HA HA HA HA
Good one!

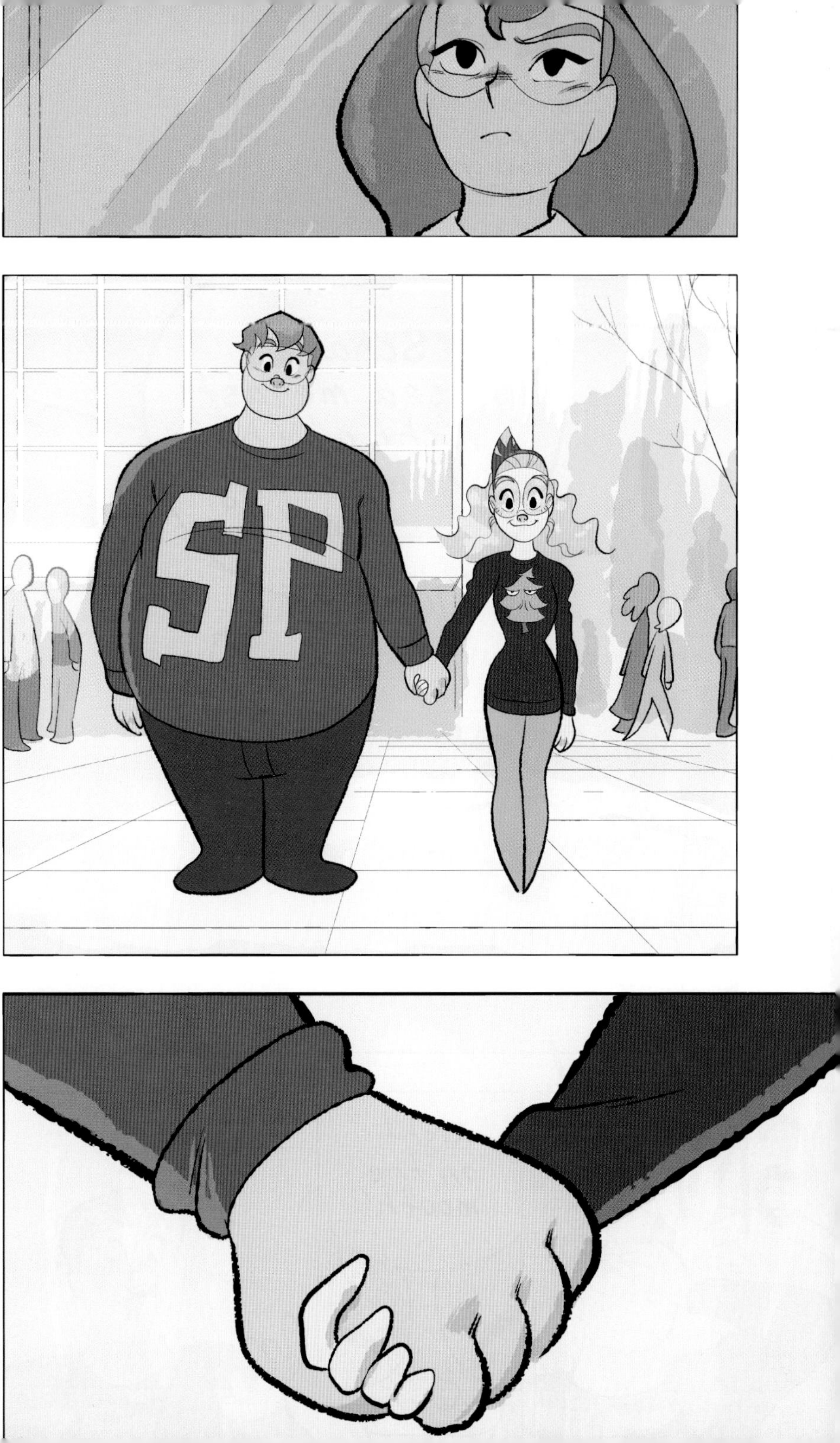
SP

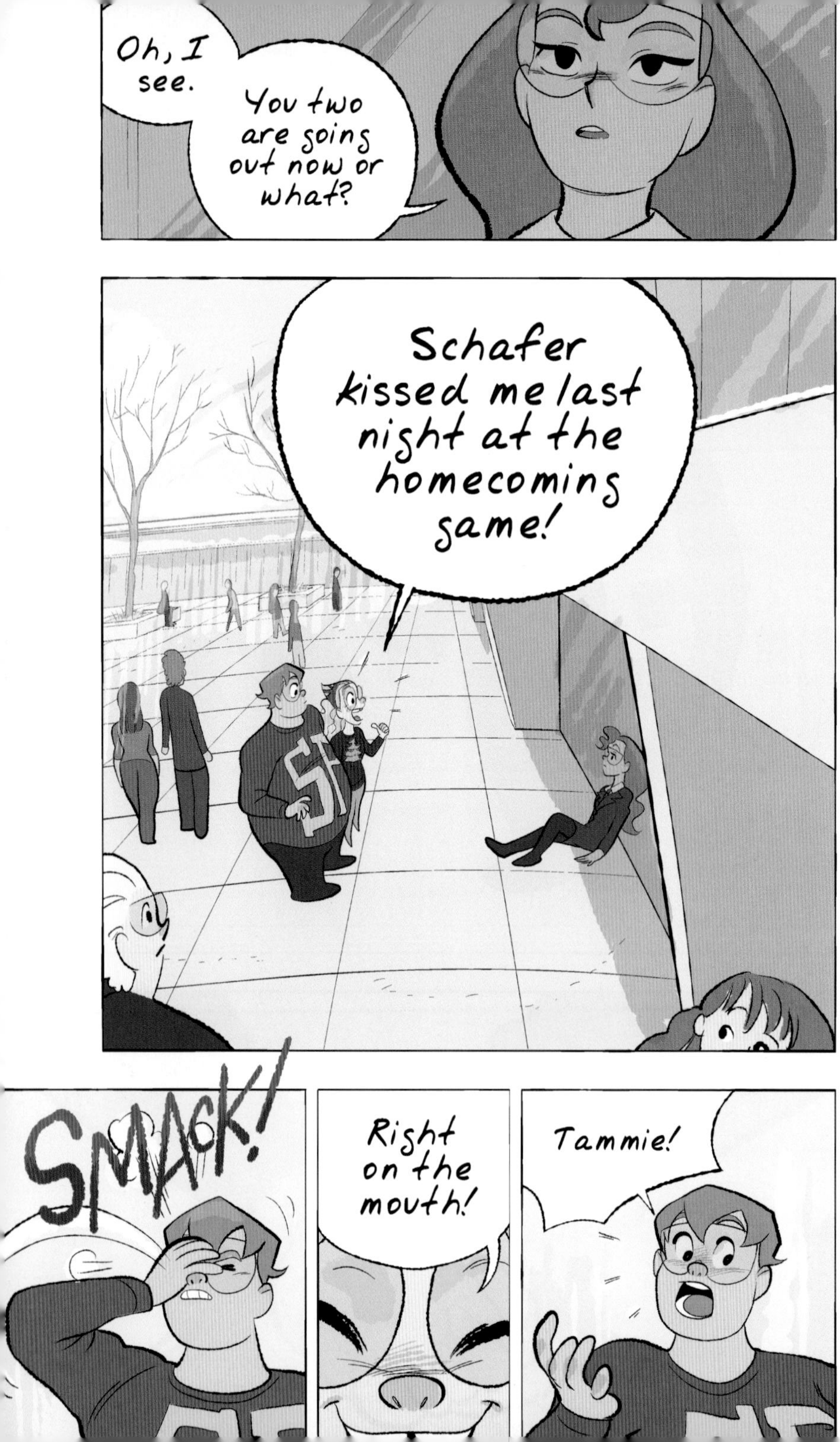
Oh, I see.
You two are going out now or what?
Schafer kissed me last night at the homecoming game!
SMACK!
Right on the mouth!
Tammie!

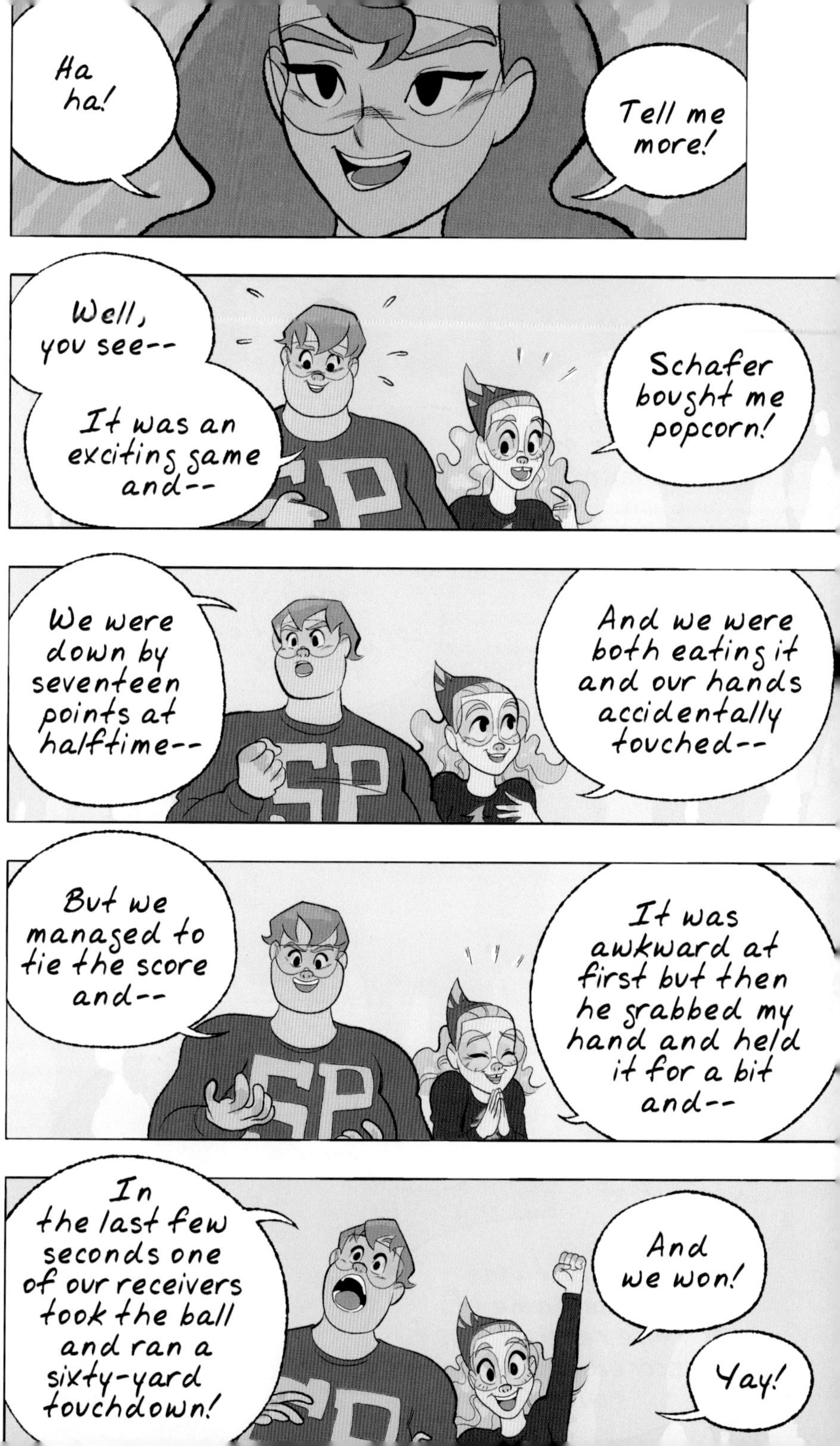
Ha ha!
Tell me more!
Well, you see--
It was an exciting game and--
Schafer bought me popcorn!
We were down by seventeen points at halftime--
And we were both eating it and our hands accidentally touched--
But we managed to tie the score and--
It was awkward at first but then he grabbed my hand and held it for a bit and--
In the last few seconds one of our receivers took the ball and ran a sixty-yard touchdown!
And we won!
Yay!

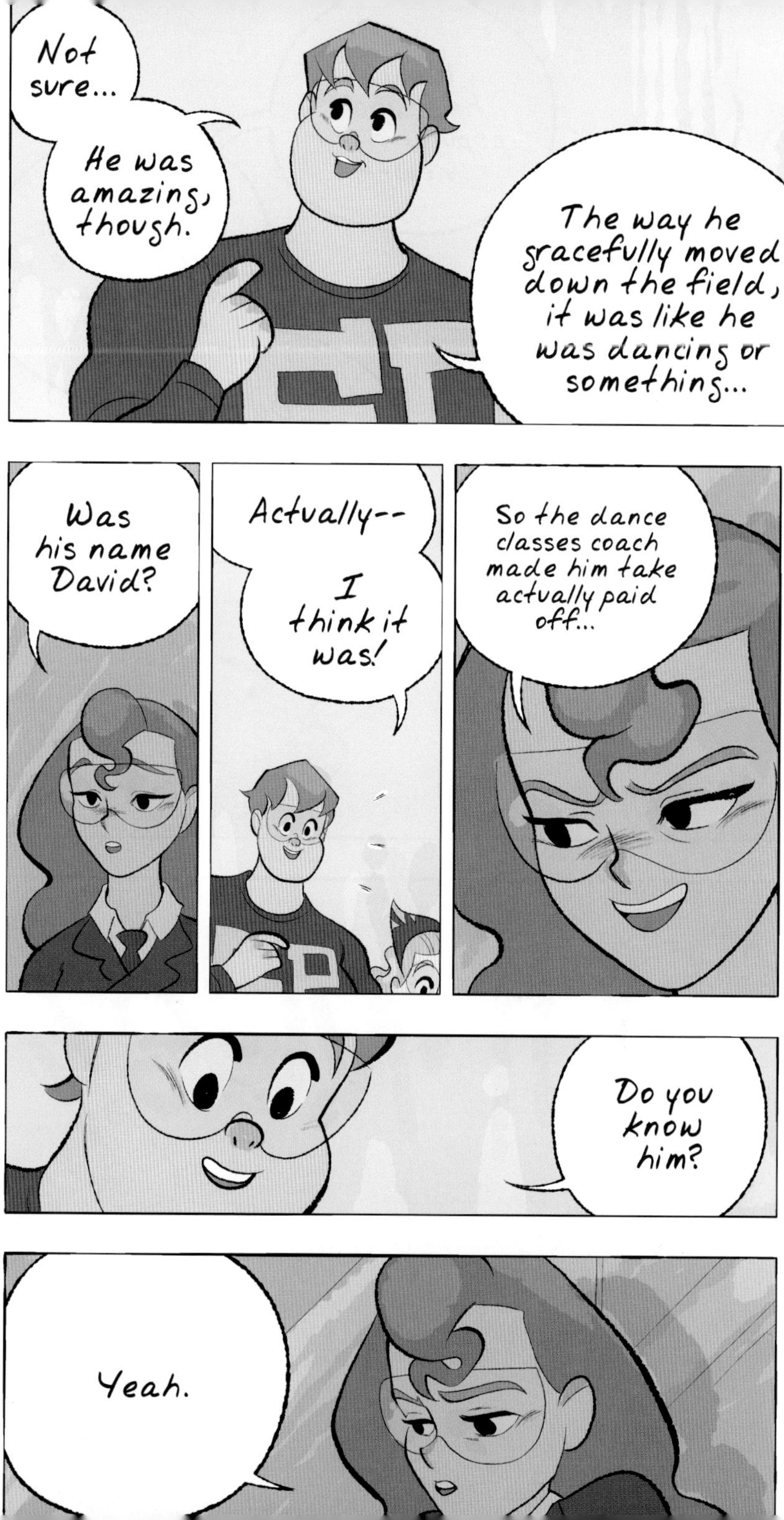

Not sure...
He was amazing, though.
The way he gracefully moved down the field, it was like he was dancing or something...
Was his name David?
Actually--
I think it was!
So the dance classes coach made him take actually paid off...
Do you know him?
Yeah.

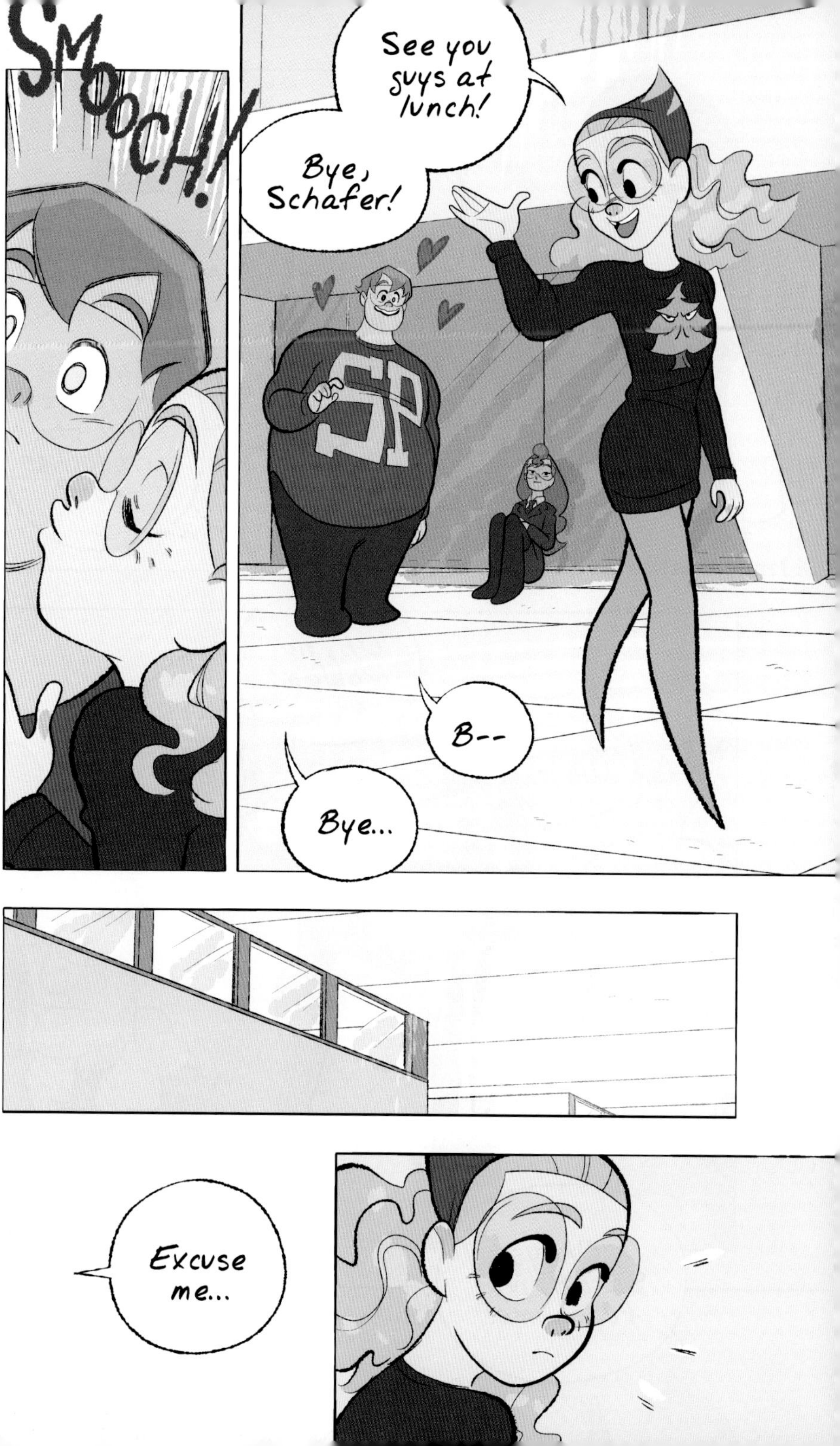
SMOOCH!!
See you guys at lunch!
Bye, Schafer!
B--
Bye...
Excuse me...

I had a dream last night...

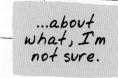

...about what, I'm not sure.

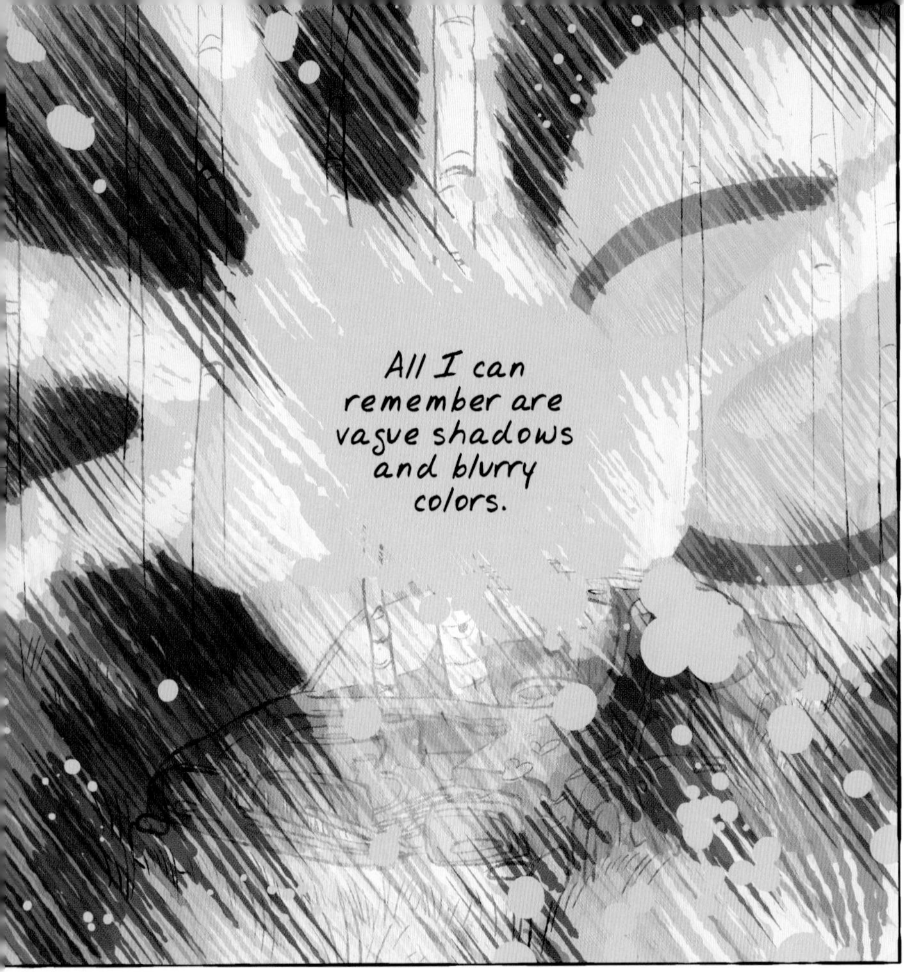
All I can remember are vague shadows and blurry colors.

It must have been a wonderful dream though because I woke up feeling refreshed and alive.

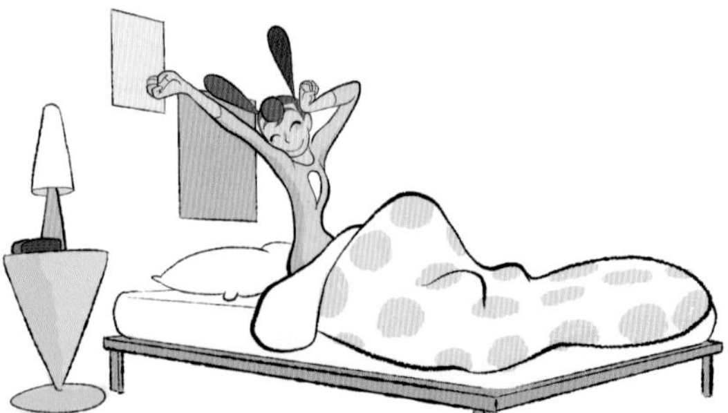

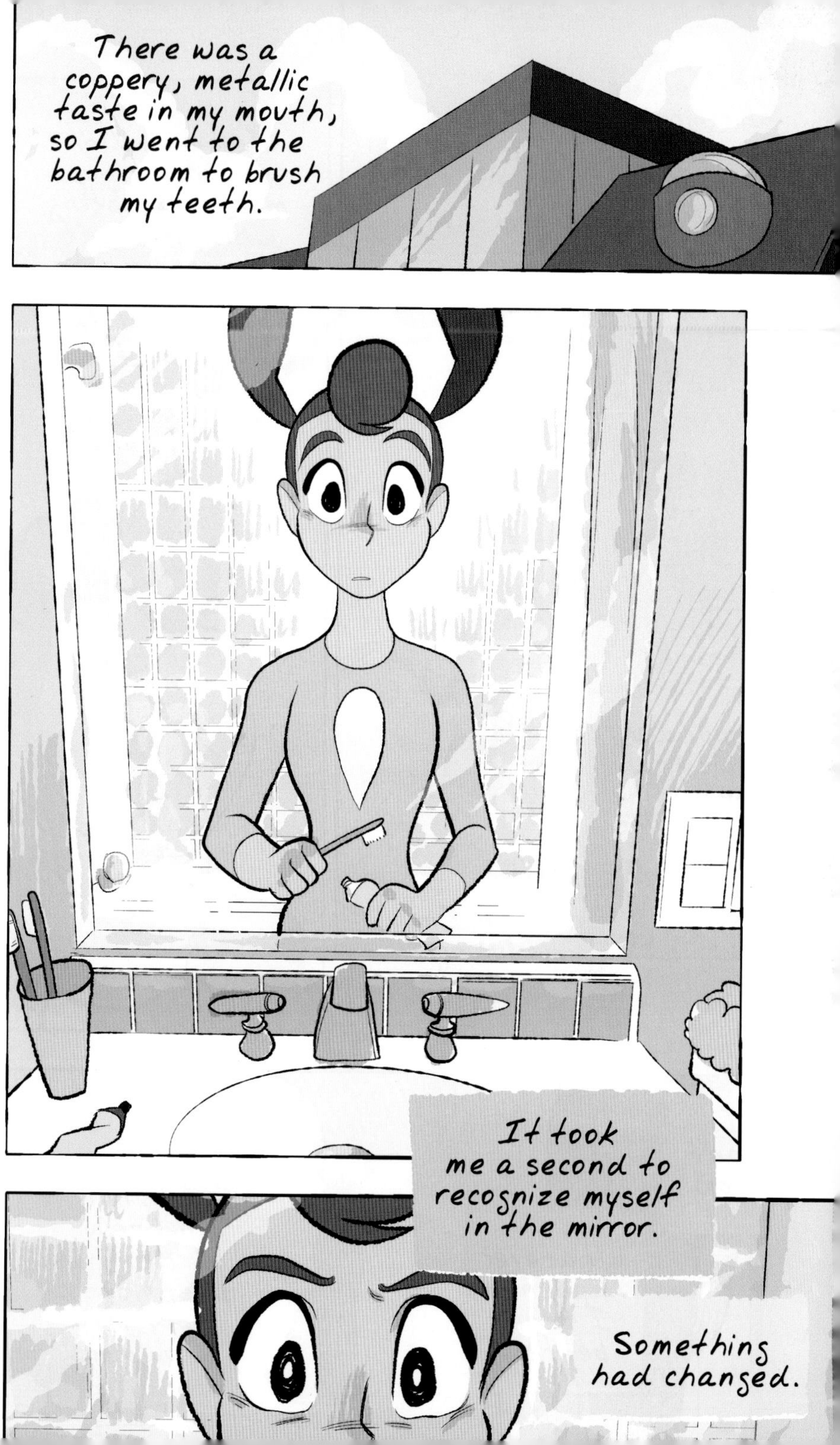

There was a coppery, metallic taste in my mouth, so I went to the bathroom to brush my teeth.
It took me a second to recognize myself in the mirror.
Somethins had chansed.

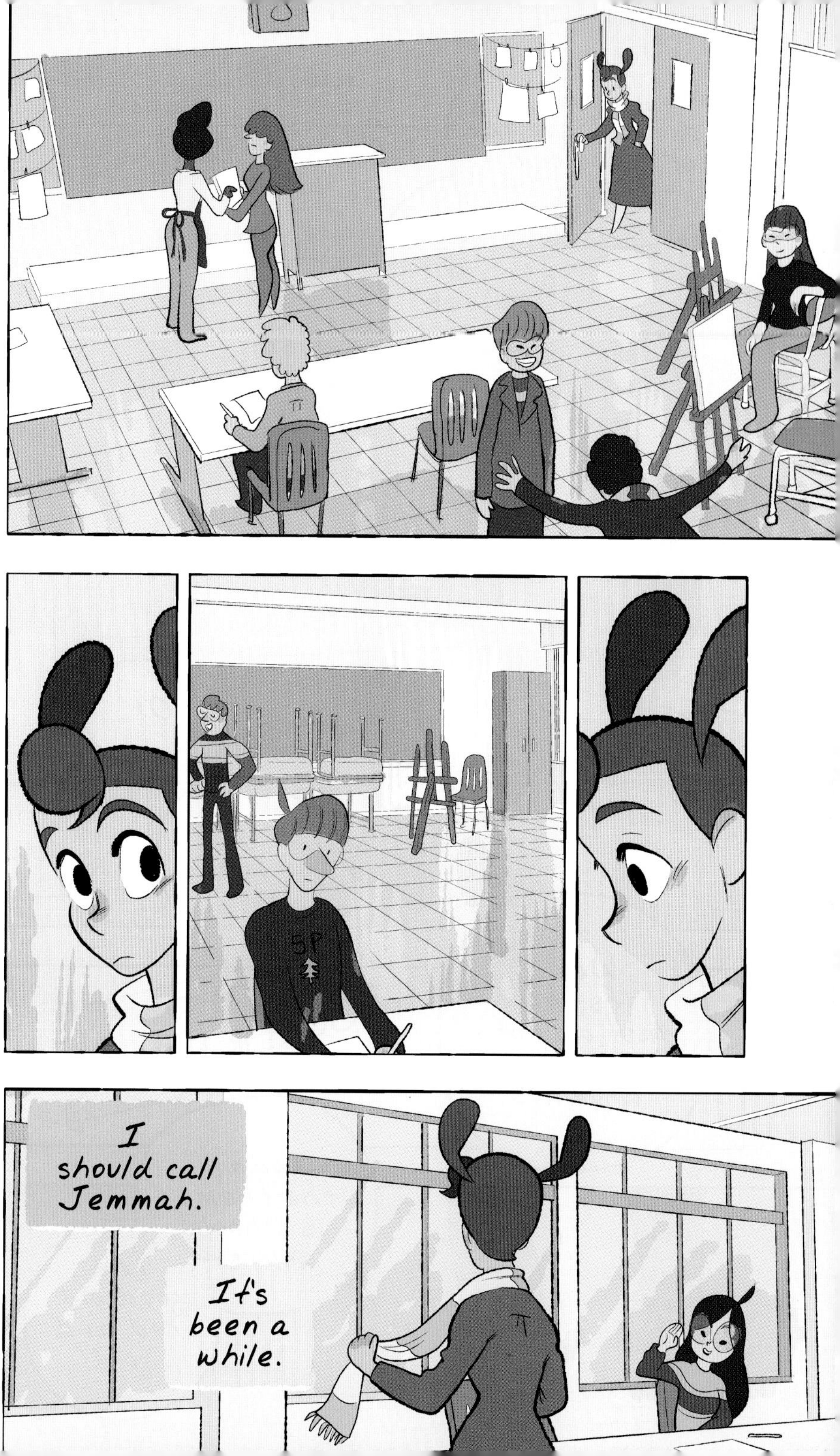
SP
I should call Jemmah.
It's been a while.

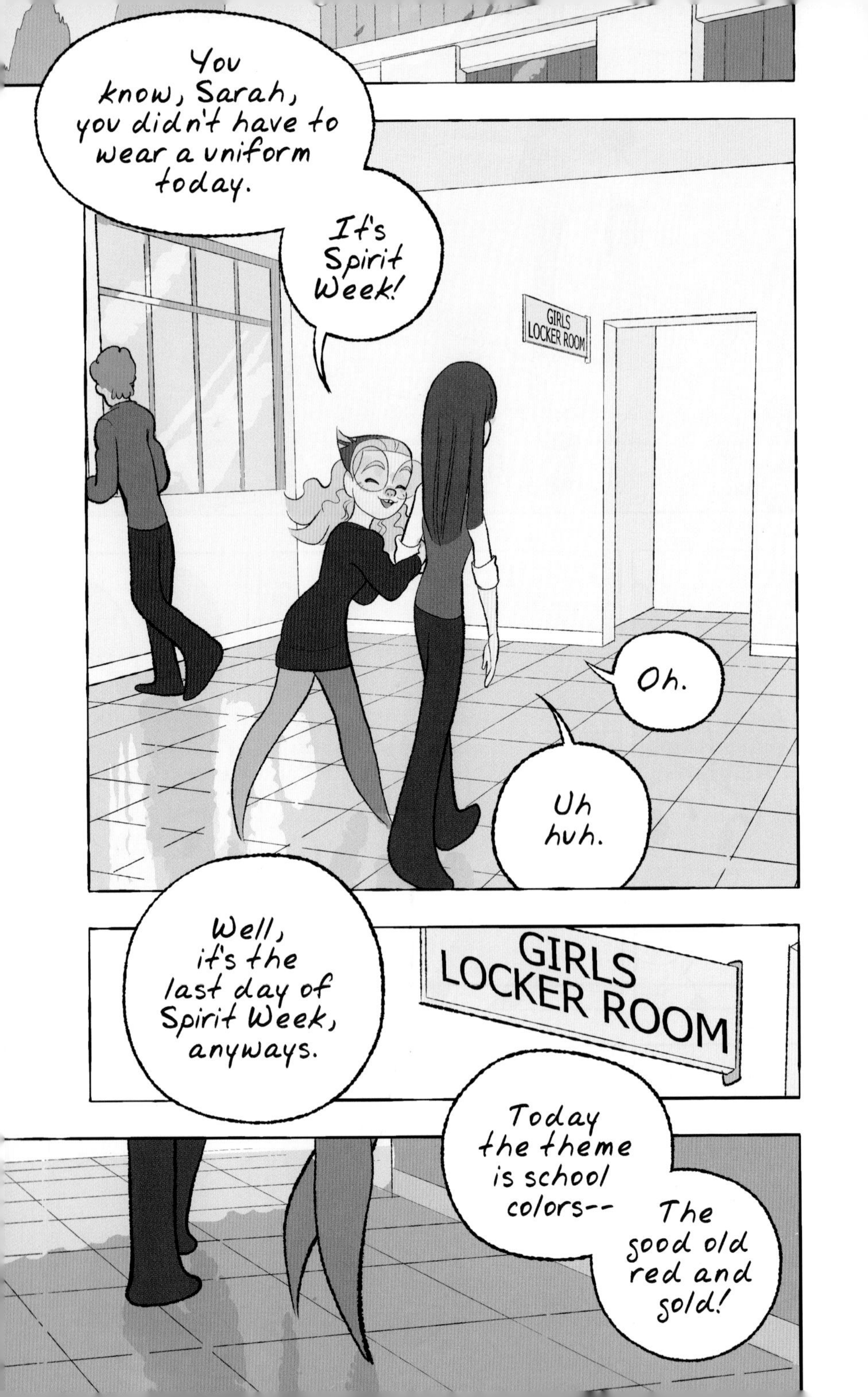
You know, Sarah, you didn't have to wear a uniform today.
It's Spirit Week!
GIRLS LOCKER ROOM
Oh.
Uh huh.
Well, it's the last day of Spirit Week, anyways.
GIRLS LOCKER ROOM
Today the theme is school colors--
The good old red and gold!

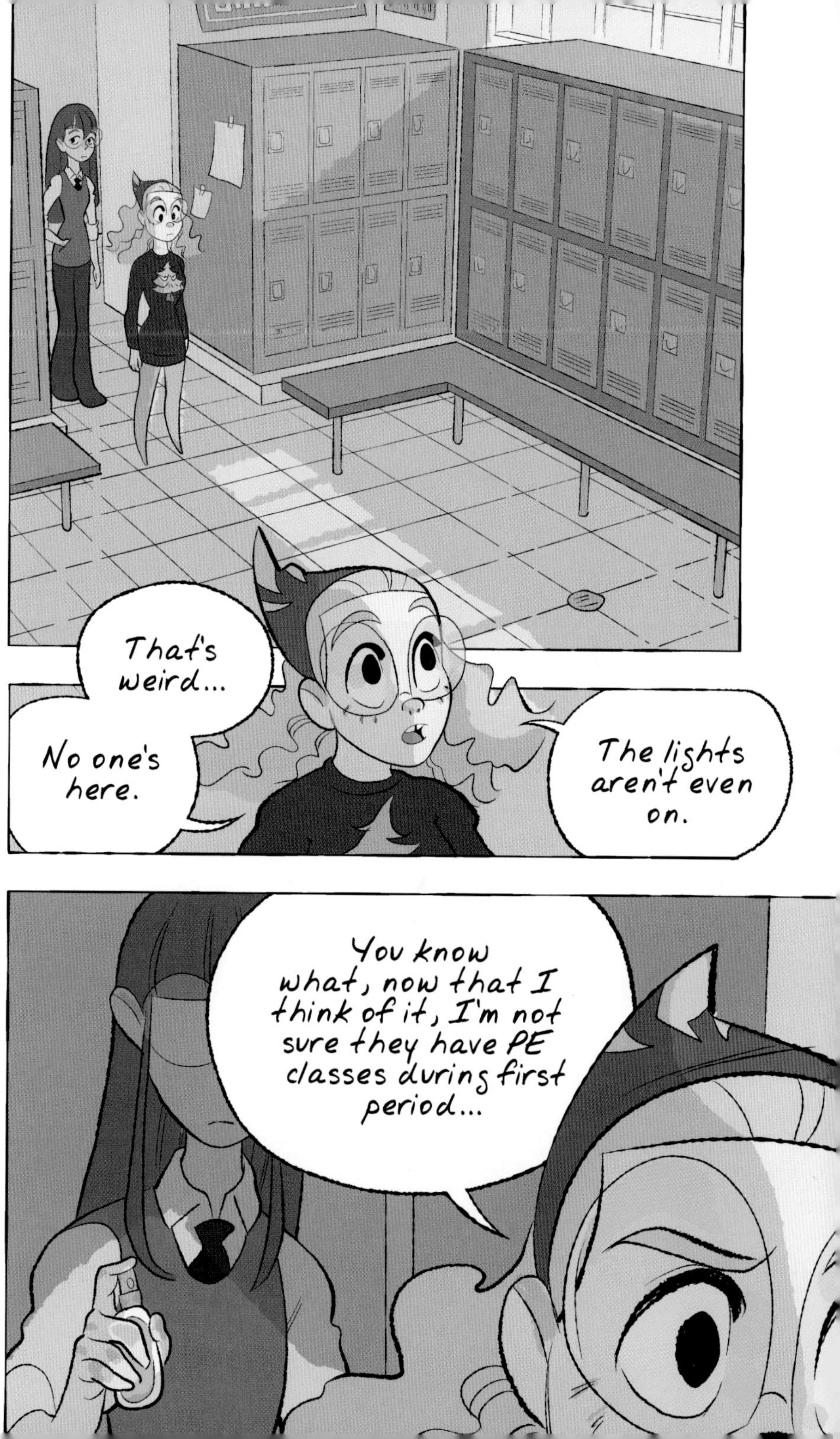
That's weird...
No one's here.
The lights aren't even on.
You know what, now that I think of it, I'm not sure they have PE classes during first period...

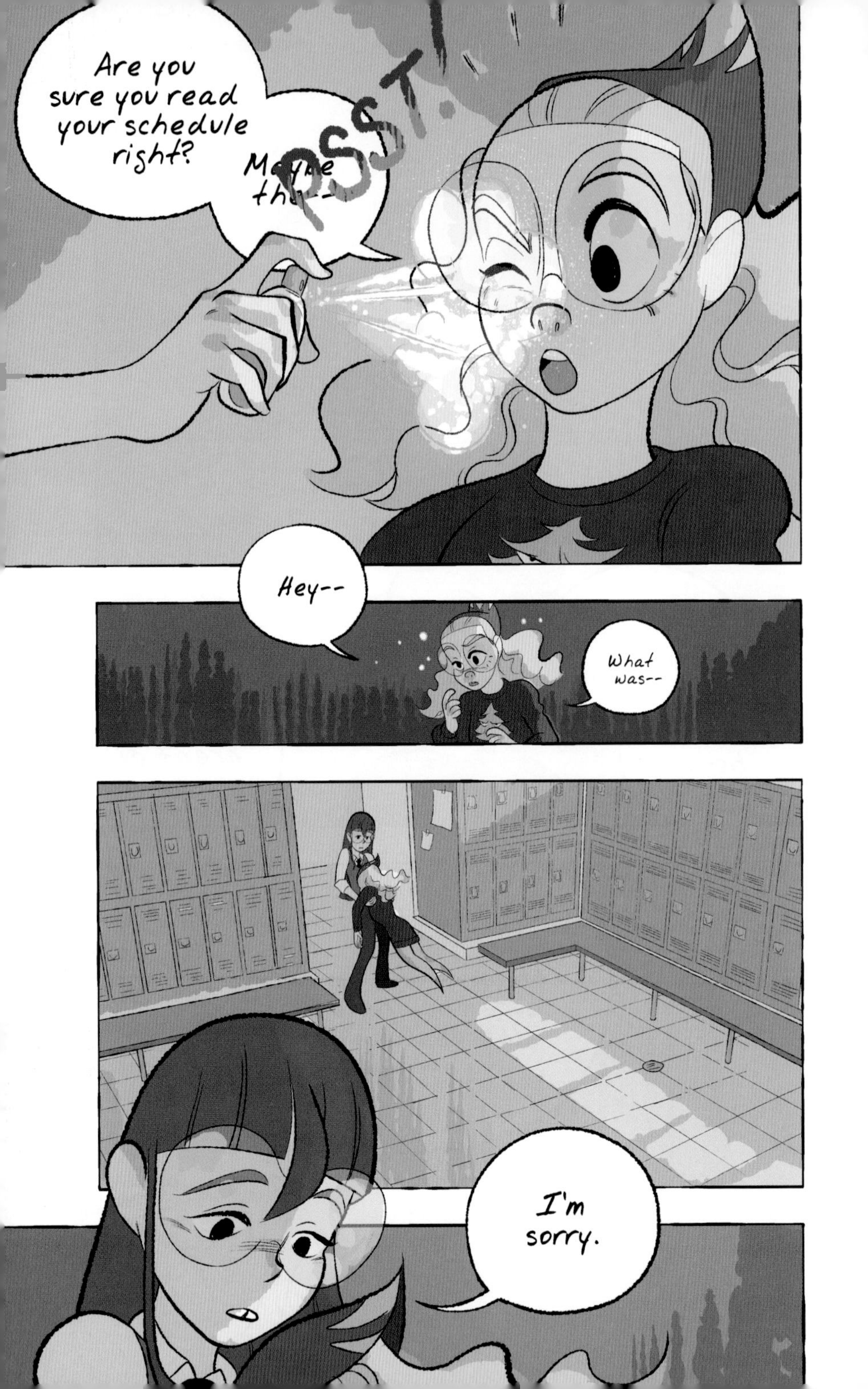
Are you sure you read your schedule right?
Maybe the--
PSST!
Hey--
What was--
I'm sorry.

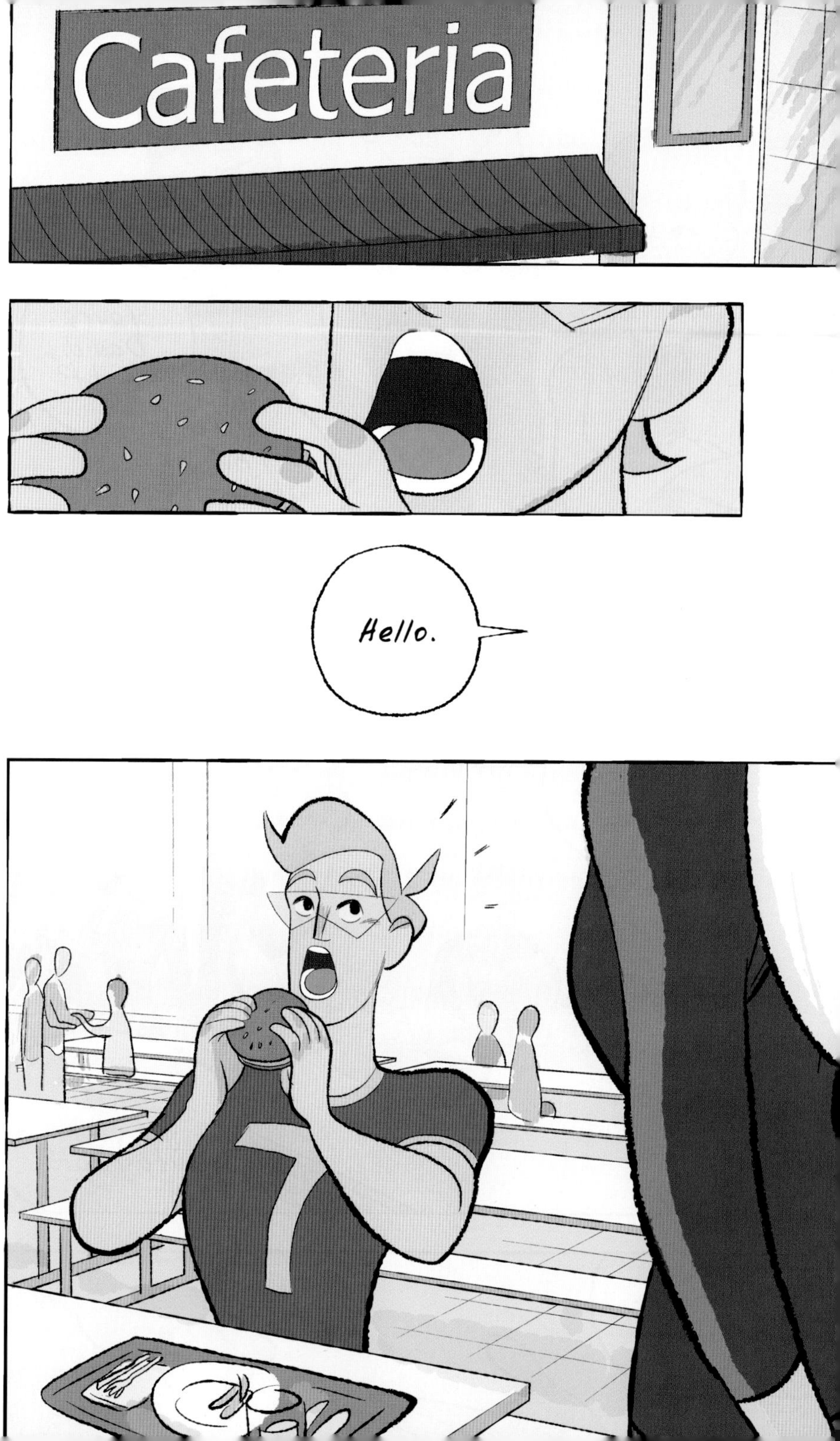
Cafeteria
Hello.

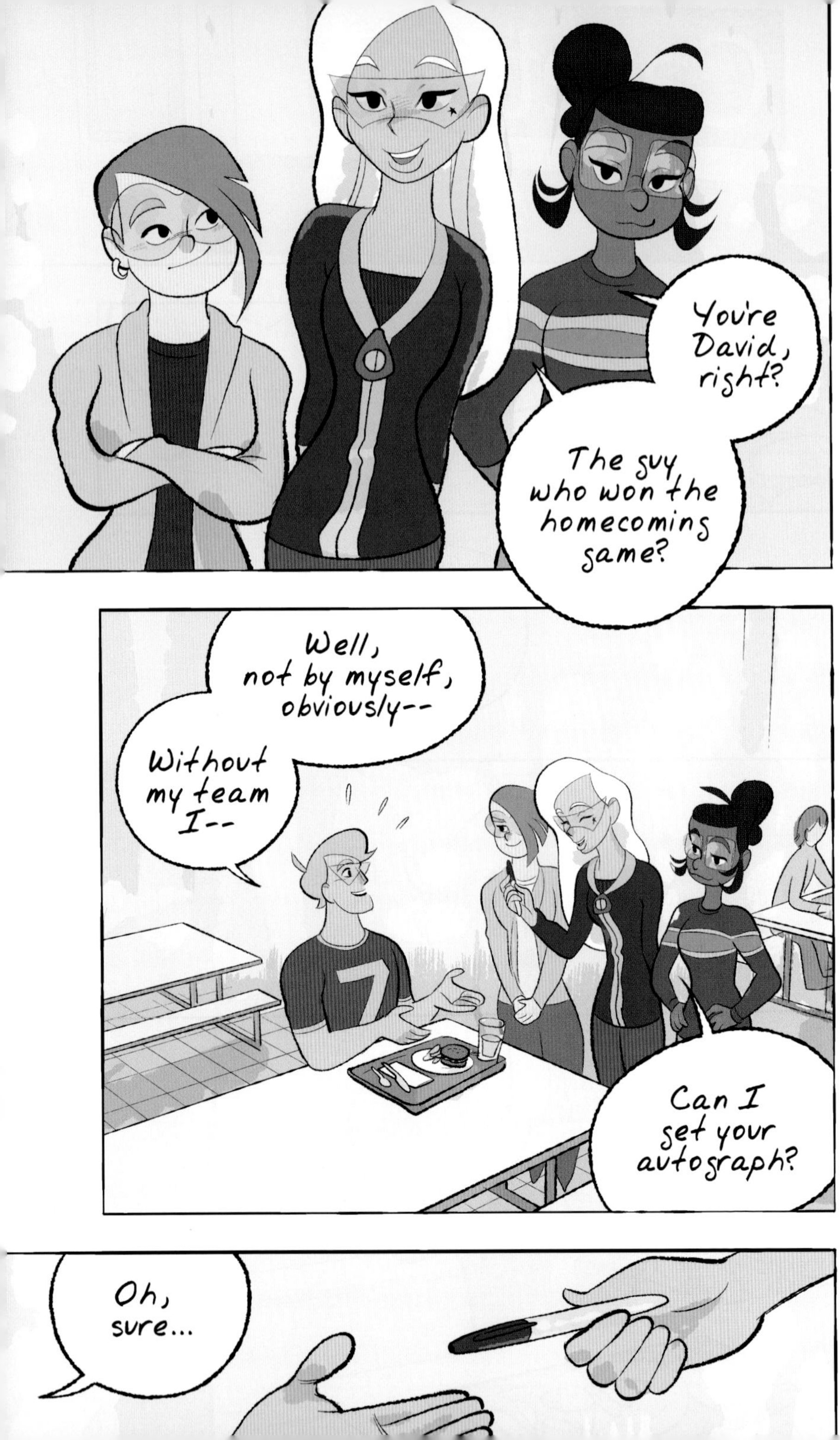
You're David, right?
The guy who won the homecoming game?
Well, not by myself, obviously--
Without my team I--
Can I get your autograph?
Oh, sure...

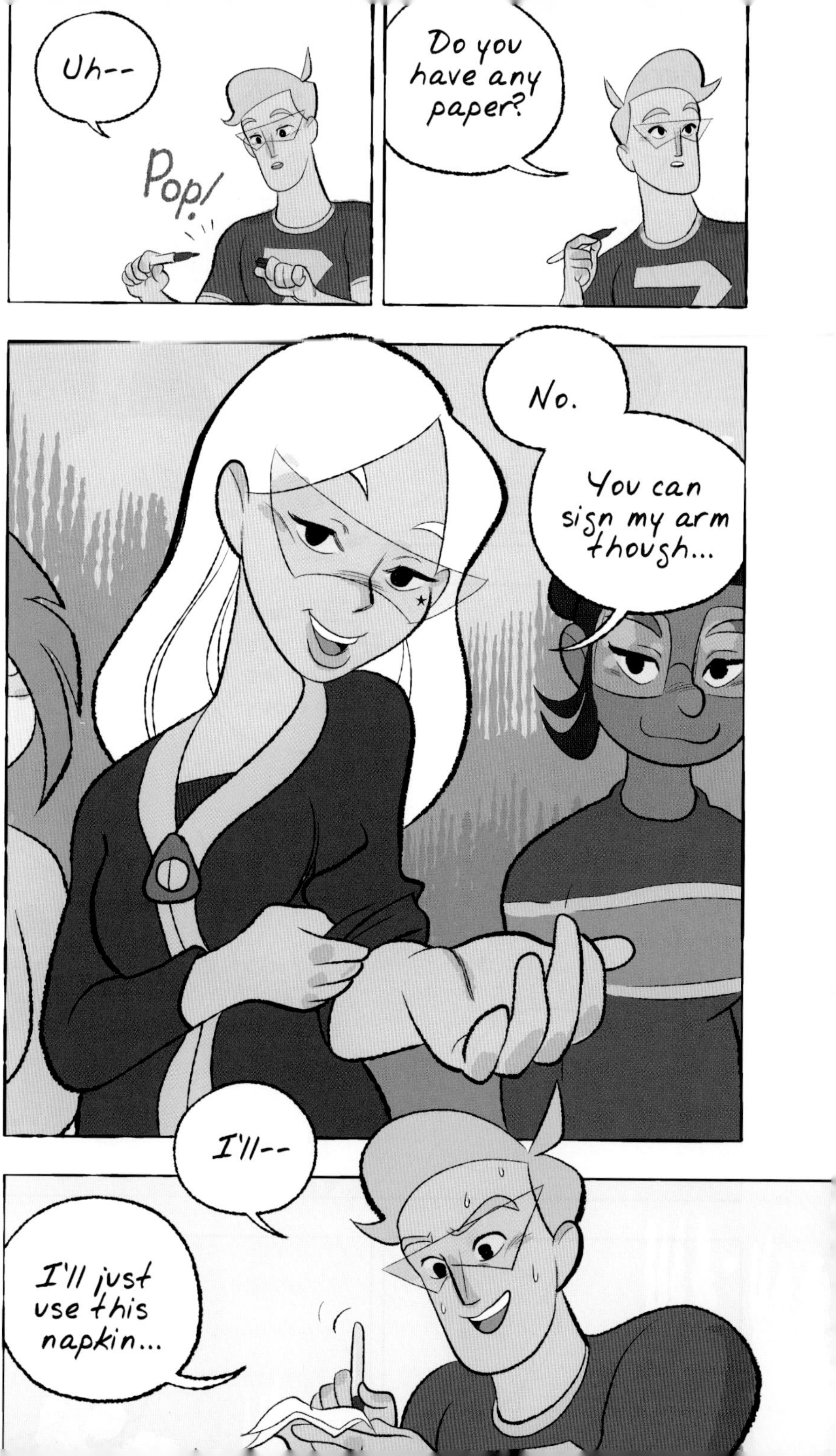
Uh--
Pop!
Do you have any paper?
No.
You can sign my arm though...
I'll--
I'll just use this napkin...

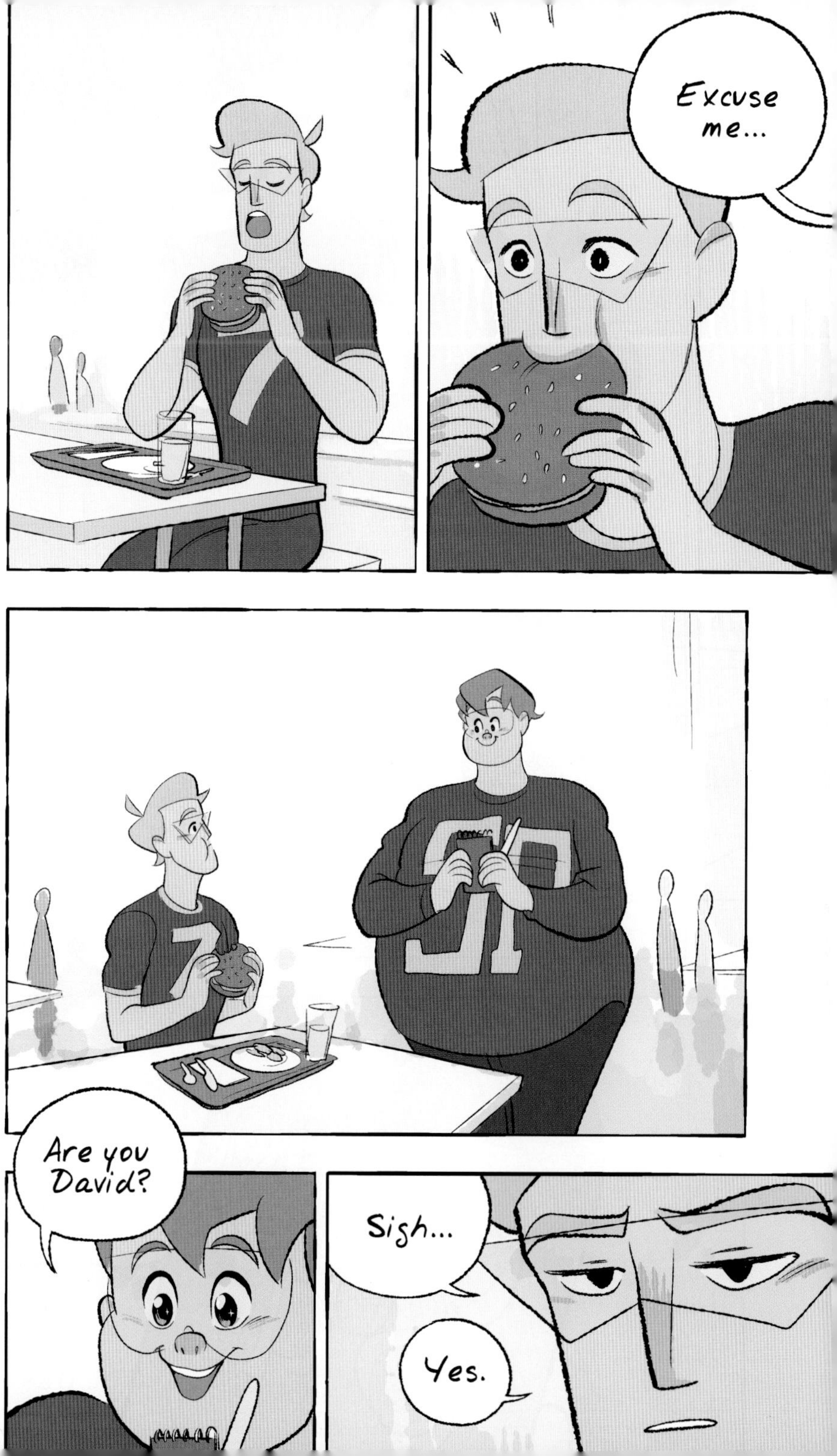
Excuse me...
Are you David?
Sigh...
Yes.

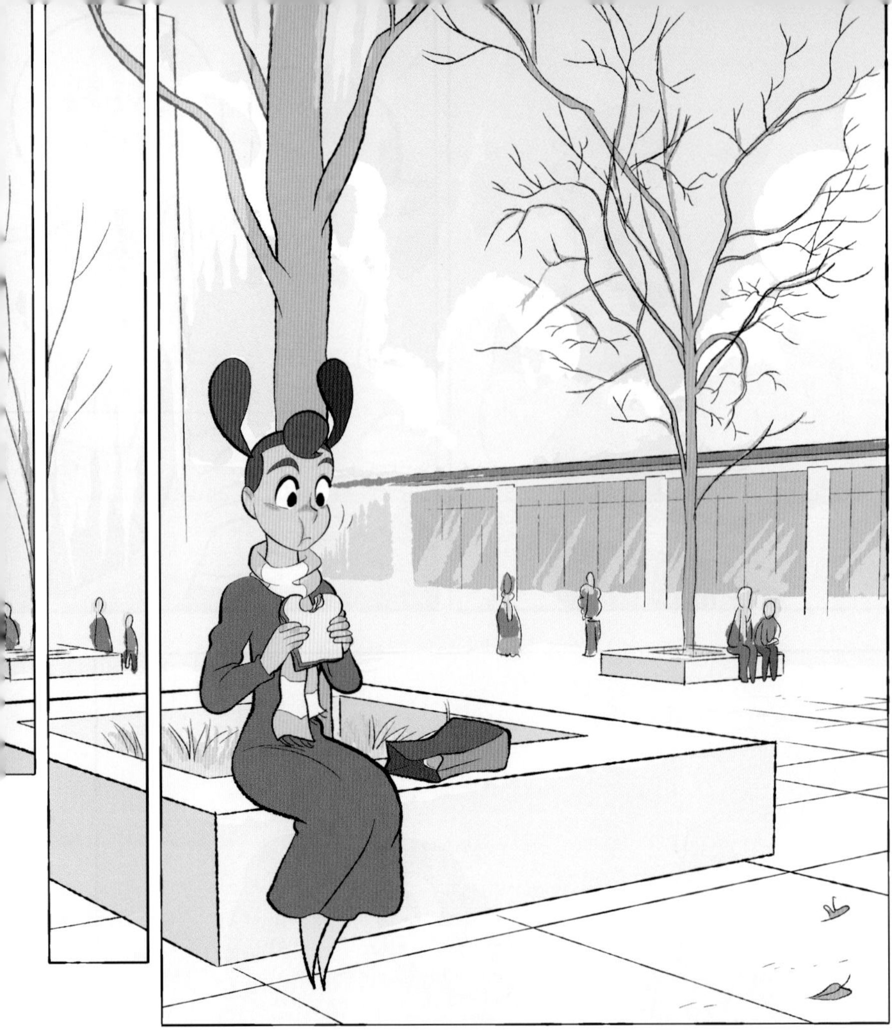

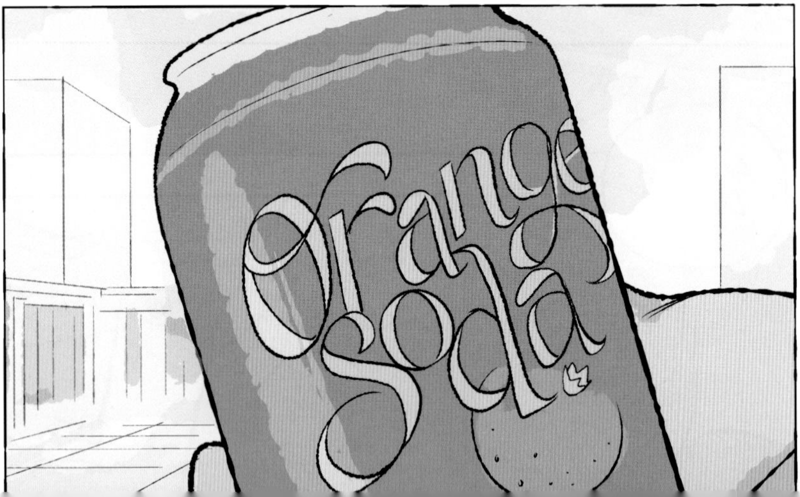
Orange Soda

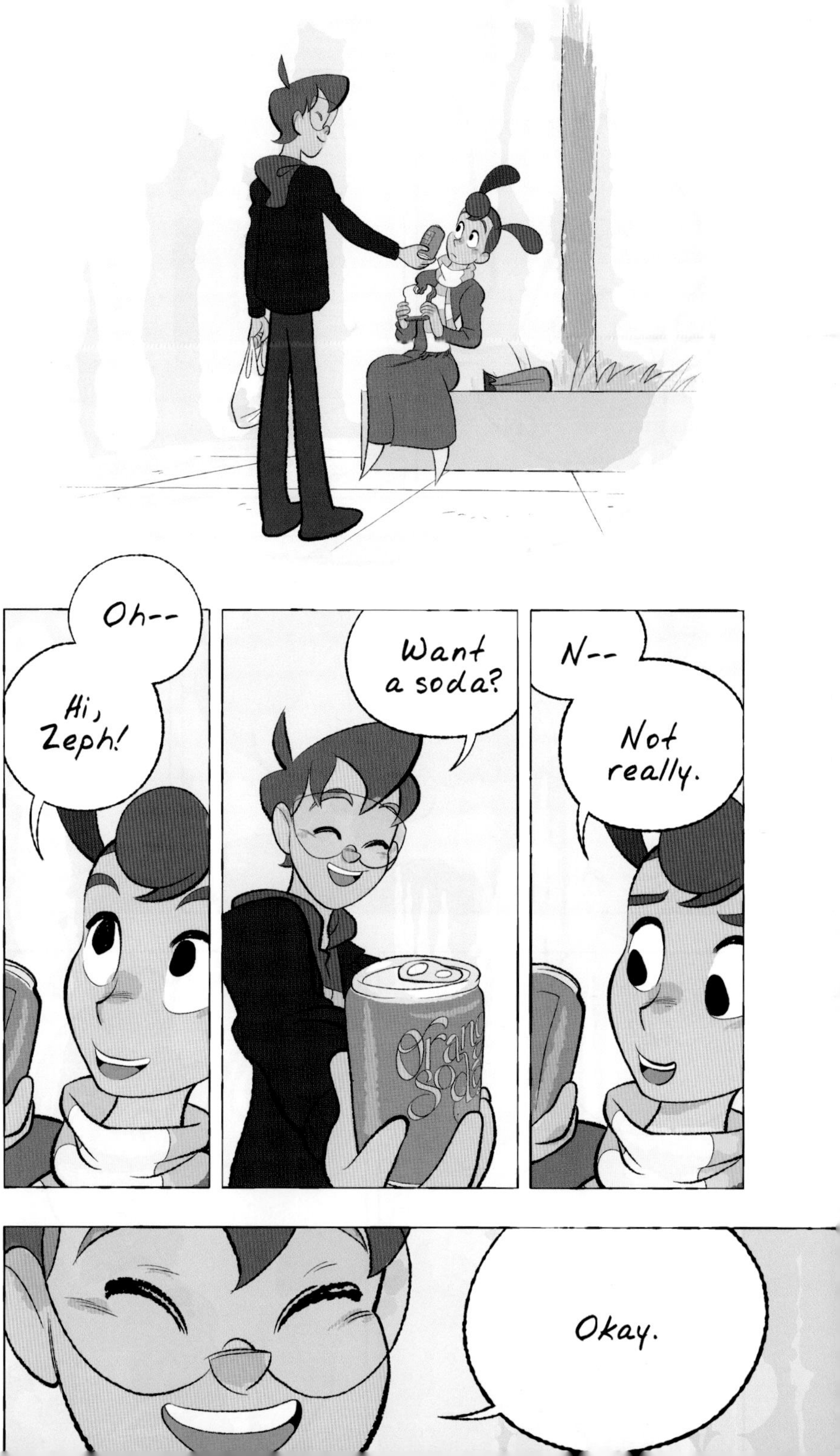
Oh--
Hi, Zeph!
Want a soda?
Orange Soda
N--
Not really.
Okay.

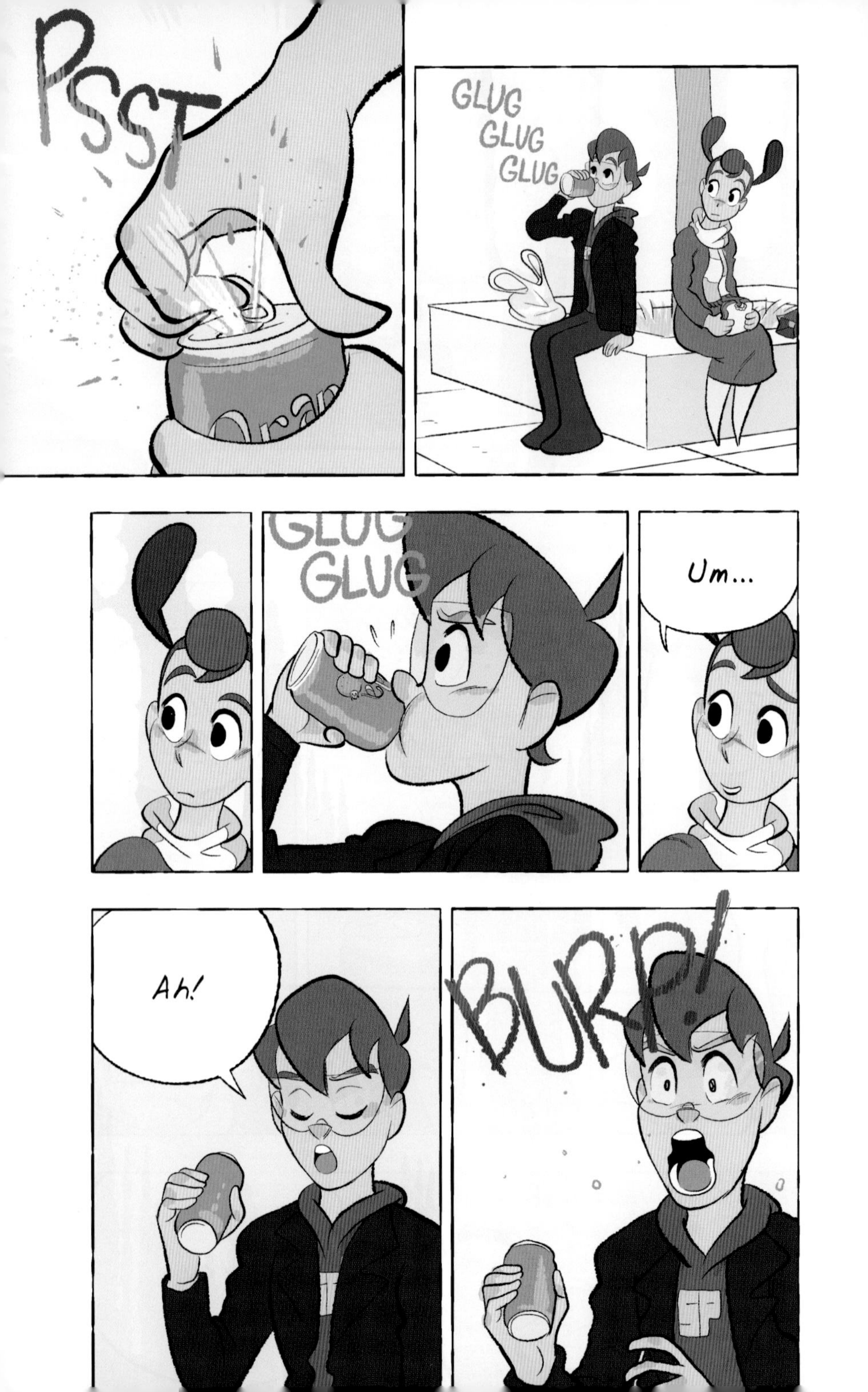
PSST
GLUG
GLUG
GLUG
GLUG
GLUG
Um...
Ah!
BURP!

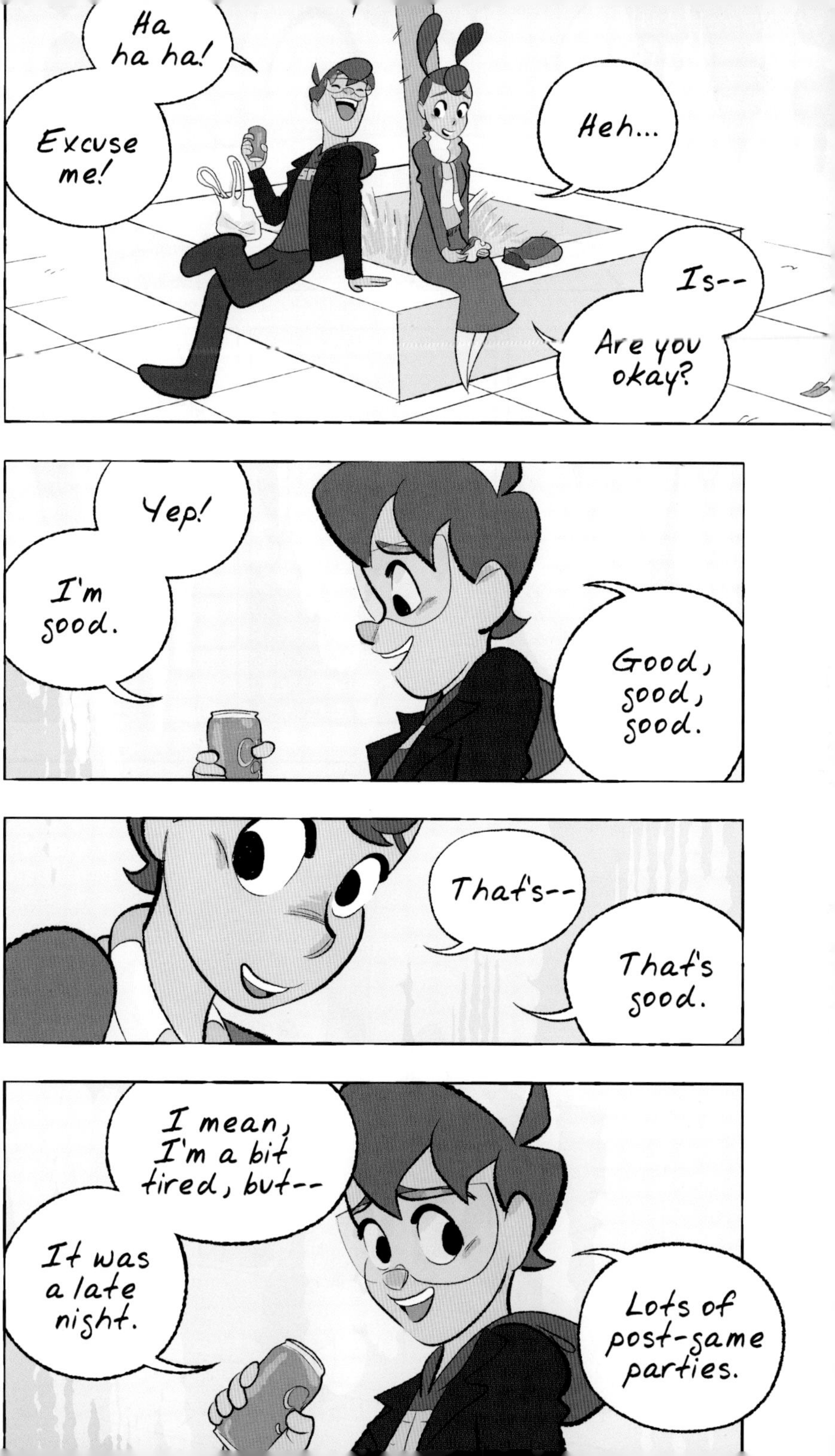
Ha ha ha!
Excuse me!
Heh...
Is--
Are you okay?
Yep!
I'm good.
Good, good, good.
That's--
That's good.
I mean, I'm a bit tired, but--
It was a late night.
Lots of post-game parties.

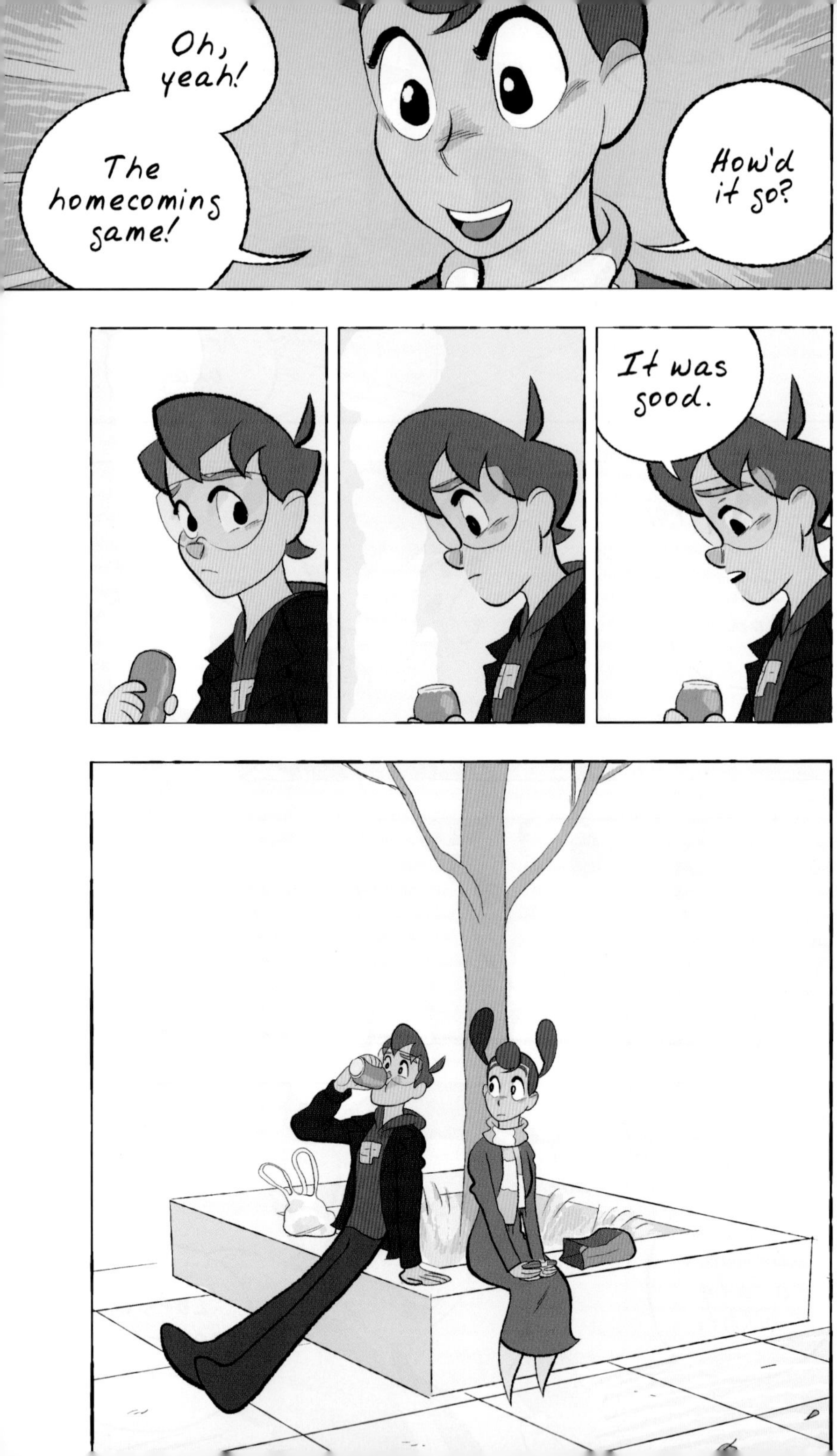

Oh, yeah!
The homecoming game!
How'd it go?
It was good.

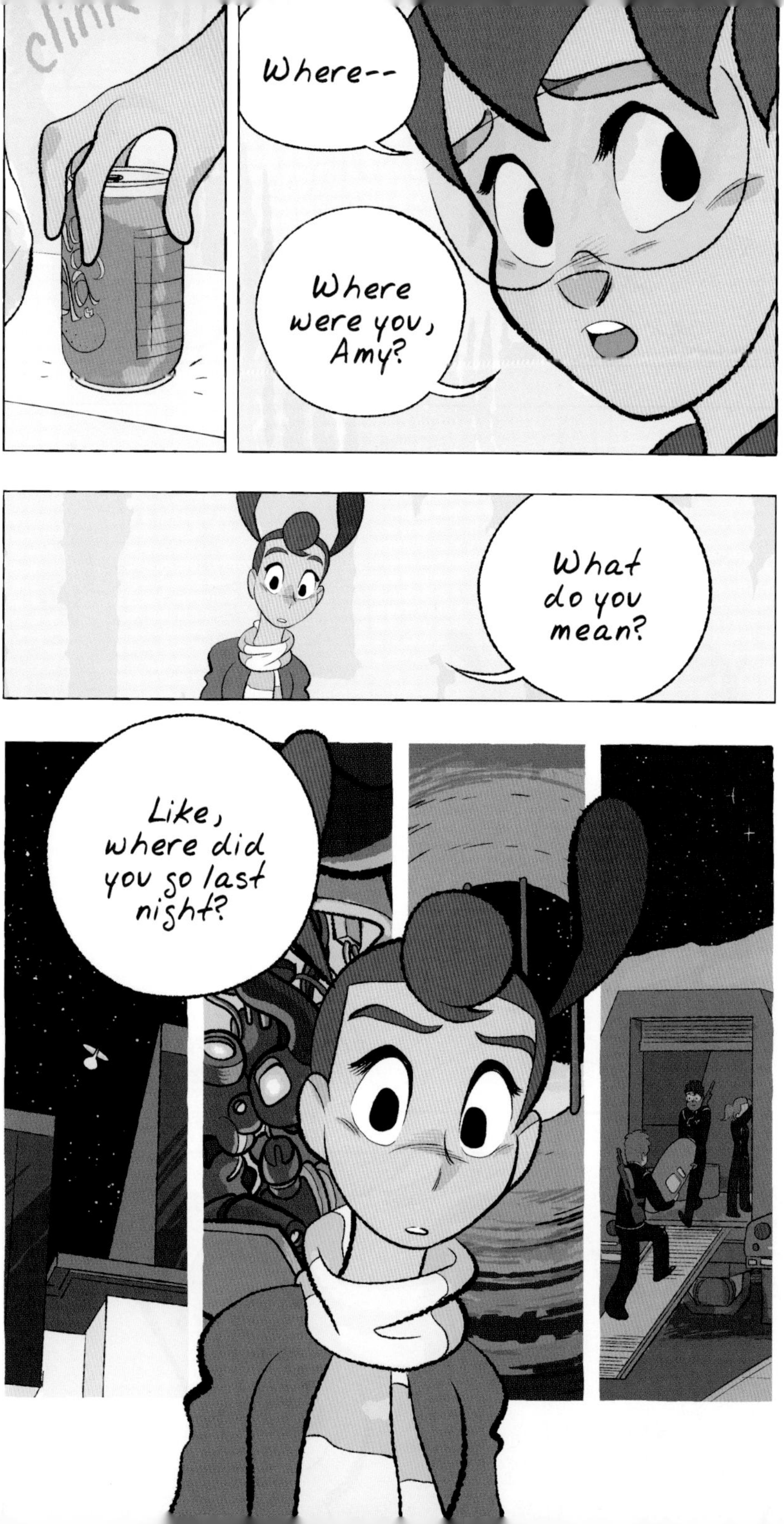
clink
Where--
Where were you, Amy?
What do you mean?
Like, where did you go last night?

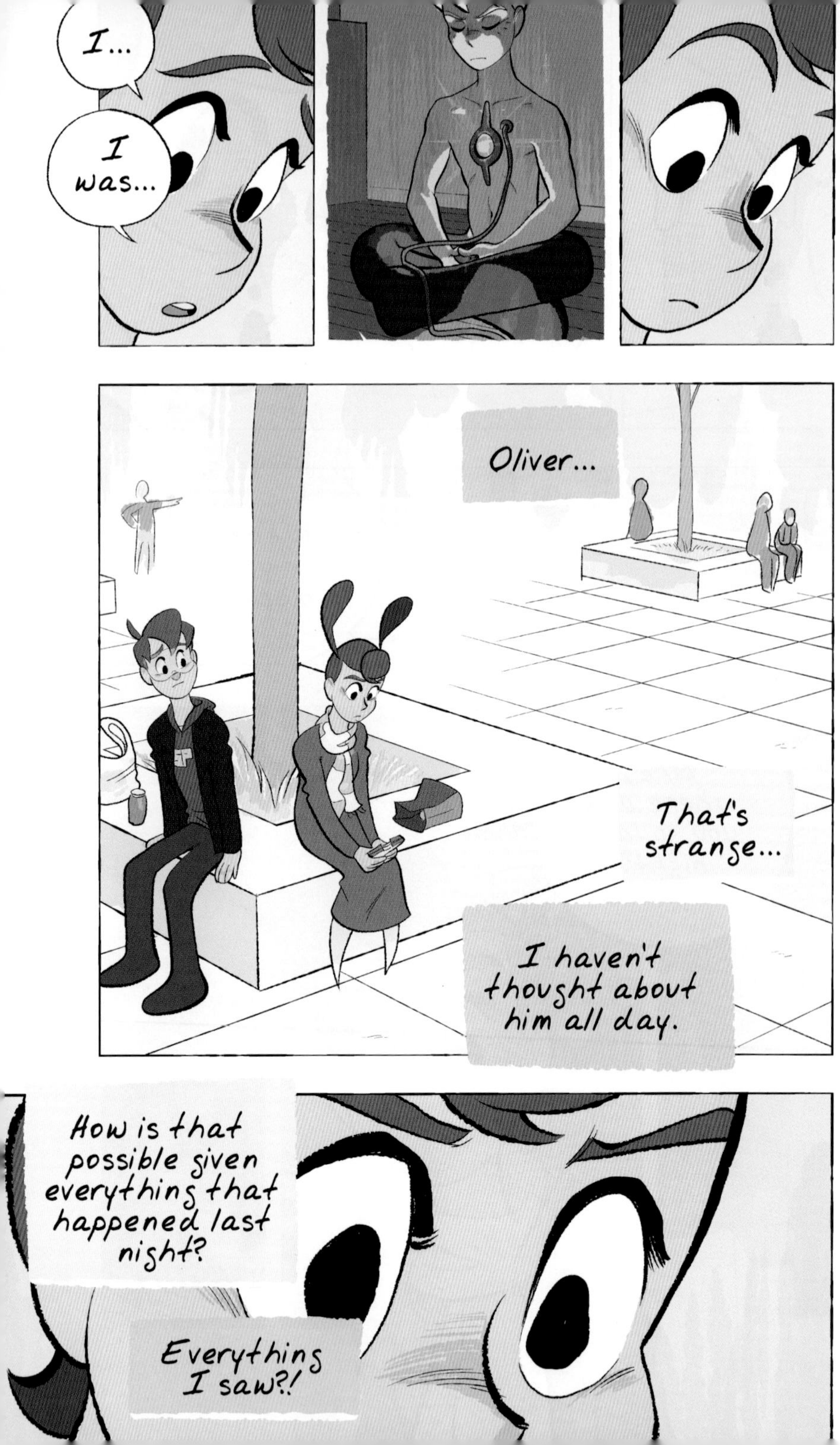
I...
I was...
Oliver...
That's strange...
I haven't thought about him all day.
How is that possible given everything that happened last night?
Everything I saw?!

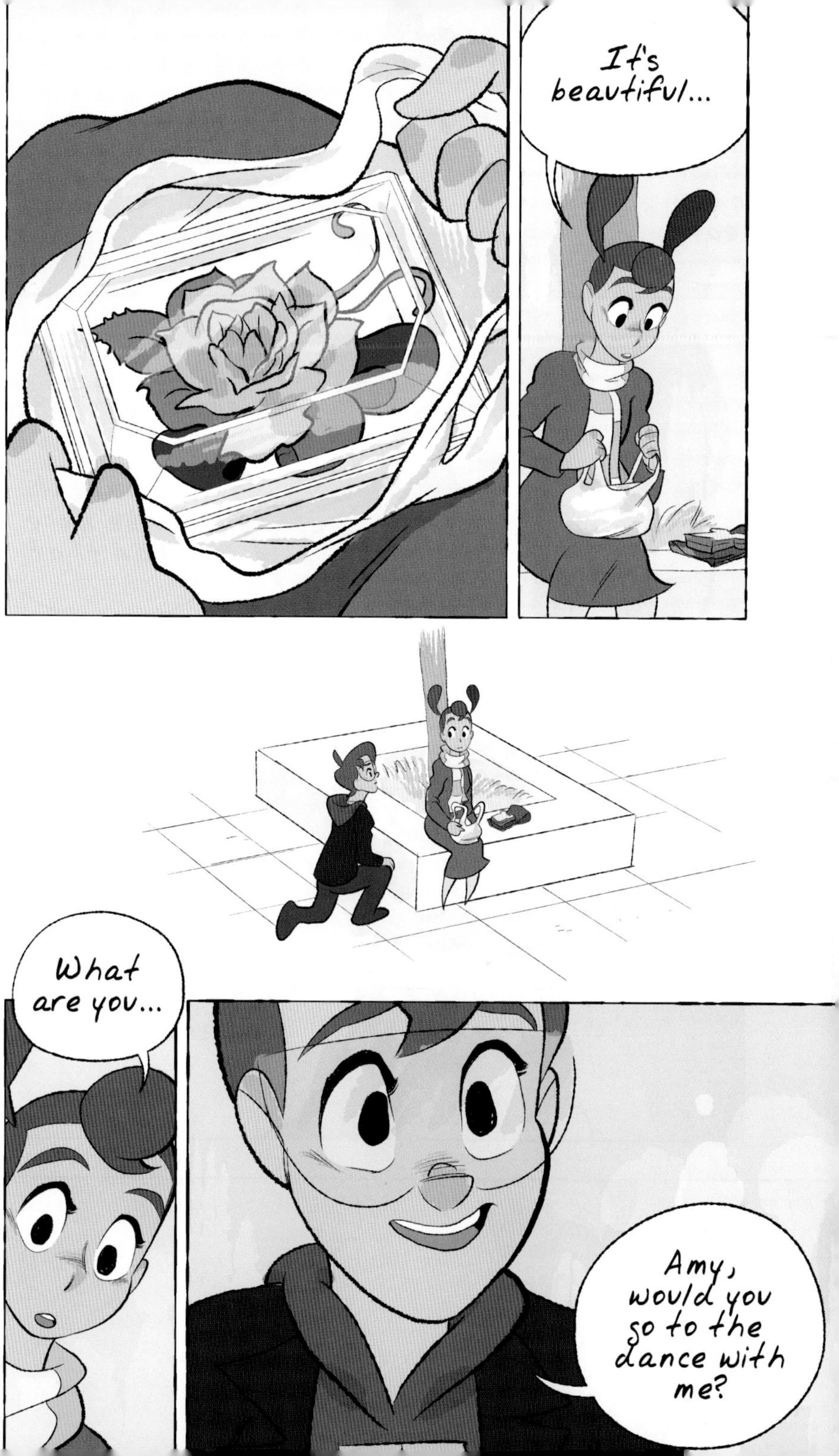
It's beautiful...
What are you...
Amy, would you go to the dance with me?

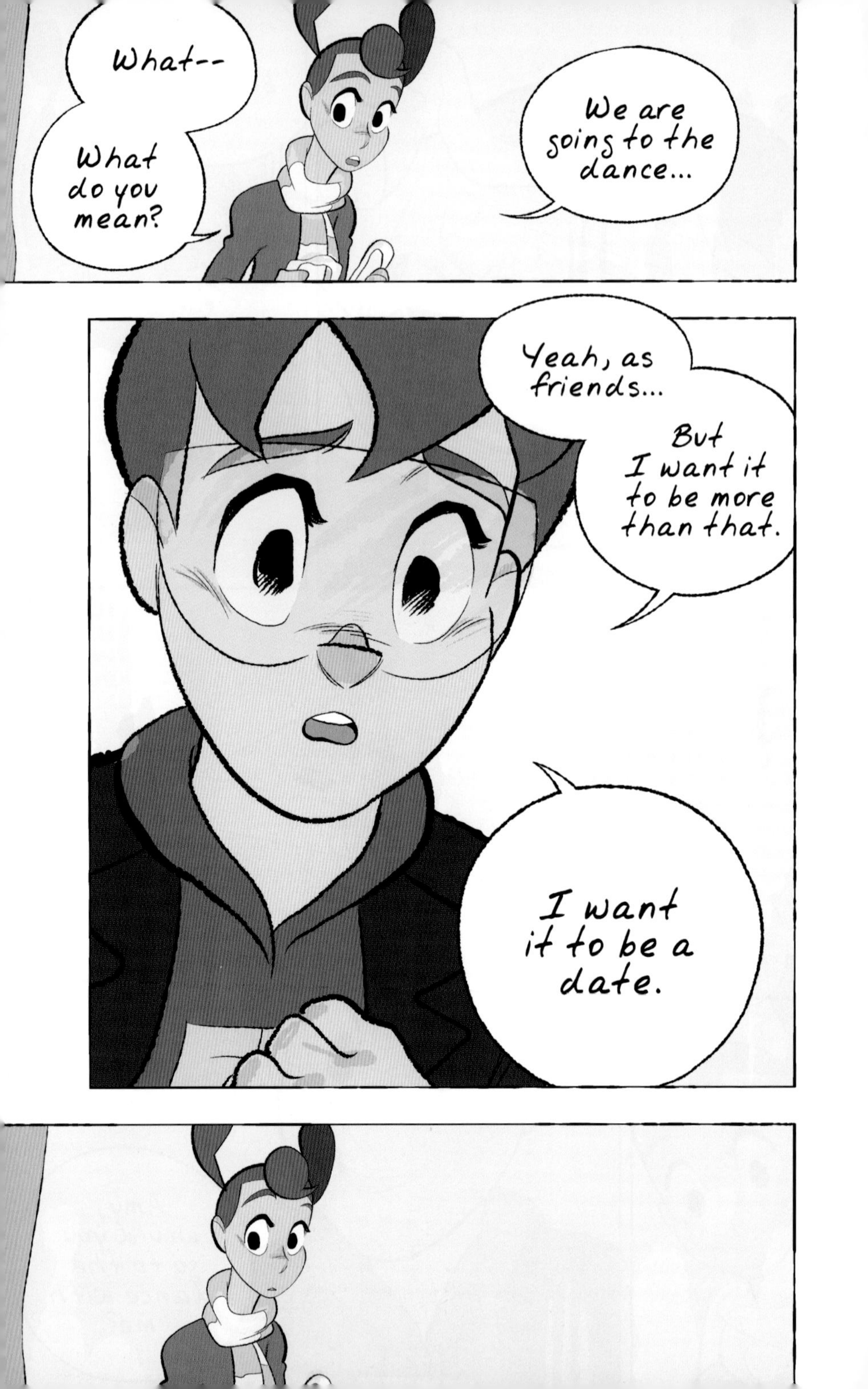
What--
What do you mean?
We are going to the dance...
Yeah, as friends...
But I want it to be more than that.
I want it to be a date.

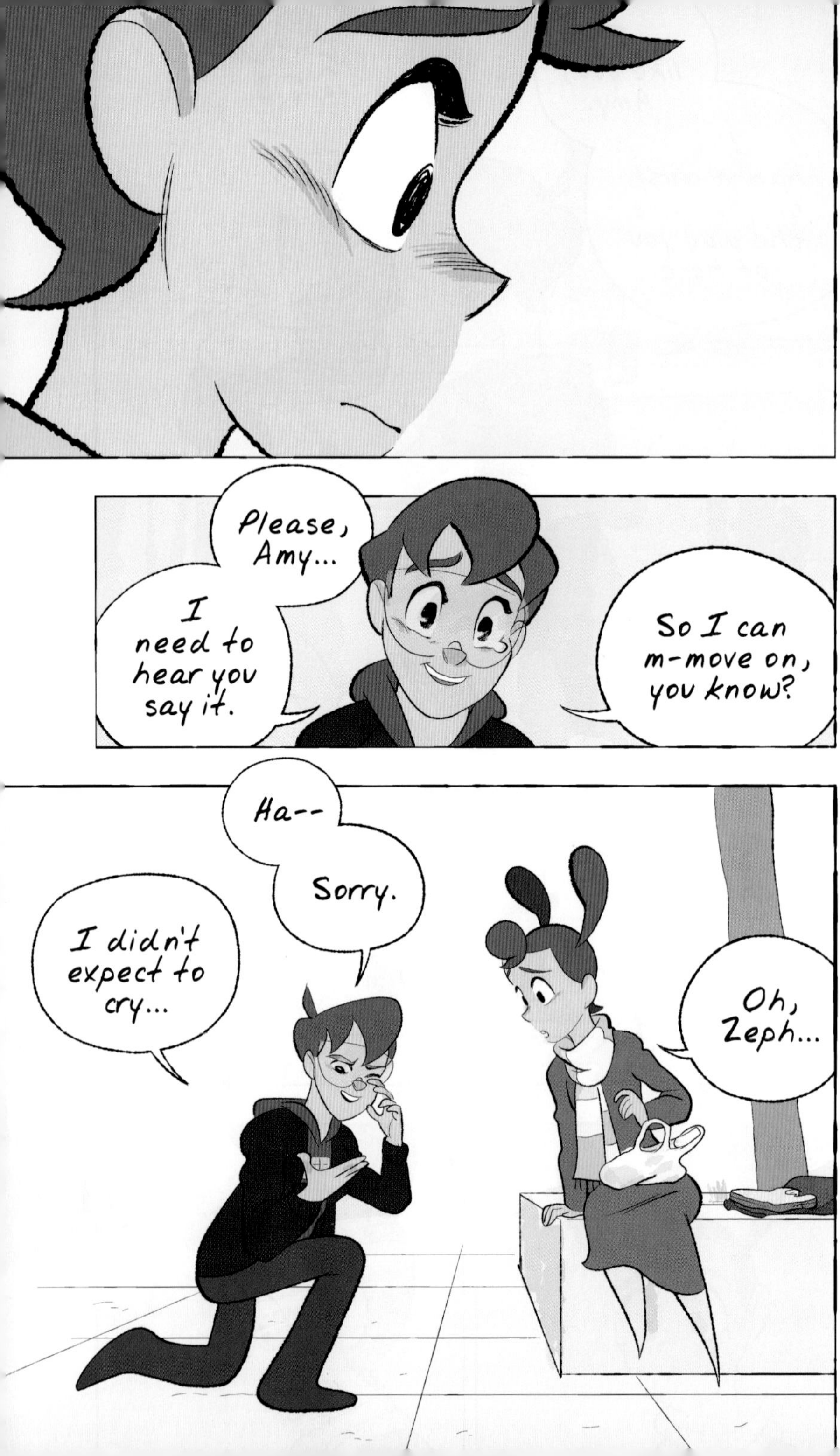
Please, Amy...
I need to hear you say it.
So I can m-move on, you know?
Ha--
Sorry.
I didn't expect to cry...
Oh, Zeph...

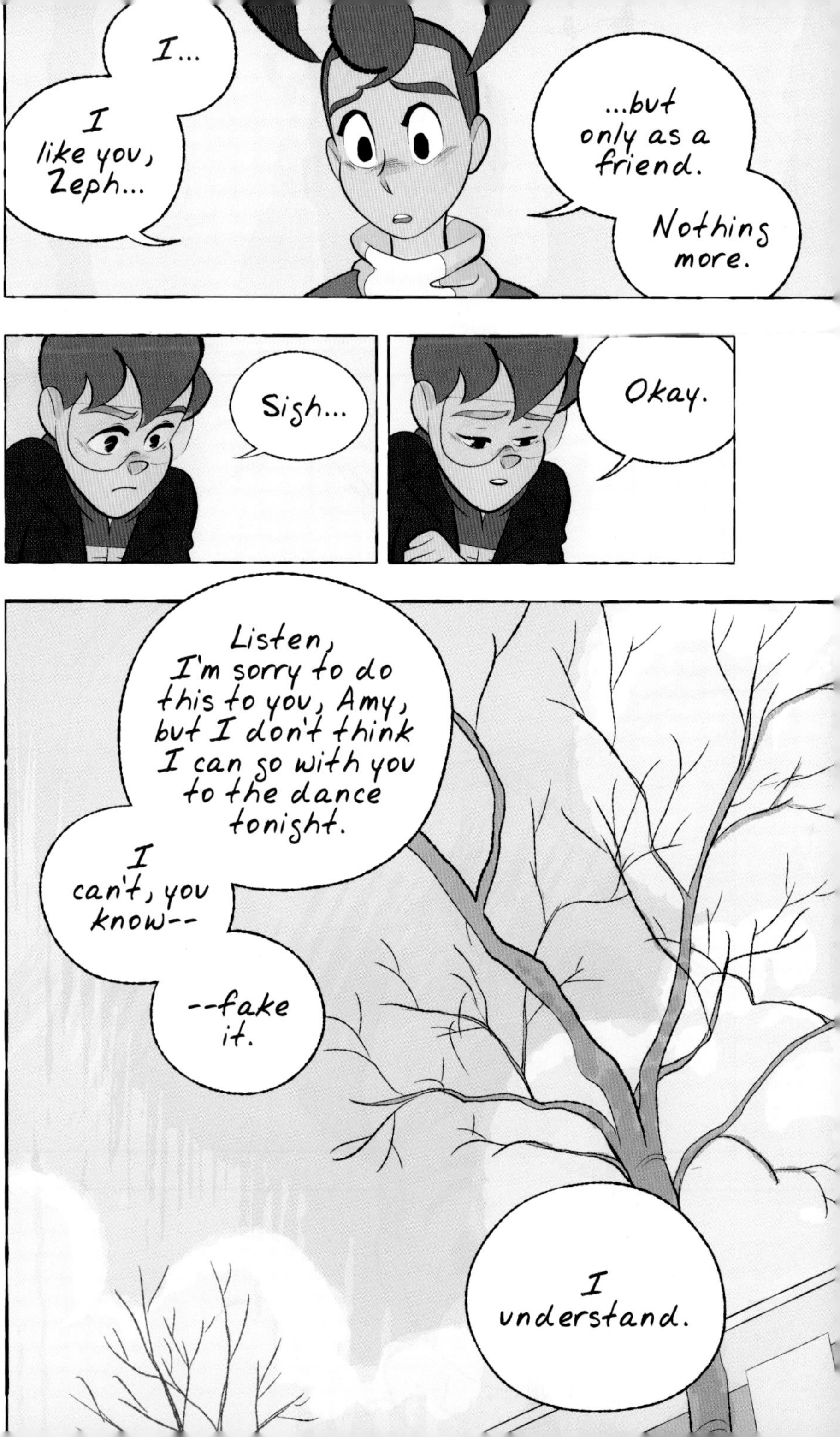
I...
I like you, Zeph...
...but only as a friend.
Nothing more.
Sigh...
Okay.
Listen, I'm sorry to do this to you, Amy, but I don't think I can go with you to the dance tonight.
I can't, you know--
--fake it.
I understand.

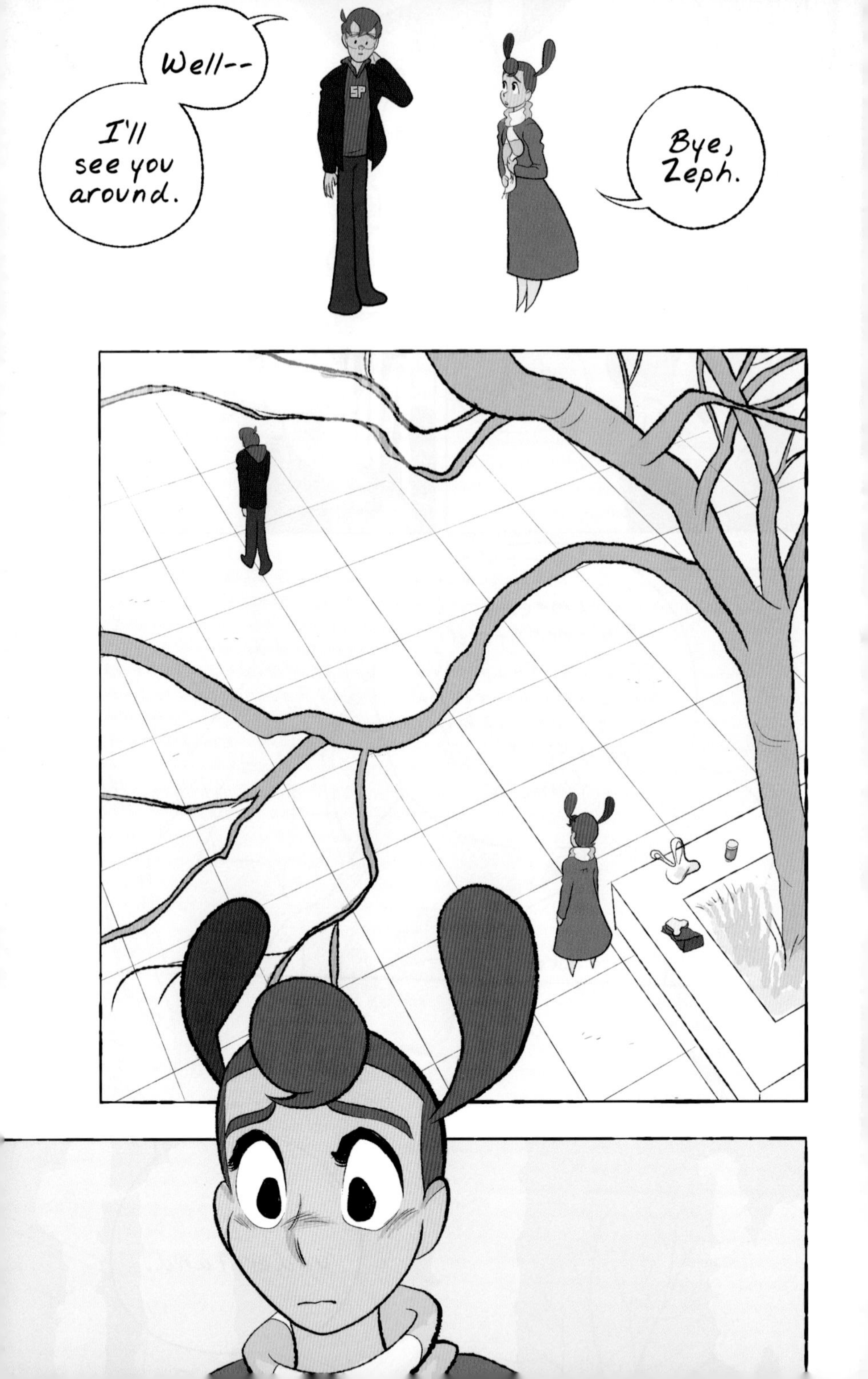

Well--
I'll see you around.
Bye, Zeph.

COMING SOON . . .

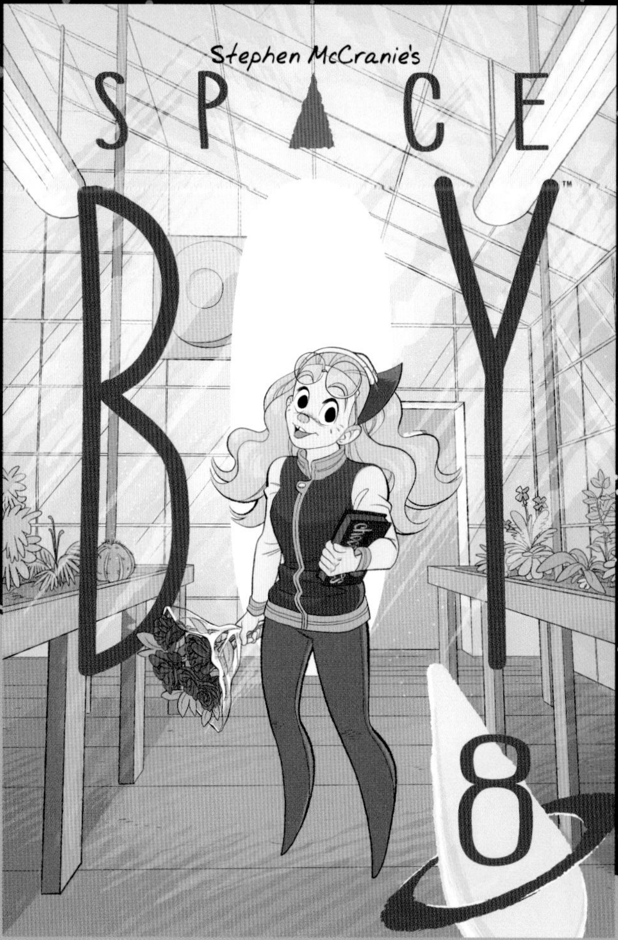

Stephen McCranie's
SPACE
BOY
8

Amy's suspicions over Oliver are put on hold when she goes to the homecoming dance with Cassie, but once there she takes an unexpected detour alone, and discovers the secret she has been looking for may have been in plain view all along. However, her discovery brings new dangers, confusion, and excitement along with it! Find out more in the next volume, available October 2020!

YOU CAN ALSO READ MORE SPACE BOY COMICS ON WEBTOONS.COM!

HAVE YOU READ THEM ALL?

VOLUME 1
$10.99 • ISBN 978-1-50670-648-1

VOLUME 2
$10.99 • ISBN 978-1-50670-680-1

VOLUME 3
$10.99 • ISBN 978-1-50670-842-3

VOLUME 4
$10.99 • ISBN 978-1-50670-843-0

VOLUME 5
$10.99 • ISBN 978-1-50671-399-1

VOLUME 6
$10.99 • ISBN 978-1-50671-400-4

AVAILABLE AT YOUR LOCAL COMICS SHOP OR BOOKSTORE. TO FIND A COMICS SHOP IN YOUR AREA, VISIT COMICSHOPLOCATOR.COM. FOR MORE INFORMATION OR TO ORDER DIRECT, VISIT DARKHORSE.COM.

Space Boy™ © 2018-2020 Stephen McCranie. Dark Horse Books® and the Dark Horse logo are registered trademarks of Dark Horse Comics LLC. All rights reserved.